OLD MONEY

Also by Kelsey Miller

Big Girl: How I Gave Up Dieting and Got a Life
I'll Be There for You: The One about Friends

OLD MONEY

A Novel

KELSEY MILLER

HANOVER
SQUARE
PRESS

HANOVER
SQUARE
PRESS™

Recycling programs
for this product may
not exist in your area.

ISBN-13: 978-1-335-00037-8

Old Money

Copyright © 2025 by Kelsey Miller, LLC

All rights reserved. No part of this book may be used or reproduced in any manner whatsoever without written permission.

Without limiting the exclusive rights of any author, contributor or the publisher of this publication, any unauthorized use of this publication to train generative artificial intelligence (AI) technologies is expressly prohibited. Harlequin also exercises their rights under Article 4(3) of the Digital Single Market Directive 2019/790 and expressly reserve this publication from the text and data mining exception.

This is a work of fiction. Names, characters, places and incidents are either the product of the author's imagination or are used fictitiously. Any resemblance to actual persons, living or dead, businesses, companies, events or locales is entirely coincidental.

TM and ® are trademarks of Harlequin Enterprises ULC.

Hanover Square Press
22 Adelaide St. West, 41st Floor
Toronto, Ontario M5H 4E3, Canada
HanoverSqPress.com

HarperCollins Publishers
Macken House, 39/40 Mayor Street Upper,
Dublin 1, D01 C9W8, Ireland
www.HarperCollins.com

Printed in U.S.A.

For M & for H

OLD MONEY

Chapter One

I know we're there before I open my eyes. I can smell it. Honeysuckle and crushed leaves and humid, summertime woods. It washes through the train car like a woozy fog.

"Briar's Green, ten minutes," the conductor bellows, and I sit up. I wasn't really sleeping anyway.

"Thank you!" calls the girl across the aisle from me—the only other person in here.

The conductor looks up at the girl, confused by this sudden outburst of appreciation. She smiles even bigger. And I just know.

"Oh!" The girl stands halfway, shouting brightly to the conductor again. "It's this car, right? These doors will open?"

The conductor nods once, then darts a glance at me. I lift my eyebrows half an inch, denying any affiliation with or knowledge of the very chatty twentysomething squirming across the aisle.

She squirms in my direction now, oblivious and beaming.

"It's a short platform," she explains. "At the Briar's Green stop."

I clock her appearance: fair, lightly freckled skin, a mass of dark curls, cutoffs and a Sarah McLachlan T-shirt (too stiff to be vintage—probably an Etsy knockoff).

"So you have to exit through the front of the train," she adds. "It's one of the oldest stations in the country."

The oldest, actually. They only replaced the wooden platform with concrete a few years ago, and only because Hurricane Sandy destroyed what was left of the original. They insisted on maintaining its original size, and somehow convinced the transit authority to preserve the old wooden overpass—a creaky, splintered tunnel sitting sixty feet above the busiest train line in North America. I don't know how many tax dollars went into saving that rickety slice of history, but I'm certain every one of them could've been put to better use. School lunches, a bomb, whatever.

"I guess it's like, why modernize?" the girl continues. "Not a ton of *train* commuters there, right?"

She tilts her head and gives me a knowing look that seems practiced.

"Right," I say, offering a shallow smile. And then, for some reason, I ask, "Are you from there originally?"

I startle at the sound of my own question, my mouth hanging ajar. God, I'm not even at the station yet, and I'm already talking like them.

"Oh—gosh, no," says the girl, laughing as though I've flattered her, rather than the opposite. "No, I've just always wanted to visit. I'm *obsessed* with the Briar."

Bingo.

A chilly prickle breaks out along my forearms, and I turn forward, my brief guilt gone and forgotten. She's one of them.

Briar's Green was always a destination of sorts. Renowned as both idyllic and elite, the village has long been considered the archetypical Hudson Valley enclave: lush, bucolic and laden with early American history—and just dazzling in the fall. It's been the subject of countless short stories and rhapsodical poems, and a whole school of nineteenth-century painters, who came to perch along its stony shore and capture the almost unimaginable grandeur of its vistas. It's also the place where, twenty years ago, my cousin, Caitlin Dale, was beaten to death by her boyfriend and left floating in a pool.

Almost twenty years ago—it'll be twenty years next month on July Fourth, 2019. Everyone seems to know that now. For the last decade, I've been the oddball who goes somber as July Fourth approaches, showing up to the barbecue with supermarket potato salad and a forced smile that makes everyone ask if I'm feeling okay. I've been hurrying home to my apartment at dusk, while the rest of Manhattan floods outward toward the waterfront, angling for a decent view of the fireworks. Nobody remembered that July Fourth was also the day of a once-infamous murder. Or they *kind* of did, yeah, but—what was her name again? Did that guy ever go to jail?

This year, though, everyone's an expert on the death of sixteen-year-old Caitlin M. Dale, honor-roll student, and captain of the JV swim team, found face down in the pool of the Horseman Club, where she and her family had been attending the annual party, on the night of July Fourth, 1999. Everyone suddenly "remembered" that Patrick Yates III (son of Senator Whitney Yates, great-grandson of the former vice president) had been accused of murder, and all but allowed to get away with it—not merely cleared of the crime, but never even formally investigated. There was hardly any investigation, period, before police declared Caitlin's death an accidental drowning, and left it at that. This, despite an eyewitness report of how Patrick Yates had hit and kicked and flung her to the ground until her skull cracked and she stopped moving. Everyone remembers that part *now*.

It started back in January, when the podcast came out. *The Club Kid* was nothing new—just a rehash of the same story reported, and recounted, and adapted for a miniseries in the first few years after Caitlin's death. After that it evolved from a scandal into a sad story from the '90s. There was a brief flurry of lurid memorial coverage around the ten-year anniversary, but for much of the last decade, Caitlin was just another vaguely tragic white girl, and Patrick was just that trust-fund Yates kid who'd once done something really bad and gotten away with it—awful, sure, but it wasn't news.

Now, apparently, it's true crime. That's how the podcast sold it, repackaging the story into a tailor-made hit for Gen Z cool kids like this girl—too young to remember the actual crime, but old enough to be outraged that it happened in their lifetime. And outraged they were—outraged but infatuated too. Suddenly, the story was everywhere again. Caitlin's school photo started popping up in the corners of tabloids, and Instagram too. Vloggers and message-board detectives argued theories about Patrick's motive, and how he got away with it. The old *Vanity Fair* article resurfaced ("A Blue-Blooded Killing in Briar's Green") and spread across social media as though it were breaking news instead of a twenty-year-old magazine article. Everyone was suddenly "obsessed" with my hometown—which, by the way, has never been called "the Briar."

"Wait," says the girl, seizing back my attention, her face suddenly lit up like a halogen bulb. "Okay, I actually read this in *middle* school."

She lifts an urgent finger, turning to rummage in her backpack, then whips back around, clutching the book. She holds it up beside her face, flashing me the cover with a confessional smirk.

I look at it, because I have to, because the only way out of this conversation is through. But of course, I know exactly what it is: *A Death on the Hudson*, by Gordon Fairchild—the book that turned Caitlin's death into the juiciest beach read of 2002. This too is having a revival, thanks to all these new—what? *Fans* of Caitlin's murder?

She's got the new edition, with its sharp, artful cover: a moonlit close-up of bare feet walking through a swath of wet, jewel-green grass. The title runs below, in spare black text, so discreet it almost disappears into the background. The original cover was glossy white, with a massive, scarlet typeface that oozed down the front. It was hideous, but at least it looked like the exploitative garbage it was. This cover makes it look like fucking Nabokov.

"I know, right? Not exactly appropriate for a twelve-year-old," the girl says, rolling her eyes. "What a little creep I was."

I look up from the book at her shining, grinning, almost-giggling face.

"You should probably keep that in your bag," I tell her.

My voice is even and completely polite—very close to friendly. But she blanches and tilts backward as though I've spit at her.

"People there don't talk about it the way they do on that podcast and . . ."

I gesture at the book. She drops it to her lap.

"And online, and all that," I finish meagerly. "It's not really like that, in the village. It's . . ."

"No, I know," the girl says, mouselike. "It's different."

No, I think. *You don't know. If you did, you'd never have gotten on the train.*

We sit, rocking in silence. In the corner of my eye, I see her nibble the edge of her thumbnail, tilting her head so that her hair falls in a curtain of curls. It reminds me of Susannah, and the reminder throbs like a headache.

I close my eyes, although I can feel the train beginning to slow. I picture the girl wandering the village, befuddled to find there's nothing actually there for her. Certainly she'll find no trace of Caitlin. No memorial benches on the village green or framed snapshots by the register at Giordano's, where Caitlin used to get pizza with her teammates after Thursday practice—her slice always doused in red pepper flakes. They don't even have signs up at the old Roosevelt barn, or Dutch Tavern, with its mottled windows, still flecked with Revolutionary musket balls, and those are things they're proud of. That's just one harmless, minuscule way the village is "different"—a word that doesn't begin to describe the icy unreality of Briar's Green.

It's a place that tourists only think they've visited. That's the best way I can put it. This girl might spend all day there, but she'll never see the real Briar's Green, because that place exists on private property—none more private than the club. She may walk the tiny village square, but beyond that she'll find nothing but pretty stone walls and iron gates. She probably knows they're all unlocked (it's part of "the Briar's" lore) but that doesn't mean she'll get past them. You know when you're unwelcome in Briar's Green. She could walk right up to the club's own gates—which aren't merely unlocked but wide-open, always—and no one would stop her. But she'd stop herself.

The train judders, and there's a deafening screech as we come to a halt. Then silence. Then the doors sigh open.

"We're here," the girl murmurs.

I turn and see her hesitant smile, nothing like the high-beam grin she had before. I clear my throat, but don't say anything. (There I go, slipping into local parlance again.)

I stand and turn, reaching for my bags, grateful to be overburdened with luggage. The bell is ringing by the time I get to the vestibule, and I shove through the closing doors and stumble onto the platform, relieved to be alone at least.

But I'm not. I turn toward the overpass, and there she is, squinting in the sunlight, thumbs looped around the straps of her backpack.

"I'm sorry," says the girl, in that same uncertain tone. "I feel like maybe—did I offend you?"

My mouth makes a vague O shape, but again, no sounds emerge.

The girl shifts her weight from one leg to the other. When she speaks again, it's almost inaudible.

"Did you, like, know her?"

I almost tell her, right then—everything, from the beginning right up until today: who I am and what I did, and what I'm going to do next. I almost even tell her why. The truth roils up inside of me, and I clench my teeth against it, quietly.

I shake my head.

"Only a little. She was older."

It's the truth and also bullshit. But that's how people talk here—in decorous lies and discreet omissions, every ugly truth cottoned in five layers of courtesy. It's true that Caitlin was a few years older than me, and thus I only knew her a little—as much as any eleven-year-old girl can know a sixteen-year-old young woman. But it's also true that one night, not quite twenty years ago, I saw Patrick Yates hit and kick and throw her down, cracking her skull against the concrete edge of the club's swimming pool. I'm the one who first saw her lifeless body in the water, and ran screaming to tell everyone—two hundred party guests, the paramedics and the police. I don't think anyone actually believes that Caitlin drowned, but I'm the one who knows.

Patrick Yates got away with murder that night, and he remains a free and happy man. And I've come home to remedy that.

Chapter Two

If Patrick Yates is "the club kid" on that podcast, I wonder what they call me. Back in 1999, the media referred to me as "the child witness," or "a minor relative of the alleged victim." I remember thinking it seemed somehow dismissive—as though I were just some little kid throwing around names.

"It's like they don't believe me at all," I'd say to my mom, over and over those first few weeks. "Nobody does."

"It's not that," she'd answer. "They can't legally identify you. Those are the only details they have. It's nothing to do with what you said."

Sometimes she'd put an arm around me, murmuring into my hair. Other times her mouth went tight, her bloodshot eyes glaring at the wall. But she always knew what I needed to hear:

"No matter what, Alice, you did the right thing."

It didn't make a difference, though. By the morning after Caitlin's death, even I understood that Patrick wasn't getting arrested on the basis of my word alone. He hadn't even been questioned yet. I'd been the one they brought straight to the station, where I stayed up half the night repeating the gruesome details of "my story." I hadn't even been allowed to change out of my party dress until some forensics person arrived to snip off a section of the hem. That's when I noticed the rusty stain on the edge of the fabric, recalling the moment by the pool, when I'd realized I was kneeling beside a puddle of Caitlin's blood. At the sight of the stain, I'd pitched forward and heaved, and the officers had grabbed me by the elbows, rushing me toward the trash can just in time.

They didn't bring in Patrick until the following afternoon, after the news broke. It was an explosive story from the start—not even the Yateses could stop that. A teenage girl found horribly dead at a country club was always going to be news. But the teenage girlfriend of Patrick Yates III, notorious rich kid with the starlet ex-girlfriend and the DUI? That was going to blow up. By noon, Caitlin was the princess of Briar's Green—a brilliant and beautiful golden child, her life cut brutally short by (according to an unidentified child eyewitness) none other than her boyfriend, *the* Patrick Yates.

When he finally did go in for questioning, at the leisurely hour of 4:00 p.m., there was a small crowd waiting for him. I watched his arrival on local news, my mom and brother seated on either side of me on the couch. Patrick crossed the parking lot, flanked by his parents, Senator Whitney Yates Jr. and Livia Wells Yates. Patrick had his father's height, but everything else was his mother's: thick hair, a diamond-shaped face and a faintly olive complexion that made him look fresh from the beach, even in February. And he almost always had a grin on his face—a big sideways smile that dimpled his left cheek. But not that day in the parking lot. His father smiled and raised a hand to the shouting reporters, but Patrick kept his head down. I felt queasy with relief when he stepped inside the police station and the door swung shut behind him—finally.

"What a joke," my brother said bitterly.

"What?" I asked.

"Well . . ." Theo scoffed. "Nothing. Let's just see what happens."

An hour later, Patrick walked right back through the door, and drove home with his parents. That's what happened.

"I know, I'm sorry, I couldn't get off the phone," says Theo. "Campaign stuff."

He shoves my last bag into the back seat of his car. The trunk is already cluttered with sneakers and soccer cleats and bottles of spray-on sunblock.

"I get it, you're important now."

I toss my tote onto the front seat, thrilled by the blast of air conditioning on my arm. Even though my older brother was twenty minutes late to pick me up, I'm happy we're together now.

"But you're going to have to take me straight there."

Theo stands back, shielding his eyes from the sun.

"Straight there, really? I thought we'd get lunch." He bends his head, contrite. "Squires? Tuna on rye—double pickles? My treat."

"*Theo.*"

"*Alice.*" He crosses his arms.

"Don't start."

"I am not starting."

We stand beside the open doors until the car begins to ding-dong, nudging us to close them.

"Got it, no time for lunch," Theo concedes, then cracks another smile. "A hug though."

Before I can reluctantly agree, he slams the rear door and wraps me in a bear hug—the kind he started doing when he became a dad. I'm still not used to it—the hugs, the elbowing, the tight shoulder squeezes. It's not that we don't love each other; it's just not how we grew up. In France, people greet each other with two cheek kisses. In Briar's Green, we nod, once, from a polite distance.

"Are you actually trying to make me miss this interview?"

"Oh, shut up," Theo says fondly. "I said I'd get you there, and I will. God help me."

I roll my eyes, but I bite my tongue and let him grumble. If I were him, I'd be grumbly too.

When I first told Theo I'd applied for a job at the club, he thought I was joking. When he realized I wasn't, he hit the ceiling. That much I'd expected—and even prepared a list of bullet points to argue in favor of my plan. It wound up taking numerous calls to convince him I was of sound mind, and doing this whether he liked it or not.

Theo gives me a final squeeze.

"I hate this. But I love you, kiddo."

"I know, and I know." I pat him briskly on the back. "Now we've gotta go."

He releases me and jogs around to the driver's side, checking his watch. His sleeves are neatly cuffed at the elbows, and he's wearing belted khakis that look professionally pressed.

"God, Theo," I say, getting in the car. "It's like you're in a congressman costume."

He shifts into Drive, smirking.

"Candidate costume," he corrects. "I know. Get this, Jules has to do my sleeves for me."

Hands on the wheel, he points an elbow at me, showing off one perfectly crisp and even cuff.

"Apparently when I do it, they look 'bunchy.' Can you believe that?"

"Uh, yeah. You couldn't do your own tie until, what? Law school?"

"One of many challenges I've faced—and overcome. So, vote for Theo Wiley. My wife rolls my shirtsleeves, but I *can* do my tie."

He waves proudly to an imaginary crowd, then drops the hand and leans sideways.

"Don't tell the voters," he adds in a stage whisper. "But the truth is I'm still pretty lousy at it."

No, the truth is that, shirtsleeves aside, he's amazing at just about everything. Fine motor tasks are basically the only thing I do better than Theo, and he takes every chance to highlight my aptitude—which just makes it worse. "Look at those shoelaces!" he once proclaimed. I was twenty-four. And he was clerking at the Supreme Court.

Theo was always an overachiever. Every school year, some teacher would ask Mom if she'd considered letting him skip a grade, not realizing he already had. But after the murder, Theo's focus hardened into something more like mission. He hadn't witnessed Patrick kill Caitlin, but he knew I wasn't lying and that everyone else was. He'd seen Patrick walking toward the pool that night—a small yet crucial detail, which dozens of other guests surely witnessed too, but Theo was the only one who reported it. Which made it even easier for the cops to dismiss it.

"I don't even think they wrote it down," he'd repeated for weeks after, muttering to himself at the dinner table.

"You did the right thing," Mom would tell him too. But for him, it didn't help.

It was the murder that changed my life, but for Theo it was the aftermath. He developed an almost pathological devotion to justice, seizing onto every wrongdoing he encountered with equal fervor—gym-class bullies, the oil industry, you name it. In high school, he lobbied the governor to shut down the Kisco power plant, which had failed to report several radioactive-steam leaks. And it worked. Theo's righteous anger successfully fueled him through college, law school and into his inevitable career as a civil rights attorney—and now he's running for Congress. All this because our family couldn't afford therapy.

"Is it round-the-clock mayhem by now?" I ask. "The campaign?"

Theo takes one hand off the wheel and waves me off.

"It's fine. It's ridiculous, but it's fine."

We turn off Station Hill Road and onto Route 9. The road is already narrow, having been originally designed for horses. But in summer, it seems even smaller: a verdant tunnel, with roadside bushes and a dense canopy of oak leaves bursting over the pavement.

Theo's phone buzzes in the cup holder.

"Do you need to get that?"

"No, but—if we're not having lunch, I should get back," he says. "I'll take your bags with me."

"Are you sure about me staying with you?" I gesture at the phone. "With everything going on?"

Theo tosses me a look that says he knows what I'm doing.

"Don't even try it."

I consider trying anyway, but this is a battle I've already ceded. Theo's one caveat to finally "approving" my summer plans was that I stay at his house. I should've told him I'm thirty-one and I'll stay wherever I like, but I agreed because, again, my brother is a litigator.

"I just don't want to . . ."

I notice something down the road and lose my train of thought.

"Is that—is that the Wishing Well?"

Theo follows my gaze, confused.

"Yeah?"

We pass the old, familiar shop—the candy store we used to go to on Friday afternoons, when they gave out soft pretzels. It's built like a gingerbread house, with stained-glass windows, and an old covered well out front that we'd all been warned not to climb on.

I'd expected to find the village center full of unsettling changes—a Starbucks where the old pharmacy stood, the candy store bulldozed for a parking lot. But the place hasn't moved a muscle. There's the old stone church with its tiny cemetery full of Dutch sailors and slanted headstones. There's the Little Village Bookshop, and the ice cream stand that served chalky softserve and amazing lemonade.

"What?" Theo asks, still confused.

"I just— How is it all still here?" I reply. "Exactly the same as it used to be?"

He snorts.

"Come on, that's the village motto, right? 'Briar's Green: Just like it used to be'"

Briar's Green literally runs by its own rulebook. It's one of a handful of colonial-era villages that still operate under their own charters. I couldn't tell you what a charter is, or why they get to have one. It's one of those remnant scraps of legislation, like daylight saving time, that everyone abides by without knowing why. But what it means in practice is that Briar's Green has its own set of laws, which—with *shockingly* few exceptions—cannot be overruled by the state or federal government.

This made for all sorts of rumors when I was a kid. We used to believe you could get arrested for blowing gum bubbles or kissing with your tongue. The reality is far less thrilling, though equally absurd. Village law is more concerned with your house and garden than your tongue. No asphalt driveways, for example. No neon storefront signs. No gates above six feet, or boundary walls below four. No invisible fencing or visible sprinklers, no barn renovations and *no* new-build homes unless village council approves your architect (it won't—I think that codicil might be sarcasm).

The village guards its visible history with an iron fist. There are stone walls here that pre-date the *Mayflower*, and countless outbuildings and haylofts where Revolutionary generals slept or ate or died from typhus. The phrase *old money* conjures images of grandeur—feather beds and gilded mansions—but in Briar's Green it looks like musty houses with worn-out floors and doors that stick in the summer. It looks like acres of neglected meadow, and knotty trees with half-rotted rope swings that one of the Roosevelts swung from as a child. No one will ever specify which—goodness, how inelegant—and if you ask, they'll feign ignorance, and slip out of the conversation. They'll know you're not like them.

"Get this," says Theo. "They're trying to establish 'tourist hours.'"

We're past the village center now, back in the tunnel of green.

"Hmm?" I say, still dazed by the time warp.

"Basically, no outsiders allowed before noon or after five,"

Theo scoffs. "I guess they've had a few more than usual this year, but it's like, sorry, these are public roads."

"Right," I say, picturing the train girl, grinning like a kid. "I met one. One of those true-crime creeps obsessed with Caitlin."

We reach a stop sign, and Theo brakes just hard enough for me to realize my mistake.

"Is that what this is about?" Theo asks softly. "All the media stuff?"

I'm already shaking my head.

"Nope. It's not. And I'm not having this conversation again."

Theo leans over, trying to catch my eye.

"Because I'd understand. It gets to me too, you know? And for you—"

"Theo."

"Especially with this whole Susannah thing."

"Theo!" I bark, turning a hard stare on him. "I said no."

He calmly closes his mouth, his eyes going soft and understanding. Except he doesn't understand. He *thinks* he does, and nothing I say will sway him. The problem with Theo's evident brilliance is that he always thinks he's right, and anyone who disagrees is wrong. And all wrongs *must* be righted. This is what makes him so great in court and an absolute nightmare at Thanksgiving.

Another car approaches behind us, forcing Theo to drive on.

We sit in the strained silence, arguing in our heads. I'm dimly aware of a pale stone wall running alongside the road. Theo sighs.

"I'm just worried, Alice," he says. "I think this is a bad decision—an unhealthy one."

"I remember," I answer as the gate appears. "It's 'an unhealthy environment,' for me. My hometown."

We pull up to the entrance. The wrought-iron spears glimmer like fresh tar in the heat, and the car fills up with the sharp, green smell of lawn.

"I'm not just talking about the village," Theo says quietly. "The village is one thing."

"I know," I finish for him, my own voice softening too. "I really do."

I nod forward, and Theo obliges, driving slowly up the path.

On that point, Theo's right—no question. I don't need him to tell me, because I know better than anyone. The village is one thing. The club is another.

Chapter Three

The club isn't as old as the village or the money in it, but it is one of the oldest of its kind in North America. And unlike others, it still maintains many of the original, overtly bigoted rules that used to be de rigueur for all country clubs. Membership is by invitation only, and it is entirely male and white. Not even wives are granted official membership, though the club does graciously permit them to use the tennis courts and pool and other facilities without their husbands present. I don't know what the club board would do if a member married a Black woman or one with a Jewish last name, but as far as I know, in the hundred-odd years the club's been standing, that has never happened.

The property is a rambling three hundred acres, and includes a golf course, a shooting lodge, stables and a riding ring, each section divided by dense swaths of the forest that once covered the land entirely. Virtually none of the member areas are visible from the outside, except for the clubhouse. It sits like a decorative box at the top of the steep, winding driveway—the highest point in the whole village.

Most American country clubs are modeled after the grand ancestral estates of the English nobility. But the Horseman's clubhouse was purportedly designed in homage to Petit Trianon—Marie Antoinette's private getaway palace, where she'd go to escape the bustle of court life at Versailles.

With its Doric columns and gleaming facade, it does have the look of a royal retreat. The clubhouse—its actual name is Brandywine, though everyone knows it as "the clubhouse" just as the Horseman Club is simply "the club"—was built with large slabs of peach-cream brick, the color of the inside of a seashell. It looks white in full daylight, then warms to a delicate pink after sunset, glowing as if lit from within. The western side is lined with four grand French doors that open onto a marble terrace overlooking the hill. Every party ends on the terrace, even in blistering winter, and that is one tradition I understand. The view is astonishing—a vast panorama of the Hudson River without so much as a treetop obstructing the scene. Rumor has it the club pays neighboring residents an off-the-books stipend to maintain their old oaks and evergreens at a specific height, so as to preserve the view.

Don't ask me how I know these things. I just do. Everyone here just does. The club has always been the center of the village. The paradox is that it's so supremely exclusive and exclusionary that most residents would never even fantasize about joining—and yet we've all been there, one way or another.

It feels as though I spent half my childhood at the club, though I know that can't actually be true. I think those memories just loom larger than most. My parents weren't members—not even close. I don't come from a "nice family," just a normal one, and that itself was a victory for my folks. They'd both grown up in households on the edge of broke, and considered themselves lucky to be merely anxious about money, rather than flat-out terrified. "It'll be different for you," Mom would say. "You'll know people."

That's why they moved to Briar's Green, although they couldn't afford it. That's why they sent us to the Wheaton School—though that would've been impossible had Theo not been such a wunderkind, accepted on scholarship at age five. I got in too, but not for free—I was just regular smart. We were two of a handful of "normies" among a sea of legacy students and the occasional celebrity kid. I grew keenly aware of the crushing cost, but my parents never seemed bothered. We were in. That's what mattered. We attended Wheaton and we lived in Briar's Green (in a rented house on the edge of the village, but still). Money worries were nothing compared to the soothing balm of proximity to wealth.

It wasn't snobbery, understand. Wealth, they believed, was the surest protection in life, and it's hard to argue they were wrong. They had no worshipful illusions about so-called American Royalty, like the Yateses or Kennedys. If anything, it was the opposite. They wanted us to know them as peers—"No different from you." But we knew the truth early on: if we were really like them, it would go without saying.

Mom and Dad did their best to give us a steady, comfortable childhood, with birthday parties and boxed cereal. But doing so in Briar's Green was nearly impossible for ordinary people, because the village simply wasn't meant for them. Mom was a bookkeeper for a handful of local businesses, and Dad worked at a financial firm in the city. It was a grunt-work position in the tax department, from which he'd never be promoted but hung on to for dear life, because working in finance—like living in Briar's Green—conferred a degree of clout you couldn't get in other sectors. It would serve us, his children, in the long term, and for my parents, it was always about our futures. They earned a perfectly fine living, but you couldn't just earn money to stay afloat here; you had to have it already.

They both worked endless hours to keep the small-but-pretty roof over our heads, never letting us know what a tenuous hold we had. Then one spring evening, two weeks after my eighth birthday, Dad collapsed in the street while walking home from the train. It wasn't the stress, the doctors insisted, assuring Mom over and over. It wasn't anything he did or didn't do. It was a freak embolism—just one of those things. "Sometimes terrible things just happen," the surgeon told my mother, gently ushering us out of the hospital lounge. "And it's nobody's fault."

Overnight, we lost both Dad and the life we'd had with him. Mom, Theo and I moved to a duplex on a wooded street in Ashborough, just outside the village. Mom had to work three times as hard to keep us under that sagging, mold-speckled roof, all while raising two grief-stricken children. She negotiated a payment plan with Wheaton, and learned basic tailoring from a library book to avoid buying new uniforms. We put them on and went back to school, for no other reason than it was important to her.

Theo and I understood then how different we really were. We were reminded each time we walked down the shaky steps of our apartment and into one of the wealthiest communities in the country—technically our hometown, but not one where we belonged. Belonging to the club was out of the question. We lacked the two prerequisites: money, and a man.

But even for us, the club was unavoidable. It was the silent center of our community, and the second-largest employer after Rippowat Prison. Everyone in the village who worked had worked at the club at one time or another. Most other normies at Wheaton were children of longtime club staffers, some of whom had been nudged into the school thanks to members. It wasn't exactly a perk, but there was an understanding that a well-liked club employee—a bartender who knew everyone's drink orders, a discreet powder-room attendant—might have a stroke of luck when applying for a spot. Such was the case with my best friend, Susannah.

Susannah's parents were both career staffers there—her mother a catering manager, and her dad the junior tennis coach. On snow days and school breaks, we often got parked in the club's breakroom, making Swiss Miss in the microwave and ignoring our homework. In summertime, the club became our secret, pseudo-day camp. Susannah and I would sneak around the grounds, making an elaborate game of hiding from members and staff. I doubt anyone would've cared except for Mr. Brody, the club's scowling, imperious butler, who had a preternatural sense for rule breakers. Like a vampire, he'd appear out of thin air the moment you even thought about sticking your gum in an ashtray. We were terrified of him, but that too was part of the fun. Really, those were the most magical days of my childhood—sneaking into ballrooms to practice cartwheels, scooping cups of maraschino cherries from behind the bar while the bartender smiled and made a big show of looking the other way. We never thought about our classmates, eating fries by the pool, charging sodas to their parents' accounts. We didn't feel different on those days. We felt like outlaws.

A few times a year, I came to the club as a guest. Caitlin and her parents, my aunt Barbara and uncle Gregory, were our only close relatives, and they frequently invited us to join them for parties or holiday festivities. Uncle Greg was a third-generation member, though he was also an exception: a warm, jokey guy who didn't golf and was married to my mother's sister—a born and raised normie. Aunt Barbara was great too, albeit a little more formal. Like many converts, she'd adopted the customs of my uncle's world and practiced them more dutifully than he, who'd been born into it. But none of them were true snobs, and they took every opportunity to include us in their very different life.

Those times at the club were nice, but not exactly fun. The Dales never seemed to notice how out of place we were, but we felt like grubby interlopers in our borrowed shoes and over-washed, too-small outfits. The members never said so, but they always let us know—those little half glances, a scoot of the chair—that they agreed.

Chapter Four

I'd like to say it feels different, twenty years later. But standing in the staff lot behind the clubhouse, I still feel like an interloper. I'm coated with a sticky film of perspiration, and my hair is already coming loose in tiny wisps. I smooth my hair into a bun, making a mental note to buy a can of proper hairspray. Everyone here uses it; I'd forgotten.

Once I'm sure Theo is gone, I head toward the staff door. I keep my head up, taking in the sights and sounds around me. This is a grounding trick I learned in therapy, when I finally did go to therapy. I rarely use it nowadays, but it was my lifeline in my early twenties—the peak panic-attack years. Whenever I felt one coming over me, I'd stop in my tracks, look around and name three things I saw—then three things I heard, smelled, felt, etc. Within seconds, my feet would hit firm ground again, and I'd be back in the grocery store or the park, back in my safe and mundane adult life.

The trouble with this place is it hasn't changed a bit since I left here as a traumatized, blood-stained child. What do I see? The hill I was standing on when I heard Caitlin screaming. What do I hear? Kids splashing and hollering down at the pool—the one that turned from blue to hazy lavender, because of all the blood. I'd forgotten that part, but one walk across the parking lot, and I've regressed all the way to eleven. So much for therapy.

I pause at the staff door, deep-breathing myself back into adulthood, and rap the brass knocker. The boom is so loud I hear it echoing inside.

"Fuck."

The door swings open and a dark-haired kid—maybe seventeen—leans out. A pale green tie hangs undone around his neck.

"Yeah?" he says, by way of greeting. He looks like he's got a trust fund and a hangover.

"I'm Alice Wiley," I say. "I have a meeting with Jamie."

I smile, still a little shaky. The kid just looks back, somewhere between bored and annoyed.

"Jamie Burger? The concierge?" I add.

He waves me into a cramped entry hall known as the boot room, having originally been used for riding-boot storage. One end leads to the clubhouse's central corridor—the gallery, they call it—and the other connects to a series of narrow passageways that run behind the walls, allowing the staff to scurry around like industrious mice, fetching and carrying without being seen. In the old days, servants entered via the subbasement—more like rats. The members only converted the boot room due to the Cold War, having decided they'd quite like to keep the subbasement handy for themselves, in the event of a nuclear attack.

"I'll take you in a sec," the kid says, grabbing a vest off a small garment rack.

"Oh no, I can find my way," I say.

"Nah," the kid says, facing a tiny wall mirror and doing up his tie. "You're not in dress code."

Excuse me? I think. I'm dressed in an all-linen outfit, sage green shorts and a white blouse.

"The shoes," he says, nodding toward my (new, expensive) leather sandals. "Your toes are showing."

My face goes instantly hot, as though he's caught me topless.

"Oh, but—sandals are allowed."

"Not for staff." He chuckles at his reflection. "Surprised Burger didn't tell you that."

"Nope, that sounds like Jamie," I mutter, more harshly than I mean. The kid pauses and cocks an eyebrow.

"We went to school together," I add in a friendly tone.

The kid seems to accept this non-explanation and turns back to his tie, a flash of something crossing his expression—snideness, maybe. Then he huffs into the mirror, yanking the tie loose and starting over. Normally I'd offer to help, but something tells me this kid's gotten more than enough help in his life.

"Fuck it," he says, dropping the tie and letting it hang undone. "Everyone's outside anyway. C'mon."

He turns toward the gallery exit—unbothered by the dress code now that he's also breaking it—and waves for me to follow.

My pulse jumps to a skittish beat as we enter the gallery—which, like everything else, is just as I remember it, right down to the smell: a potent mix of carpet cleaner, burnt coffee and extinguished candles. This is the artery of the building, providing access to three private dining nooks that no one ever uses, and the beautiful, wood-hewn bar, unofficially reserved for cigar-smoking men after a day of skeet shooting or golf. The western side opens onto the club's four palatial ballrooms, known simply as the yellow room, the green room, the blue room and the pink room.

Memories hit like waves in a rising tide, and I bat them away with small talk, asking the kid dull questions and nodding at his dull answers. His name is Cory Amos. He's never heard of the singer. His dad golfs here. That's who got him the doorman job.

"Do you like it?" I ask absently, my neck craning as we pass the blue room. (*Eyes forward, Alice. You're fine.*)

"It's fine," Cory answers. "It's whatever."

As a rule, member kids can't work at the club, but doorman duty is the exception. That gig is typically reserved for teenagers (boys, specifically), and it's both a privilege and punishment.

Parents use it to humble their spoiled kid after wrecking a car or setting someone's beach house on fire. Personally, I think sticking some shitty, entitled teenager at the front door is more punishing for everyone else. But the practice continues because it's tradition. And there's nothing the club values more than tradition.

"Is Jamie a good boss?" I ask, recalling Cory's sneery little chuckle.

"Burger?" Cory replies. "Uh, sure?"

There's that look again, and this time I can read it. Not snideness, just plain old snobbery. Cory may be humbled by this public-penance job, but he'll always feel superior to the likes of Jamie Burger. I used to feel the same way, but for different reasons.

Jamie was my childhood classmate, and Theo's best friend. Like Susannah, he was the child of a club staffer, and a financial-aid student like me. All of us normies understood we were outsiders, and most of us knew to keep our heads down. But Jamie was the kind of kid who handled insecurity by making a loud, obnoxious joke of himself. He was always pretending to fall in gym class or walking into homeroom doing impressions nobody understood. You couldn't even make fun of him. Kids would call him "Jamie Hotdog"—a nickname both mean and meaningless—and he'd laugh out loud, as though he got the joke and *loved* it. It was bad enough putting up with him all day, and then I'd come home to find him hogging the TV with Theo. Jamie wasn't the *worst* part of my childhood, but he was certainly the most annoying part. The fact that I'm actively trying to work for him feels even stranger than trying to work for the club.

"Shit," Cory hisses as we near the yellow room. "Hang on."

He ducks into the ballroom, and I hurry behind him.

"What?" I whisper, my heart thudding though I don't know why.

Cory stands against the wall, fumbling with his undone tie.

"He's such a dick about this stuff," he mutters.

"Who? Jamie?"

Cory shakes his head, annoyed, pointing his chin toward the doorway. A figure walks past, moving briskly—a brief, uniformed blur in my peripheral vision.

"Him," Cory mouths, his blasé expression turned alert and anxious.

I recognize that look. But—no. He can't mean *him*.

I step sideways, peeking through the open doorway.

"No way."

He's at the other end of the gallery now, nearing the back stairs. But even at this distance, and even with his back turned, I recognize Mr. Brody.

"I know," Cory murmurs. "He's been here since I was a kid."

I step back, agog.

"He's been here since *I* was a kid."

"Wow," says Cory, in a full, astonished voice. "That's insane."

On second thought, I think I'll leave Cory to fiddle with his tie, and go find Jamie's office myself. I open my mouth to tell him so, but Cory turns to me, his face shifting from incredulous to intrigued.

"Wait, what's your name again?"

Something's clicked.

"Alice," I say, one foot shuffling backward—just an inch, but the sound echoes in the cavernous room.

Breathe. He doesn't matter. He probably doesn't even know about Caitlin.

Cory seems to smile slightly. Of course he knows. He's from here.

"Alice what?"

Stop. Look around. What do you see? What do you hear?

But it's too late, the room is already throbbing. The walls pulse around me, in time with my galloping heart, and even though

I know it doesn't matter if he knows my last name—it doesn't matter if he knows *exactly* who I am—I need to leave, now, before he asks another question.

"I've got a meeting," I manage, heading for the doorway.

I move as fast as possible, though the air already feels like thick molasses, each step a clumsy effort. I grasp the door frame, pulling myself around it and into the gallery, and as I do I dare one split-second glance back at Cory, and there it is: recognition, spreading wide across his face.

Then I turn the corner, and the world goes black.

Chapter Five

July Fourth, 1999

I have bits and pieces from the night of the murder. "Flashbulb memories" is the term my first therapist used, but I never entirely agreed with that description. Home-movie clips would be a closer analogy, but even that's too tidy. I remember the fruity stench of blood. I remember wet grass slipping through my toes as I ran across the hill. I remember the sounds she made.

"Ah-hah!" Caitlin called from inside her closet. "Found it."

She stepped back, holding up the dress. It was cool white and shimmery, with a stiff, poufy skirt.

"I got it last year for Spring Fling." She held it in front of her. "But then I had to skip it."

She made a pouty face, rubbing the opalescent fabric between her fingers. Her nails were painted baby blue.

"Oh yeah, you got mono!" I said, my voice loud and chirpy.

Caitlin turned her head and gave me a sideways smile.

"Good memory."

I shifted on my feet, cheeks prickling.

"Anyway, it's not really *me* anymore. But . . ." Caitlin held the dress out at me, the skirt gently rustling.

"Oh. Um."

"You don't have to. I just thought it would be so cute on you."

I stood awkwardly in the middle of her messy room—partly because there was nowhere to sit. Every surface was covered in clothes, including the unmade bed. The real issue though, was that I couldn't sit in my own dress. It was the same one I'd worn last July—a cap-sleeved shift that fit just fine a year ago—before my body turned so suddenly, horrifyingly pubescent. I was somehow both longer *and* rounder, and my shoulders had seemingly widened by a foot. After getting dressed that evening, I'd come out of my room crying, stuffed into the dress like a human wearing doll clothes. Mom had insisted I looked lovely, but I knew she was just saying that because it was too late to find something new.

My face was still red when we got to the Dales' house, and Caitlin whisked me to her room while she got ready.

"No pressure," she said now, still holding out the shiny dress. "Totally get it if you don't wanna change. My mom used to pull that with me all the time, and it drove me *bananas*."

I looked at it, swinging on the hanger like a silver bell. A tiny smile crept over my face.

"Yeah?" Caitlin grinned back. "You sure?"

I nodded.

"I love it."

"Yay!"

Caitlin ushered me into her en suite bathroom, leaving the door ajar—possibly by accident? I wasn't sure. Among the older girls at school, casual nudity seemed to be a signifier of cool-girl friendship. I'd once seen Caitlin doing a crown braid for one of her swim-team friends, wearing nothing but her swimsuit, rolled down to the waist. I'd relayed the anecdote to Susannah, realizing as I spoke how creepy it made me sound—like I'd been spying. But Susannah had grabbed my arm and whispered, "I *know*, Anna told me! That is *bananas*!"

That was Caitlin. She was the trendsetter on whom we all spied, picking up her mannerisms without even noticing. "Bananas" was a Caitlin thing. So were crown braids. That fad had picked up so suddenly that even she noticed. ("It's *so* embarrassing," she'd told me at Thanksgiving, murmuring in a confessional tone. "You know why I do my hair like that sometimes? So I don't have to wash it. It's my gross-day hairstyle.") I'd relayed this to my fellow sixth graders, and soon all of us were showing up with unwashed, floppy braids that looked nothing like the honey-gold crown on Caitlin's head.

It wasn't just us. Everyone was a little obsessed with Caitlin—teachers, parents. *Keep your eye on that one*, they'd say. As if we weren't already. Caitlin was the one they trotted out for school tours and included in every Wheaton catalog. Caitlin wasn't an academic whiz kid like Theo, and she didn't win every award. But she was the unchallenged star of our school. And that was *before* she started dating Patrick.

Allegedly dating, that is. They hadn't gone public, but everyone knew. It had started sometime after Christmas break, though we couldn't pinpoint when. Patrick had reportedly given Caitlin a ride home in January, and someone claimed they saw them making out at the multiplex later that month (this though was unsubstantiated). The whole thing was just a rumor until February, when Patrick sneaked out of the senior section during assembly, and ducked into the junior rows, sitting in the seat directly behind Caitlin's. He'd held a finger to his lips, then leaned forward and quickly squeezed Caitlin by the shoulders. She'd glanced back, guffawed at him, then rolled her eyes and faced forward, but with an enormous smile. At that point, I don't think anyone was looking at the stage.

The whole school remained riveted by Caitlin and Patrick's public flirtation. People turned to watch whenever they so much as walked down the hall together. I'd even overheard two teachers discussing them behind me in the dining hall: "Did I hear that right? Caitlin Dale and—" "That's what I'm told. Thought she was smarter than that."

I'd been startled by the comment, especially from a teacher. I kept it to myself (and Susannah, of course), but I'd been dying for an excuse to tell Caitlin. And then to say something like:

Can you believe that? What does that even mean? And then to ask her everything about her and Patrick.

"How ya doing, babydoll?" Caitlin called to me.

"Uh," I answered. "Yeah."

I was panicked. I'd wrenched myself out of my own dress, but it turned out hers didn't fit much better. I'd gotten it on, but the zipper wouldn't budge. The bodice gaped open behind me, revealing my whole back and the top of my (embarrassing, babyish) underwear.

I peered through the open the door, desperate for help, but unable to ask her. Caitlin was bent over her vanity, applying eyeshadow with her ring finger. Her own dress that night was a pearl-colored slip that swung about her ankles. Her hair was loose—messy in the good way—and dappled with sunny highlights. She fished through the tubes and pencils on the vanity, plucking out a tin of plummy lip tint. She dabbed it lightly on her lips, pausing for a moment to smile at herself in the mirror.

"Is Patrick Yates your boyfriend?" I blurted out.

Caitlin jerked up, genuinely startled. I was too. Sometimes thoughts would burst from my mouth before I could catch them—usually the most embarrassing ones.

"Shit, Alice!" Caitlin cracked into laughter. "You sound like my mother!"

"What do you mean?"

She bent back down to the mirror, rubbing her lips together and giving her hair one last shake.

"Me and Patrick—she's up my ass about it."

"Okay," I said, unable to stop myself. "But is he your boyfriend?"

"*Ugh*," Caitlin gave an exasperated laugh. "Yes, but that's between us. Do *not* tell my mom."

I grinned. This confirmation was thrilling enough. *Between us* was even better.

"Of course not." I straightened up, trying my zipper again. "Why?"

Caitlin breezed into the bathroom, sighing.

"God. I don't know."

She took me by the shoulders, turning me toward the mirror, and started working the zipper up.

"It's not just *her*, y'know, it's everyone. It's just like—" Caitlin caught my eye in the mirror. "You know who Patrick is, right? His dad and his grandfather, and all that?"

I dropped my chin, and Caitlin laughed.

"Right." She leaned back, considering the bodice, still mostly undone. "You've got swimmer's shoulders, lady."

I hoped it was a compliment.

"Anyway," she continued, "I know everyone acts like they're not impressed by stuff like that, but it's bullshit. They totally are."

"Totally."

She glanced up, cocking an eyebrow at my reflection.

"You know his mother had the Lincoln Lodge torn down last month?"

My eyes widened in the mirror.

"*No.*"

The Lincoln Lodge was an old stone house on the edge of the Yateses' property—so called because Abraham Lincoln once spent two months there, recovering from pneumonia. It was one of the village's most treasured landmarks, not to mention a federal one.

"And . . ." Caitlin leaned down. "She put in a helipad."

I gaped, speechless.

"That's like a little airport, but for helicopters," Caitlin added.

"I know," I answered automatically—I'd never heard the word in my life. Helicopters? You weren't even allowed to ride dirt bikes in Briar's Green.

"But—how did she get permission?"

Caitlin smirked.

"Who says she asked?" She tugged the dress upward, trying the zipper again. "She could've replaced it with a burning cross and the whole village would be like, *Oh, what a lovely barbecue.*"

I swallowed, uncertain. Was I meant to laugh? Which part was the joke (or was she not joking)?

"I'm not saying they're like that." Caitlin held my gaze again. "But you know what I mean, right?"

"Totally," I repeated, not having a clue.

"Good." She smiled. "Breathe out, Alice."

I did. In one quick motion, Caitlin pushed hard between my shoulder blades, using the other hand to yank the zipper all the way up. I lurched forward, gasping, then steadied myself. When I looked up, Caitlin was beaming at me in the mirror.

"I knew it."

This time, I saw it too. The dress was too small, but still a hundred times better than my old one. I looked different. I looked mature—or nearly there.

"Okay, it's official," said Caitlin "You're a babe."

She pinched the back of my arm lightly, and I beamed, thrilled by the casual intimacy of it—like I was one of her real friends. Caitlin leaned down again, leveling her reflection with mine.

"Hey," she whispered. "That thing about the lodge. I don't mind if you tell your friends. But you didn't hear it from me, 'kay?"

I nodded, still grinning. Caitlin put a hand on my shoulder. I remember the cool grip of her fingers. I remember the tiny chip in her baby blue polish.

"All right, babydoll." She gave me an excited squeeze. "Shall we?"

Chapter Six

"More ice?" Jamie Burger asks.

I pull the bag away from my nose. It's mostly cold water now.

"I'm fine," I say. "How's your shoulder?"

"Oh." He looks at it, shrugging. "All good."

There's a beige smear of my makeup above the left lapel of Jamie's suit jacket. The collar of my blouse is speckled with bright blood. We look like children who've been dragged into the principal's office, for a fight that neither of us won. In fact, we are two thirtysomething adults who, quite simply, walked into each other. That's it. In my haste to get away from Cory's suspicious face, I'd stepped through the ballroom doorway just as Jamie was speed-walking past it, heading to the boot room to find me. It was slapstick—a classic Jamie Hotdog move.

Jamie shifts in the wooden swivel chair behind his desk—an antique behemoth that takes up two-thirds of the room. The walls are lined in 1970s wood paneling that bubbles out in spots, making the room feel even smaller than it is. Jamie himself almost hits the ceiling when standing. He was always the tallest kid in class, and now I bet he's the tallest adult in most rooms. Physically, Jamie really is the scaled-up version of his sixth-grade self. Still lanky, same sandy-brown hair, and densely freckled skin.

"I forgot about that," he says. "Your, uh, fainting thing."

He says it lightly, as though it were a hobby I once had. In fairness, it's not completely unjustified. If slapstick was Jamie's annoying habit in middle school, then fainting was mine. It started about a month after Caitlin's murder—I'd just pass out every few weeks, seemingly at random. Mom kept taking me to the doctor, who kept saying there was no evident *physical* cause, but that much we all knew. All I could do was choose desks at the end of the row (my classmates learned to leave one open), so I wouldn't fall on anyone. The fainting spells eased up with time, and by senior year they'd stopped entirely.

Until today, when I stepped into the gallery without looking, and crashed into Jamie Burger—his shoulder bone, specifically.

I'd come to only seconds later, but was still fairly dazed. Jamie had sent Cory for a first aid kit, then guided me to his office, where I'd briefly panicked again after he pointed into a closet and told me to sit down. This, Jamie explained, *was* actually his office—although it had been a coat closet originally. So he wouldn't take offense.

"I don't faint anymore," I tell Jamie firmly. "Really. That hasn't happened since high school."

Jamie nods slowly.

"And the office—you know, it's great, but you might take the coat hooks down," I say, gesturing at the wall. "That'll throw people off."

I smile at my own little joke, hoping he'll follow my lead, but he stays quiet. This is the most uncomfortable job interview I've ever had, and it hasn't even started.

"Jamie, honestly, it's not an issue. I just haven't been here in a while."

Blood tickles inside my left nostril and I hold my breath, stifling a sneeze.

"And it's really hot," I finish, squeakily.

Jamie gazes at the desk, considering. This part is new—this

contained, professional Jamie Burger. I've never heard him go this long without talking.

"I get it," he says finally. "It's not that. I'm just sort of stunned that you're here."

"What do you mean?" I fire back. This part I'm prepared for. "I applied for the job. You called me."

"Yes," he says evenly. "I thought you'd explain."

"Explain what? You're hiring a summer assistant. I am a *career* assistant, and I need a summer gig."

"And you couldn't find one in the entire city of New York," Jamie says, almost laughing. "You had to apply for a minimum-wage job in Westchester. Here. Come on, Alice, do I have to say it?"

"Okay, I'm overqualified, but—"

"Come *on*."

Jamie levels his gaze. I hold it for a long beat, then drop my shoulders.

"Fine," I say, exhaling. "Look, do you know what a reparative experience is?"

Jamie shakes his head no.

"It's— Shit, it sounds so gross saying it out loud. I've basically spent the last decade in therapy, trying to get this place out of my system. I've spent pretty much all my money too, by the way. And it was completely worth it, but—there's only so much you can do on the couch."

I pause, eyeing him. Jamie's hands are knit together tightly, his shoulders and eyebrows visibly tensed. I carry on.

"To really process a trauma, you need to do the legwork. A reparative experience is like—it's like when you go to the park where you got mugged, and have a picnic or something. You have a good time, and then you aren't scared of the park anymore. You're not avoiding it, and thinking about it constantly." I take another long pause. "I've been waiting for this chance, Jamie. I saw this job listing and it felt like fate. I could find a better one, you're right, but—this is the one I need."

I look into my lap, horrified at the landslide of emotion and vulnerability I've just unleashed.

Even more so, because it's almost all bullshit.

It *is* true that I work as a personal assistant, and that I was looking for a job. My last one ended in May, when my employer—an ex-supermodel, expecting her second child—decided to move back to the UK. She'd given me a healthy severance and three months of insurance coverage (a stipulation I require in all employment contracts). I usually don't need to use the cushion, nor do I need to job hunt. I'm good at what I do, and having done it for ten years, I can reliably count on word of mouth to find me a new position within a week or two. But again, this year is different than others.

I don't know what compelled me to poke around job listings online—I didn't have a plan at that point. But it must have been forming in the back of my mind, or else I'd never have searched for jobs in Briar's Green. The truth is I've never felt the need to "repair" my relationship with this place, and certainly not with the club. It's true I've done a thousand hours of therapy; I found my first therapist six months after landing my first full-time job. But no one's ever suggested I needed to get on a train and return to the scene of the crime in order to truly heal from it. Reparative experiences are great for some people, but I think any mental-health professional would agree that this place is toxic.

Yet it's also true that when I saw the job listing—barely two hours after Jamie Burger posted it—I knew I would apply, and that I'd get it. I knew I was going home this summer, and I knew exactly why.

"Right," says Jamie, when he's able to speak. "Well, since we're putting cards on the table, I should give you a heads-up on something."

He straightens up, the old chair squeaking.

"It's a shitty gig."

I straighten now too, cocking my head.

"Okay?"

"Technically, you'd be a 'floating admin,' but really, you'd be helping me update the club's operating systems."

I glance reflexively at the giant, old computer monitor on his desk.

"Not that," Jamie says. "I mean, yes, computers. But I mean *all* operations. Dining reservations, function-room bookings—all the basic admin stuff. Oh, and a website."

"Sure." I nod, then pause. "Wait. The club has no *website*?"

Jamie leans back, chuckling.

"When I say we're out-of-date, I mean straight-up analog. Think rotary phones. Think Brody."

I nod again. It's fine. I was alive for dial-up.

"That's the other thing about this job," Jamie continues, sitting forward. "It won't last."

"Right, it's just this summer, I know. The listing—"

Jamie shakes his head.

"I'd be surprised if it lasted through July. I got *very* reluctant board approval to make this hire. They don't want the place 'modernized'—none of the old guard do. Especially not this summer, with everything going on here."

Jamie sits back, drumming his fingers on the side of his chair.

"I can't tell," I say after moment. "Do I have the job?"

He shrugs, eyebrows raised, his whole body skeptical.

"I can't think of a reason not to hire you. Not a good one, anyway."

I feel myself smiling. I'm sitting here blood crusted, and he's got a stain the size of my cheek on his jacket.

"Aside from the dry-cleaning bill?"

Jamie glances at his shoulder.

"Oh no, I'm going to sue," he deadpans. "You've got the job, but I'll see you in court."

"Sounds good." I nod, standing and extending a hand. "Tomorrow then?"

This time Jamie does follow my lead, standing to shake my hand with a tight smile.

"Nine a.m. Oh, but no sandals. I'll send you the dress code."

I'm floored by how smoothly this whole thing's gone. I guess part of me expected *worse* than just a head-on collision, a fainting spell and a bloody nose.

I pick up my bag and shuffle around my chair, heading through the open door.

"Alice?"

Something sinks inside me before I even turn around. When I do, Jamie is standing with his arms folded, his ears slightly pink.

"About this summer—the thing I said, about everything going on here?"

I look at him, lost. Finally, he spits it out.

"Sorry, I just have to ask. You do know about Susannah, right? I mean, about—"

"Oh! Yes!" I answer, far too brightly. "Definitely."

"Okay. Great. I just had to—"

"Of course."

We stand there nodding vigorously at each other.

"I didn't know if you were in touch," he says, a splotch of blush emerging on his forehead. He lifts a hand, rubbing at his hairline. "Sorry, no. 'Course you're not."

I smile through a wave of sadness. It's nice to hear someone else say it.

"No. Not in years. Not since before she moved back here."

I leave it at that, as though Susannah's move and our estrangement had nothing to do with each other—just coincidental timing. This sends another wave of heartbreak through me. I wish it were that simple.

Chapter Seven

Ten days after the murder, village police held a press conference and declared the investigation closed. Caitlin's death, they said, was an accidental drowning—no evidence of Patrick's involvement or of foul play. It was a tragedy, not a crime. The murder allegations were "a misunderstanding, at best."

Susannah appeared at my bedroom door that evening, carrying her sleeping bag. I hadn't called her—I hadn't spoken at all in hours. But just the sight of her filled me with immeasurable relief. She slept on the floor by my bed that night, and for the first time in days, I slept too.

Susannah slept over at least once a week for the rest of the summer. She never asked me about the murder and I never wanted to talk about it, but I'd wake from screaming nightmares almost every night. Susannah would sit up, bleary but calm, and grab me by the wrist, gently shaking me back into reality. I'd crumple to the floor with her and let it all spill out—the horror I relived in perfect detail each night: Caitlin's needle-sharp shrieks, the crack and thud of fists against flesh, the way I'd somehow known I was too late, even as I ran to her.

Susannah listened, every time—although it was a story no eleven-year-old should hear. Only later did I realize how terrifying it must have been for her, sitting knee to knee with me in the throes of acute PTSD.

As a recovered, functional adult, I'm ashamed for putting her through that, but the fact is, without her, I'd never have recovered or learned to function. I only made it to adulthood by following her there.

Susannah was a stalwart, even as a kid—the type who committed and never looked back, whether it was field hockey or friendships. When we returned to school that fall, she stuck by me—sometimes literally pulling me to her side when I drifted back a step, walking behind her and hiding my own face behind her mass of curls. Everyone else seemed to wish I'd vanish too. Teachers wouldn't even call on me, and if I so much as raised my hand for the bathroom pass, the whole room froze as if a ghost had spoken.

"Ignore them," Susannah would say, like it was that easy. For her, it might've been. Susannah never bothered much with other people's opinions, even when they applied to her. She didn't care about being a normie, or blush if someone mentioned that her dad was their tennis instructor.

"They're *insulting* you," I'd hiss.

"How is that an insult?" she'd reply, not even lowering her voice.

Sometimes it drove me up the wall—this relentless maturity and confidence. But I counted on it. Susannah was the only one who still saw me as Alice after I became "the child witness." I leaned on her character and unshakable sense of self—herself *and* mine.

In truth, I probably leaned on it a little too long. Each passing season felt a little less surreal, and though I wouldn't say I had a normal adolescence—what with the spontaneous fainting and all that—I had moments of normal. I made friends, I kissed boys, and squished into the backs of cars with a pack of kids, all of us in hysterics. But those were occasions. Susannah was my constant. She was the one with whom I laughed the hardest. She was the one who baked birthday cookies and quizzed me on French verbs, even though she took Latin. She daydreamed of her bright, ambitious future—psychologist or city planner, maybe married but no kids—and in doing so, reminded me that I had a future outside of this place too. And on bad days, when the nightmares returned and I retreated into darkness, it was still she who tugged me into the present.

I'd have done the same for her, of course, and whenever I did get the chance to be the supportive one, I supported with all my might. When she got dumped by the lifeguard from her summer job at Mirror Lake Camp, I was there ten minutes after she called. When she hit a deer with her dad's car, driving home from SAT prep, I came (and brought Theo to deal with it). I was there when she got rejected by her second-choice college in the city. Two days later, when she got accepted by her top-choice school in California, *with* financial aid, I was there again, with a cake. I'd be going to the first state school within driving distance that accepted me. Yes, I envied her getting to leave Briar's Green and start fresh in a place where normies were just the norm. But the fact that we'd be separated was the part that crushed and terrified me. I never let on though. Susannah had borne enough of my terror—and because of that, I knew, I would be okay.

And I was. We both were, miraculously, and so was our friendship. If anything we grew closer in college, shrugging off the cast of our childhood bond and reshaping it into something more balanced. The normal moments stretched out into normal months and years, both of us stepping into adulthood on opposite sides of the country, holding one another's hands via cell phone. Yes, I was surprised when Susannah decided to stay in California and take a position at a San Francisco marketing firm (since when was *marketing* her plan?). But plans changed, I understood. I was busy falling into my own unexpected career, having been poached from my temp job at a SoHo hotel, by a guest—a director in town for a two-month movie shoot, in dire need of a second assistant to manage his personal calendar and keep his minifridge stocked with Lean Cuisine.

Susannah and I still talked constantly, swapping stories from our days in real time. ("I'm picking up sneakers for my boss, and you won't believe what they cost!" "I'm trying a Pilates class, because all anyone talks about here is Pilates. You won't believe how much *it* costs.") But then our days got busier. Our lives got busier. Twenty-five felt different than twenty-one. By twenty-six I'd landed my third full-time-assistant position, and realized that I was both good at this job and content in it. I'd swapped my silver flip phone for a smartphone the size of a brick, and an auxiliary laptop I kept fully charged in my backpack at all times, along with my passport, running shoes and a backup cocktail dress sealed in a freezer bag. My life had gelled into *my* life, unrecognizable from the one I'd shared so intimately with Susannah. The same was true for her, I knew. I could hear it when we talked—all the names I didn't know, the promotions and new apartments she could've sworn she told me about.

Things slip through the cracks when you're three thousand miles apart, and those cracks can quickly widen into chasms. Our constant calls became intermittent voicemails, and eventually, unanswered texts. At first it just seemed like we kept missing each other—the time difference and everything. But at some point, the silence became a tense silence. I didn't know why, but I didn't worry about it. Maybe she was just extra busy with her own new life, and all the Pilates and corporate jargon I didn't understand. I knew we'd sort it out whenever we did find time to talk.

We didn't though. A month passed, and then three more. And then she called me late one night and told me she'd gotten a new job back home, working for the Yates Foundation.

"I— Sorry, the water's running, hang on."

I was in the bathroom, floss wound around my fingers. I blinked at myself in the mirror. I looked down at the phone beside the sink. Susannah's name looked up at me. I turned the faucet off.

Do over, I thought. *I misheard.* "Hey," I said, picking up the phone. "Okay, what did you say?"

Susannah's sigh came garbled through the speaker.

"I said it's the Yates Foundation. I'm going to be director of communications."

Her voice was flat. Not hesitant, not defiant. Nothing.

"I don't get it," I said, part of me still certain I'd misunderstood.

"It's been in the works for a few months," she said. "I didn't want to tell you until it was official."

My legs felt cold and wobbly. I sat on the edge of the bathtub, clutching the sink.

"Patrick isn't involved in the foundation," Susannah continued. "Neither are his parents. I made sure of that, obviously."

I shook my head in silence. None of it made sense. No part of it was obvious.

"His uncle is chairman, but even that's mostly a title," she said, a bit more relaxed. "It's quite independent from the family at this point."

"Oh?" I said, my voice loud and craggy. "Is it quite?"

A heavy breath came through the speaker again, tickling my ear.

"Was that a *sigh*?" I almost laughed. "So sorry, am I being quite tiresome?"

"You're being unfair."

Fury burst like a firecracker in my chest.

"Are you actually joking? You call me at midnight, out of the blue, and tell me you're going to work for the Yateses. And—"

"For the Yates *Foundation*."

"And it's been 'in the works' for *months*. For months, Susannah! Without telling me! *I'm* being unfair?"

"Yeah," she spit back. "Unfair, and completely selfish."

I stood up, speechless, still clutching the sink.

"You think I *want* to pick up and move?" she barked. "Start a new job across the fucking country?"

"Well. Okay, why are—"

"Because my parents asked me to," she said, her voice breaking. "My mother *begged* me to. Okay? My dad's barely mobile after the last back surgery, and she can't take care of him alone anymore."

She was really crying now.

"It's not like they can afford help, you know? I'm it. They need me. She actually said that, Alice. 'Please, I need you.'"

I forced myself to breathe. I pictured Gloria Joyce's face, as familiar as my own mother's. How many times had she given me dinner? How many birthday cards had I gotten with goofy little notes to "our second daughter"?

"Shit," I winced. "I'm sorry. About your parents, I mean."

I heard her turn away from the phone and blow her nose.

"Look, it's fine, you didn't know. And I'm sorry for not calling sooner. It's been chaos. I had to drop everything."

Something about her voice—some thread of hesitation. I pictured her on the other end, blinking slowly as she spoke. Susannah was a bad liar with an obvious tell. She'd start blinking uncontrollably the second she started saying something false. It was hilarious—in high school, she actually practiced on me, trying to stop the reflex. The best she could do was slow it down, which made the giveaway even more obvious. She'd start blinking in slow motion like a sleepy kitten, whenever she tried to fudge the details or tell even a minor fib.

"Right," I said, trying to put my finger on it. "Chaos, I'm sure."

"Yeah, breaking my lease, finding a new job. God, is there *any* chance you could be cool with this?"

I faced myself in the mirror, my mouth agape and incredulous. Susannah continued before I could answer.

"You know, I only applied because it was local. But honestly? The foundation's great—the people are great."

There it is, I thought. *There's the bullshit.*

"It's a huge step up too," she added. "If I stayed here, I wouldn't make director for five years."

Her voice brightened as she carried on about her exciting new role. Gone was the pretense of a chaotic, last-minute move. Gone was the somber tone and stress over her parents, so desperate for her help. That might've been true, but she certainly hadn't "dropped everything," and fled across the country to pitch in. She'd taken her time. "It's been in the works for months," she'd said. I imagined leisurely interviews, some higher-up flying out to have lunch with her. Had she even applied, or had they been courting her? And if so, had she balked even once at the thought of working for them?

"Wow," I said, interrupting. "Congrats on the dream job."

Susannah stopped.

"What?" she said. "I don't follow."

"It sounds like a great career move, really. You could've just told me that," I said. "You could've just told me the truth, I could've handled it."

She inhaled sharply.

"You know what, Alice? I don't think you could."

From there, we were off to the races. I called her out for eliding the truth about this new job. I told her it was obvious she'd compromised herself, and she clearly knew it too. Why else would she avoid telling me? Why blame it on her parents, like a child? It wasn't blame, Susannah said; it was responsibility—something she claimed I knew nothing about it. She laid into me about my stunted, selfish mindset. *Yes*, what happened was terrible, but it was time to move on. She wasn't going to spend the rest of her life avoiding the village, and she certainly wasn't going to turn down an opportunity like this out of some childish sense of loyalty to me.

"Okay, fine!" I shouted—we were both shouting by then. "Forget me, what about Caitlin?"

"What about her?! She's dead and it's awful, but Jesus, what am I supposed to do?!"

"Literally, work *anywhere* else maybe?" I answered through hot tears. "Take *anyone* else's money."

"These people didn't kill her! They didn't know her! And shit, Alice, you barely knew her!"

I went still, standing straight-backed in the middle of the bathroom, my nose and eyes streaming.

"What the hell does that mean, Susannah?"

She sniffled on the other end, crying herself.

"You—"

She cut herself off, pausing for a breath. I could hear her thinking, then deciding to say it.

"You act like Caitlin was the most important person in your life, and that her death was the most important thing that happened to you. The most important thing that happened, period."

My head felt numb and unwieldy on my neck. I shook it silently, not knowing what to say. She was just completely wrong.

"I remember listening to you talk about her one night a few years ago—maybe on her birthday, I'm not sure. And I suddenly thought, *Caitlin's the one who died*. This isn't just a thing that happened to *you*, Alice Wiley."

"A few years ago?" I finally replied. "You never said anything. I wish I'd known how you felt."

A sad, ragged laugh came through the phone.

"No, you don't, Alice," Susannah said. "I love you, but that's bullshit. You wanted my support, my validation—my actual thoughts and opinions? Not so much. Not if they challenged yours."

"That's not true," I answered, stunned and mumbling. "That's not fair."

"Fine," she sniffed. "Fine, you win, you've got dibs on *fair*. I'd rather be honest than fair anyway."

Chapter Eight

"Piggy attaaaaaaack!"

I see a blur of blond hair as Simon leaps off the couch. I reach back, catching him just as he crash-lands onto my back.

"Simon!" Jules steps out of the kitchen, sponge in hand, looking her youngest in eye.

Simon relaxes his choke-hold grip around my neck and slithers off my back, giggling.

"We always do piggy attack," he shouts.

"But we always *ask* first, right?" Theo calls from the kitchen sink, hollering over the clatter of dishes. I've arrived on Dad's Spaghetti Night. The house is steamed up with garlic and pasta water.

"Right!" Simon hollers back, flopping onto the couch.

"What else do we do?" Jules asks patiently.

"I'm sorry, Aunt Alice, and are you okay?" Simon says, his head dangling above the carpet.

I've been kneed in the kidneys by a flying six-year-old. I may never stand upright again, but I'll be damned before I lose my reputation as Cool Aunt Alice.

"Yeah, buddy! Just give me a warning next time."

I extend my palm for an upside-down high five. Simon slaps it, then falls off the couch on his head.

Simon is the baby of his family, and it suits him. He's like a golden retriever puppy: jumpy and destructive, but you simply can't get mad at him. Isaac, his older brother, is just as sweet, but in the opposite way: a sensitive, thoughtful kid—the kind who notices everything.

"Are you sure you're okay, Aunt Alice?" Isaac asks. "You're sitting kind of funny."

He pauses by the dining table, dirty plates in his hands, watching me. Isaac is also a bit of a worrier.

I straighten up and smile back, nodding. I feel a hand patting my foot and look to see Simon beaming up at me from under the coffee table.

"Aunt Alice, may I please have a piggy attack, please?"

Jules and Theo's house is always a mess, but it's ten times nicer than the condo we grew up in. Two bedrooms, two bathrooms and an honest-to-God basement. It has a brick walkway out front, and a driveway where the boys are always leaving their bikes, even though the garage is right there. It has a front *and* backyard, and a kitchen floor with not one single missing tile.

It also has a massive mortgage and a roof they're always staring at. Whenever I see Jules and Theo on the front lawn, hands on hips, muttering about shingle, I simply swell with pride. I can't help it. Theo's life is far more modest than the one our mother wanted for him, but it's also better than she could've dreamed of. I just wish she'd gotten to see more of it.

"Hey," says Theo, stepping out of the kitchen, drying his hands on a dishcloth. "You okay?"

"Yeah. You?"

"Yep."

This is how we talk about mom. She died three years ago—cancer, quick and awful. By the time she was diagnosed, the disease was so entrenched that surgery was ruled out and other treatments were deemed too great a strain for her body to endure. She was in hospice ten weeks later, and died four weeks after that. We hadn't even adjusted to the fact that she was sick, and suddenly, she was gone. Years later, Theo and I still haven't found actual words to talk about it.

Instead, we stand in the messy, loud living room watching Simon and Isaac flick LEGOs at each other while Jules checks emails at the dining table, sipping peppermint tea and reminding them not to aim for the eyes. I give Theo the mom-would-have-loved-this nod. He gives me the don't-I-know-it clap on the shoulder. That's that.

"Let's get you settled." Theo nods toward the hall, where my bags sit heaped by the basement door. "Big day tomorrow."

I peer at him, knowing full well that "get you settled" means "carry your bags to the basement, then hold you hostage with a lecture." But I do have a big day tomorrow—and a busy night tonight, though Theo doesn't know that part. If I'm squeezing in a lecture too, I'd better get it out of the way.

"Say goodnight!" Theo calls to the boys, waving me to the basement door.

"What?! No!" Simon bellows. "We were gonna do the puzzle she brought!"

"She has a job now, buddy," Theo calls, heading downstairs. "She'll be here all summer."

My neck goes hot and prickly as I descend the carpeted steps. All summer. Unless I get fired first.

"It's nothing fancy," says Theo, hitting the light switch at the bottom of the stairs. "But Jules did jazz it up a bit. And I know everyone says this, but the foldout's actually very comfortable."

I look around, once again knocked out by the suburban domesticity. It's a classic shag-carpet basement, complete with a plastic tub of Christmas decorations and a dehumidifier moaning in the corner. A tinny drip echoes from the narrow bathroom, and the wood-paneled walls look identical to those in Jamie's closet-office. But the room has indeed been cozied up. The foldout's made up in crisp white sheets and a set of jewel-toned throw pillows. There's a nightstand on each side where Jules has placed two table lamps that light the room with a buttery glow.

"It's wonderful," I say, and I mean it. "Thank you, Theo. I'm glad I'm here. This was the right call."

He nods at the room, a blank expression on his face.

"Hey," I say, leaning sideways to catch his gaze. "Don't know if you caught that, but I said you were right. About staying with you all."

He nods. "Of course. You're family, Alice. We don't have much of that left." He turns, somber, and locks eyes with me. "I just wish you'd tell me what you're really doing here."

My breath catches. I grasp at my stash of prebaked answers—the stuff about reparative experiences and closure, or something like that—but I can't quite get ahold of them. So I just look back at my brother and nod. We stand there, listening to the thump and holler from upstairs. Theo turns to leave. He waves good night without looking back.

I wait until the house is still and I'm that certain everyone's asleep. Then I reach under the bed, pull out my smallest suitcase and turn the dial on its tiny combination lock. It's light—the only things in here are four pairs of shoes lined up in vinyl shoe bags, and beneath them, my laptop and thick manila file of printed forms. They're already signed and notarized, I just need to do a once-over for typos before I bring them to the police station. Tomorrow is my first day of work, and I already have lunch plans: I'm filing a request for all police records related to the death of Caitlin Dale.

This is just a first step, and mostly ceremonial. I don't expect to get much from village PD (and I loathe the idea of asking them for anything), but I need a public record showing that I tried. I'll likely spend the rest of my life in some degree of legal trouble over what I plan to do here. I don't *plan* to break the law, but if I have to, I won't hesitate—I won't mind a bit.

I'm getting Patrick Yates. That's what I'm really doing here.

Starting tomorrow, I'm going to scrape the whole village for evidence. There's plenty of it out there—plenty of mouths kept politely shut all these years, many of them glugging cocktails at the club right now. Maybe there's even some physical evidence locked up in somebody's dusty old safe.

How I'll get any of this, I don't know. I've got some ideas and I've got the summer. All I know is I have to try, and I have to try *now*, when all eyes are on the village again. I'll get whatever I can, and then I'll report it—not to the cops this time, but to everyone. I'm going to the media and those creepy murder fans to tell them what I know and what I saw twenty years ago. I'll tell them another thing too: my name.

I flip the last form over and stack it on top of the others, closing the file. I slip it carefully into my tote, then lift the bag and tuck it between the bed and the nightstand. I look down at it for a moment, then lean over, tutting at myself, and zip the tote bag shut with its tiny, decorative zipper. My eyes are dry and clicky, but I'm exhausted in a wired way. I lie back, settling into the fresh sheets and firm, new-smelling pillow.

Make no mistake—I want Patrick Yates locked up and legally demolished. I'll involve law enforcement eventually, but I can't go to them first. I reported Patrick "the right way" back when I was the child witness, and I failed. I can't let that happen again. I need to make it impossible for his family or this village to protect him this time. Because this time, unbelievably, the stakes are even higher.

I pull out my phone, open Instagram, my thumb navigating automatically to the post—the one I stare at every night, sometimes until I fall asleep. It's a macabre ritual, like picking at a wound until it bleeds again. But I do it—I've done it every night for the last four months, because some small, pathetic part of me still thinks it might be gone. *Maybe she's deleted it. Maybe it was never there.*

It's there tonight though. The picture appears before my eyes, each pixel of it painfully familiar and still unthinkably strange. Susannah faces the camera, standing on a beach beneath a dusky sunset. Her dark, black-coffee curls have been ironed straight and lightened to a warm chestnut. Her cheeks are pink from the sun, and she's laughing hard, eyes closed and mouth wide open, showing her molars. She holds her left hand up, displaying the ring.

The man with his arms around her waist looks freshly tanned too—but then, he always did. His head is bent against her shoulder. He wears a reverent smile. His eyes are closed, but even so, he's instantly familiar. I'd know Patrick anywhere.

Chapter Nine

"And over here's the library. Usually dead this time of day." Jamie opens the door. A fire is crackling in the old stone hearth, despite the fact that nobody's in here, and also, it's June.

"Don't tell me they still keep it lit all summer," I whisper. It's approaching eighty degrees outside, and it's barely 10:00 a.m. "Have these people heard of climate change?"

"Yes, they do, and no, they have not. You don't have to whisper in here, by the way."

I shake my head, embarrassed. The library was a no-kid zone when I was growing up, and we all knew to keep silent even walking by, lest we disturb one of the cranky old men who camped out there all afternoon, napping beneath the *Wall Street Journal*.

"Old habits," I say, speaking up.

Jamie nods, understanding, and waves us back into the lobby.

"You might want to keep quiet about climate change though."

Jamie is taking me on an orientation tour that I don't need. I told him as much when I arrived this morning, hauling my bulky tote bag and wearing Jules's shoes. Jamie sent me the dress-code document last night, attached to an ominous one-line email: **Okay. Here it is.** Reviewing it this morning, I understood. As a female staffer, there are two types of shoes I may wear: oxford lace-up or penny loafer, "white only." I'll have to hit the mall later, to find a knee-length skirt in "buff khaki," "buttercup" or—wait for it—"true white." No pockets allowed. Today I'm making do in Jules's beige oxfords, which are both too long and too narrow for me, and a skirt which is *regular* khaki and has one back hip pocket.

"But it's sewn shut," I told Jamie. "Purely decorative." Then he told me my shirt wasn't white enough.

I'm now wearing a club-issued polo shirt, in the signature crème de menthe green. My white blouse—with its non-regulation-gray buttons—is stuffed inside my tote, hanging from one of the hooks in Jamie's office. I'd hesitated to leave my bag, filled as it was with all my police forms. But I didn't have much choice. Jamie had given me the shirt and pointed me toward the break room, saying I could change there and leave my bag in any open cubby. I'd paused, and he'd looked at me with concern and confusion—a combination that looks a lot like suspicion.

"Or my office, if you prefer to leave it there?" he'd added. "It's not locked either though."

"Perfect," I'd said, feigning relief. "Some things never change!"

Now I remember though—*nothing* changes. The clubhouse is just as it was twenty years ago. The further we get into orientation, the more I recall: the toilet in the powder room that was always running (still there, still running). The grill menu, with the same four lunch items: turkey club, Caesar salad, blackened chicken and the clam chowder that no one ever orders. Even the ashtrays are still here, as is indoor smoking.

"They sued the state over the ban," Jamie explains, as if this is a totally normal thing to do. "Indoor smoking is now legal in all of Briar's Green. Legal *again*, I guess."

He heads toward the center of the lobby, moving a hair faster than his usual fast clip. I have to speed-walk to keep up with his long-legged strides, my shoes skidding on the felted green carpet.

"Are you serious? The whole village?"

"Yeah, but don't worry. They only smoke in here."

Jamie narrates as he goes, pointing to the far-right corner.

"Cloakroom's still there, next to the powder room. Fire exit's in the back. Reception desk is on the left—not to be confused with the *old* reception desk."

He stops in the middle of the lobby, facing the grand marble staircase that swoops up to the second floor. There's a small door carved into the base of the stairs, and in front of it, a matching marble desk, topped with a tidy vase of lily of the valley. Jamie gestures to it, lowering his voice.

"You remember the deal with the old desk, right?"

"It's haunted."

"Ha ha."

"It's electrified, and anyone who steps foot behind it will be zapped to death."

The old reception desk was another subject of several childhood rumors—all started by the club itself. The real story was that marble had been crumbling off the side of the staircase for sixty years, and no one wanted to pay for all those tiresome safety repairs. Better to simply use the funds on a new reception desk, and keep children away from the old one with ridiculous horror stories.

"Do they still tell the one about the secret room behind it, where they torture kids who run by the pool?"

"Yes, and the archive full of cursed jewels and skeletons." Jamie deadpans. "But seriously, don't go back there. It's coming off in chunks now."

I nod soberly.

"Okay, second floor." Jamie heads up the staircase, narrating as he goes. "We can skip the guest rooms—mostly just mice in there. Fire exit's on the landing, left end of the hall is the airing cupboard, and staff steps are on the right. Sorry for rushing this."

"We really don't need to do this at all, Jamie," I say, clutching the banister, steadying myself on the slick, worn marble. "I know where the fire exits are."

The village is militant about fire safety laws, not for the sake of its citizens, but its precious old properties. I guess I'd be worried too, what with all the indoor smoking and roaring, unattended fireplaces.

"We really do," Jamie counters, marching up the steps. "If you break an ankle on the staircase I need to be able to say I told you it was slippery and uneven."

"Roger that," I reply, still grasping the banister. Jamie nods me along.

"The grill starts serving Bloody Marys at ten, and I need us off the floor by then." His voice rebounds off the marble and he drops into a murmur. "They're fussy about staff tours 'getting in the way.'"

They, I have gleaned, are the club's old-guard members and its almighty board. Jamie may be concierge here, but he's not one of them—far from it. His dad had worked on the overnight maintenance team, and Jamie started there too, at eighteen, chipping away at a hospitality degree during the day. But he was always aiming for management, and having grown up in the clubhouse, he knew the place inside-out. He'd proven a unique and invaluable resource, trusted by both members and staff, and soon he'd worked his way up so high that even the board had to agree—with great reluctance—to create a senior position for him.

"*Concierge* isn't really the appropriate title," he explains as we walk down the long corridor that comprises the club's second floor. "But that's the one they agreed on. After nine board meetings."

I laugh. He looks at me, eyebrows raised.

"I'm not joking."

"God," I say, half whispering again. "It's like they *enjoy* wasting time."

We stroll briskly past the row of guest rooms that line the upstairs hall—originally meant for overnight shooting parties and debutante balls. They're cramped and stuffy, and the members never use them, but they're always made up with fresh linens nonetheless. These people enjoy waste, period.

Jamie sighs, shrugging lightly.

"They sure do. Staff stairs are down here." Jamie points us down the hall, continuing. "Before me, it was just Brody running the show, and they were fine with that. They loved it—all his formalities, rules for the sake of rules."

"I remember," I say, still chilled thinking of him. "An etiquette for everything. 'Always time for manners.'"

"Exactly. Can't put out the newspaper until it's been ironed by hand," says Jamie, adding darkly, "That is also not a joke, by the way."

But it still makes me snort with laughter.

"God, and then what? They all shared the one copy?"

"No, it just sat there all day!" Jamie whisper-shouts. "People get the news from their own papers—or phones or TVs. That's the point, it was a lot of needless ceremony and zero efficiency. The younger members started to complain, and eventually forced the board to bring on some new management. 'Additional' management, not replacement."

He gestures at himself.

"So, it's like Brody's the monarch and you're the prime minister."

"Basically. If the monarch still retained the right to decapitate someone for pouring wine from the bottle without decanting." He holds up his hands. "I mean no disrespect to Brody. I get it—we're here to serve our members, and the old-school crowd still likes doing things the traditional way. But the newer folks expect a little more service for their $50k. They want Wi-Fi."

That, they still don't have. Currently, the club operates on a hodgepodge of spreadsheets and leather-bound ledgers. If a member wants to book a function room, they have to call the front desk and be transferred to the events manager (or more likely, his voicemail). If they want to reserve a tennis court, they have to call a different number to speak to the recreation manager (who, as it happens, is often outside). There is no such thing as online booking because nothing is online. Every form, list and menu is saved on paper, and most important records are written by hand—Mr. Brody's, specifically. If a member needs to update their phone number, he must go in person to Mr. Brody's office and dictate it to him while he inscribes it in the register. This is the kind of inefficiency that *they* hold dear. It's tradition.

My job as "floating admin" is to streamline and digitize operations just enough to make life easier for the newer members, without disturbing those who still prefer to do things the old, annoying way.

"So, install an online booking system, and—what?" I ask, following Jamie down the spiral staff staircase. "Scan the paper records?"

He stops at the bottom, thinking.

"Uh, yeah. I guess that's the bulk of it." He gestures to the doorway, leading out of the staff hall and into the gallery. "I told you, you're overqualified. I was just going to hire a college kid."

"You thought you needed a *college* kid for this? Simon could knock this out in a day."

Jamie pauses, frowning.

"Simon," I repeat, my little joke hanging a little awkwardly now. "Theo's son—the younger one."

"*Oh,*" Jamie says, shaking his head. "Right, no, I— Right."

He heads into the gallery. I watch him for a moment, then hurry to catch up.

"Sorry, I spaced for a second," Jamie says as we pass the pink ballroom. "Theo and I don't hang out much anymore."

"What? Really?" I ask, taken aback. "He didn't tell me."

Jamie shakes his head dismissively, looking ahead.

"Nothing to tell. I work here, and he's doing his whole—" Jamie gestures in the air. "Our paths don't cross a lot."

He's so flat and inscrutable that it takes me a moment to put two and two together: Theo's becoming a big shot, and Jamie's a concierge. It's only now occurring to me how odd it must be working here, not just as a former staff kid, but a former Wheaton normie. He must cross paths with lots of old schoolmates, but no old friends.

"I guess you see Susannah though," I blurt out into the silence. "She must be here a lot."

"Hmm?" says Jamie, his face briefly, and reasonably, alarmed. "Oh. Not much. They don't really—I mean, holidays, yes, but they don't really—"

"Jamie." I smile, patting his arm. "Relax. And *please* slow down."

He stops short, his shoes scuffing softly on the felted carpet. We're nearing the end of the gallery, and I glance toward the lobby, ensuring it's still empty.

"The whole thing is beyond weird already," I say, quiet but still smiling. "You can't possibly make it weirder."

He winces—a proper wince. And then he checks the lobby too. "Wanna bet?"

Jamie waits until we're back in the office and sitting down, and then he tells me: the wedding—Susannah's wedding to Patrick Yates—is happening here.

"*Why?*" I demand, no longer keeping quiet. "Why would she—why would *he?*"

I grip the arms of my chair with clammy fingers.

Jamie sits with his hands folded.

"So, you didn't know then."

Now I recall the little exchange at the end of our interview yesterday. Jamie double-checking that I knew "about Susannah" and "everything going on here."

"Not *that* part. I knew they were getting married here, but not *here*. The wedding announcement said Briar's Green."

Announcements—I'd read three of them. One in the *Times*, one in the *Hudson Valley Journal* and one in the Wheaton alumni newsletter. They'd all been revoltingly breezy, as though this were any other charming couple, not a murderer and a woman voluntarily marrying a murderer. And none had said anything about the club.

"Well," Jamie says, tilting his head. "This is the usual Yates wedding venue. His parents, his grandparents, all of them."

I glare across the desk.

"I'm just *saying*," he says, hands flying, a little whine in his voice—a little of the old Jamie Burger. "Trust me, I get it, but if you think about it from their side—Alice, quit looking at me like that. From their side it's like, if he doesn't get married here like everyone else, then how would it look?

Respectful? Rational? The only reasonable thing to do?

Every inch of me wants to argue, but he's right. To them it would look like acknowledgment—maybe even an admission of guilt. Patrick, of all people, getting married here, of all places (of all summers), is a great way to demonstrate how unbothered he is.

"Alice, I apologize," Jamie says calmly, a professional again. "I should've been more explicit. If this changes things with the job, I understand. No harm, no foul, you can just leave."

I turn my eyes downward, giving his desk a hard stare. *I see a leather blotter*, I think. *I smell shoe polish and oiled wood. I hear someone hitting tennis balls outside.*

"When is it exactly?" I ask, breathing slow breaths. "I know it's August, but—"

"Second of August."

I exhale in a gust. The second of August is pretty much July.

"It doesn't change anything. Of course I'll stay."

Jamie looks incredulous. "Really? Because she'll be here more than usual. With wedding stuff."

I shrug—a little forced, but I pull it off.

"It's fine. She'll be out there, planning centerpieces or whatever, and I'll be—" I pause. "Actually, where will I be? When I'm not 'floating'?"

Jamie bows his head and gestures to me—to exactly where I'm sitting. I look at the desk again and see the blotter's been nudged to one side and the computer monitor to the other, making space for my laptop. I'm not sure where my knees are supposed to go.

"It's tight, I know," Jamie says, scooching up in his chair. "I'd find you another closet, but this is the only one with an internet hookup. And without asbestos."

I feel the paneled walls closing in. How am I going to get anything done? Any of my *real* work? I picture it: Jamie on one side of the desk, yakking with Susannah's wedding planner, and me on the other, investigating the groom.

Jamie's face is shifting into that curious-suspicious look I noticed earlier.

"It's fine," I repeat in a game voice. "It'll be fun."

Jamie's eyebrows lift just slightly. *Too* game—I try again.

"It'll be fun *and* weird. But I mean it, the wedding changes nothing about the job. I'm here to do spreadsheets and scanning, so—" I nod, trying to put a period on the end of this conversation "—where shall I start? Who's first on the list?"

The suspicious look holds for one more second, then Jamie cracks a smile.

"Pretty sure you do know this one."

And immediately, I do.

Chapter Ten

"Ms. Wiley," says Mr. Brody. "What a pleasant surprise to see you again, here."

He sits behind his desk in a high-backed wooden chair, unblinking and still.

"I don't think I've actually been in your office."

I titter under my breath—a pathetic, mousy sound, but Mr. Brody makes every human nervous. It's basically his job.

"Not quite what I meant," he says. "Do come in though."

I cross the threshold of his dusty lair, the air turning suddenly cooler and damp. Mr. Brody's office is on the subterranean level—the downstairs hall, most members call it. It's a long, low-ceilinged corridor running from one end of the clubhouse to the other, mirroring the gallery above (but with shabbier carpeting and fluorescent lights). On the north end is the door to the women's locker room, and the exit toward the tennis courts. On the south end is the men's, and the exit toward the pool. Mr. Brody's office sits tucked discreetly in between them, the door unmarked and painted to match the grove-green walls.

The room appears to have been modeled after the library upstairs, with two floor-to-ceiling walls of bookshelves, and everything painted the same flat, nearly black navy. It looks crisp and sophisticated in the large, tidy library, but down here it just makes it feel more like a cave they'll find your bones in. Mr. Brody's office is five decades of messes layered on top of each other. Every surface is covered with old papers and ledgers, and my throat is already tickling with dust.

"I understand you're here to 'streamline' us," Mr. Brody says as I sit in his creaky guest chair. "Oh, no need, dear."

He makes a lifting gesture—which, for some reason, I obey, leaping to my feet and standing silent and appalled. Mr. Brody smiles without teeth, then continues.

"I can't speak for the rest of the staff," he says, touching a hand to his chest. "But my system is quite all right as is."

I seriously beg to differ. Good luck finding anything in this pit.

The truth is I had hoped to do just that. I'd been counting on it. I have a list of my own—a running tally of places and people to search for evidence, and Mr. Brody is near the top. He may be a figurehead now, but in 1999, he really did run the show. He approved every new hire, inspected each menu and table-setting, and personally supervised every club party. The Christmas Revel, the Hunter's Ball, even the annual ice cream social for children twelve and under—Mr. Brody would be there, standing guard outside the ballroom door, surveilling the merriment with a resolute scowl. "Dear Mr. Brody," my aunt Barbara used to say. "Always keeping us on our p's and q's."

It wasn't just the staff he kept tabs on, and it wasn't just at parties. Day or night, Brody was the first to flag a dress-code violation, or catch kids sneaking into shuttered dining rooms to practice Britney Spears choreography (Susannah and I were busted, twice). He could sniff out a disruptive drunk at a dinner before they got out of hand, and swiftly dispatch a server over with a tray of petits fours—the tacit signal that someone at the table had perhaps had enough.

And at the big parties, which started with cocktails and ended in blackouts, he kept the chaos contained. People didn't roam much during cold-weather gatherings, preferring the fire-warmed ballrooms to the rest of the drafty clubhouse. But at summer parties, with all doors flung wide, Mr. Brody kept a close eye on comings and goings—especially on guests of particular value and/or concern: A-list members, known troublemakers and teenagers. In July 1999, Patrick Yates was all three. I imagine Mr. Brody had eyes on him all night.

I don't expect him to tell me anything. He was one of the few staffers the police interviewed about Caitlin's death, and he clearly didn't tell *them* anything—in fact, I'm almost certain he lied. Brody guards the club members because he worships them. He's built his life around his role as their most trusted servant. And the members do trust him. About that much I'm certain. Each December there's a quiet flurry of traffic outside his door as one by one they slip inside to deliver his Christmas card, always visibly thick with cash. Some are thicker than others, but everyone gives him a card. Everyone knows Mr. Brody holds the literal keys to the clubhouse—he's the only one with a set. Everyone knows he's the club's de facto record keeper, and writes everything down. And here's another thing we all know, though I've no idea why: Mr. Brody's door is the only one that's ever locked.

I know he's got something in here—some incriminating record or scrap of evidence. I'd pictured it tidily locked away in a drawer or safe—secure but close at hand, like an insurance policy. I'll admit, I got the "tidy" part *quite* wrong.

Mr. Brody clears his throat with a performative little *ahem*, and I snap back to attention.

"I don't want to interfere," I say, hearing myself shift into the formal tense that he prefers. "Perhaps you could walk me through it. Your system."

"Not necessary," Mr. Brody shoots back.

"Right, we'll start with your computer." I glance at the monitor, unplugged and shunted to the side of the desk. "When did you last update it?"

He shakes his head.

"Computers are for losing things."

"Mr. Brody," I say, tilting my head and folding my hands in front of me—a fighter's stance in Mr. Brody's world. "I do understand your reticence, but we will have to get things a bit more organized."

I glance at a stack of ledgers beside his desk, the lowest ones buckling, their bindings dry and beginning to crack.

"I'm afraid Jamie's insisted," I finish simply.

"Then he's mistaken," Mr. Brody replies, standing as he speaks. This is my signal to retreat politely (and quickly), or risk never being allowed through the door again.

"You'll forgive me for being direct," he says, gesturing toward the hallway. "But I've a full schedule this morning."

I pause. He pronounced it *shed-yule*, the English way—or rather the way that Anglophile Americans who've never been to England pronounce it. It's an affectation. Affectations are distinct faux pas, not only at the club, but in all of Briar's Green. "Putting on airs" signals that you are not of the elegant class, and worse, that you're trying to fake it—so preening and pathetic it would be uncouth to even acknowledge your gaffe.

I don't acknowledge it. But I don't leave either.

Mr. Brody fusses with papers on his desk, making a performance of getting back to work. I wait until he looks up again, jutting out his chin, his face taut and full of loathing. I smile back, polite as ever.

"I'm also quite concerned," I say, gesturing to the same stack of dried-out ledgers, "about your safety. And the safety of our members, of course."

"Nonsense," he scoffs, as close to flustered as I've ever seen him. "What on earth do you mean?"

"I would have to check the current village codes, but given the age of the building, and its electrical system—" I glance up at the buzzing light bulb dangling overhead "—I'm fairly certain this office presents a significant fire risk. In its current state."

At this, Mr. Brody's mouth drops into an unguarded scowl. He looks at me hard—but it doesn't work the way it used to. Now, I just look back, waiting until he finally speaks:

"Then we must remedy that."

Chapter Eleven

July Fourth, 1999

We followed the Dales to the club in our own car, and Mom parked in the staff lot, skipping the valet as usual. I sat hunched forward in the passenger seat, leaning into the last gasp of cool air from the air-conditioner vents. Theo's tie had come loose on the drive over, and he was still fumbling with it, cursing in the back seat. Mom was pretending to ignore it, fixing her lipstick in the rearview mirror, already visibly tense. She glanced at me with a small, apologetic smile. *Would you?* I got out and knocked on Theo's window. He muttered one last expletive and got out.

"Fine."

Theo had just finished his first year at the upper school, which required ties on formal days. He'd failed to learn to tie it himself, but I—the cat's cradle master of the lower school—was a natural. By the end of the year, I'd learned a handful of knots by heart (there was always some ridiculous tie fad with the Wheaton boys), and kind of enjoyed my weird new hobby, if only because Theo sucked at it. It made him grouchy, asking me for help, but it wasn't as bad as asking Mom.

He stood in front of me, lifted his chin, resigned. "Not half Windsor," he hissed. "It's gotta be four-in-hand."

"Huh? Why?"

I knew why. The same reason he'd started wearing Dad's old watch, even though it was broken. The same reason he'd let his hair grow shaggy, fighting off Mom's scissors all summer. Because all the upper-school boys did—because Patrick Yates had decided it was cool.

"Four-in-hand looks *just* like half Windsor," I said. "No one can tell the difference, it's just harder to do."

"They can tell," Theo answered, a thread of sadness in his voice that caught me off-guard. "Please?"

"Okay," I huffed. "Quit moving."

He was right. No normie would see the difference—no normie would even bother to look at his tie knot. But everyone in the club would.

Caitlin and her parents were waiting on the clubhouse steps, chatting. They all cheered when we came around the corner, as if we hadn't all left their house fifteen minutes earlier. The three of them made a showy fuss over me in the borrowed dress.

"Just darling," Aunt Barbara said, then corrected herself. "And so grown-up."

Caitlin winked at me and mouthed, "Perfect." Uncle Greg bent to give me his elbow, and everyone laughed. It was embarrassing, but in a good way, somehow, and I felt a bubbly excitement as we entered the club.

The lobby was a crush of bodies: women in white and men in black suits—required dress code for July Fourth. I hung back by the door, stifled by the fug of perfumed body heat, letting the others walk ahead. Caitlin, I noticed, had looped a raspberry-pink shawl over her elbows—a thin, silky thing, hanging low across her back.

Aunt Barbara noticed too. She put a hand on Caitlin's arm.

"Sweetheart," she whispered. "The shawl."

Caitlin shrugged. Aunt Barbara raised her eyebrows. A silent exchange passed between them, and just seeing it from four feet away made me hold my breath and look sideways. They whispered at each other for a minute, and then Aunt Barbara called my name.

"Alice, dear." I turned to see her beckoning me with a smile. Caitlin had her arms crossed.

I scurried over and Barbara put an arm around my shoulder.

"Alice, would you please escort your cousin to the cloakroom?" she asked. "I would, but I fear the humiliation would kill her."

She reached out with her satin clutch, playfully whacking Caitlin's arm. Caitlin suppressed a grin, rolled her eyes, then cracked.

"*Ugh.*" Caitlin groaned, dropping her head back. "Such a drama queen, Mommy!"

She shrugged the shawl off with a performative sigh and took my hand. Aunt Barbara waved us toward the cloakroom, blowing a kiss.

"I thought nonwhite accessories were okay," I said, as Caitlin guided us through the crowd.

I looked back, searching for Mom's face. She normally kept close tabs on us at the club, but when I caught her eye across the room, I could tell she wasn't worried. I was with Caitlin.

"What?" Caitlin said after a pause. "Sorry, did you say something?"

She was scanning the crowd too, I realized. Looking for Patrick. My stomach did a giddy flip.

"The shawl," I said, gesturing to the offending pink accessory draped over her arm.

"Oh," she said, paying attention now. "Well, technically no, they're not allowed. But literally no one cares except my darling mother. Oh, and him." She smirked, nodding toward the corner of the lobby. "He cares. 'Dear Mr. Brody.'"

I followed her gaze. He was standing apart from the crowd, hands behind his back, in his formal vest and jacket. He looked more formal than the guests.

"He hates me," I said, thinking of the putrid scowl he'd given me the last time we'd crossed paths. Susannah and I had been in the break room doing the assigned reading from *Great Expectations*, with our feet propped up on a metal folding chair. Mr. Brody had spotted us from the hall and made some icy comment about our grotesque manners. Thinking about it made my back go straight.

"Oh, honey," Caitlin guffawed. "He hates us all."

We found the cloakroom unattended, and all the racks empty.

"In July? *Quel surprise,*" Caitlin said, poking her head in. "Guess we'll have to fend for ourselves."

She stepped into the little room and took a hanger off the nearest rack.

"*Shit,*" a small voice whispered behind me, making me jump.

I whirled around, relieved, then irritated. It was only Jamie Burger.

"Oh my God, don't sneak up on people!" I snapped at him.

"I wasn't!" Jamie whined back.

He was dressed in an odd, cobbled-together outfit, comprised of his school jacket, a dress shirt that must have belonged to his dad, and a pair of dark wool trousers. His forehead was prickled with sweat, and his obvious discomfort made me more conscious of my own ill-fitting dress, squeezing tight with every breath.

"Hi," Jamie said to Caitlin. "I can help you."

He stepped into the doorway, glancing at me sideways—already being weird.

"I'm sorry, do you work here?" Caitlin asked, a slight amusement in her voice.

"Not usually, I'm just helping tonight," Jamie babbled. "The coat person was sick, I think? My dad works here—but not at parties, he does maintenance. He'll get me later, but I get to stay for the fireworks."

He paused, staring at Caitlin like a stunned deer.

"I hung my shawl here." She gestured slowly to the rack. "Hope that's okay, Jamie?"

Jamie's whole face had gone pink now, so bright and blotchy on his freckled skin that it looked like he had a rash. Caitlin gave him a moment to find his words, then smiled.

"Great." She pointed to the doorway he was blocking. "We'll let you get back to work."

"Oh wait!" Jamie exclaimed, grabbing Caitlin's wrist as she passed. "I need to give you a token!"

"Ow!" Caitlin yelped suddenly. "You're hurting me!"

She yanked her arm back, rolling her wrist and giving Jamie a wide-eyed stare.

"What the *hell*, Jamie," I hissed.

He sputtered wordlessly, looking back at her with abject alarm.

"I didn't—" Jamie's voice came out raspy. "I'm sorry."

He inhaled sharply and I realized he was on the verge of tears. And then the tears appeared, shimmering in his eyes.

"All good," Caitlin said in a cool tone. "We've got to get back."

She put an arm around my shoulders, pulling me along.

"Alice," she said in a stage whisper. "That's not your little boyfriend, is it?"

"What?" I spit back, glancing over my shoulder where Jamie stood, still well within earshot.

Then I realized—that was the point.

"God," I answered, projecting with all my might. "No *way*."

Caitlin squeezed my shoulder, suppressing a laugh as I shouted in her face.

"Good."

The crowd was moving now, the party migrating into the yellow ballroom for cocktail hour.

"I can't *believe* him," I said, speaking normally again. "Is your wrist okay?"

"Hmm?" She looked at her arm, then smiled. "Oh no, that's just my little trick. Some guys can't take a hint, you know?"

I had no idea. A hint about what?

"Totally," I said.

Caitlin side-eyed me, amused. She dropped her hand from my shoulder and gave me another confidential little pinch above the elbow.

"Just remember," she said. "They scare easy."

Chapter Twelve

I pull up to the police station ten minutes into my lunch break, pleased to find the visitor's lot empty (*Quel surprise*, says Caitlin's voice in my head). Theo and Jules have loaned me their beat-up Volkswagen for the summer. The "grocery-store car" they call it—not because it's the color of a hothouse tomato, but because it can't be trusted for more than local errands. It brings a smile to my face, parking this red, rumbly eyesore outside village PD. I must admit, I'm smiling a lot more than I expected today.

Mr. Brody sulked in silence all morning, scribbling and shuffling papers on his desk while I sorted through two rows of ledgers on his shelves. He'll answer direct questions, but as far as his "system" goes, it seems I'm on my own to figure it out. Three hours in, I started to worry I'd been wrong about him keeping secrets. All I'd found were a dozen old address books, a wine inventory and some mail that had fallen behind the books. I dropped the Discover card offer on his desk and told him I'd be back after lunch.

Walking away from the office, it dawned on me that he hadn't left it once. Mr. Brody is usually everywhere—a constant presence in the clubhouse, gliding from room to room like a specter. He'd left the members unattended all morning—unheard of—just to keep an eye on me.

I still don't know what he has, but clearly it's in there, and it's worth guarding. All this, and it's only my first day.

The police department is not exempt from the village's strict aesthetic codes. From the outside it looks like a woodland cottage. Gabled roof, white dormer windows, an oil lamppost. No garish floodlights here, thank you, and no security cameras on the facade—in the lobby, if you must.

I breeze into the station, greeting the young officer at the desk with a "hello" so cheery that I startle myself. I pause in the doorway, about to apologize for startling *her*, when the officer breaks into a wide smile and replies in an even brighter voice.

"Good morning!"

She's young—maybe twenty-four—with a smile that makes her look even younger. She stands at a computer desk behind the tall wooden barrier separating the waiting room from the rest of the station. Her reddish hair is pulled into a tight French braid. She is not what I'm used to seeing in this police station. Or any police station.

"How can I help?" she chirps, still smiling (genuinely, I think). I roll with it.

"Nothing major." I shrug, crossing the room and swinging my bag forward. "Just a Freedom of Information request."

The phrase sounds ridiculous in my casual tone, but Jessie doesn't seem to notice.

"Ooh, a FOIL, okay!" she answers. "Looks like you came prepared."

I thunk down my file of forms on her desk—one for each record I'm requesting: forensics reports, evidence inventories, medical exam notes and all police interviews, including my own. Thanks to New York's Freedom of Information Law, I have the right to request such records—but the law says nothing about making it easy. In other jurisdictions I could do this on my phone. In Briar's Green, you have to bring your printed, signed and notarized papers in person, between the hours of noon and 2:30 p.m.

"Look at you," says the officer, eyeing my file. "ID?"

I hand her my license and she takes it with another proud-of-you grin.

"I'm Jessie, by the way," she says, then taps the nameplate on her chest. "Officer Applebaum, if anyone else is around, but—"

She shrugs at the empty room with a goofy face, and I laugh because she laughs. Then she looks down at my license.

"And you're Alice . . ." Her mouth drops slack. "Oh."

She looks up, checking my face.

"Oh. Okay."

My heart starts bouncing as I watch her open the file and look at the first sheet of paper—the names written on it.

"Right," she says to herself—and then to me, more firmly. "Right. This might take a few minutes."

"I've got a few minutes," I tell her.

It's almost refreshing—someone acknowledging that they know me and my whole horrifying story. No one else in the village would be so direct; that's not how gossip works here. People don't address things directly. They just find a way to let you know what they know. Your wife leaves you for her lover in the city, and next month you get a Christmas card addressed to you alone, rather than "Mr. and Mrs." You return from a month of bulimia treatment, and whenever you go to a dinner party now, the host pulls you aside, whispering with performative discretion, "Feeling all right?" And if you do—or even *see*—something really bad, then everyone simply looks away. You don't exist, and that ugly business never happened. Why on earth would you say such dreadful things?

The truth is everyone knows who killed Caitlin—everyone knew back then too. It was a massive crime in a tiny village, and about two hundred of the most powerful residents were standing about ten yards away when it happened. The police interviewed eight of them.

The investigation was quick and dirty—though to be fair, the scene was chaotic before they arrived. The fireworks were still going when I came running up the hill, screaming and bloodstained. The crowd on the terrace turned to me and froze for several seconds before slowly reanimating. One of the members ran into the clubhouse to call 911, and another one—a surgeon—sprinted past me toward the pool, barking for others to come help. A handful of men pulled Caitlin's body from the pool and tried to resuscitate her, which only served to pump blood and pool water (both potentially useful evidence) out from her insides. Uncle Greg was stumbling toward the pool like a zombie, trying to push through the group surrounding him. Aunt Barbara was somewhere, screaming.

The pandemonium went on for twenty-five minutes before the police arrived. It was July Fourth, the busiest night of the year for them—perhaps their *only* busy night. As we say in the village, you can't get a speeding ticket on Independence Day. From afternoon on, the village cops are patrolling for private (and illegal) fireworks, bonfires and sparklers. It's a whole other kind of pandemonium, with half the village ratting out the other, and cop cars zooming up and down Route 9, sirens blaring. If there's one thing our police force knows how to do it's bust up a lawn party.

A violent crime scene, not so much. When the officers finally arrived that night, they quickly scrambled to section off the pool, and in doing so, only muddled things further: clearing away lounge chairs, stepping in bodily fluids and tracking them across the cement. Meanwhile, the clubhouse was left unattended, and the party quickly cleared out. By the time they came up to take statements, half the guests were already gone, and the rest were reaching for their purses and jackets, *terribly* sorry they couldn't help more. The officers did get a few on-site interviews, all brief and seemingly random: a handful of members, Mr. Brody, some servers and Theo (but only because he'd insisted on giving one). I was still in shock—parked between him and Mom in a corner of the pink ballroom, wrapped in a crinkly emergency blanket—and even I remember thinking something seemed off. What about the others? Were they all going to the station? Would the police talk to them there?

Even for inexperienced cops, it was a meager pantomime of effort. It was as if they already knew that Patrick's parents would intervene—and perhaps they already had. Whatever deal they made was clearly done before Patrick went in for his own interview the next day. The rest of the investigation (all seven days of it) was even less convincing. They never returned to the club to see the grounds during daylight. They let them drain the pool to be cleaned and reopened, no need to wait. They did conduct some further interviews, but the only people they called to the station—where the press remained camped out—were those the press already knew about: Liv and Whitney Yates, Aunt Barbara, Uncle Gregory and Alex Chapman—Patrick's alibi.

Alex is the only one I'd like to speak to myself. He was Patrick's best friend, and the one who vouched for his whereabouts during the murder. I know for a fact they're still close—Alex was even there for Patrick's proposal. According to Susannah's Instagram post, "Chappy" is the one who took the picture. He's a long-shot to say the least, but he's worth the effort.

My aunt and uncle—no. Not worth it. I haven't seen or spoken to them in twenty years, and I don't need to. I already know what they have to say.

Patrick's parents I'll steer clear of. They were never potential sources, of course, but I did consider them targets at first. They're the ones who scuttled the investigation—that part's not even an open secret so much as a generally accepted fact. Whit Yates was the youngest of an old-school generation of politicians—the kind who thought greasing palms was only polite and that Marilyn Monroe had it coming to her. And with a son like Patrick, he was used to throwing money at the problem, be it a stolen speedboat, a bottle of someone else's pain medication or a party prank involving said opioids, which landed two other teenagers in the ER.

That incident had raised a few eyebrows, and gotten a little more than the usual finger-wagging coverage in the tabloids. Whit Yates was confronted while leaving a fundraiser at the Met one night—stopped cold in his tux by a handful of reporters asking for comment on his son's alleged use of a drug that some doctors now claimed was more lethal than morphine. Where had he gotten the pills? Was it true one of the kids he'd dosed had needed to be resuscitated? And why was Patrick, son of Senator Whitney Yates—a self-proclaimed admiral in the war on drugs—facing no criminal charges whatsoever? In response, Whit Yates had offered a polite half smile and a shake of the head:

"Boys will be boys."

Then he'd literally waved them off and walked away. He hadn't even noticed one of them had a cameraman with them. It was the kind of moment that would've gone viral today—the tux, the blithe smile—and even in the late '90s, it left a good scuff on Yates's burnished reputation. But it didn't amount to any actual consequences. It just underscored the fact that families like the Yateses didn't face the same sort of consequences as everyone else. People tutted, shook their heads and changed the channel.

I dug up the clip on YouTube last month, while gathering tidbits on Whitney and Liv. But to my surprise (and dismay), it wasn't as galling as I'd expected—two decades and a raging opioid epidemic later. The callous comment just read as clueless. Whit Yates, with his crisp tuxedo and salt-and-pepper hair and that easy, unbothered wave—he seemed more archetype than human. He had the same toothy charm as Patrick, but none of the simmering vitriol beneath. He seemed like someone who knew he was untouchable.

He was probably right, I realized—even more so these days. Whit Yates is a *former* senator now, but a profoundly influential one. He and Liv still put their might and money behind their favored candidates, and a photo of them at a fundraiser is considered a potent endorsement. Age has made them even more immune to criticism. *They grew up in a different time. That's how people talked back then.* (They're not nearly as old as everyone seems to think. Then again, they do live in the land of indoor smoking, and golf at a whites-only club.) Furthermore, they're even wealthier than they were in the '90s, now that Liv Yates has inherited her own family's legendary fortune—and the dubious title of "fourth-largest private landholder in New York state." In other words, I don't stand a chance against the Great Yateses as an entity—and frankly, I'm less interested in them. Patrick's the one I'm after.

"Alrighty!" Officer Jessie announces, startling me back to the present. "All set here."

I stand, twisting the sour look on my face into something like a smile.

She slides another paper across the desk.

"Confirmation doc—that's yours to keep," she says, talking in her sing-song voice again. "Just need your filing fee. That's four hundred dollars, and yes, we do take cards."

Of course it is. Of course you do.

"Processing time is ninety days," she continues. "But I can't imagine it'll take that long."

"Right," I say, handing over my credit card. "Slow summer."

"Oh, it's not even that," she says, tapping her keyboard. "No, archived records take forever. But case records like *these*—"

She stops, her eyebrows raised, with a tiny but audible gasp. Her hand jerks up toward her mouth, but she forces it back down. This girl has got to get a better game face.

"I'm so sorry." She shakes her head, her voice lower—older now. "I just, I saw the case information."

She gestures to my file of forms, closed beside her keyboard (*their* forms now).

"And I recognized your name." She winces. "I shouldn't have—"

"It's okay," I say, quickly and quietly, placing a hand on the desk. "It's fine, it's not really a secret that I'm—"

I bend my head, looking pointedly at the file.

"I certainly don't expect to be anonymous in *here*."

I give her a little laugh, but she just blinks at me with a look of grave concern.

"Of course you are," she says, distressed. "I mean, I'd never discuss—not with anyone in here. Not like that, like gossip."

She sighs and taps the space bar, embarrassment drifting across her face.

"No, I know the case, obviously. But I was little when it happened. And my family wasn't really a part of that scene, you know?"

She taps her nameplate: Applebaum. Suddenly, I'm embarrassed. All those parties I attended with the Dales, thinking *I* was an outsider.

I nod.

Jessie cracks a smile.

"I'm just saying, it's not like you walked in here and I thought, *Ah-hah! It's her! She's here to get the case reopened!*"

My stomach leaps into my chest, and I look around instinctively, ensuring we are indeed alone. But Jessie's laughing now.

"No, Alice, I recognized your name because I used to go out with a friend of yours," she says, relaxed into her cheery self again. "Well, a friend of your brother's."

"Oh." I peer at her, catching up. "Oh! Jamie Burger, yeah!"

"You remember him?"

"He basically lived on our couch in high school, so yes," I say, continuing without thinking. "And I'm actually working for him this summer, at the club."

Her eyes go wide.

"Wow."

"It's a temp gig," I add. "Anyway, yes, I still know him."

We nod at each other silently. Am I dealing with Jamie's friendly ex or Jamie's ex who happens to be friendly?

"Me too—still friends, don't worry," she chuckles, answering my thought. "You kind of have to be around here."

"Small town." I shrug.

Jessie points at me.

"Small *village*," we say together. A bit of local semaphore.

We both laugh more than necessary, relieved to have the awkward, whispery moment behind us. Jessie double-checks her computer screen and hands my credit card back to me. She asks me to say hi to Jamie, and I tell her I will. I zip my bag shut, and look up to say goodbye and thanks, but Jessie's face has changed again. Still friendly, still wide-eyed, but with a brittle tension.

"Are you?" she asks softly. "Are you trying to get it reopened?"

I look back, speechless. Her eyes are locked on mine, her face so clearly trying to say something, and for the first time, I can't read it.

"I don't know," I answer. "Maybe."

"I just wondered," she says, eyes still steady. "Because, as I'm sure you know, there will be a public notice of this request."

What?

"It's village law," she says, nodding. "Anytime someone requests records, they put a notice in the local newspaper. Usually within the month."

I nod slowly, trying to think.

"Alice?" Jessie tilts her head, pulling my focus back. "It might be sooner than that. Slow summer. You know?"

I step back, my body pulling me toward the door, wanting to move—to get going on *something*.

"Right," I say, taking another step. "Thanks for reminding me. I'll—I'll keep an eye out."

I turn, hurrying for the door, glancing back as I pull it open. She smiles.

"I will too."

Chapter Thirteen

"You didn't," says Theo. "*Fire* codes?"

He peels the paper top off an aluminum take-out container. The salad inside is packed tight, covered with fat slices of red onion and studded with olives.

"I did. Oh man, is that Giordano's?"

"Obviously." He stacks the salad on top of the pizza box, sliding it across the kitchen island. "Jules, are you hearing this?!"

"Huh?!" she calls from the hallway bathroom, where she and Isaac are cleaning his fish tank.

"Alice caught Mr. Brody in a fire violation!"

Jules comes in, drying her hands on a washcloth.

"Impressive," she says, picking a cherry tomato off the salad. "You got two, right?"

"Three," he replies, and points at me. "You haven't seen her around a Giordano's salad. She's a beast."

I nod, my mouth full of olives.

"I'm *hungry*," Simon moans from the dining table.

"Two seconds, buddy!"

"Do you even know what's in the fire codes?" Jules asks, bent over the silverware drawer.

I take a victorious sip from my sweaty can of Diet Coke.

"No, but there must be something in there about not having that much crap on the floor. Flammable crap, no less."

Simon hoots from the table.

"Aunt Alice said the c-word!"

I choke on soda.

"*Excuse* me, I did not!"

Theo slaps his thigh, clutching the counter in silent hysterics.

"'Crap'" he murmurs. "'Crap' is the c-word."

Pizza nights are usually a once-a-month occasion. Most nights, the whole family cooks dinner together—a ritual established both for budget reasons, and to ensure some guaranteed family time in a household with two parents who work very full-time jobs. Jules is a lawyer too, specializing in environmental policy ("Thank God *one* of us is making the big bucks!" they often joke). In fact, Jules has always been the primary breadwinner, and makes a fairly good living for someone in her field. A few years back, she was poached from her firm by the Fisher King Group—a local organization with worldwide renown, thanks to its clean-water initiatives. It's often cited as "the group that cleaned up the Hudson," though, Theo always insists, "it's Jules who *keeps* it clean."

"Cheers," she says from the end of the table, holding her soda aloft. "To a successful first day."

The others follow suit, Simon cheering loud as a foghorn, Isaac elbowing him in the ribs. I give Jules a thankful smile and she nods back warmly. Jules, I suspect, is the one who got Theo to mellow out my summer job. She knows all about the murder, of course, and she's no fan of the club. But she didn't grow up here, and doesn't have the baggage Theo and I do, or the WASPish instinct to avoid it. My sister-in-law is a no-bullshit New Yorker, who thinks baggage is something you're supposed to unpack.

"Seriously though," Theo says, reaching for another slice of pizza. "Do you really expect to 'modernize' Mr. Brody?"

There's a thud beneath the table.

"*Hey.*" He looks at Jules, who glares back. "What? I'm not trying to be a party pooper. Simon—okay, enough."

Simon cackles through a mouthful of pepperoni slices.

"'Pooper,'" Jules explains, and turns a look on Simon.

"I'm just saying it's a big ask," Theo continues matter-of-factly. "Any change is a big ask at that place. It's a lot to put on a summer admin."

He sips his soda, muttering.

"I don't know what Burger thinks he's doing over there."

There's a bitter undertone in his voice, and it grabs my attention.

"What do you mean?" I ask lightly.

"Nothing." Theo shakes his head. "I haven't seen him in a while."

It's the same tone Jamie had in the gallery this morning—that stilted nothingness that's meant to sound unbothered.

"He mentioned that," I continue, still keeping my own voice casual. "What happened?"

"Nothing," Theo repeats, shrugging. "Just—he's still there, still serving them, I don't know. Not the guy I thought he was."

I look at Jules, alarmed: *What the hell does that mean?*

She lifts a hand, rolling her eyes: *Don't bother.*

I pick up my pizza, backing away from the touchy subject. Then I see Isaac across the table, looking at Theo with worried eyes. I tilt my head, catching his gaze in the silence.

"Guess I'm the pooper now, huh?"

Simon erupts into laughter, spraying tiny bits of pizza across the table, and everyone starts yelling at once—the silence decidedly broken.

I stay up late again that night, lying on the foldout bed, waiting until they're asleep. I don't know why, but it feels wrong to work on my investigation while they're awake up there, brushing teeth and slamming doors, and shouting at each other about slamming doors. All their wholesome family noises just make me feel more like a criminal liar.

It's after eleven when I pull out my laptop. *Just a liar*, I think. *Not a criminal one—not technically.* Then I log into my new, secret email account and email the private investigator I've paid to dig up personal information on Patrick Yates and his associates.

Re: A.C. contact info

Alice—

Got the address and phone numbers, as requested (see attached). My two cents, let that sleeping dog lie. Looks like a biter to me. —J

Private investigation may be legal, but it's easy to forget that when your PI is Jeremy. All his emails are like this: one part information, two parts ominous metaphor. Jeremy is what people around here would call "quite the character." But he's good at his job. I emailed him before I came to Briar's Green, thinking at first that maybe I should pay a professional to handle the whole thing. I knew he'd done gigs for two of my former employers. I have no idea why, and I gather that's part of what makes him good—$350-an-hour good.

The $350 is actually his low-end fee. He made a point of telling me when I first reached out:

And I typically charge a premium for high-profile guys. Higher risk, etc. But I don't know how much help I'll be on this one. Rich folks are one thing, but old money's different.

Another term for Jeremy is *paranoid cliché*. We exchanged a handful of emails before I officially engaged him for up to three hours of "light touch" work. (Basic data pulls. No boots-on-the-ground stuff.) I then had to set up a new email account specifically for his correspondence, and agree to "destroy" the account once our work was done. Further, I agreed to use it only on my laptop—never on my phone. Jeremy doesn't do phones, and will only call or text during "life-and-death situations."

Again, I'm not going there with this guy. I'm not getting run off the road for this one. Copy?

I told him I did indeed "copy."

Okay boss, I'm on it. I'll get you a background in a few weeks. Like I said, don't get your hopes up, but if there's anything useful out there, you'll have it. Anything comes up in the meantime, just ring the bell.

Jeremy's an expensive oddball, but I need someone to track down the intel I can't—the stuff I can't even file a request for. Patrick's lived a whole life since the murder, and I know it hasn't been squeaky clean. He was a tabloid topic too, those first few years. "Patrick Boozes on the Beach Weeks After Girlfriend's Suspicious Death." "Bad Boy Yates Kicked off Campus After Frat Photos Leak." "'It Got Nasty!' Blue-Blooded Brat Pack Parties Hard at Patrick's 21st." They really wore out that "blue-blooded" angle.

Eventually though, they got bored with him. As Caitlin evaporated into old news (tragic, but old), so did Patrick's infamy. The details got murky in public memory, and the longer he walked around free—dating models, clubbing in Corfu, hitting the odd charity gala—the more people assumed he had a right to. Patrick skipped out on his last semester of college, taking the trust he'd gotten access to upon turning twenty-one, and moving to Silicon Valley, where he'd run around dumping chunks of it into random start-ups like coins in a slot machine. When, five years later, one of them actually succeeded, Patrick was suddenly a tech mogul—despite the fact that all he'd done was buy himself a title. Five years after that, he'd moved back to New York in semiretirement, even wealthier than he'd been before. He bought one of the old Astor mansions on a wide swath of riverfront property, abutting his parents' own land—quietly tripling his family's footprint in the village. And when his uncle stepped down from the Yates Foundation—one year after Susannah began working there—Patrick quietly took his board seat.

Those are the broad strokes of the last twenty years. I'm counting on Jeremy to fill in the dirty details—and I know they're out there, even if they didn't make headlines. Patrick managed to live quietly for a while, but *The Club Kid* and the "murder fans" ended all that. Now he's back in the tabloids, and still boozing on the beach with the same old blue bloods—one of them at least.

"Billionaire Patrick Yates's Boys Night Out in Naples." I saw the *Daily Mail* post this evening, just after leaving work: Patrick and two other men, bottles dangling from their hands, outside a bar. It's one of a few small items they've run this week, following Patrick and Susannah's "summer getaway." Thanks to the Google Alert I set up for Patrick's name (among others), I've been following the trip too. According to the *Mail*, Patrick and Susannah have opted for a joint bachelor/bachelorette trip, cruising around southern Italy "with a group of their closest friends." The whole thing reeks of PR, particularly since all the "close friends" pictured are clearly Patrick's pseudo-celebrity friends: models, a DJ, a celebrity stylist—names I vaguely know. Today's post is the first one with a face I recognize: Alex Chapman's. It's a grainy, low-lit photo, and his name's not in the caption. But he's standing beside Patrick—right where he always was.

I forwarded the piece to Jeremy, and asked him to get me Alex's contact info, including any workplace numbers and his home address. Realistically, the only way I'll get ahold of him is by showing up at his door.

I open the attachment of Jeremy's email, my pulse picking up as I scan the short page. The work address has a Manhattan zip code, but it's a PO box—no office listed. I can't be sure, but it's a good bet that he works from home. And the home address is local—in Briar's Green, barely five minutes from the club. He's still got a local cell number too.

"Fuck it," I say to myself, and whip out my own phone, dialing.

This is silly—not strategic. I don't even know what I'll say if he answers, and anyway, it's not even 6:00 a.m. in Italy. I should wait. I shouldn't do this—not while he's yachting around the Mediterranean with Patrick.

But I let it ring. I'm smiling, excited—I can't help it. The phone clicks and a robotic voice tells me to leave a voicemail, then it beeps.

"Hi," I say, inhaling sharply. "Alex, this is—"

I stop just short of saying my name. I sputter for a moment, then try again.

"Alex, hi. I'm a fellow graduate of the Wheaton School, reaching out to congratulate you, and the whole class of '99, on the twenty-year anniversary of your graduation. We'd love to hear what you've been up to since then, and discuss your recollections from your time at Wheaton. And, in particular, the friendships you made there."

I feel my lips begin to twitch and quickly hang up, slapping a hand to my mouth, giggling and giddy with adrenaline.

"Oh my God," I laugh into my hand. "Oh my God, oh my God, what is wrong with me?"

I collapse back on the bed, looking at the number on my outgoing calls and bursting into laughter again. I feel utterly ridiculous. But I'm not scared—I'm not even worried. Odds are, Alex will simply delete the message at the first mention of Wheaton, assuming I'm one of those chipper alums who call for a hand-out ten times a year—albeit a little more awkward than most. And on the off chance he does call me back? Well, mission accomplished.

I think about Jeremy's warning: *Let this sleeping dog lie. Looks like a biter.* He's probably right. There is no reason to believe Alex Chapman will talk to me—no reason to believe he won't threaten me himself. But I just don't think he will. I have the oddest feeling that, if I ask just the right questions at just the right moment, Alex will answer. I don't know what makes me think so—or, I do, but it's also ridiculous. It's Alex's face in the photo. I pull the article up on my phone, zooming in to look at it again. It's small and slightly blurry in the dim light, only partially visible behind Patrick's shoulder. Alex isn't smiling.

Chapter Fourteen

July Fourth, 1999

Caitlin vanished for the first time during cocktail hour. All the teenagers did.

Every party began in the yellow ballroom, kitted out with bar stands and a shrimp-cocktail spread that no one ever touched. Families would sit together at dinner, but here, everyone split off into their demographics. Kids my age hung around in corners, sometimes playing UNO or passing around a Game Boy until Mr. Brody confiscated it. The adults shuttled between conversations, the volume rising slightly with each round of drinks. With their parents pleasantly sloshed, the older kids would start to dip out, meeting up for their own private gatherings on the back steps or the tennis courts.

Sometimes I'd see them from the terrace—a cluster of them smoking at the bottom of the hill, or a couple making out in the trees beside the pool. But it wasn't much fun, spying on my own.

Susannah never came to parties—no staff kids did, unless they'd snagged some little one-off job like Jamie had, filling in at coat-check for twenty dollars and unlimited sodas. I knew most of the kids playing games in the corners—I was friendly with some of them at school. But they had their own social circles at the club, and I knew without asking that they were closed to me. So that night, like most nights, I spent cocktail hour leaning against one of the open French doors, drinking Shirley Temples and half watching the room like a dull TV rerun I'd seen a dozen times. I wish, just that once, I'd paid closer attention.

I do know from various news reports that Caitlin was with Patrick for at least part of that hour. They were seen on multiple occasions by multiple guests, though no one recalled specifics—they were just darting around the clubhouse together, like the rest of the teenagers. Nobody noticed the looks on their faces, their tones of voice or whether they were holding hands or not.

I'm guessing they still were at that point—though perhaps not in front of people. Whatever conflict arose, I don't think it had even begun yet. The one thing I do recall from that point in the evening is the moment they both returned. It was just before dinner, and she appeared first, slipping in through the doorway and weaving through the crowd to join her dad, chatting with a group at the far end of the ballroom. She looped her arm through Uncle Greg's, laughing at something he said. Her cheeks were flushed with a candy-apple shine.

Patrick came in just a minute later. A ripple of quiet went through the crowd, and all conversations paused, just for a breath, as he walked through the door—his own face glowing too. Everyone was talking again, pretending not to look at him, but stepping out of his way. The party seemed to move around him as he ambled across the room—hands in his pockets, chin high and head cocked, the right side of his mouth turned up, as always, in that delicate smirk. It looked both obnoxious and utterly dashing. I'd never thought of a boy as sexy, but I knew Patrick was something other than cute or handsome, and that it made me feel pleasantly ill. I could see, objectively, that his suit was too big and his shaggy hair was dirty. But Patrick had a preternatural confidence—the same kind Caitlin had—that made everything he did or said or wore seem exactly right. Even that fussy little four-in-hand knot.

He stopped beside his mother at the French doors, barely thirty feet away from me. Liv Yates was locked in conversation with an older woman, a martini held casually at her side. Patrick lifted it from her hand—gently, but with no attempt to hide it—and turned to take a sip.

Just as the glass touched his lips, he noticed me staring. His eyes locked on mine and he froze, as if I were a ghost.

Two heartbeats and it passed. The fear dissolved, his face relaxing back into its easy grin. I watched him tip his head back, draining the martini glass, Caitlin's words echoing in my head: *They scare easy.*

Chapter Fifteen

Two weeks later, on a Friday morning, I drive to Alex Chapman's house. I head out early, the morning blissfully cool after a long night of rain. By the time I reach Bramble Bush Road, where Alex lives, the sun is blazing and the air is as thick as a wet wool blanket.

Alex never returned my voicemail—my little impromptu alumni-relations message. I'd woken up the next morning seized with anxious regret, feeling like a fool for the impulsive call—and even more foolish for thinking Alex might be receptive to me. I hadn't even blocked my number. What if he did listen to my whole, awkward message, with the cryptic allusion to recollections from '99, and in particular, his friends? What if he told Patrick? *Wouldn't* he tell Patrick? And wouldn't he put an end to all this somehow?

But two weeks later, nothing. I was still punching in at work (with an honest-to-God time card). My call hadn't caused even a minor stir—*nothing* I'd done so far had. They hadn't even placed the notice in the paper about my FOIL request. I'd checked the *HV Journal* every day before work, but the only items in the public-notice section were road-work announcements and summer library sales. All that fretting I'd done, imagining my very presence would make waves. It hadn't made a ripple in the village—let alone Italy.

The *Daily Mail* ran two more little items about the Italian getaway, though in terms of photos, they stuck to the famous friends—all of whom I stalked on social media obsessively, searching every selfie and champagne-toast shot for evidence of something amiss. It never appeared. Neither did Alex.

I'd gotten that funny feeling again, and emailed Jeremy, who confirmed it. The rest of the group was still cruising around Italy, but Alex flew home ten days ago, alone. **Last-minute booking. Rome to JFK, and first class too,** Jeremy wrote. **That's a $5k fare. Old money or not, I call that a red flag.** I think so too, but there's only one way to find out.

I turn onto a sun-dappled stretch of road, slowing to a crawl and scanning for Alex's gate: 84 Bramble Bush Road is one of only a dozen homes up here, on the crest of the hill. It has nearly as grand a view as the club—which sits, conveniently, just on the other side of the woods, connected by a narrow footpath. Members sometimes use it for riding, and every year, without fail, some member kid takes a golf cart up there and winds up getting stuck on a tree root. Bramble Bush isn't technically club property, but they treat it as such since nearly all the residents are members.

Alex, however, is not. I checked the member rolls myself (one perk of working in Brody's office). His parents still are, but Alex never joined. It might mean nothing. I have to remember that. On balance, all these tiny details that *feel* off are nothing compared to the facts I know.

Alex was a classic Wheaton kid—a lacrosse-playing type whom everyone called "Chap" or "Chappy." Patrick's inner circle was larger than most, but Alex was near the center of it, and often a party to his misdeeds. He was in the passenger seat when Patrick got his DUI on Martha's Vineyard. He was nearly arrested himself when he and Patrick were busted on the Hudson, playing a game of speedboat chicken that ended with a sloppy crash and a shattered knee for Alex. And those two incidents were just their greatest hits.

The night of the murder, Alex told the cops that he and Patrick had been in the men's locker room doing coke—something they were rumored to do a lot of together. I would've believed the story myself, had I not seen what I saw. Alex was unable to produce the coke in question, and therefore was neither arrested nor charged. He was, however, admitted off the waitlist at Princeton two months later—where Patrick himself was going to college. Where Patrick's father had gone too.

I pause beside a moss green fence, checking the map on my phone. This is it all right, and as I inch forward toward the gate, I see a car in the driveway. My heart leaps and I pull over, rolling down the windows and idling a few feet away. The house is a charmingly weathered colonial, on a rambling stretch of land. I sit for a moment, looking at it and breathing. I need to be calm when I knock on his door.

I see white shutters. I hear early-morning birds chirping. I—

But I see something else now. Alex Chapman's front door opens and a child runs out—a little boy in swim trunks and chunky sandals. A woman leans out the door, calling for him to come back, to get his swim bag. The boy ignores her, zooming around the yard in a wide circle with his arms out, singing loudly to himself. He reminds me of Simon. The woman retreats into the house, leaving the door open, and a moment later, a man appears.

"Georgie boy!" he calls, coming out onto the steps. "George, c'mon, get your stuff so we can go."

He stands watching, hands on hips, until the boy zooms back toward the house. The man starts to turn back too, but then he pauses, shielding his eyes from the sun. He's looking at me.

"Morning," he says and waves, neither friendly nor unfriendly.

I stick my arm out the window, waving back. But I can't make myself speak.

The man waits another moment, then goes back to the house,

glancing over his shoulder. He is tall and heavyset, with broad shoulders and very blond hair. And he is not Alex Chapman.

I sit back, waiting for it to click—the obvious explanation that just hasn't occurred to me. There's got to be one. I grab my phone, pulling up Jeremy's email. Either I mixed up the address or he got the wrong one. But, no. This is 84 Bramble Bush, and according to current property records, 84 Bramble Bush belongs to Alexander C. Chapman. Furthermore, he has no other known residence. This is his home. So, what are these people doing in it?

"Hello there," says a cool voice to my right.

"Oh!" I gasp, whipping my head toward the passenger window, yelping even louder. "Oh God!"

At first, I just see the horse, and then the person on it. She's dressed in jodhpurs and a white, sleeveless blouse. I duck a little, waving out the window.

"Sorry, hello. I was—"

Then I see who I'm talking to. Liv Yates sits serene and sweatless in the saddle. Her hair is tucked into a low bun, and she's smiling a closed-lip smile.

"Everything all right?" she asks.

I try to nod.

"Are you sure?" She casts a glance at the car, the old engine wheezing.

"Yes," I eke out.

It's not just me. This is the effect she has on everyone. *Regal* is the word most people use, but that's too simple. Liv Yates is mesmerizing, in the truest sense of the word. When she looks at you, you don't blink. And though her husband is the prototypical politician right down to the tilted-head wave, Liv Yates is not anyone's idea of the politician's wife. And it's not because of her striking self-possession or her unapologetic snobbery, or the fact that she rides horseback down the middle of the road at eight in the morning. It's that she does it without making a sound.

"Car trouble?" she asks politely, though I've already answered, twice.

"No," I say softly, and something shifts in Liv's bright eyes. *Ah*, I realize. *Not the answers she wanted.*

"Some other trouble then—forgive me. Not my business?"

She dips her head, the curve beneath her cheekbones sharpening as her taut smile deepens. This time, she doesn't wait for me to answer.

"Oh dear, I certainly hope not." She gives me a teasing, wide-eyed look. "Can't say 'hello' to you without a lawyer present—I ought to know better!"

Liv drops the face and laughs a tuneful chuckle. It skitters down my back like a bug.

"A *joke*, dear," she says. "And barely. Good gracious, your face."

I have no idea what face I'm making. I can't even feel my face.

"Ah well," Liv Yates sighs, resettling herself in the saddle. "You were always a sensitive thing."

Liv holds me frozen in her gaze for another endless moment. Then her back straightens and she squeezes the horse with her thighs.

"You're over the property line," she says as the horse strolls onward. "I'd move that car before someone makes a call."

I watch until she reaches the downslope on the other end of the road. At last, she descends out of view and my body unfreezes, my shoulders dropping with such force that my head wobbles. I drop back against my seat, still staring down the road in a daze.

My phone buzzes in my hand, and I jump, fumbling to catch it. It's a text from Jamie.

Hey, can you come in early? 8:30?

I check the time and see it's already 8:08. Even if I—

Actually, do you have a second now?

The second text appears barely a minute later, instantly followed by a bubble beneath it as Jamie types another.

I start typing a reply, but the sound of distant chatter interrupts me, and I look up and out my window toward Alex Chapman's house. The family reappears in the doorway, hauling overstuffed beach bags. The little boy bolts toward the silver SUV in the driveway, opening the back door and shouting for the others to hurry—something about wanting to get a good spot.

My phone vibrates. Jamie's name appears. I punch the accept button, answering in a quiet growl.

"Jamie, I will call you back."

"Did you get—"

"Five minutes. Thank you, goodbye."

I hang up and toss my phone on the passenger seat. The family's car is turning now, heading down the drive. I get out and walk quickly toward the front gate, watching it open as the car approaches.

"Hi there!" I call casually, smoothing the front of my skirt. *Buff khaki, see?!*

The car stops. The man and woman stare at me through the windshield, concern and irritation plain on their faces. They exchange a few words I can't hear, then the woman rolls down her window.

"Can we help you?" she asks, eyeing me.

"Yes, I'm *so* sorry to bother you," I say—warm, but appropriately embarrassed. "I was coming to see an old friend—a classmate."

She blinks at me.

"I grew up here," I continue, thinking on my feet. "I'm just home for a visit and thought I'd surprise him. Alexander Chapman?"

"Who?" she asks, angling her head. "Say again?"

"Alex Chapman," I repeat, taking a step closer. "This was his house."

This is his house, I think. *This is where his car is registered. And he checked it out of the midterm parking lot at JFK last Tuesday. Don't ask me how I know.*

The woman shakes her head, brow furrowed.

"I'm afraid I don't know that name."

The man mutters beside her and she holds up a hand to quiet him, still looking at me.

"You don't mean the Cabots, right? They're across the road, a little further down."

I shake my head.

"Chapman," I say one last time, but she's already turned back to the man. He speaks quietly to her, still gripping the wheel, glancing at me sideways.

"No, I *hear* you," she says to him, then looks back at me. "I'm sorry, we can't help you. And we're running a bit late."

She rolls up her window and pulls out onto the road, the gate closing behind her with a soft click.

Probably going to the lake, I think idly, walking slowly back to my car. I imagine them meeting up with friends, spreading out blankets on the shady side, apologizing for being late. This odd woman just showed up in the driveway, asking about some "Chapman" person.

I pause beside the driver's side door, thinking. The unknown family in Alex's house is strange enough. What's stranger still is that they've never heard of him. Most people *know* most people in the village—names, at least. I haven't lived here in over a decade, and even I know which Cabots the woman meant.

My phone buzzes in the car, though this time it doesn't startle me. I'm too preoccupied to startle. I turn slowly, still puzzling, and lean in through the window to pick it up, neglecting to actually look at it. I lean back against the car, holding it at my side until it buzzes one more time. I shake myself back to reality, finally checking the screen—it'll be Jamie again, wondering where the hell I am.

But it's not Jamie. It's not anyone. It's not a phone number at all—just ten asterisks in a row. If it weren't for the message, I'd assume it was spam or some robo-text. But there's no doubt a person sent this.

Get back in your car and leave.

I stare at it, not quite registering the words. And then one more appears.

Now.

Chapter Sixteen

I arrive at the club fifteen minutes later, parking in the staff lot and doing my hair in the car. I pin it into a smooth French twist and spritz my hairline with hairspray. My hands aren't shaking; my pulse remains unhurried. This is what I've been waiting for.

Yes, I've received a fairly threatening anonymous text, from someone who was clearly watching me, and for all I know, still is. I'm scared, sure, but right this minute, I'm relieved. Turns out I made a ripple after all.

"Alice?" Jamie calls, and I lean over, looking through the windshield.

He's leaning through the staff door, his jaw set and so tense I can see it from here. He waves me over impatiently, and I nod, getting out of the car.

"You didn't call me back," he mutters as I step into the boot room.

I start my calm, practiced reply, but he cuts me off.

"Never mind, it's fine. Listen, Patrick and Susannah are here."

"*What?*"

Jamie lifts a finger, shushing me. My voice is loud in the tiny staff entry.

"*Here* here?" I whisper, pointing at the floor. "Or Briar's Green."

"The club. They're here for the walk-through. For the wedding. I tried to tell you."

"The wedding is in August! Aren't they in Europe?"

"Yeah, no, they were. We were supposed to do this next month with the planners. I guess— I don't know! She just called this morning and here we fuckin' are."

Jamie is clearly on the edge of panic. I'm starting to get there myself.

We speed down the gallery to the break room.

"Where are they now?" I ask, trying to triage.

"They had breakfast at the grill," Jamie says. "Just finished. His parents are coming too, by the way."

Right, I think. *One of them on horseback.*

We reach the lobby and turn into the staff hall behind the reception desk. I quickly dig out my time card and stick it in the mouth of the punch-in clock on the wall, then follow Jamie into the break room.

"Coffee?" he asks. "Have you eaten?"

"Huh? No, thanks, I'm good."

He goes to the coffee machine anyway, grabbing a paper cup and punching buttons until it clunks to life. His hands, I see, are trembling.

"Hey," I say. "Jamie, what are you worried about exactly? Is it the walk-through?"

He gives me the coffee I didn't ask for.

"You're not going to faint again, right? If you see him?"

Ah, got it. The thing he's worried about is me.

"No." I shake my head, smiling—I'm offended, but I get it. "I can handle an awkward run-in, okay?"

Jamie nods, though he's definitely not buying it.

"How about you stay inside the office for the day, just in case. You can have it all to yourself!"

"Are you serious?"

"If you need the bathroom—"

"I'm not hiding behind your desk all day, dude!"

Jamie huffs and closes his eyes.

"I knew it was a mistake, having you work here," he mutters. "Of all fucking summers."

I open my mouth, all remaining anxiety wiped out by righteous outrage. I take a step closer, preparing to let Jamie Burger have it. But then I hear a familiar voice behind me.

"Knock, knock," she says.

I look over my shoulder. Susannah is standing in the doorway of the break room.

"They said I should just come on . . ."

She trails off at the sight of my face. Her own face turns a shade whiter, her mouth slackening. Even the coffee machine goes silent.

"Susannah Joyce!" Jamie crows. "Hey!"

He gives her a jovial smile, his panic tucked away in an instant.

"Jamie, hi, I'm so sorry about this," Susannah answers warmly, the look of dread wiped off her face. "It's so last-minute, I know—terribly rude."

She's dressed like an Easter egg, in a soft blue top tucked into a pencil skirt the color of an eraser. Her lightened hair is even lighter after weeks of Mediterranean sunshine, and still ironed pin straight.

"Oh, quit minding your manners. It's fine!" Jamie puts down his coffee and goes to her. "Been a while, huh?!" he continues. "I haven't had the chance to congratulate you in person."

Susannah glances sideways at me, a nervous laugh escaping at the mention of her engagement. Jamie keeps talking—tossing out chitchatty comments, as if coaching us along: *Do you hear how I'm making my voice normal? Why don't we all try!*

"How've you been?" Susannah asks him, making an attempt. "How's the season going?"

"Good! Busy!" He looks at me. "Good thing we've got Alice with us this year."

I watch Susannah's face closely. Is this news to her?

"Wow. Amazing," she says in a vacant tone, her eyelids fluttering.

There's the blink. There's the terrible liar I know.

"Hi, Susannah," I say, firm and polite. "Long time."

"Yeah, gosh," she says, her words half-inflated, drifting across the room like a week-old balloon. "What's it been? Three years?"

It's been over four, but whatever. I'm not interested in playing make-believe nostalgia anyway. Not with her.

"I actually have to dash. I'm due at Mr. Brody's office."

"Oh!" Susannah says, visibly relieved as I brush past her through the door and into the dark staff hall. "Well, it was great to see you. We should get coffee sometime."

I stop, cringing at the floor. Fake plans? We never did that bullshit. It fills me with such aching sadness that I want to sit and weep on the spot. Instead, I turn around and lie politely back to her, because that's the normal thing to do.

"That would be great."

Mr. Brody greets me from behind his newspaper.

"Good morning, Ms. Wiley. I'd invite you in, but you don't typically require an invitation."

I'm never actually "due" at Mr. Brody's. I make a point of showing up at random, in the hopes of catching him away from his desk—so I can finally have it. Thus far, it's been a wildly unsuccessful tactic. I always arrive the moment he happens to be taking a break with his paper or catching up on bookkeeping. I then huddle in the corner with my scanner and laptop, converting his useless papers into useless PDFs, while he sits at his desk, contentedly guarding it like a mother hen.

This morning though, I have a better idea.

"I'd like to finish these menus today," I tell him, surveying the shelves in question. "Then move on to table seatings."

"I daresay you won't have time."

"Daresay I might, if I devote the day to it."

Jamie wants me out of sight. What better place to tuck myself away?

Mr. Brody lowers the newspaper, a look of unmasked annoyance on his face.

"I'm afraid not, Ms. Wiley. I've allowed this invasion, but I can't have you loitering all day."

I shrug.

"The sooner I'm through these, the sooner I'm out of your hair."

He launches into some retort, but I cut him off.

"Anyway, it's busy upstairs today, what with the walk-through."

Mr. Brody's mouth freezes, then shuts.

"The wedding walk-through?" I say. "Patrick and Susannah arrived at nine."

"At nine o'clock this morning?" Mr. Brody says, springing to his feet.

"Yes, I assumed you knew," I say, maintaining a tone of mild confusion. "The Yateses should've joined by now."

He folds his newspaper with an exasperated sigh, his decorum slipping in his irritation.

"Strange that I'm the one in need of 'organizing,'" he scoffs, straightening his vest and examining himself in the small mirror beside his desk. "Your old friend Jamie can't seem to schedule an appointment without informing all relevant parties. Perhaps if he actually wrote things down."

With that, Mr. Brody storms out to go barge into the walk-through—to which I'm sure he was deliberately *not* invited.

Alone at last with his desk, I jump into action, pulling out drawers. I'm being sloppy—he'll know I was rummaging—but I can't risk taking time to be careful. He could come back at any moment, and if he catches me in the act then the club will actually have a good reason to fire me. The desk is a heavy old oak piece, big as a ship and full of compartments. I tear through the smaller ones at the top, finding nothing but old golf pencils, paper clips and dust. I lean down and pull out a slightly larger drawer, which is full of blank printer paper, dry and crinkled at the edges.

A pair of voices approach in the hallway, and I freeze. The conversation passes, and then I hear the distant clunk of the north exit door swinging shut. I pivot in Brody's squeaking chair and reach for the largest drawer—my hand pausing as I notice the keyhole at the top. My heart sinks. I kick myself for being disappointed over something I should have anticipated. There's only one key for this lock, I'm sure, and it's upstairs in Mr. Brody's pocket. Just for the hell of it, I reach down and yank the handle.

The drawer flies open with a heavy clang. I clap my hand to my mouth, looking down at the row of leatherbound books, the slim spines face-up in a neat line. No dust on these ones.

I lift one out slowly. My heart beats in my ears as I open it. It's a diary, and it's not new. The first entry is dated March 10, 2001.

> G.A.'s dinner guests included H.W. and D.T. Charlie informed me of the latter's late arrival, approximately 8:40 p.m., and I—

I skim the rest of the page: a dry but specific play-by-play of a private dinner party, beginning with cocktails in the bar and ending with cigars in the library, before the guests left shortly before midnight, in various makes and models of cars. I have no idea whose initials these are, or why their dinner was relevant, let alone their cars. I flip ahead, scanning the next entry and the one after that. There has to be something. Whatever's in these books must have been important enough for Mr. Brody to keep them in his desk for eighteen years. *But not important enough to lock?*

I hear a rumble from above as someone pushes open one of the heavy ballroom doors.

The walk-through, I think. *Can't they walk a little slower?*

Moving quickly now, I check the rest of the diaries. They're lined up chronologically, the most recent one from just last year. I pull them out one at a time, scanning the pages for the dates or initials I need. F.S. plays tennis with W.Y. in August 2017. E.I. books the pink room for a two-day meeting in January 2014. Some of the coded entries are more easily deciphered than others. I'm briefly alarmed by a 2007 account of an auction attended by a P.C. and H.C., who arrived with several "SS officers." It takes a minute before I realize P.C. is President Clinton, H.C. is Hillary and "SS" stands for Secret Service.

I reach for the last diary, the first page dated 1998. I flip through, my hopes deflated—no 1999 records in this drawer. The thought repeats in my mind and I pause, holding the book open. I lean down, peering at the tidy row of books. *No 1999 records in this drawer.* 1998 to 2018 are all accounted for. There's only one year missing.

The sound of voices upstairs interrupts again. The walk-through must have finished in the pink ballroom—the one at the end of the gallery, beside the basement stairs. I picture the group strolling out together, Liv Yates still dressed in riding boots, discussing table arrangements with Susannah.

I slot the book back in the drawer, shove Brody's chair back into place and scoot back to the stack of menus near my scanner. I open my laptop, just as the door swings open. It isn't Mr. Brody though.

He stands there, one hand on the doorknob and the other holding a single sheet of paper.

"Hi?"

Jamie doesn't answer. He looks at the sheet of paper, then takes a step toward me and holds it out, just far enough for me to see what it is. A cold wave rolls down my body.

Jamie speaks at last.

"Were you ever going to tell me?"

Chapter Seventeen

"No," I answer.

My voice is calm and consciously neutral, but Jamie is still taken aback.

"Are you being serious right now?"

We're back in Jamie's closet-office, where he can comfortably berate me. I can see the strain it takes to keep his voice low.

"It's nothing to do with you, Jamie," I say. "Why would I bring it up?"

I don't know how this happened, but I know I haven't done anything wrong. I need to act like it.

The letter sits between us on Jamie's desk. It's a single sheet of stationery, emblazoned with the village seal. The header reads: "Police Department of the Village of Briar's Green."

My FOIL request has been processed—and approved. I am invited to make an appointment at my earliest convenience, to view the following materials:

Death Investigation Report: Case No. 8488, Caitlin M. Dale, July 4, 1999

P.E. Contents & Inventory: Scene Investigation, Case 8488

Statements: Witnesses and Secondary Parties, Case 8488

Interview with John H. Brody: July 4, 1999

Interview with Barbara C. Dale, July 6, 1999

Interview with Gregory H. T. Dale, July 5, 1999

Interview with Patricia C. Wiley, July 6, 1999

Interview with Alice K. Wiley, July 4, 1999

Interview with Patrick S. Yates III, July 5, 1999

Et al.

I'm fairly confident these notices don't typically list the specific records in a citizen's request. Then again, I imagine, they usually don't mail them to the citizen's boss.

The letter has my name on it, but the envelope—sitting open beside it on the desk—is addressed to Jamie directly: "Jamie Burger, c/o The Horseman Club."

"Why would you bring it up?" Jamie guffaws. "Alice, I'm not a dumbass."

"Jamie," I hush him with a hand to my lips, nodding toward the lobby. "They're still here."

He shuts his eyes and sucks in a sharp breath.

"I never planned to involve you," I murmur, a hint of Liv Yatesian coolness in my voice. "I have no idea why this letter came to you, but I certainly didn't use the club address on my paperwork, let alone your name. It's a personal—"

"I knew it was something like this," he hisses, jabbing a hand at the letter. "What is it, a new investigation? Are you trying to get him charged?"

"Whoa, Jamie, you're making some very big assumptions."

"Yeah," he spits. "Because you're not telling me shit."

I startle back into myself, any pretense of cool professionalism gone. For a moment, we just glare.

"This is really inappropriate," I say, unblinking.

"Goddamn right it is."

Jamie throws up his hands and turns away, muttering to the wall.

"I knew you were full of it the day you came. All that bullshit about closure. Day One, I knew."

And yet, I think. *You gave me the job anyway.*

Silence stretches out between us, until a tinkle of laughter floats in from the lobby. Mr. Brody will be escorting Susannah and the Yateses out. I imagine him calling Susannah "Ms. Joyce" and bending his head in a polite bow.

"You should go home," Jamie says.

"What? Are you *firing* me?"

Jamie doesn't answer. He shoves the letter across the desk to me.

"You have no legal recourse, Jamie," I say, pulling Theo tricks out of my hat. "You know you were never meant to see this letter, and if you terminate me over—"

"Jesus, Alice." Jamie recoils. "Just go home, take a day off, whatever."

He drops into his chair, done. I pick up the letter and tuck it into my bag, leaving, but taking my time about it.

I cross the staff parking lot, my body loose and rattling with adrenaline. As I unlock the car, someone calls my name and I jump.

"Do you have a second?"

It's Susannah.

"Sorry," she adds.

I look down and force a few deep breaths. I should tell her no—no, we're not going to have our first conversation in four years right this second. I want to be ready for that conversation, and right now, I'm the opposite of ready.

I clutch my key in my fist and walk over to her.

"I just wanted to—" she begins, halting when she sees my face. "Is everything okay?"

I stop, leaving a good five feet between us.

"Not sure how to answer that, Susannah."

I can see Patrick on the clubhouse steps. He's talking with Cory. They're laughing about something.

Susannah follows my gaze.

"Okay," she says, looking back at me, uncertain. "I just wanted— Sorry. I was hoping to—"

"Suze?" Patrick calls to her. "All good?"

He and Cory are both looking this way now, the smiles and laughter gone.

"Yup!" she answers brightly. "Two shakes!"

Two shakes?

Susannah takes a quick step forward and grasps my left hand, hard. "I really would like to get together, Alice," she says very quietly, her eyes wide and searching mine. "Okay? Soon?"

"Sure," I say, flabbergasted.

"When?"

"Uh. I guess—"

"Susannah?" Patrick calls again. His eyes shift toward me just for a second.

(*They scare easy.*)

"I'll text," says Susannah, releasing my hand.

As she walks swiftly toward Patrick, I run a finger over the tiny half moon in my palm, where her thumbnail dug into my skin. The depression is already fading, but I can still feel it there.

Chapter Eighteen

"Hey, stranger, what are you doing home?" Theo leans out of the kitchen, a sandwich in his hand. "Guys, look who's here."

Isaac and Simon come out of the dining nook, Simon with a Joker-smile of jelly on his face.

"Hi!" I say, loud and cheery, feigning pleasant surprise. "What are *you* doing home? All of you?"

"Um," Isaac says portentously, stifling a grin. "No swim camp today. We got sent home."

"Davey Holland diarrheaed in the pool!" Simon bursts out. "It was so—"

"That's okay, bud!" Theo interjects.

Theo and Jules take turns on days like this: snow days, sick days, diarrhea-pool days. It's a fair-share parenting policy they adopted from Ruth Bader Ginsburg and her husband. Theo makes a point of saying so in every interview—adding that no one gave Ruth extra credit for picking up her kids occasionally.

"We're doing PB&J," says Isaac. "Want one?"

"Absolutely," I say, dropping onto the couch.

"I'll make it!" Simon yells. The boys run into the kitchen, jars banging on the counter.

"What's up?" Theo asks, taking a bite of his sandwich. "Everything okay?"

I peek into the kitchen.

"Patrick," I mouth to Theo. His face freezes, midchew.

"They were at the club—he and Susannah. The Yateses too."

"Wow," he says, sitting.

That's nothing, I think, recalling the rest of my morning: the family, the text, Liv Yates on a horse. *That's not even the headline.*

Isaac brings me a lopsided sandwich and a handful of potato chips piled on a plate. He sets it on the coffee table, along with a glass of ice water.

"*God* that looks good," I say, meaning it.

Isaac and Theo snicker at each other as I pick up the water and gulp it gratefully down.

"Can I get the mail, Dad?" Isaac asks, and Theo nods.

"I call the paper!" Simon shouts, bolting for the door, determined not to be left out of anything, chores included.

"Did you talk to them?" Theo asks.

"Only Susannah. It was pretty fucking awful."

"Damn, I bet it was."

Simon and Isaac come bounding back inside, swinging the door open too hard. It slams against the wall. We both wince and Theo swears under his breath.

"Come on, guys, we talked about this."

He sighs and goes to assess the damage.

I put my plate on the coffee table and sink back into the couch, relieved for a moment of semisolitude. If I still have a job tomorrow, I'll go to it. If not, I'll make my appointment at the police station. I still can't believe they approved my request. Sure, they ratted me out to Jamie at the same time, but still. There's got to be another catch. It doesn't seem—

"Wait," I say, sitting upright. "Theo, wait."

I get to my feet. But I'm too late.

Theo stands beside the open front door, holding the newspaper. He walks slowly back to the couch, his eyes still on it. He drops it on the coffee table.

Public Notice: Briar's Green Police Department has processed a request filed by A. Wiley under the NYS Freedom of Information Law (Article 6, Sec. 84–90).

"Theo," I begin, but he stops me with a hand.

"God, you know what?" He looks at the paper, surprised, almost smiling. "I was thinking, *What's she doing at the club? What's the plan there?* Because obviously, there *was* a plan"

Now he looks at me.

"Okay, Alice? I wanna be clear about the obvious part. Even the boys know you're not here for some temp job."

I stay quiet, keeping my cool. Although I don't have much left today.

"But it never occurred to me you'd go back to the cops," Theo says, hardening. "Those cops."

"I didn't want to worry you," I say, and Theo gives a gasping laugh.

"Well, good news, I'm a hell of a lot more than worried now," he says, taking a seat. "I think I'm getting close to scared, to be honest, so how about you just tell me. Please. Please tell me what you're doing here."

"I'm just—" I reach for the words. "I'm looking for information. About Caitlin, and what happened."

"Right, I got that much." He snorts, eyeing the paper. "And what are you planning to do with it?"

I look at him.

"Tell?" I turn my hands up in a tired shrug. "Get Patrick charged? Get the case reinvestigated properly, somehow?"

"Uh-huh." Theo nods, his knee bouncing. "So, to get a case reopened, you need novel or compelling evidence. *Legally* compelling, I mean. It's extraordinarily rare. And when it does happen, it's all over the press."

"I don't mind, Theo." I shake my head. "I'm telling the press anyway. I'm going public as the witness."

Theo's knee stops. He tilts his head, searching me. I hear my own words repeating in my head, my voice so light. I *don't mind.* I'm *going public.* As though I'm the only one involved—the only one affected.

"So, you thought this through before you came here," Theo says, putting the pieces together. "You know they're going to have eyes on you, right? Now that this is public?"

I nod.

"Which means they'll have eyes on this house," he concludes.

I nod again, my chest caving in beneath a wrecking ball of guilt.

"Well, that's rotten, Alice," Theo says simply. "This whole thing is ridiculous and rotten as hell."

I hear the boys spatting in the bedroom, Isaac telling Simon to quit it. Their voices are so, so small.

"I'll go," I say, looking into my lap. "I'll go to the Inn—today."

"No. I'm not kicking you out," he says, a tired look on his face. "Not because you're my sister—that's why I insisted before. *We* insisted. Now I'm insisting because if you walk out of here, I'll be up all night waiting for the phone to ring. And I've already spent half the nights of my life awake, worrying about you. You here is bad. But you out *there* is worse."

He stands, ending the conversation.

"Okay," I mumble. "I guess. If you think that's best."

"What's best, Alice, is you back in the city," Theo says, then catches himself. I watch him consider taking it back, and then decide not to. "Get away from the club and all those awful, *legitimately dangerous* people. If you really give a shit about me—my kids, my family, the only family you've got left—that's the best thing you could do. Second best is staying here."

Chapter Nineteen

I drive to the police station at 6:00 a.m. the next morning. I gave up on sleeping three hours ago, got up, showered and picked up my phone to leave a voicemail on the village PD courtesy line, requesting my appointment. Then I had a better idea: fuck the appointment.

I shove the station door open, bleary-eyed, my hair still hanging damp.

"Well, hello again!"

It's Officer Jessie behind the desk. I nearly scowl at the sight of her bright, friendly face (*It's 6:00 a.m. Can't I get a dour stranger?*), but then I catch myself. Jessie may be a puzzle, but she's also a village cop. If she wants to play nice, I should play along.

"All right, Officer, tell the truth—do you actually you live here?" I give her a suspicious grin, shuffling across the linoleum. "Or is it just—"

Another head pops up beside the metal cabinet. This officer has a stack of files in the crook of one arm, and a dirty look on his face. There's my grumpy stranger.

"I'm on overnights this week," Jessie says, laughing at the joke I didn't finish. "I'm on until nine—you just got lucky again."

Lucky, right. I wonder what she'd say if I told her I got kicked out of my job yesterday, and that my brother's only keeping me around because he's worried people are watching me, and he's right. *Get back in your car and leave. Now.* Maybe I'll show her the text and see what she thinks about my current luck status.

"Everything okay?" she asks as I approach the counter. I see her clock my wan, insomniac face and quickly paste a smile on it.

"Yeah! Everything's great actually. Look what I got yesterday." I pull out my approval notice and place it proudly on the counter. "Heck of a lot faster than ninety days, huh? It went to the wrong address, but you know, mistakes happen."

I hold my friendly expression, watching her face for a reaction—any hint of knowing. She angles her head, knitting her eyebrows—the very picture of confusion.

"Doesn't matter," I breeze on. "Anyway, I know I'm supposed to make an appointment, but I was in the neighborhood. Any chance I could take a peek now?"

The other officer glances over his shoulder, his dirty look aimed at me now.

"Well, it's not how we usually do things, but . . ." Jessie taps at her computer. "But if I can find your file and if you're done with it by nine?"

I nod. Fine. Sure. Whatever's in that file, it won't take three hours. It's probably just a piece of paper that says, "Made ya look!"

"Great!" says Jessie, game as ever. "Just give me a minute to print and— Oh golly."

"What?" I ask, trying to see the screen.

"Nothing, it's just a bit larger than most. I might need more than a minute."

Jessie's eyes narrow on the screen as she scrolls—and scrolls and scrolls. She nods at the visitor's bench, still looking at the screen.

"Why don't you grab some coffee and just hang loose a second."

I wait a beat and then I do as she says. There's an old percolator on the table beside the bench. I pour myself a scalding cup of coffee, watching as she clicks around. Somewhere in the back of the station, the printer hums to life.

It's nearly forty minutes before Jessie calls me back. Sun is streaming through the front window, painting bright, golden stripes across the floor.

"This way."

Jessie smiles, stepping down from her desk and swinging open the little half door of the barrier, nodding me toward the back. I check my watch, wondering if I've made a mistake.

"Maybe I should come back," I say. "If there's really that much, I don't know if I'll finish by—"

"No worries, I'll show you the way," Jessie says, waving for me to follow.

Cautiously, I do. Jessie leads me down the same narrow hall I walked the night that Caitlin died. It doesn't unsettle me this time. I'm getting used to things being eerily familiar.

"Voilà," says Jessie, opening the door to a windowless room.

There's nothing inside but a table, and two tidy stacks of files.

"I'll leave you to it," she says, turning on her heel. "I'll be up front when you're done. Don't rush!"

I watch her go, puzzled.

Later, I remind myself. *No time for that.*

I settle at the table, looking at the files, each of them nearly a quarter-inch thick. I slide one off the top of the nearest stack, take a breath and open it.

The first sheet is labeled "Scene Report: Death," and includes a date and time stamp at the top. The rest of the page though, is filled with a series of black rectangles where paragraphs should be. Confused, I turn the document over, then flip through the sheets beneath it—all similarly covered in blocks of black ink. A tiny line of text at the bottom catches my eye:

> This record has been partially redacted by authorized parties, in accordance with the law.

I could almost laugh. It's printed on every page of every record—nearly all of which have been so thoroughly redacted that they're rendered virtually meaningless. The death-scene report includes Caitlin's name, the phrase "found unresponsive" in the middle of the page, and "declared dead" floating in the middle of a black blob toward the bottom. The rest of the page is all blob.

I go through the other files, and eventually do start laughing. I've *technically* been given access to everything I asked for—the autopsy report, lab results, the interviews—albeit with some "partial" redactions. My fingertips are stained with ink by the time I close the last file, lightheaded from laughter. I'll be pissed later, I know. Right now, I'm just relieved to have found the catch.

"Well, jeez, sorry I used all your toner," I say to Jessie, stepping back into the lobby. "Do you have any wipes, by the way?"

I lift my hands, twiddling my blackened fingers. Officer Grumpy looks up from the file drawer. Jessie blinks, frowning.

"Oh!" she says after a moment. "Makeup wipes! I've got some in my bag."

She reaches for a backpack beneath the desk, unzipping and searching compartments. My loopy mood begins to fade, watching her dig around—the one person in here trying to help.

"Never mind, it's fine." I shake my head, turning for the door. "I was just—"

"No, no, it's in here somewhere."

She waves me back urgently, still rummaging.

"Really," I say. "I should get going anyway."

"Ah! Bingo," she says, pulling a small, half-crushed box from her bag. "Still got a couple."

She opens the box and turns it sideways, showing me the pink packets left inside. But she doesn't hand it to me.

"Perfect. Thanks." I search her smiling face, glimpsing something behind it now. "Did you need anything else from me?"

"Nope," Jessie says, her smile still hard and masklike. "Not unless you'd like your copies."

"Of the records?" I ask, dipping my chin. "I think I'm good."

The other officer shoves a drawer shut, looking through his remaining files. Jessie's head turns toward him slightly, but her eyes stay on mine.

"You have a legal right to keep a set of copies, physical or digital," she continues. "Personal use only, of course. They're confidential, and not admissible in court."

I look back at her suddenly unreadable face. What is she saying? What am *I* supposed to say?

"Okay?" I say slowly. "Can I think about it?"

"Sure!" Jessie says, the strange tautness melting from her face. "You've got thirty days, no hurry. Oh, here you go."

Jessie hands me the box of wipes.

"Go ahead—only two left. Looks like you might need them."

I take it carefully, mindful of my stained fingers. Something slides against the inside of the box as I place it in my own bag—something small and hard.

I feel my own face change now. I see Jessie see it happen. She glances at the door, urging me out with her eyes.

"Happy to help!"

Chapter Twenty

July Fourth, 1999

The game began at dinner. I didn't start it, but it was my fault. Everything that happened between dinner and the pool was my fault.

Through sheer luck I wound up sitting with Caitlin, at a different table than the rest of our group. At most parties, club protocol required guests to sit boy-girl-boy-girl, and never beside a relative—but July Fourth was meant to be "informal." The dinner bell was rung at the end of cocktail hour, and everyone scattered from the yellow ballroom and into the green and blue rooms, hoping to claim one of the tables by the open terrace doors.

Theo had scurried ahead and managed to nab one for us. He beamed with pride as the rest of us followed, Caitlin whooping and Uncle Greg applauding, holding out a chair for Mom and then for Aunt Barbara. Only then did we notice the table was two seats short. The awkward moment passed in a flash as Caitlin took me by the hand, saying we needed some girl time anyway.

"Are you sure?" I asked as she walked us across the room.

"*Bien sûr*, babe."

She squeezed my hand, pointing to a pair of open seats at the corner of a long table by the fireplace.

I felt like a contest winner. An intimate dinner with Caitlin—

not just my incredibly cool older cousin, but the topic of endless, fawning speculation among all the lower-school girls. I would play it cool, *obviously*, but this was my chance to get answers to our many important questions. For instance, how did she make her hair look like that—messy but not dirty? And what face wash did she use? And was it true she shaved her legs with men's BIC razors? Maybe she could show me how to shave mine if my mom said yes? And was she in love with Patrick yet? Did they have sex?

I took my seat, cringing at myself and my perverted brain.

"Hey," Caitlin whispered—not sitting herself, but bending down. "I'll be right back, okay?"

"Oh, uh-huh," I said, my dream deflating before my eyes.

Caitlin was scanning the room—for Patrick, I realized. As if hearing my thoughts, she looked down and gave me a little wink. Then she turned to go, fluttering her fingers in a covert wave. Excitement bubbled up again, buoyed by the sort-of secret she'd sort of let me in on.

She came back quickly that first time—maybe ten minutes later. I remember, she said something about the salad not being out yet, and that she'd just pop out again real quick. By the time she returned, they were serving the soup. Even then, she didn't take her seat. She just leaned over it, resting her forearms on the back of the chair.

"All good?" she asked. "You need anything?"

"What? No." I was instantly defensive.

"Aw, babydoll, I'm standing you up," she said in a wheedling tone. "Are you lonesome over here?"

"*No,*" I protested. "No, I'm totally fine."

She leaned closer, glancing at the others at the table—all ensconced in their own conversations.

"Patrick's just having a bad night," she said, dropping into a whisper again. "Fighting with his mom or something."

"About the martini?"

She paused.

"Hmm?"

"Nothing," I said. "Never mind."

A server brushed by with a tray of soup bowls. Caitlin stood, giving my shoulder a squeeze.

"Listen, five minutes," she said. "For real."

It was more like forty. The soup was long gone by the time she returned, and half the table had finished their entrees. I sat before my untouched slab of pale chicken breast and oversteamed vegetable medley, sinking into what my mother called a "grade A sulk."

I felt the cool weight of Caitlin's arm on my shoulders as she slid around the back of my chair, finally taking her seat.

"Honey, I'm home!" she trilled. "Aw, sweetie, you didn't have to wait for me to eat."

"I didn't," I groused. "I'm just not hungry."

My tone was so sullen that it would've gotten me a warning at school. It didn't seem to register with Caitlin. She took a long drink from her sparkling water.

"I don't blame you," she said, eyeing the pallid chicken on her plate. "Gag me."

It stung, somehow—the way she wasn't noticing my foul mood. I crossed my arms, although it made the dress feel even tighter. I turned my face away, in case I started crying.

"You don't have to keep checking on me," I said, not looking at her. "I don't need a babysitter."

Anxiety pinched me between the ribs—I'd gone too far. I'd let my mouth get away from me again, and said the most babyish, embarrassing thing. No wonder Caitlin kept running away. Of *course* she didn't want to sit chatting with me. She probably couldn't stand me. And now I'd made it worse by deliberately being rude.

I whipped around, already spewing apologies—but Caitlin wasn't even looking at me. She was grinning at Patrick, who was two tables away, reclining in his chair, the way boys did in class. He mouthed something to Caitlin that I couldn't make out, and she tossed her head back in peals of muted laughter. She replied with a silent "No way!" and gave him a scandalized look as she reached for her glass and took another deep sip. I saw then how flushed she was—blushing all over, from her cheeks to her clavicle. My stomach tumbled over as I caught a glimpse of a small, ruddy mark on the side of her neck.

"Do you and Patrick have sex?"

Again, the words flew out of my mouth of their own volition. Caitlin lurched forward, eyes popping, as though I'd just vomited all over the table.

"Did you really just ask me that?"

I shook my head, speechless. It made Caitlin laugh even harder.

"What is this?" she cackled. "Truth or Dare?"

"I'm sorry," I said, all the blood in my body surging up to my head. "Oh my God, I'm sorry."

"Are we doing Spin the Bottle next?" Caitlin said, still overcome with laughter.

It happened then: a hot flood of tears streamed from my eyes, and I looked into my napkin, unable to stop them.

"Oh!" Caitlin cried. "Oh, honey!"

She scooted her chair closer.

"Alice! Oh my gosh, I'm kidding. Hey, shh, it's okay."

It was too late though. I was crying for real, like the baby I was. My shoulders trembled, tears plop-plopping on the skirt of my dress, leaving small, silvery stains.

"Come on now, hey." Caitlin put a firm hand on my shoulder. "Deep breath."

A white-haired woman was looking at me from across the table, her gaze somewhere between concerned and repulsed.

"Does she need her mother?" the woman asked Caitlin quietly.

Yes, I thought. I needed mom to take me home, help me get out of this awful dress and sit on the couch watching the *Twilight Zone* marathon in pajamas with me until I fell asleep.

"Oh no," Caitlin answered politely. "She's fine."

She waited for the woman to look away. Then she picked up her glass of sparkling water.

"Here," she murmured. "Have a little sip."

Without thinking, I took the glass and did as she instructed. My head jerked up as a sharp, floral flavor hit the back of my throat.

"It's nothing," Caitlin said before I could ask. "Just gin and soda."

I looked at the glass, putting a hand to my mouth.

"Don't worry, it's pretty light," Caitlin said, smiling at me. "Just a couple sips. It'll help."

I looked at her—the pity all over her face. I could have broken into sobs. Caitlin would've gone to fetch Mom, and I'd have begged her to take me home, and she would have, there and then. And none of the rest would've happened. All I had to do was cry.

But I didn't. Instead, I took a breath and looked Caitlin in the eye. I pictured Patrick—the way he'd drained the martini glass—and leaned my own head back, taking a long, dramatic drink.

"Um, okay," said Caitlin. The pity was gone from her face. Now she watched me with slightly nervous eyes.

Good, I thought. The alcohol spread warm across my chest. I remembered what she'd said to me in her bedroom earlier—that movie-dialogue line. I leaned over and put on my best Caitlin voice.

"Do *not* tell my mother."

Caitlin laughed again, but it was different this time—a laugh at my joke, not me.

"You got it," she said. "Cross my heart and hope to die."

Caitlin took her glass back and raised it for a sip. She paused, holding it just short of her lips, considering. Then, instead of taking a drink herself, Caitlin extended the glass back to me. She raised her eyebrows.

"Dare?"

Chapter Twenty-One

I turn out of the police-station parking lot, make a left and floor it. My hands shake as I grip the wheel, glancing in the rearview mirror. I don't know what Jessie's given me, but I know it's something. I have something.

It's barely a ten-minute drive to get home, but I can't wait that long to find out what it is. I reach the village center and park in the near-empty lot beside the grocery store. I pull the little box out of my bag and open it. It's a thumb drive. I knew it. I *knew* it.

I pull out my laptop and slot the drive into the USB port. It takes an eternity to load the drive's contents, and when the files finally appear, I see why. Because it's everything. Jessie has given me absolutely everything.

The records are all tucked into zip files—a dozen or so in each. Each PDF inside is labeled with what looks like a random string of characters. You can't tell what an individual file contains until you open it. At first I wonder if Jessie obscured them on purpose, but my guess is she didn't have time for that. There are more than sixty files in here—more than I even requested. She must have been dragging and dropping the entire time I was in there with the redacted files. *(Don't rush!)* And she'd handed them over to me right in front of another officer.

Why? I wonder. But that's for later. For now I have reading to do.

I sit in the parking lot for over an hour, the car and my laptop growing uncomfortably hot. It's nearly ten thirty when my phone rings.

"Alice, where are you?"

"Jamie? I'm just— Where are *you*?"

There's a loud, metallic clatter in the background, and someone starts shouting.

"Here!" he barks. "Everyone is here but you!"

The person shouting in the background shouts something about "goddamn salad tongs" and I realize Jamie is in the clubhouse kitchen.

"Right but—yesterday," I begin, unsure if he can hear me over the racket. "I thought I was fired."

"What? No. But you are extremely fucking late," Jamie replies. "Can you be here before eleven?"

I slump back in my seat, fiddling with the touchpad on my laptop. Can't I just be fired for a day?

"I'm actually out on an errand," I say. "I'd have to go home first. I'm not in dress code."

"What are you wearing?" he counters. "I mean—it doesn't matter. If you're wearing clothes and in the tristate area, please come to work as soon as you can."

My computer wheezes, exhausted and overheated. I give up.

"Okay, yeah," I sigh, ejecting the thumb drive and closing the laptop. "But what's going on?"

"I don't have time, Alice. Can you please just get here, and bring a pound of lemons?"

"What?"

Jamie's voice is muffled for a moment, and all I hear is the muted cacophony around him.

"Sorry," he says. "Ten pounds of lemons. I have to go."

I catch on quickly once I'm at the club. The member lot is packed with cars, and half the golf carts are gone. Crossing the staff lot, I can hear the thwack of tennis balls—at least two games going—and the distant shriek of kids at the pool. There's a tinge of grease in the air—the snack bar is getting a jump on things. An hour from now, a throng of wet, ravenous children will line up for burgers and curly fries. And their parents will be drinking in earnest. Hence, the lemons.

Jamie calls this "The Descent." It's the unknowable day when high season truly begins. Jamie explained it to me a few days in: the early days of summer are typically quiet, with maybe a dozen members on-site at any given time. And then, suddenly, they arrive en masse—usually on a Thursday, sometime in late June.

"Like Thanksgiving," he'd said. "Except you don't know the day in advance. And there are never any leftovers. And no one says, 'thank you.'"

I get it now. Coming through the boot room, I can already hear how full the clubhouse is. I head to the kitchen first, sacks of lemons swinging from each hand.

"Hello?" I say, pushing the door open with my shoulder. The kitchen is as chaotic as it sounded.

"Thank God," says a sweating line cook, diving for one of the bags. "The rest go to the grill."

I take the back way, using the staff hall. The gallery would be faster, but I'm in shorts, sneakers and a wrinkled pink shirt. The only dress-code violations I'm not breaking is the no-pockets rule. I stashed the thumb drive in my bra, too nervous to leave it in the car, though now I'm just nervous that it'll fall out.

"Alice!" a voice calls behind me. "Wait up!"

Jamie jogs toward me, with Cory in tow. I drop my hand to my side, perching the lemons on my hip in an awkwardly casual pose. Jamie doesn't notice—all he sees are lemons.

"Thanks," he says, taking the bag and handing it to Cory.

"Grill. Go," he orders. Cory nods and marches onward like a soldier to the front.

"You." Jamie points at me. "Freight elevator. Let's go."

★ ★ ★

The lemon crisis began with an unexpected flood of Tom Collins orders. The drink is always on the menu, but today it's all anyone wants.

"Every year, it's something like this," Jamie explains, shoving an ancient key into the ancient elevator operating panel. It jolts to life.

"In 2016 we ran out of gin. Fuck, man, that was a day."

He recounts the great gin disaster as we descend to the cold-storage room where the kitchen staff keep a backup stash of frozen lemon juice. ("We have to ration fresh. When martini time hits, we're gonna need those twists.") Jamie's so jacked on manic energy he's practically bouncing on his feet.

"You're not fired, by the way," he says, as the elevator bumps to a stop. "But—we need to talk."

The elevator doors clank open and Jamie leaps forward, running toward the freezers.

"Later though," he calls, his voice echoing in the dark. "When they're gone."

They never leave though. They just keep coming. The Descent is an endless, lawless day, with the whole staff working overtime and some of them not even staff. Jamie and I return from cold storage to find Cory by the elevator, waiting with some blond kid I've never seen before. Without a word, they swoop in to help unload the tubs of frozen lemon juice, all of us running them down the hall like vital organs to all the suffering, Tom Collins–less people at the grill.

The rest of the day is a sweaty blur. I spend most of it in a golf cart, ferrying coolers of lemon juice to the satellite bars set up around club grounds, with the help of the blond kid—who, it turns out, is both Cory's brother *and* thirteen years old.

"It's cool!" the kid tells me. "Cory said it's okay as long as they don't pay me, because of child labor."

I drive him to the staff parking lot and tell him to call his dad, wondering how many laws I've broken, serving cocktails mixers from a vehicle, with a minor, in ninety-two-degree heat.

I go inside for a bottle of water and somehow end up carrying a pallet of them to the snack bar. The snack bar needs napkins, so I hike up the hill and go in through the basement door, where an attendant pops out of the men's locker room with a wild-eyed look, implores me to fetch more mouthwash, then disappears before telling me where to find it. I ask a grill server who tells me to ask the valet, who tells me to fuck off because he's on his first break in six hours and he just wants to finish his sandwich in peace, *please*.

"Sorry," he says after a moment, a fleck of tuna on his lip. "Long day."

That's when I look at my watch and realize it's almost 6:00 p.m.

"Holy shit, what happened," I say to my wrist.

"Right?" the valet answers, wiping his mouth. "Worse every year."

I knock on Jamie's open office door and lean in.

"Got a minute?"

I'm officially gross, my skin tacky with dried sweat and a Picasso-esque sunburn on the left side of my body from my afternoon in the golf cart. But Jamie's even more wrecked. He's reclining in his desk chair, eyes shut, mouth ajar and clutching the armrests with a white-knuckle grip. He looks like he's fallen asleep on a roller coaster.

"Hi. Hey." He jolts forward, shaking himself awake. "What's wrong, what happened?"

"Nothing. I just thought we could talk."

"It's not about Matthew, is it?"

"Who? *Oh*." Cory's brother. Feels like that happened a month ago. "You mean the child bartender I drove around without a seat belt? No."

I risk a smile and sit down.

"Look," I begin.

"You know what?" Jamie says. "I know I said we should talk, but—another time. I really don't want to get into it."

"Okay. I do though."

He takes a bracing breath, beginning to protest. I raise my voice above his.

"Jamie, I came home to get Patrick charged with Caitlin's murder. I'm here to— Well. What I—"

I hear myself starting to hedge. If I'm telling him the truth I'll have to tell it all, plain and messy as it is. I clear my dry, throbbing throat.

"It's exactly what you think it is. I'm trying to fix it—get the whole thing reinvestigated properly. *I'm* reinvestigating. I hope the state will too, eventually—or the county. But I'm, like, forty steps away from that. It's a huge deal getting a closed case reopened—even with all the publicity this year. I mean that helps, but the village certainly won't reopen the case unless they're forced to. And in order to do that you either need 'compelling evidence,' or—"

"Or a judge," says Jamie quietly, slouched back in his chair. "Yeah, and even then they can appeal."

He drums a finger on the desk, rubs his eyebrows and sighs.

"I looked into it once."

"What?" I lean forward, wide-eyed and open-mouthed. "When?"

Jamie shrugs.

"Years ago. Briefly," he adds. "Not like that."

He raises his eyebrows, pointing at me with his chin. Not like *my* wild, rambling plan.

"*Why?*" I ask him, still stunned.

Jamie looks up, his eyes narrowed—offended.

"Why the hell do you think, Alice?" he murmurs. "Did you think you were the only one who remembered what happened?"

In the silence I can hear the distant, tipsy roar of cocktail hour in the clubhouse.

"Okay then," I say, whispering too. "Then you understand."

He nods.

"You should've told me though. Me, of all people."

At this, I drop my chin and give him a look.

"Come on." I smirk. "I take your point, but no way would you have hired me if I walked in here and told you all that."

Jamie stands, buttoning his jacket, looking toward the door. Dinner service will be starting soon.

"Yeah, maybe not," he concedes. "Still wish you'd told me though. I would have have helped."

I watch, speechless, as he steps sideways from behind the desk, heading for the door. He pauses in the door frame for a moment.

"Yeah," he says, nodding to himself more than me. "I'm helping."

Chapter Twenty-Two

July Fourth, 1999

I spun around, arms up, ballerina style. When I stopped, the room kept moving.

"You are amazing!"

Caitlin took my hands and spun us both around. The band was loud and the dance floor was crowded, and we were in the middle of it.

I didn't quite remember dinner ending—only that we'd been among the last to leave our table and head into the pink room for dancing and dessert. I didn't know how much I'd drunk from Caitlin's cocktails, but at some point I stopped worrying about getting in trouble and realized I enjoyed the pleasant frenzy tumbling through my body.

The game of Truth or Dare had escalated into an all-out competition, the two of us taking turns daring each other. I'd put salt in someone's coffee. She'd hung a teaspoon from her nose. We'd both asked the band for song requests ("Happy Birthday!" "The Macarena!") and run away giggling. Then Caitlin coaxed me onto the dance floor, daring me to twirl.

Now we were both spinning. The band was playing some old jazz standard, and we sang out lyrics when we knew them. ("No, no, they can't take that away from me.") I stumbled backward into a couple behind me, and Caitlin reached out, yanking me toward her, apologizing through laughter.

"Time out!" she declared and pulled me through the crowd, suddenly producing a glass of water.

"Drink the *whole* thing," she shouted over the music, leaning me against a wall—blissfully cool against my back. "I'll be right back!"

I nodded, lifting the glass, forcing the water down. When I lowered it, I saw Aunt Barbara, standing with Caitlin on the edge of the dance floor. Her head was bent close to her daughter's face as she spoke, and her eyes were hard and searching—angry in a way I'd never seen before. The water roiled horribly inside me as I watched them in their quiet argument: Barbara inching closer, Caitlin looking away, her thumb and middle finger picking at each other.

There was a brief blip of quiet as the band ended one song and swung into another, and in it I could hear Caitlin snap at Aunt Barbara. "He's right," I thought she said, but wasn't sure. Then the music resumed and Caitlin spun away from her mother, striding toward me in a hurry. I caught sight of my own mother then, standing beside Theo at the coffee station, their faces in identical flat frowns. Then Caitlin had me by the hand again, walking me out of the ballroom.

I remember the silent walk down the gallery. I remember waiting outside the cloakroom while Caitlin got her shawl. I remember her saying we needed fresh air, and the sudden wave of tiredness that came over me.

"It'll help, I promise," she said, bending over with a hand on my shoulder, so close I could smell the liquor on her breath and a hint of her violet perfume.

"It's my turn, right?" she said, smiling. "Come on. What's my dare?"

Chapter Twenty-Three

I get to the restaurant twenty minutes early, but Susannah is already there. She waves to get my attention—as if I could miss her sitting at that table, smack in the center of the room. I wave back and sidle through the crowded restaurant, the whole place so boisterous with chitchat it sounds like one big birthday party.

Adelina's, I growl at myself. *What the hell was I thinking?*

I wasn't, really. I'd been caught completely off guard yesterday, when Susannah texted: Just circling back about lunch! Two weeks had passed since that strange moment in the parking lot, and I hadn't heard from her. I'd started to worry—she'd been so insistent, squeezing my hand—and then her text appeared. I'd written back immediately: Tomorrow? Adelina's? It was the first restaurant that that came to mind, and now I realize why. I was probably seventeen the last time I was here. And I was definitely with Susannah.

"I just can't believe it," Susannah marvels, surveying the room. "It looks exactly the same."

Growing up, Adelina's was the special-occasion restaurant, reserved for major milestones: graduations, big birthdays, the day I finally got my license after failing the road test twice. There were nicer, more culinary, restaurants in town, but Adelina's had a dressy, festive vibe, with its gilded chandeliers and cushy velvet chairs. It also had an outrageous chocolate lava cake—a dessert

I'd believed Adelina's invented. Even after I learned it was a '90s restaurant staple, I maintained that Adelina's was the finest—well worth the forty-minute wait.

"Smells the same too," I reply, taking my seat, suddenly overcome with the scent of sautéed garlic, browned butter and the charred edges of last night's steak au poivre—a trio so familiar that it stuns me like a spell.

"They haven't changed the menu! Look, the ham salad. Remember?"

She reaches over, tapping on the menu in front of me, and the light catches the gleaming, gray diamond on her finger. I nod and sit back, the nostalgic haze clearing. I glance over, taking in the rest of Susannah's prim new look: her hair is freshly blown out and barretted. She's dressed a notch too formally, in a creamy shift and pale yellow jacket. I'm not positive, but I think she's even wearing pantyhose. This is not Susannah Joyce, with the big hair and vicious laugh. This is the future Mrs. Patrick Yates.

I have a thousand questions for her: *Why did you come back early? Why did you want to see me so badly?* Above all: *What the hell happened?* But I'm not asking questions today. Today was her idea. I need to be listening when she tells me why.

"I already ordered the lava cake," she says. "Well, two."

I feel my own surprised smile.

"I was worried they'd run out!" she says with a big shrug, her fingers splayed cartoonishly—a flash of the old her.

I let myself laugh. And, with hesitancy, she does too. The knot in my chest slackens as the both of us break down in quiet hysterics.

And for thirty miraculous minutes, everything's fine. It's very close to fun. We both order the house salad: a pile of iceberg lettuce, delivered with a gravy boat of tangy, pink dressing and silver bowl of garlic bread. My stomach is still too anxious for me to eat much, but the rest of me is having a surprisingly great time. We chat. We swap memories from Adelina's, and talk about how weird it is that the village still doesn't even have a Starbucks. We sidestep the touchy subject of family, and other than that, it's oddly comfortable. Then, Susannah forgets herself.

"How's work these days?" she asks.

"At the club? It's fine. It's—"

"Right," she says, touching her fingertips to her forehead. "I meant, before you— I forgot for a second. We just saw you there."

Both of us stare at the table, the sound of that "we" setting in like a storm. And that's the end of lunch.

"Susannah," I murmur. "We don't have to tiptoe around him. All right?"

"I was just trying to be sensitive."

"I know," I say evenly. "But what's the point, right? I'd rather we just talk about it honestly."

Susannah looks panicked—a wholly unfamiliar expression on her face. When did she get so *fragile*?

"I'm not saying, you know—'show me the dress!'" I continue. "But if he comes up? We can't avoid the subject all summer. Susannah, I'm working at your wedding venue."

She coughs out a laugh.

"Fine," she nods at the table. "Fair. No tiptoeing."

"I know that's how we're supposed to behave, here in 'the Briar.'"

I roll my eyes and mime a snooty laugh.

"What?" Susannah tilts her head, confused.

Shit. Shit, what is wrong with me?

"Nothing, just this—" I think fast. "It's this stupid thing Jamie says. It's a joke."

She raises her eyebrows, but, like a gift from God, the lava cakes arrive before she can respond.

"Wow," she declares, eyes fluttering.

"Seriously," I say, lifting my spoon. "So, we've covered work on my end. Jamie Hotdog is my boss, et cetera. Your turn."

Susannah nudges her cake, feigning relaxation.

"Um, good. Great, in fact," she says to the plate. "All those years I spent trying to climb the ladder—I never realized how satisfying a job could be."

I try to say something nice, but I can't even dredge up a platitude.

"I love it, is the truth," Susannah says. "I mean, it's not forever. But it's great for now."

She glances over with a bashful smile. The old Susannah was ambitious and proud, and now she's all apology. Anger flashes through me as I think about how small and flat and *meek* he's made her. And she allowed him to.

"Are you thinking of moving on?"

"No, I mean after kids," she says. "We'd like to start soon."

The words come out in a startling rush as though she's been holding them in.

"Oh," I mumble, numb and horrified. "Uh-huh."

"Yes, that's the plan," she continues, still in that odd, propulsive way. "I'm going to step back."

"Stop working, you mean."

Now I hear the pressure in my own voice. We're not yelling at each other, just speaking very firmly.

"People do it, Alice," Susannah says, her voice twanging with restrained defensiveness as she loses her grip on it. "People raise their children."

"*Excuse* me?"

I scoff—a loud, disgusted scoff—and both of us glance around the restaurant, checking to see if anyone's noticed the fight breaking out in the middle of the room.

"Alice, please don't do this."

"Do what, Susannah?" I hiss. "What am *I* doing?"

The urge to shout is so intense it aches like a cramp in my throat.

"You're right, I shouldn't have said anything," she cedes in a crisp, polite tone. "About anything."

"Why not?" I'm shaky with rage, more adrenaline in my

veins than blood. "'People do it,' right? Totally normal choices you've made."

Susannah props her elbow on the table with a clumsy bang, dropping her forehead into her hand.

"I don't know why I thought this would go differently."

My breath comes out in choppy laughter.

"Me neither!"

Susannah looks around again—embarrassed now, by me.

"Look, Alice, this is not what I came here to do. I apologize, okay? I know this is sensitive."

The word hits like ice water.

"Sensitive," I repeat. "Susannah, you are engaged to a murderer. You are talking about having children with a murderer."

On the edge of my vision, our server approaches, then quickly changes direction. Susannah and I are still as statues, almost head-to-head.

"Alice," she says, nearly inaudible now. "You don't know wh—"

"Yes, I do, Susannah. I know exactly what I'm talking about. You know I do."

Then, another miracle: Susannah crumples inward, a hand covering her face. A tear free-falls into her lap, and then another. My anger dissolves, and I realize this is it—this is my window. I reach through it.

"Susannah," I say, reaching for her other hand. "Tell me. What is happening?"

"That's not what . . ." she whimpers, a ragged inhale cutting her off.

"What? What is it?" I squeeze her hand, willing her to squeeze back. "Please, I want to help."

"Stop." She sits up, shaking her hand out of mine. "Enough."

Susannah breathes in, composing herself. She dabs her face discreetly with her napkin, then tucks it back in her lap.

"He forgives you. Okay?" She looks me in the eye, resolute and calm again. "That's what I came here to tell you. He forgives you."

Chapter Twenty-Four

"She said *what?*"

Jamie gawks at me over his beer. I take a deep drink of my own.

"I don't get it," Jamie continues. "He forgives you for what?"

"I think, all of it?" I shrug. "Reporting him? The entire public-accusation thing?"

Jamie squints and shakes his head.

"That's all I got, dude."

I twist sideways in my seat, wedging my back into the corner of the booth. The Martha Washington is one of the oldest operating pubs in the state, and the owners take great pride in their genuine-replica booths, modeled after the original colonial ones. It's a charming spot, but there's not one comfortable seat in the house. I have to suck in and bend over to get into a booth, and Jamie—who stands a foot taller than any of our founding fathers—has to fold up like an accordion just to get his legs under the table. But the Martha is twenty minutes outside the village and the food is both bad and overpriced, so it's reliably empty. Thus, it's become our meeting spot.

"Do you think that's actually why she wanted to have lunch?" Jamie muses.

"No idea," I answer, downing my beer. "But I don't know why she's doing any of this."

I unfurl myself from the booth and wriggle out, waving at the faintly smoggy air. There's a tiny fireplace in the back, as old as the Martha itself—and a health hazard, I suspect. It snaps and spits all night, producing more smoke than flame. But it smells nice.

"I'm getting another." I lift my glass. "Want one?"

"Sure," he says, still squinting into space. "'He forgives you.' God. So weird."

It's nice to hear someone else say it. It makes me glad, again, that I agreed to let Jamie help.

At first I said yes because I had to. Once you've told someone about your semilegal, amateur crime investigation, you can't just leave them out of it. And Jamie had insisted. He'd even told me about his ex-girlfriend, a village PD officer, whom he suspected *might* be able to help. He wasn't sure how much, but he *would* be willing to ask. I'd thanked him for the gallant offer—then watched the blood drain from his face as I told him Jessie and I were old pals. And that he had a lot to catch up on.

I'd filled him in on my busy first week, including the FOIL request, the useless redacted files and the unredacted ones Jessie had quietly stolen for me. Then, the bad news: those files were pretty much useless too.

I'd gone home after The Descent and combed through every file on Jessie's thumb drive. I'd stayed up half the night, reading and rereading, certain I'd find something—if not a smoking gun then smoke at least. But no—not a whiff. All the records demonstrated was how meager (and meddled with) the investigation had been. The interviews were half-assed and perfunctory. The death-scene report was so scant that half the form was just blank lines. "Decedent was unresponsive. Medics confirmed death at scene, suggesting possible drowning." Even I knew that was ridiculous. Sure, drowning might be a "possible" scenario, but no one arriving on that blood-soaked scene would have "suggested" it first. And as for all that blood, it hardly got a mention. In the section labeled "Evidence Observed/Collected" there was a single line: "Fluid samples (type pending)." The end. That's what really shocked me—the literal bloodlessness. I had seen and smelled and felt that blood beneath my shoe. I'd heard the sticky sound it made when I leaped back in horror, realizing what I'd stepped in. For God's sake, I left bloody footprints. How do you overlook that, even if you're *trying* to look the other way?

I'd grown angrier with each read-through—mostly at myself for thinking I'd find something, except proof of what I already knew: the case was bullshit. Individually, the records might've looked like appallingly shoddy policework. But on the whole, the investigation just looked fake.

"And there was nothing about the Joyces, right?" Jamie asks when I return from the bar. "The cops didn't call them?"

I shake my head, gently plonking a fresh beer beside his first one, still sitting two-thirds full.

"It would make sense," he continues. "They were career staffers. They knew everyone, right? Hal Joyce—he taught all those kids. He was like the *cool* tennis coach, remember? If anyone—"

"Yes, Jamie, I really do get it." I speak with all the patience I can muster, which is not a whole lot. "It *would* make sense to interview more staffers, in a normal investigation. In a good one, they'd probably call everyone. But this one—"

"Was bullshit." He nods and cracks a warm smile. "I got it. You wanna sit?"

I scoot into the booth, my hand still tight around my beer.

"Susannah's parents were both off anyway," I grouse—but now he's got me thinking about it. "I obviously asked her about all this a million years ago."

Over and over again: Was she sure her parents weren't at the club? Had either of them ever said *anything* about Patrick? Or Caitlin? Or anyone they knew? I felt bad, grilling her, especially because I already knew the answer.

"They were down the road, waiting for the fireworks. They got a spot by Northern Lights that year, so—"

Jamie nods, his amused smile softening.

"Good spot. Ice cream adjacent."

I bend my head—we both get it. The club's fireworks display is the only one sanctioned in Briar's Green. You can technically see it all the way from the village square, but to get a proper view you need to stand somewhere along the edge of Route 9—and you will be standing, unless you get out early enough to claim one of the good spots. If you nab the patch of grass by the ice cream stand, you spread out your blanket and camp out all day on it. You wave like a champion when your friend drives by in her mom's car, gawking at you through the window. You drink four strawberry lemonades, then sit in agony for an hour, waiting for the next designated family member to come take their turn, then you run across the parking lot to Squire's Deli, praying it's the nice guy behind the counter and he lets you use the bathroom without buying something first. Even if you get stuck with the mean guy, it is absolutely one of the best days of your summer.

Jamie knows all this—no need to explain. He nods again with great sincerity, and the anger firing in me dissipates. It's not for him.

"Anyway," I say, breaking the brief silence. "Even if the cops had called them, it wouldn't have mattered. Those interviews were a joke. Aside from mine, I mean."

Reading the transcript of my own police interview had been a masochistic exercise that conjured up details I'd gladly forgotten. The cops had prodded me along with ever-more-pointed questions: Was it hard for me to make friends at Wheaton, given my "different" background? Had I felt jealousy toward classmates, and if so, how did I handle it? Was there alcohol in my house—my apartment, rather—and was I often left alone with it, when my single mother was out at one of her three jobs?

I wanted to print out the transcript just to set it on fire. But the truth is, it's the only record with any real value. It proves they were, in fact, capable of interrogating someone.

"Can I take a look at the drive anyway?" Jamie asks (again). "I'm not doubting you. I'm just thinking—fresh eyes."

I sigh and drop my head back, forgetting how shallow the seat is. My skull whacks painfully against the back of the booth.

"Fine." I wince, dropping my voice. "I'll bring it tomorrow. I don't have it on me."

This is a lie. But I need to sleep on it. I trust Jamie, but part of me is still hesitant. Until a few months ago, I trusted Susannah too.

"And I'm telling Jessie, obviously," I add—though it's only just occurred to me. "She stuck her neck out, getting me that info. I don't know if she'd appreciate me handing it over to her ex-boyfriend."

Jamie smiles into his beer.

"She won't mind. We're friends."

He rubs at his hairline—a reflex I now recognize. Jamie may have grown out of his adolescent self, but he still goes red when caught in an awkward conversational corner. Whenever we're approaching one, his hand goes to the forehead in a gesture of sudden concern. Part of me wants to tell him—but not tonight.

"What happened there anyway?" I ask, smiling. "Jessie's great."

"Jessie's twenty-seven."

"And? You're thirty-one, it's not exactly May–December."

"A *young* twenty-seven," Jamie says, meeting my eye again. "You're right, she's great. We're just not in the same place."

Jamie makes a great show of adjusting in his seat, physically moving on from the topic.

"You thought anymore about calling your aunt?"

"Nope."

Jamie gives me a parental look.

"I get it," he says, clearly not getting it. "What they did was—cold."

Cold. Even for a born-and-raised Briar's Greenian, that is a dazzling understatement. What my aunt and uncle did was eviscerating—almost as devastating as the murder itself.

We'd all drawn close in the immediate wake of Caitlin's death, especially Mom and Aunt Barbara. Those first few days, Mom spent every waking minute on the phone, trying to keep her shattered sister afloat—even with me clinging to her like a petrified barnacle. But something shifted when the case was closed, and Patrick was cleared. The phone stopped ringing, and Mom went stone-faced. She wouldn't say why, but I found out soon enough.

They didn't believe me either—not anymore. Barbara and Gregory released a brief statement, thanking the police for their efforts and asking the press to kindly withdraw. They'd chosen to side with the village, and go along with the official nonsense story about a tragic accident. Caitlin had been drinking, and she drowned. As for my story, they declined to comment. Perhaps they'd decided I was simply confused, or maybe they thought I lied. I never found out, because they never spoke to me or my family again.

"Not even when Mom got sick," I tell Jamie. "Theo called Barbara, like, ten times. Nothing. Not even when she died."

Jamie takes this in, a curdled expression on his face.

"Understood." He nods once. "I shouldn't have asked. Sorry."

"Don't, it's fine." I wave off the apology like a gnat. "Next."

Jamie drums the table nervously with his fingers. Then something hits him.

"Hey! What about Gordon Fairchild? The writer guy."

"*Why?*"

I feel my nose wrinkle at the very thought of approaching Gordon Fairchild—the best-selling sleazemonger behind *A Death on the Hudson.*

"What do you mean 'why?' He was a member—he wrote the book. Who knows what he knows?"

"I think anyone who *read* the book knows what he knows," I fire back. "Or anyone who listened to *The Club Kid*. So basically, everyone. Besides, he's getting so much press right now—with that fancy new edition."

"I saw that." Jamie nods. "With the feet on the cover? What is that?"

I hold up my hands.

"It's gross—it's more money in his pocket. Anyway, I'm not calling him up and giving him another story to tell in his next profile, or whatever. I think he's gotten enough content out of this."

Jamie sips his beer, shrugging.

"Just saying. You wouldn't even have to use your private-detective guy. You could probably find Fairchild's info in Brody's office."

I nod, looking down at the table, pretending to consider this. The fire crackles in the background, even louder in my sudden quiet.

"What?" Jamie asks. He waits. He puts his beer down and tries again. "Alice, what?"

I picture the drawer full of diaries. All except for 1999.

"Okay," I say softly. "There's something I haven't told you. Something I found in Brody's office."

Jamie leans closer.

"I didn't tell you because—I mean, Jamie, I know you want to help. But this is your job. I don't want to—"

He stops me with a wave.

"*Psssh*. Are you kidding? You've spent, like, three hundred hours in Mr. Brody's office. I figured you weren't scanning wine lists the whole time." Jamie leans, eyes wide again. "So did you find it?"

I hesitate another moment, then cave. He's right; it's been three hundred hours. I can't waste all summer down there.

"No." I sigh. "I found the drawer, but 1999 is missing."

"Huh?" Jamie's face turns perplexed. "What do you mean? *All* the '99 reports?"

"Reports," I repeat slowly. "You mean his diaries. That's what's in the drawer."

"Oh God. Brody's little daybooks? No, he keeps a record of the day's events, because he thinks it's part of the job."

"Stop, what? How do you know all this?"

"Because he told me! He thinks it's part of *my* job too. He gave me a whole song and dance about it when I got promoted. All the bullshit about keeping a daily record for posterity—but, of course, nothing indiscreet." Jamie mimes a Brody-esque frown. "'If it shouldn't be spoken of, best not write it down.'"

I sit, trying to parse through this Brodyism.

"It means you leave the bad stuff out," Jamie translates. "You save that for the incident report. I'm guessing you haven't found that yet."

I've never even heard of it.

"What's an incident report?"

"Seriously?" Jamie asks, looking genuinely incredulous. "It's—yeah, it's exactly what it sounds like. Brody writes up every member infraction for the board's review."

"All of them?" I sit back. "Every incident?"

"Every incident he knows about—so, yeah, probably most. If it's bad enough, the member has to sit before the board."

"All because of what *he* says happened."

Jamie shrugs again.

"The great and powerful Brody. Anyway, something involving a dead body? I'd say that got written up real quick."

A wild surge of hope floods through me—then passes in an instant.

"And probably got thrown in the fire, on the orders of the great and powerful Whit Yates."

Jamie bobs his head, weighing this.

"Could be. But Brody's more of a keeper than a tosser."

You don't say.

"I'd have guessed the desk too." He points his beer glass at me. "But you know that shelf behind—"

Jamie goes still, his mouth frozen midword.

"Oh shit," he says, a smile coming over him. "No, dude, I know where it is." He looks at my glass. "Don't finish that." He puts down his own half-drunk beer and digs for his wallet. "We're going back to the club."

I check my watch. It's almost 11:00 p.m.

"I know," Jamie says, reading my thoughts. "We've got to try now, when the clubhouse is empty."

"Try what?" I said firmly, not moving. "Where are we going, I need a noun."

Jamie looks up, beaming.

"The secret room," he says. "The archive."

Chapter Twenty-Five

"Wait, Jamie." I chase him across the staff parking lot. "The archive is *real*?"

He yanks open the door to the boot room, flicking on light switches.

"The story about the secret room," I press. "Behind the old reception desk. You're saying—"

"Yeah. That one's true."

I stand, stunned for a moment, picturing the little door discreetly carved into the base of the staircase. Of all the silly rumors, I'd never have picked this one to be true. The "secret room" story was one of those macabre bits of lore that gets darker with every telling.

Legend had it that behind that door was a long, hidden hallway, leading to a secret room called "the archive." We thought of it as a kind of glamorous crypt where the members kept their secret treasures and held initiation rights and (depending on who you asked and how old you were) had clandestine orgies. The real thrill was that the entrance was a hiding spot in plain sight. If you were in the right place at the right time, you might catch someone sneaking in or out of it.

"The sex part is bogus," Jamie says, raising a hand. "I *think*."

We walk down the gallery, the green carpet shadowy in the dim security lights.

"But the secret part is real," he continues. "I only found out when I got promoted. No one's allowed in there without written permission from Mr. Brody or the sitting board chairman."

"Not even you?"

"*Specifically*, not even me," he says. "It's in my contract. 'Concierge's purview shall not extend to private meetings, private records or any some-such stored in the clubhouse archive.'"

"And you signed that?!" I'm dizzy and slightly breathless, both from excitement and from jogging to keep up with him.

"Trust me," Jamie says soberly. "It's no weirder than the other caveats in my contract. I'm also not allowed to ride any horses at the stable."

"Damn, so you have to bring your own horse?"

I'm practically giggling with nerves. Jamie nods, acknowledging the joke without laughing.

"You know, Susannah swore she saw the door open once, when we were, like, nine," I say as we approach the lobby. "When Brody was going in after hours."

"Bullshit. Like he'd leave it sitting open."

"No, I mean just for a second, as he was closing it. She said she saw steel walls?"

"Huh." Jamie nods sideways. "That actually tracks. I always heard it was connected to the old bomb shelter downstairs. That also exists, by the way."

I gawk at him, speechless.

"I'm not allowed in there either, even if the Russians invade."

A single floodlight illuminates the lobby. At the old reception desk, we both instinctively pause.

"Wait, is the electrocution thing real, too?" I whisper—half kidding.

"It's not that," Jamie says, looking at the door. "Shit, Alice, I don't think this is gonna work."

He points to the door. It's easy to miss at first glance. It doesn't have a doorknob or handle, and the facade is made of marble, allowing it to disappear into the stairs.

"What? I don't—"

"Closer," Jamie instructs, pointing harder. "There."

Now I see it. It's only visible thanks to the shadowy floodlight. Just as I remembered, there's no knob on the door. But there is one tiny lock.

Chapter Twenty-Six

It's past midnight when I get home, slipping in through the basement door so I don't wake anyone. I'm still wide-awake and wired on the cocktail of excitement over the archive, and dismay over our failed attempt to access it. It turns out Mr. Brody's door isn't the *only* one in the clubhouse that locks. We tried pushing at it, then peered at the discreet keyhole tucked into a tiny notch in the marble. It was old and gummy on the edges, but the center had been rubbed clean, and you could see it had been used. We tried Jamie's elevator keys, just for the hell of it, but it was obvious we weren't getting in. Jamie was quiet and pissed off when we left—but I can't bring myself to be upset about it. Just the fact that the archive exists feels like evidence of something.

I sit on the carpet and open my laptop. I check my email, where there's nothing but ads for pre–July Fourth sales and a credit card bill. I log out and log into my *other* email account, thrilled to find an email from Jeremy waiting for me.

A—

Chapman is in Briar's Green, or at least his phone and credit card are, and that's all I can tell you. Anything else would take boots on the ground, which, for the third time,

I'm not doing with these folks. I can't tell you what those people are doing at his house, but there's no record of anyone but him living there since he took ownership. Feel free to connect those dots yourself.

As for that text you got, there's no way for me to trace a number that's been starred out. I will say I'm familiar with scrambling services, and the ones that do it like that are not cheap. It ensures the number won't appear as spam, and it gets people's attention. It's showy—not the kind of move a Patrick Yates-type typically makes. Either it's him, and you've got him scared, or it's someone else who wants you to get in your car and go.

I'd consider doing so. In case it's not clear, Alice? That's a warning shot. Most people don't get two.

—J

PS: Background coming soon, sorry for the holdup.

I read it again, trying to parse out how much of this bluster I should take seriously. I haven't gotten another text, and I haven't fled town. If anything, I've dug in deeper since the morning I drove up Bramble Bush Road. I think of my ill-gotten police records, and my covert meetings at the Martha with Jamie. I've driven to work every day in my loud and highly visible old car. If someone did want to fire a shot at me, they'd have no trouble aiming. And I'll admit, there's something oddly reassuring about the suggestion that I've got Patrick Yates scared. Isn't that another way of saying I'm on the right track?

The feeling's still there when I wake up in the morning, after a few fitful hours of sleep. It feels as though my brain's been powered on all night—overheating, fans blasting—and it takes a moment to remember *why* I feel this edgy mix of glee and paranoia. The day comes back to me in bits and pieces as I dress and climb the stairs.

"Morning, sunshine." Jules leans out of the kitchen. "Didn't think we'd see you up this early."

"Aunt Alice!" Simon shouts from the table. "Are you babysitting tonight? Can we watch the dirty movie?"

"What? Oh—" I turn to Jules. "They keep talking about *Dirty Dancing*? That's a no, right?"

Jules rolls her eyes.

"That *is* a no, Simon. Next year, maybe," she calls, then turns to me. "Somebody's older sister told them about it. I think they just heard the word *dirty*."

She hands me a frosted Pop-Tart, cold and wrapped in a paper towel.

"Sorry, out of plates. Theo had to head out at the crack of dawn." She bends to grab detergent from under the sink. "I promise it won't be this chaotic once we get past the fundraiser."

"You're coming, right?" Isaac asks from the table. "It's at Giordano's, and you can have all the soda you want for free."

Jules chuckles behind me as I head into the dining nook.

"Yeah? Does that include Shirley Temples?"

"I think so," says Isaac, just as Simon says, "Yes!"

I sit and take a bite of my Pop-Tart, making a pondering face.

"Okay then. If it's cool with your dad, I'm in."

"Of course it is," says Jules, and I turn to see her curious face.

I guess Theo hasn't said anything about the newspaper. Or the conversation that followed—the one where he said if I really cared about him and his family, I'd leave town altogether. He and I have barely spoken since. Thankfully, we've both been out of the house so much that no one's had a chance to notice that things are a little weird.

Jules punches buttons on the dishwasher and it turns on with a swoosh.

"Tuesday," she says, watching me. "You'll be there, right?"

I nod. I guess I have to. Skipping the fundraiser would make things ten times weirder.

Remember, Mom used to say. *This is just a chapter. Not the book.* She'd remind us of this whenever we got bogged down in some petty school drama or struggled through a class we loathed. It might feel all-consuming, but in a matter of weeks—months at most—this chapter would pass, and we'd be onto the next. It never felt true in the moment, but she was always right.

I tell Jules I'll clear up the breakfast so she and the boys can head out for early camp drop-off. I promise Simon we'll watch an awesome movie, and make a note on my phone, reminding myself to tell Jamie I can't do the Martha tonight. Until Simon mentioned it, I'd completely forgotten I was hanging with the boys so Jules and Theo could go out for their anniversary (I'd also completely forgotten their anniversary). I feel a guilty prickle as I tidy the kitchen and bundle up the trash—filled to the brim with take-out containers. I hadn't noticed until now, but I guess things have been more hectic than usual these past couple weeks.

I leave for work, hauling the trash and recycling to the bins at the end of the driveway before I go (another thing I haven't been helping with). My car (the one they've loaned me indefinitely, for free) is parked on the street just beside the mailbox. The front is hanging open like a tongue, the inside piled with what looks like a week's worth of mail. I reach in and pull it out, cradling the small stack of envelopes and catalogs in the crook of my arm. I dump the pile on the passenger seat—I'll bring it in later, I've got to get going. That's when I see the two pieces on top: one, a wide, decorative envelope, and the other a sheet of white paper—no envelope or postage at all.

I lift the envelope first. It's thick and ivory colored, hardly any signs of travel on it. Then again, it hasn't traveled far. It's addressed to Jules and Theo Wiley. The return address says "Joyce" and lists the address of Susannah's childhood home, where her parents still live.

It's a wedding invitation.

I look at it, not feeling a thing.

I see black lettering. I hear cicadas. I smell oil on the pavement.

I drop it on the pile, my brain whirling into overdrive, producing possibilities, desperate to find a reason: a mix-up or an oversight. Maybe Susannah's parents sent it by mistake. Maybe it's *not* a wedding invitation somehow?

I lift the sheet of paper next, my mind still on the invitation. The paper is folded in half, crisp and unwrinkled as though it's only just been left in the mailbox. I unfold it and see there are only three words written on it, printed in blocky capitals. When I read them, I forget the invitation entirely.

TAKE CARE, ALICE.

Chapter Twenty-Seven

July Fourth, 1999

The night was moonless and deep dark. I could barely see the slate steps in front of me as Caitlin and I trekked down the rear path, away from the clubhouse. I remember the roar of the party behind us, growing fainter as we descended the hill. I remember wishing I was there, even if I was in trouble.

"Done!" Caitlin called to me.

She stood at the bottom of the steps, her white dress like a beacon in the darkness. She raised her arms, triumphant, one kitten heel in each hand.

That was the dare I'd given her: to walk down the rear path barefoot. Not exactly daring, but I was losing steam. It seemed like hours had passed since the Macarena.

"Might be easier if you took your shoes off too," said Caitlin. "The grass feels amazing actually."

I shook my head.

Caitlin extended a chivalrous hand as I neared the bottom.

"Mademoiselle?"

I wobbled on the last step and she grasped my wrist. The alcohol sloshed in my stomach.

"Okay there, babydoll?"

"I'm fine."

"You want to go back up?"

"No."

She had that look of gentle concern on her face again—that babysitter look. I could feel myself about to snap again, but then, over her shoulder, I caught a glimpse of bright blue light. I smiled.

"I've got a better idea."

No one used the pool at night, but they kept the underwater lights on anyway. Caitlin said it was "très gauche," and that the club should know better. People only lit up their pools at night to show everyone else they could afford to. She was probably right, but all I could think was how pretty it looked. The pool was painted a vivid white and emitted a luminous aura, lighting up the mist that drifted off the surface and softening the edges of the night.

"But what did he say exactly?" I asked.

Caitlin chuckled, rolling her eyes.

"He didn't like, 'ask me out,'" she said. "Guys don't really do that, you know."

I nodded. Of course I knew, *obviously*.

Caitlin sat at the pool's edge, leaning back on her hands at the top of the steps, her feet in the water, resting on the top stair.

"Maybe boys your age do that," she said. "Have you had a boyfriend, Alice?"

"What? No?"

I was leaning against the fence, hoping Caitlin wouldn't ask me to sit with her. Even if I managed to get on the ground without breaking the dress's zipper, I'd have to ask for help to get back up (the mere thought made me flinch with embarrassment).

"No!" I said again, and Caitlin chuckled.

"No? Not even that kid in the cloakroom? I bet he's asked you out!"

"Oh my God."

I covered my face with both hands as Caitlin howled.

"You can tell me! I *promise*, I won't tell your mom."

"I swear to God, I have never had a boyfriend."

"Okay, okay, if you say so, babydoll." Her laughter eased and she gazed into the water. "Anyway. It's different when you're older."

How? I wanted to ask. *Specifically how?*

Caitlin went quiet, watching the water, as if she too was looking for the answer. Reflected light played across her face in little splashes. Finally, she spoke.

"You just start hanging out, and then—yeah . . ." Caitlin trailed off, her expression unreadable. "At some point, he's your boyfriend."

Now I rolled my eyes. Something about the embarrassment made me feel drunk again, and bold.

"But how do you *know* then?" I asked.

This was the part I didn't get. How did you know when the "hanging out" part was over, and you and the boy became something official? Nameable?

"Like what happens, exactly?" I pressed.

A smile crept onto Caitlin's face.

"Uhhhhh, I—" She cut herself off with a laugh. "Hey!"

She whipped her head toward me, mock outrage in her voice.

"Hang on, are we doing truths now?"

I shrugged, but my face went hot.

"Busted!" She pointed at me. "We're doing dares, and it's *your* turn. I dare you to come put your feet in with me."

I started to protest. No, the game was over. We were just talking.

Caitlin shook her head, eyes shut.

"Nope, that's the dare." She grinned. "Seriously, the water feels *so* good."

"I don't feel like it."

"Too bad, babe, it's a dare!"

"Fine," I muttered, shrugging again. "You win, I don't care."

"Aw, c'mon!" Caitlin paused, biting her lip, then leaned

toward me, dropping into a whisper. "I'll tell you 'what happens, exactly.'"

She wiggled her eyebrows.

"Shut up!" I shouted. "I don't *want* to!"

Everything seemed to freeze, Caitlin included. For an instant, she looked just like my mother. The look on her face was the same one Mom got the time I told *her* to shut up. It was a look of astonishment more than offense: *I didn't know you could do that.*

"Well," Caitlin said. "Alrighty then."

Now the game was really over. I covered my mouth, instantly sorry.

Caitlin took hold of her dress with one hand, grasping the railing with the other. As she stood, her feet skidded slightly on the underwater step. She made a little whooping sound, gripping the railing.

"Wait," I said, rushing over, desperate to make up for my gaffe. "It's slippery, I'll help you."

"No worries, I'm—"

Caitlin lifted one foot out of the pool, and the other one slipped again, sliding sideways on the step. It happened in an instant: her eyes and mouth opened wide, a look of panic seized her face and she dropped her skirt, reflexively reaching for my shoulder to steady herself. I registered her hand a second too late, lurched sideways under the force of her grasp, and then my feet stumbled one over the other and I was falling toward the pool. Just before I hit the water, I heard Caitlin gasp.

Chapter Twenty-Eight

"I don't understand," says Jamie, holding the paper. "It came with the wedding invitation?"

"*No,*" I hiss. "They were both in the mailbox, but the invite was mailed. This was just *left.*"

"On the same day as the wedding invitation."

"Maybe?! Or maybe the person left it this morning, and just stuck it in with yesterday's mail."

"Which had the wedding invitation in it."

"Jamie!" I shut the office door firmly. "Please stop saying 'wedding invitation.' That's a whole other whatever—I can't even think about that yet. I'm still on the unmarked note."

He raises his eyebrows.

"I don't think it is 'a whole other whatever,'" he says simply. "I think it's pretty obvious, this came from Patrick too. Maybe not him personally, but you know—on his behalf."

I shake my head. It doesn't feel like him. I think about Jeremy's email—him saying it didn't seem like the Yateses' style, making overt threats. Then again, Jeremy also said most people don't get two warnings. I guess I'm the exception.

After reading the note, I ran back into the house and packed my things. I called Jamie and said I'd be late, and he'd understand when I got there. I called Jules and said something had come up and I was really sorry but I couldn't babysit tonight. I told her it was a work emergency, and I'd be staying in the village tonight, possibly longer. Jules was more alarmed by my urgency, brushing my apologies aside and asking if everything was all right—could she help? I felt monstrous. I told her no, and not to worry—I would explain later. I tucked the note into my tote bag and left the rest of the mail on the kitchen island, the wedding invite included.

I drove across the village and checked in at the Alcott Inn, a chintzy bed-and-breakfast near the train station. It's overpriced, designed for weekend tourists who want to stay somewhere "authentic"—which is to say it has no air-conditioning. But it's the only place that had a room available immediately.

"If you don't think this is Patrick, who do you think it is?" Jamie asks.

"I don't know. I'm thinking Alex Chapman, but I don't know."

"Chapman? Why would—"

"I don't know."

"Right." Jamie looks up, appraising me. "Look, you got out of the house. That's what matters. Let's just get through the day and think. Deal?"

Weary, I nod.

"We can compare notes later," says Jamie. He sits forward. "By the way, I've got another idea about getting into the archive. I'll explain at the Martha."

I shake my head.

"Let's take a night off from the Martha."

Jamie looks deflated.

"Seriously?"

"Seriously. I don't have room in my head for another idea."

This is true, but it's not the real reason. The real reason is I'm scared. I can't stop looking over my shoulder. I don't know who left that note in the mailbox, but they've won this round.

I spend the afternoon in Mr. Brody's office, trying and failing to lose myself in the mindless admin work. I feel his icy glare on me the whole time, and the feeling stays with me even when I leave the room. In the gallery, in the powder room, in the staff lot after work—I can't shake the itchy sense of being watched.

I drive straight back to the Alcott Inn, desperate for my little room with its lockable door.

But there's someone waiting for me there too.

"Alice, my God," says a voice as I turn onto the landing.

I stop in my tracks, gasping aloud.

"Oh!" she says. "I'm so sorry, honey. I didn't mean to startle you."

It's Jules. It's just Jules.

"You're wound up tighter than he is." She pulls me into a bracing hug. "The two of you, I swear. Your lives would be so much easier if you just learned to say 'something's wrong.'"

"Something's wrong," I say into her shoulder, numb and flat-out exhausted. "Come in."

The Alcott's rooms are color-themed—like the ballrooms at the club, but the effect is far less subtle here. My room is wallpapered in a crimson floral print, the floor is layered with faded burgundy rugs and the four-poster bed sits at the bleeding center of it all, topped with a scarlet canopy.

"I don't even want to ask what they're charging for this room," says Jules, looking around.

She's dressed in bike shorts and a boxy blue T-shirt that might be one of Theo's. My first thought is she must have pretended to go to the gym to come see me. But then I see her ruddy cheeks and the water bottle in her bag and remember that Jules is a grown woman who doesn't sneak around and lie to everyone. That's my thing.

"How'd you know I was here anyway?"

I flop down into one of the overstuffed armchairs in the little seating area beside the windows. I reach over and crank open the nearest one, letting in a muggy breeze.

"Well, I saw my old car parked out front this morning. So that was my first clue." She cranks open the other window. "My office is two streets down."

"God," I mutter. "Small town."

"Small village. As they say."

I shut my eyes and prop an elbow on the chair, dropping my head heavily against my hand. Maybe I'm not being paranoid. Maybe everyone in the village *can* see me.

"I'm sorry about leaving like that," I say. "And shit, I'm so sorry about your anniversary."

Jules sits across from me and takes a long drink from her water bottle.

"Don't be," she exhales. "I was *not* up for putting on heels and going out tonight anyway. And neither was Theo. He's probably passed out on the couch right now, while the boys tear the house apart."

"Or watch *Dirty Dancing* on YouTube."

She gives me a closed-lip grin.

"Anyway, that's why I'm here. Theo told me about the argument."

I shut my eyes—I don't have room in my brain for this either.

Jules sits forward in her chair.

"I didn't press him for details, and I won't press you. I've got two brothers *and* a sister, okay? Someone's always furious about something; it's called having a family. But Alice, believe me, he feels awful."

"Oh," I say, in a toneless voice. "Really?"

"*Awful,*" she repeats. "He came home, and he's like, 'Where's Alice?' I said, 'Well, honey, she called me and said she was leaving this morning. Any idea why she didn't call *you*?' And he just fell apart."

This raises my eyebrows.

"Oh yeah." She nods, continuing in a sad-Theo voice. "'We argued. I was a jerk, I overreacted.' I said, 'Okay, so call her!' But he just—you know."

She shakes her head and sits back.

"Look, it's no excuse. But things ramped up fast this summer. Campaigning has become a full-time job—a *second* full-time job. And between us, I think he thought it would be easier."

I snort. I bet he did. Theo who blew through the SATs like a word jumble.

"Still." I fiddle with a loose thread on the arm of the chair. "I think it's best I'm out of the house."

Jules stands with a breezy smile, pulling her bag onto her shoulder.

"Well, honey, you're wrong."

"No, like you said, it's a busy summer. It's not a good time for visitors, and I—"

She lifts a hand, refusing my rebuttal.

"Nope, sorry, don't peddle your WASP bullshit here. If you need a breather, *fine*. But you don't stay in a hotel in your hometown. You stay with your family and have a fight, and then guess what? You get over it."

She waves me onto my feet, and I stand, sighing like a child as she scolds me like one. She takes me by the shoulders.

"You know if this were any other moment in time, he'd be the one here saying this, right?"

She gives me a little jostle. And something comes loose.

"I saw the wedding invitation."

I say it to the floor, scared to see her face.

"Oh God, *that* nonsense," Jules says, scoffing. "Talk about WASP bullshit."

I wait, confused. Jules looks back with an astonished half smile.

"It's because of Theo. Because he's running for office. It's one of those ridiculous, old-school courtesy things."

I stare through her, trying to do the math.

"Whit Yates is a senator. Theo's running for Congress. Local-politician hat-tipping, blah blah blah—just what they do around here. I thought you knew all that stuff."

"But it came from Susannah's parents," I reply, though even as I say it, I realize I'm almost certainly wrong.

"Right, that's tradition too," Jules says, folding her arms. "'Mr. and Mrs. So-and-So invite you to the wedding of their daughter.' The bride's family traditionally pays for the wedding too, but I gather that's not the case here. I don't know the Joyces, but I'm guessing they're not in a position throw a black-tie reception at the club."

My stomach sours at the thought of it. I bet Susannah's parents would have loved to throw a wedding for their only child. A modest one, yes, with a cake from the bakeshop and Susannah in her mom's old dress. I wonder if the Yateses even asked before they booked the club.

"So," I say slowly. "You're going to decline?"

Jules's eyes pop.

"Me? I'm not even dealing with it. It's on Theo to figure out how to say no—while still tipping his hat back or whatever. It's a lousy position to be in, but he's the one who wanted to go into politics. Is that why you left? Because of the invite?"

"No," I say, meeting her eye. So there's *one* truthful thing I've told her.

"*Good.* And maybe you do need a breather. But talk to your brother, all right? Let him apologize. I mean it, this is not the year for dramatic silences. You two can do it your way on the next fight. This time I'm butting in for the greater good."

"Deal," I say, my voice dry.

She pulls me in for one last hug—the solid, whole-armed kind that disarms me every time, and makes me want to ask her where she learned it. She lets me go and I open the door for her, leaning heavily against the frame.

"Will we see you next week?" Jules asks in the hall. "I know you don't really celebrate. I just thought you might want to be together this year."

I frown, not understanding. "The fundraiser?"

"The Fourth, Alice. Next Wednesday is the Fourth."

"*Oh.*" I shake my head, sputtering. "No, of course, I just—I forgot what day it was."

"Time flies," Jules says, a sad smile.

"Yup. And the fundraiser's Tuesday. I didn't *forget* forget."

"No pressure," she says. "For the fundraiser or the Fourth. Just—keep in touch, okay?"

"Of course. Absolutely."

"And get some sleep."

I close the door at last and step out of my work shoes, kicking the oxfords into the little closet without bothering to unlace them. I turn on the shower to warm up while I undress. Even the sound of it makes me smile with drowsy relief. I reach back to unzip my skirt, instinctively patting my pockets before remembering I don't have any.

A soft rattle comes from across the room. I look over at my bag, slumped on the floor against the frilly armchair. My phone vibrates inside of it again.

It can wait. If it's Theo, if it's Jamie—it can all wait. I step into the bathroom, the calming rush of water blotting out all other sound.

Three restless minutes later I emerge, clean but unrelaxed, and hurry across the room in a towel, my hair dripping all over the rug. I fish my phone out and there they are again—a row of stars where a phone number should be. And beneath it, another row. And another, and another, and another.

And then the phone rings again. This time, I answer.

Chapter Twenty-Nine

Two days later, on another early morning, I drive up the Taconic to Westchester County Airport. It's not yet 5:00 a.m. and the two check-in gates are closed. There are only four flights listed on the departures screen, the next one scheduled for seven twenty-five. It's a small, regional airport that runs a handful of short-haul commercial flights between cities along the East Coast. The rest of its clientele are private fliers and corporate employees who depart directly from their respective hangars, bypassing the terminal entirely. The sheer lack of lines makes flying through Westchester an eerily easy experience.

My footsteps echo on the freshly mopped floor as I follow the signs for security. This area is also empty, except for two guards chatting beside the conveyer belt. Just past the security area, there's a shuttered souvenir store, a magazine stand and in the corner, a tiny coffee shop with three café tables. Alex Chapman is sitting at the last one, waiting for me.

He lifts his chin by way of greeting, hands wrapped around a paper cup of black coffee. He wears a fleece vest over his T-shirt. His face is cheesy pale and studded with black stubble. He doesn't look like someone who spent last month cruising the Italian coast, but I do recognize his face as the same one photographed in Naples: solemn and set, his mouth a flat line.

"Don't bother getting coffee," he says when I reach the table, his eyes on the cup. "It's burnt to shit."

His blue eyes, I notice, are bloodshot.

"Are you gonna sit?" he asks mildly. "I don't have that much time."

He doesn't seem like the person who called me the other night either. He'd been panting and frenzied when I answered the phone, like someone fresh from a screaming fight. He'd exploded at me: What did I want? What was so goddamn important that I'd tracked down his fucking home address?

I'd gathered myself as quickly as possible, unsure where or how to begin. It hadn't mattered though. As soon as I found my voice, Alex cut me off.

"Not on the phone!" he'd barked, pausing. "Tuesday. I'm on an early flight out of Westchester. Because of you."

Now Alex sits before me, somewhere between abashed and indignant.

"So, are you going to ask me questions, or . . . ?"

I watch him for another few seconds, still adjusting to his wilted, bloodless affect.

"Where are you going?"

"Upstate," he answers. "Rehab. Third time."

He sits back, taking a shallow sip from the steaming cup.

"I thought—you said you were leaving because of me?"

"Yep." He nods. "They're shipping me out again, because of you this time."

I shake my head, confused. He raises his cup toward me in a grim toast.

"I'm not an alcoholic. Patrick is—a sober one now. *For* now. I've seen him clean up twice before, and it never lasts."

Alex sneers into his cup.

"I'm a better fake. I do it full-time."

"What does that mean?" I ask delicately. *What are we doing here?*

He takes a breath and then, with great deliberation, Alex unravels, bit by bit, before my eyes. The story spills out of him with hardly any prodding. It's like he's had the whole thing queued up and ready, just waiting for me—for anyone—to come along and push the button.

Alex and Patrick had indeed been close in high school, but by their graduation, Alex was growing weary of being the constant sidekick. Thanks to their reckless antics, he'd already fucked up his knee *and* any shot of getting into an Ivy League school. Patrick, he'd noticed, had paid no such price. Either way, he figured, they'd have one last drunken summer, then they'd go off to college and real life would begin. But Alex's life changed forever, the night he served as Patrick's alibi.

"It never occurred to me back then," he says. "You don't think about consequences like that when you're seventeen."

"Did Patrick ask you to confirm his story?" I cautiously interject. "Or was it his parents?"

"What?" Alex answers sharply. "That night? Both of them. All of them. But it's not like—"

He stops, scrubbing at his forehead, mumbling to himself.

"What's that?" I lean forward.

"It's not like they *asked*," he repeats, his anger surfacing again. "Nobody pulled me aside and said, 'Tell the cops you were with him or else.'"

Alex looks at me affronted.

"It was like—I'm just standing there, and Patrick's talking to his parents, saying we were doing coke in the locker room. And at first, I'm thinking, 'Coke? Shit, where was I?' Like I don't even know why he's telling this story. I thought—"

"Wait," I cut in again. I have to. "Just to be clear. Are you saying it's not true?"

Alex's face goes from irate to confused.

"You were *not* with Patrick during that time frame?"

He looks at the wall, then back to me, his brow knit tight.

"Are you recording this?"

"No," I answer quickly. *Shit, why am I not recording this?*
"If you are," he says a bit louder, "I do not consent."
"I'm not recording," I huff, pulling out my phone and dropping it face up on the table.
"Fuck it. Doesn't matter," he says, more to himself than me. "*No*, I was not with him. Yes, I lied. All clear now?"
I nod, speechless, my whole body beating with adrenaline.
"Where were you?" I squeeze the words out.
"Fuckin' passed out in a bathroom stall," Alex replies. "We'd been going pretty hard that week—last hurrah, whatever. I didn't even want to drink at the club party. We'd been up the whole night before, and I literally remember thinking, *Shit, I just wanna go to bed*. But we always got shit-faced at those things. It was like a rule. So yeah, I was tanked by dinner." He shrugs. "Then I went to the bathroom and next thing I know, I wake up falling off the toilet."

He chuckles at the table, his face briefly lifting, then slowly sinking into a mask of bewilderment as he continues, following the memory.

"And then I clean up and go back upstairs, and the music's stopped and everyone's—everyone's running around, and it's like, I can hear all these voices but can't tell what anyone's saying? And Patrick's there, in the gallery with his folks, and he just sort of pulls me in, the way he does. The cops weren't even there yet, and already he's telling this story about the coke and the sauna in the locker room, and then they all just—" Alex tilts his head, slowly. "They just turn to me. And I don't know what's going on, but I know what they want me to say. They want me to say yes to all of it. I didn't have a choice."

I turn my head, hearing the distinct note of self-pity in his voice. "You did though."

Alex stiffens and looks back at me through lowered eyelids. I'm starting to realize how backward I had it. Alex is more than willing to talk to me. He just doesn't want me to talk back.

"Yeah, okay, I had a choice," he says. "And I made it, and I paid the price."

"The price," I repeat, my own patience thinning now. "Alex, I'm sorry but—come on, you didn't get a drug charge. You got to go to Princeton. You're hanging out on his yacht."

Alex pulls his lower lip in, nodding at the floor.

"I'm not 'hanging out' anywhere. I'm a paid employee." He flicks a glance upward, checking my face. "I go where he goes. That's how it works."

I freeze, seized by a sudden, vise-tight panic. What if *he's* recording? What if he's not alone? I look behind me at the empty coffee shop and the empty terminal beyond. I can barely hear the security guards chatting in the distance. When I turn around, Alex has a small, satisfied smile on his face.

"Guess you didn't know that part."

"What do you mean you go where he goes? What do you do for him?"

"Uh," Alex says, looking up. "Let's see, back in San Francisco, I was his 'house manager.' After the first rehab trip, I was 'sober companion,' for, like, a year. The second rehab, they had me go with him, so that was another title change—I can't remember. Then we moved back east, and I think I've just been 'consultant,' ever since." He shrugged. "It's just what they put on the checks. Really, I'm just Patrick's full-time friend."

"Why though?" I ask, still puzzling it together. "You mean so you can—what, keep an eye on him?"

"Yeah." Alex bobs his head. "And so they can keep an eye on me. A little of both."

"I don't understand."

"Yeah, well." He rubs his eyes with his thumb and forefinger. "Took me a few years too. But that's why I got to go to Princeton—my big prize, right? I show up at the dorm and guess who's my roommate? Then he's going to California, and they book me a ticket too. At first it's a gift, and then it's a favor. 'Won't you keep him company? We hate to have him out there all alone.' It's incremental. And by the time you realize what's happening, you're a fuckin' hostage."

Hostage. That word cuts through the fog.

"What about your house?" I blurt out. "Who are those people? The family living there."

"Christ," Alex says, half laughing. *"Tenants."*

I picture the woman's furrowed brow as she called to me from her car—the man beside her, eyeing me through lowered lids.

"They said they didn't know you. They didn't recognize your name."

"Yeah? I don't know theirs either. My management company handles the details. If they clear the renter, I sign the lease." He shrugs tightly. "I think the guy works up at IBM? I don't remember, they've been there a while. I know his company's paying, and they pay on time."

I take this in, nodding. I can see his patience dwindling further.

"So, it's a rental property," I state. "And the renters don't know your name because—"

"Because who gives a shit? Because I don't live there, and they don't personally hand me a check every month. The rent goes to my property managers, who take their 25 percent and transfer the rest to my business account. Ya got me, I'm an absentee landlord. Is that what you came here to talk about?"

Alex shuts his mouth quickly, eyes scanning the room. I keep mine on him.

"Where do you live then?"

He leans forward, eyes wide, a tiny jaw muscle flickering.

"Nowhere. Are you listening? I live wherever he lives—in whatever pool house or cottage or little detached suite they stick me in. I am a permanent guest."

Alex lifts his eyebrows at me, a soft warning in his voice.

"That house is my only source of income that isn't entirely controlled by them. I don't have some bottomless trust like

Patrick, okay? I got *some* money from my parents and I put it all into that house, because I saw the writing on the wall. The money the Yateses pay me goes into a bank account that's managed by *their* finance people. The house money is separate. It's not a fortune, but it's secure."

He stops himself, swallowing, taking a deliberate pause.

"It's the one thing I have that they didn't give me. But they can damn sure take it away if they want to. I think you know that."

I look at his white, wild-eyed face, and think of Liv Yates gazing down at me from the back of her horse. I can't fathom how she got word to him so fast, but like Alex said—I know she could if she wanted to.

"So you sent that text," I say. "Liv told you to scare me off, and you did."

"*I* wanted to scare you off." He holds my gaze and nods, once. "Yeah, I sent a text. You'd called my phone—left that creepy fuckin' message. Then you showed up at my house. Liv Yates didn't make me do anything. She doesn't care that much about you, or me."

I'm not sure he's right about that.

"So she just happened to be riding by your house. The morning after I called you."

"Maybe," Alex says, sitting back, slowly deflating. "For all I know she rides there every day." He leans back. "I'll tell you one thing though. That phone call fucking *ruined* the Italy trip." He leans back.

He chuckles at this. I sit quiet, unsteadied by yet another sudden shift in his demeanor. Anger I expected. Paranoia too—perhaps a hint of buried remorse. But Alex is all those things and more, and none of it is buried. Every reaction is right there on the surface. Jeremy's right. If he were a dog, he would bite.

"What happened?" I ask finally. "When you got my message?"

"That's the thing, I didn't," Alex says. "I didn't get to it first. Patrick did. He was up before everyone, doing his fuckin' sunrise meditation. And someone's phone starts ringing—wrecking his precious moment of peace. So he gets up, starts looking around the boat, and there it is, stuck between two cushions on the back deck. Must've fallen out of my pocket the night before. He's all pissed off, coming to bring it to me—and then he notices the number."

Alex gestures to me across the table.

"Local number. I've got one too, but it's not so common, area code. So he barges in and asks who's calling me from our village, when it's midnight there."

Talk about paranoid.

"And I have no idea, and I'm basically still asleep, so I just play the message—and holy shit!"

Alex cracks up again.

"His face, my God. You hit all the buttons. Mentioning 1999 and Wheaton. And the way you kind of fumbled the names? Something like, 'Hi Alex, this is, um, uh, Alex?' Did you do that on purpose?"

"What?" I ask, completely lost. "No, obviously not. Why?"

"Because 'Alex' and 'Alice' sound pretty much the same on a voicemail."

I pause, catching up.

"He *knew* it was me?"

The thought feels like ice water down my back.

"He was flipped out enough to get the call traced. And that was the end of vacation."

Alex catches his breath.

"They had me on a plane two days later."

"First class," I say, not thinking. Quickly, I add, "I bet."

"Every time." Alex sniffs. "Know why? Because the flight crew keeps tabs on first-class passengers. They greet you by name. It's like flying with a nanny."

He nods, reading my face.

"I know, cry me a river. Anyway. Everyone went ho[me]. Patrick and Susannah were supposed to stay a few weeks [lo]nger, but I guess he pulled the plug on that too. The trip [was] supposed to get them away from all the media hype, and—you know, the anniversary. But, no dice."

I sit, taking it all in. I can feel a thousand questions for[ming] as my brain wraps around this scenario, and what it may or may not mean.

A garbled voice booms out from the terminal behind u[s and] both Alex and I look toward it, startled.

"That'll be my flight starting check-in," Alex says. "You[']r[e] lucky. If it wasn't so last-minute, they'd have flown me private."

He reaches back, rolling a small suitcase around from behind the chair. He unzips the front pocket and pulls out a printed itinerary.

"Did you know this is the airport where JFK Jr. and his wife took off from?" Alex asks idly. "When they crashed, I mean."

I pause, disarmed by both the comment and the blasé tone.

"Yeah," I answer in a mumble. "Her sister too."

Alex nods absently, scanning the itinerary.

"Why did you call me?" I ask, watching him closely. "I mean, why now? After trying to get rid of me."

"You filed a police request," he says. "Pretty clear what your end game is here."

Alex cocks his head, looking at me sideways.

"I'm not saying you'll pull it off—and I don't want details. But I'm done." He pauses, as though reconsidering. "You're right. I had a choice back then. I guess I wanted to make a different one this time."

He pops the handle on his suitcase and stands.

"Wait, Alex," I say, turning in my seat. "I don't understand, why are they sending you to a rehab?"

"Like I said, I'm good at faking it. So I did. I had a few benders, fucked up the guest house." He shrugs. "It didn't take much convincing. I think they're all relieved to know I'll be locked up and under guard for the next thirty days. At least."

I start to ask why *he'd* want to go, but that seems instantly, abundantly obvious.

"Well, bye," he says, reaching for a baseball cap in his back pocket and shaking it out. "I hope that helped with—I don't know, whatever you're doing. Don't tell me."

He puts the cap on and turns swiftly toward the terminal, the suitcase rumbling behind him.

I stand abruptly, banging my chair into the table behind me. I apologize to the cashier as I run past.

"Alex!" I call, my voice echoing off the terminal ceiling.

He turns, perturbed, but only mildly. I slow to a walk.

"Did you leave a note in my brother's mailbox?"

Alex squints, his mouth a circle.

"Did I— Your brother? You have a brother?"

"Yeah, he went to Wheaton too," I say, knowing Alex would never have noticed him back then. "Theo Wiley? He's running for Congress."

"Okay? Good for him. Look, I have to go."

"Alex, wait. Can I call you?"

"No," he says simply. "They take your phone."

"After, then. When you're out."

He doesn't answer—just looks at me.

"You'll need more than me," he says, finally. "You need to talk to other people."

"Who?" I press, closing the gap between us.

"Anyone," Alex murmurs. "But I'd start with the parents."

"*Caitlin's* parents?" I ask, my volume ratcheting up. "Why?"

"Just—" Alex hedges. "I don't know. But Patrick went to see them after the case was closed."

"What?" I whisper. "*Why?* At their house? What did he say? Alex you've—"

"I don't *know*," he repeats sharply, holding up his hand again. "He told me the day he went to see them, and then his dad shut him up."

I feel breathless, my mind whirling like a top.

"Okay." I nod. "Who else?"

Alex tuts, a flare of aggravation crossing his face.

"Like I said, anyone. Members, club staff, anyone who was there. Jesus, I'm not the only one who lied that night."

"I know," I say automatically, still only half hearing him. *Patrick went to see Gregory and Barbara?*

"And Alice," Alex says, and I snap back to attention. "New York is a one-party consent state."

I stare at him, lost. He presses his lips together, looking sideways again. Then he leans over.

"Next time, record."

Chapter Thirty

July Fourth, 1999

I was flailing underwater, desperate for air. I fell hard into the pool, and my dress whooshed up and wrapped around me in tangled layers. I heard the muted scrape of my shoes against the bottom. This was the shallow end, I knew, and yet I couldn't get a foothold. I struggled toward the surface, just inches above, but couldn't reach it—an actual nightmare come true. I batted at the shimmering fabric around my head, kicking for the floor, and a white-hot panic took hold.

Something caught me by the hair, yanking me sideways. My hands flew up and found it—Caitlin, dragging me by the scalp. Still submerged, I grabbed on clumsily, my nails digging into Caitlin's wrist and forearm. She pulled and pulled and finally, she got me over to the stairs.

"Alice! Jesus, are you okay?"

I sat, gasping, on the steps, and Caitlin crouched beside me. She put a hand on my shoulder, the other still gripping the railing. The bottom of her dress swayed gently underwater.

"Hey." She shook my shoulder, touched my cheek. "Say something, honey."

I whacked her hand away.

"What the hell?!" I shrieked, frightened by my own strangled voice.

I bent over, seized by a burning coughing fit.

"I'm so sorry. It was an accident." Caitlin looked dazed with shock. "Holy shit, I thought you were drowning!"

"I was!" I shouted. "I almost drowned because of you!"

"Alice, oh God, I'm *so* sorry."

"I'm going back up," I muttered, heading for the gate.

"Wait, wait, let's find you a towel," Caitlin called after me. "Then I'll take you back."

"I don't need you to take me! I don't need your help drying off, Caitlin. I'm not some little kid."

It was automatic anger—the kind that just spewed out, unplanned and unintentional. But there was something so satisfying about the shock on her face. And this part, I remember, I did intend:

"Go find your boyfriend, you fucking bitch."

I wheeled around, pushed the pool gate open and stomped across the grass toward the rear path.

I listened for Caitlin's footsteps behind me, waiting for her to call my name. When she didn't, I felt proud. Then nervous. Then, with each step, a little more scared. All I could hear was the zip-zip-zip of the sodden dress fabric rubbing against itself.

I reached the path at the bottom of the hill and nearly keeled over on the first step. My shoes were ruined and coming apart, and I yanked them off. The slate steps, still warm from the hot day, felt soothing against my feet. The dress though was heavy as armor—I had to pause and catch my breath as I neared the top of the path.

I heard music and chatter from the clubhouse, picturing Mom and Theo inside, enjoying themselves. I'd go sit in the car, I decided. Let them get worried and come looking for me. Let Caitlin come looking, racked with guilt, maybe even crying by the time—

Caitlin's scream tore through the night.

I froze—not scared, just confused. It wasn't *quite* a scream, but something like it. An animal, I thought, or some ordinary mechanical sound, echoing off the hill. Or maybe—

Another shriek, much longer than the first. The kind that starts out high and then goes higher. The kind I'd never heard in real life. It was Caitlin, and she was terrified.

My body turned before I could stop it, and I saw them: Caitlin and the man. No, I realized, not a man—Patrick. They were inches from the pool, arms entangled, twisting and shuffling.

They're dancing, I thought. *Some funny, made-up dance.*

I stood still, observing in a dreamlike state: Caitlin kept trying to pull free, bending forward and throwing her weight back, then angling sideways to knock him off balance. She was taller and agile, but he had her by the wrists and from the sounds she was making, I could tell she was both hurt and frightened.

I could hear him too, grunting and gasping as he strained to drag her back toward him, and then a furious bark that might've been an expletive as he let go of one arm and grabbed her other one in both hands. He jerked the arm upward and turned, rotating her with him as he forced her upright. She stumbled toward him with a piercing cry of pain.

Not dancing. Not fighting either. It was an attack. Patrick was attacking her. I knew it for sure now, seeing his face: his white teeth gritted, his sharp jaw tensed. His eyes were so open, so unnaturally wide that even from where I stood, I could read intent in them. It was simple recognition—some ancient instinct in me that knew the look of lethal threat. He was trying to kill her.

With her free hand, Caitlin shoved Patrick in the chest, and he roared into her face with feral rage. Stunned, she faltered, her muscles slackening, and in that instant, Patrick brought his fist down across her face. The crack was so loud, it echoed.

I started running. I ran without thinking, heading for the patch of trees on the steepest part of the hill. This little grove served as a deterrent, urging people to stay off the treacherous slope and use the path instead. I'd sprinted through it countless times; Susannah and I used to race against each other, to see who could make it through fastest without falling. I knew I could make it to the pool quicker that way. But I also knew that I was already too late.

Chapter Thirty-One

I arrive at Theo's fundraiser on time and overdressed, in a crisp, black dress and full makeup. My hair is pinned up in a tight bun, so heavily hair-sprayed that it looks like glazed pottery and smells like a gas station.

"Aunt Aliiiiiiice!" Simon screams, spotting me before I'm even through the revolving door.

He comes barreling across the bustling restaurant, Isaac close behind. I may be on time, but Giordano's is already packed.

"Guys!" Jules calls, emerging from the crowd. "Hey, guys, easy!"

She looks between the two of them, then pivots to me with a warm smile.

"Sorry, they've had three hundred sodas apiece." She puts a plastic cup of wine in my hand and gives me a careful, one-armed hug. "You made it."

Jules steps back, taking in my outfit.

"And you look *amazing*."

"I look like Posh Spice!" I laugh, glancing at the crowd behind her—all shorts and ponytails. "I thought 'casual' meant, like, *business* casual."

Jules beams around the room. Even she's less dressy than I am, in fitted jeans and black ankle boots.

"I know, it's like a keg party," she says, grinning. "Wait 'til you hear the band."

"There's a *band*?" I look around again. It's not just packed; it's standing-room only. "Where's Theo anyway? Signing autographs?"

"He's in the garbage!" Simon says, and he and Isaac both giggle madly.

"He's talking to some local news folks out back," Jules says, pulling Simon toward her for a squeeze. "No room in here, so they're doing press by the dumpsters. Very glam indeed."

She nods toward the rear of the restaurant.

"Get some food, okay? Pizza's in the back, and— Hey, Simon. *Simon*, give her a minute."

But the boys have had it with the grown-up talk. Simon paws at my arm like a puppy, and the both of them start yammering about pizza and the pinball machine, and how I *promised* I'd show them how to get the bonus ball. Still talking, they pull me into the restaurant by the wrists. Jules protests, and I call over my shoulder to her.

"You eat, I've got this. I brought quarters!"

Her frown turns into an affectionate smile.

"Super Aunt!" She lifts her cup. "In heels and all!"

The truth is I just want to get away from her. Another minute and she'd notice the hollows under my eyes, or catch a look on my face. *Everything okay?* she'd ask. And what the hell would I say?

I texted Jamie before leaving the airport this morning. I needed another day off—last-minute, I knew, but he'd understand when I told him. I sped back to the Alcott and emailed Jeremy, asking if he could get current contact info for my aunt and uncle. I figured I could budget for one more hour of his time (though every day at the Alcott is another great leap toward my credit card limit). I knew Barbara and Gregory weren't on social media, and they made a great effort to unlist their information after Caitlin's death, hoping to make it harder for the media to reach them. I knew Theo tried Barbara when Mom was ill, and presumably still had her number—but asking him would only lead to a bigger conversation. After my big conversation with Alex this morning, I needed a beat before having another one. Especially this one.

I never really got over what Barbara and Gregory did, choosing to side with the village. The family schism was its own tragedy. For two years after, I would duck down in my seat when we drove past the turn-off to their road, or stopped at the traffic light beside the Little Village Bookshop, where Aunt Barbara used to take me on paperback sprees. It was a dismal relief when they finally left the village. They moved across the river—Nyack or somewhere, and got divorced soon after. I heard Uncle Greg had moved to their ranch in Santa Fe, and eventually remarried. I had no idea where Barbara was, and I made an effort not to wonder. I knew it was selfish, but it seemed unthinkably cruel that I'd already lost my father, seen my cousin killed, and now two more members of my dwindling family had walked away willingly.

Theo forgave them faster than I did. The second Isaac was born, he developed an instant, overwhelming compassion for all parents. He refrained from expounding too much in my presence, but I knew Caitlin's death had taken on a whole new shape for him: "The idea of my child dying in pain and fear? It's unbearable. It actually hurts to think about it." I got it too, eventually, and my anger burned off. Barbara and Gregory had lost Caitlin forever. Given the option, what parent wouldn't "choose to believe" the less violent version of their child's untimely death?

Jeremy got me the info in just a few hours. (These people aren't hiding. They're just not on Facebook.) Uncle Greg's address is still in Santa Fe, though he and his wife also maintain residences in Provence and Naxos. Aunt Barbara, however, is still unmarried and still lives right across the river. Gobsmacked,

I pulled up her address on Google Maps. I could be there in twenty-five minutes—twenty, if traffic was good. Jeremy had sent both a cell and landline number for her, and I called the cell immediately, riding a molten wave of outrage.

"It's Alice." I said to her voicemail, breathing hard. "Your niece? Call me."

Then I hung up as hard as I could.

Hours later, I'm still riding that wave of fresh anger, though it's finally starting to crash. I perch on a bar stool, sipping my tepid wine and watching Theo wrap up his speech. He stands on a small stage, set up on the side of the restaurant, a row of decorative glass-bottle windows behind him.

"Some see a congressional seat as a step toward higher office," he says. "If elected, I intend to take my seat and stay there, because that's where I can be of use."

I've heard variations on this speech before. It's a good one that's gotten even better with practice (and professional speech writers).

"I don't aspire to rise through the ranks of our country's political system. Anyone can see that system's bent. The best I can do is pitch in to help fix it. That's what I've devoted my whole working life to: trying to help fix it. Trying—but mostly failing. I'm running for Congress because there, I'll stand a chance at failing less."

On cue, the crowd breaks into applause, and Theo smiles.

"Thank you all for being here. And now, the greatest college band of all-time—" he leans into the mic "—the Xennials!"

He steps aside, welcoming the band. Everyone cheers as they launch into a familiar '90s pop song—I've almost placed it, when something catches my eye to the right of the stage: a baby blue cardigan, layered over a white, tennis-style dress and accented with a tiny pink purse. She's dressed like an Easter egg again, but that's beside the point. What the hell is Susannah doing here?

Chapter Thirty-Two

"I wondered if I'd run into you." She speaks so softly I can barely catch a word over the music.
"Why are you here?"
"Wow. Nice to see you?"
"Likewise," I deadpan. "What are you doing here?"
Susannah's shoulders drop and she looks at me wearily.
"I'm not staying, okay? I only have ten minutes. Can you just—I'm too tired to do this tonight."
The guy on the bar stool beside mine turns at the word *tired*, and immediately slides off his seat, gesturing for her to take it. I expect her to protest, but she smiles sweetly and accepts the seat.
"Is it going to be like this all summer?" Susannah asks, smoothing the hem of her dress.
"Probably." I shrug. "I think this is just how it is now."
"That's really sad."
I say nothing. She's right. Our friendship still aches like a phantom limb. It just never occurred to me that she felt it too.
A server pops up behind the bar, holding a bottle of red wine.
"Refill?"
I hold out my cup automatically.
"You too?" he asks Susannah.
"No," we both say automatically, surprising the server. "She's allergic to red," I add.

Susannah eyes me, perturbed at me for remembering. One sip and she breaks out in silver-dollar hives. *Trust me*, I think at her. *I wish I could forget too.*

"Thank you." Susannah smiles at the server. "Water's fine."

He plunks down a sweating jug of ice water, leaving Susannah to fill her cup. She holds the pitcher gently to her temple before pouring. Another thing Susannah can't tolerate is heat—and it's considerable in here, between throngs of people and the pizza ovens running full blast.

"Why are you wearing a cardigan?" I ask. "It's like eighty degrees outside."

It comes out rude, but not as rude as my real question: *Why are you dressed like a Stepford Wife?*

"We're having dinner with his parents. All this wedding chaos. I'm going from here."

My back straightens and my eyes go to the door.

"He's not here," she adds. "Do you really think . . . ? Never mind. I shouldn't have come. I wanted to congratulate Theo in person, but whatever. Another time."

She gulps down the water, ice and all. I look over to a dense cluster in the crowd where Theo stands surrounded, merrily chatting.

"Yeah, I guess you might not get a chance to at the wedding," I say, and take a pointed sip from my own cup.

"It wasn't me," she sighs. "It was my in-laws, okay? He was on *their* list, not mine. It was a gesture—a professional courtesy."

"A heads-up would've been nice."

"If I'd known, I'd have given you one!"

"Right." I nod, still looking across the room. "You're saying his parents have their own invite list *so* long that you didn't even notice my brother was on it."

"Alice, their list has three former presidents on it." She reaches for the pitcher of water, refilling her cup. "There are something like four hundred people invited to this wedding—about twenty of whom I actually know."

Surprise ripples over my surly expression, and I turn to look at her.

"Yeah," Susannah says, an acerbic tinge to her voice. "And half had already RSVPed."

She downs the water, clearly wishing it was white wine.

"Sorry?" I ask, catching her odd phrasing. "They *had* RSVPed?"

Susannah glances at me and does a quick double-take, her face mirroring my confusion.

"Before the dates changed," she says slowly. "Didn't Jamie—I called this afternoon. He didn't tell you?"

"Wait." I stop her. "Wait. The *wedding* date?"

"Yes, we had to move it up. Jamie didn't tell you? I said it was fine if he did."

"I was off today." I brush this aside. Jamie's not the issue. "Moved up to when? And why?"

My heart thrums, my mouth already going dry.

"I'm not supposed to say anything yet, but—" She exhales. "*Vanity Fair* wants to cover the wedding. And with their schedule—the photos, the interviews—we had to move everything up by a week."

She rolls her eyes to the ceiling.

I'm so relieved that I laugh aloud. Not a pregnancy. Just a magazine story.

"So, the wedding's July twenty-seventh now," Susannah says, eyeing me, thrown by my sudden laughter. "It's chaos, like I said. We only just sent the invitations, and now— God, *what* is so funny?"

I've started laughing harder, imagining the mayhem—this wrench thrown into the summer plans of every socialite north of the Mason-Dixon, *and* three former presidents.

"Nothing," I wheeze, my eyes watering. "You're going to put East Hampton into a recession."

Susannah cracks a small smile.

"All those canceled reservations," she murmurs woefully. "All those Pilates classes."

I clap a hand over my mouth, sputtering wine.

"*Easy*, Alice." She glances around with a polite smile. "Everyone will think you're drunk."

"Right," I say. "And everyone knows that never ends well."

Susannah catches it before I do. Her smile slumps. For a moment we'd slid back into our old rhythm, but now we're back in reality.

"I didn't—" I stop, correcting myself. "I'm, um, gonna check the bathroom line."

I didn't mean it. That's what I almost said.

"Alice." Susannah's face is stony. "I'd like to get lunch again. Or coffee, or something."

I don't answer right away, unsure what to make of this frosty invitation. What is this, another message from Patrick? Some other bomb she'd like to drop over salad?

"Another lunch date, really?" I slide off my stool, suddenly exhausted. "Because the last one went so well? Whatever you have to tell me, I can handle it here. We don't need to ruin another meal."

"I guess it does seem ridiculous. It sure *feels* ridiculous every time I do this."

Do what? I wait, tipping my head toward her, eyebrows raised.

"I'm just trying to make up, Alice. I'm trying to—be friends again, somehow. I don't think I could live with myself if I didn't. I'm just *trying*. That's all."

The band kicks off another bouncy tune—another vaguely familiar melody I can't quite place, and Susannah takes the cue.

"Forget it, I'll drop it." She adjusts her purse strap and flicks her hair back over her shoulder. "I can't deal with this now anyway. Just—bye."

"Fine," I say, stopping her as she turns. "A coffee though."

Susannah softens the slightest bit.

"And not this week," I quickly add. "I'm slammed with work."

I shift on my feet, knowing how phony the excuse sounds—and how futile. Susannah knows what week it is.

"I'm sure you'll be busy with appointments and dress stuff, and all that. But—"

"Of course," Susannah says, a strange, sharp pity in her eyes. "I'll find the time."

We nod a silent goodbye, and I watch her clip-clop toward the revolving door in her beige kitten heels. The idea of spending the murder anniversary with the murderer's fiancée is so macabre I could almost laugh again.

And that's what she is, I remind myself. *For now.*

I really will be busy these next few weeks—just not with my day job. With the wedding moved up, I'll have to move faster. This morning with Alex had felt like a breakthrough. He'd given me leads; he'd said Patrick was scared—it felt like real progress. Now it just seems like a hazy conversation I had with a scorned ex-friend (and current employee), who'd willingly lied his way into rehab—or else, was lying to *me*. Either way, I still have nothing tangible. I still need to get my hands on "novel or compelling evidence"—the kind that makes headlines and gets cases reopened. The kind that gets weddings called off.

That part is even more crucial now. Otherwise, the wedding itself is going to make headlines. Somewhere in Manhattan, there's a team of magazine editors already earmarking space for it in some thick, glossy fall issue. The same magazine that published "A Blue-Blooded Killing in Briar's Green," not quite twenty years ago.

I wonder if they reached out to the Yateses' publicity reps, or if it was the other way around. Patrick's never given a personal interview, and therefore never had to answer any awkward personal questions. And people want them more than ever. It'd be a coup for the magazine, getting that exclusive. But Patrick would get even more. He'd get a whole new story.

Chapter Thirty-Three

The morning of July Fourth dawns warm and bright and uneventful. Just how I like it—business as usual. The anniversary is always easier when I can maintain a regular workday routine—no easy feat on a national holiday. Each mundane task is a soothing respite amid the laid-back revelry around me. I'm not a fan of unstructured time in general, but on July Fourth, I simply cannot do relaxed. Invite me to your beach day; I will destroy it.

Jules texts me early, reminding me that I'm invited to join them at home, for a low-key day of board games and Chinese takeout, with *The Twilight Zone* marathon on in the background. This is the July Fourth ritual that Mom, Theo and I fell into after Caitlin's death, and part of me aches to say yes. But then I think of the note in the mailbox (its tidy folds and chilling brevity: *Take care*).

I get to work early, but the club is already decked out in festive bunting, and bustling with party prep. The groundskeeper and his team are setting up space for fireworks, and delivery trucks are clustered at the top of the hill.

I can hear Jamie on the phone as I approach the office. It's not even 9:00 a.m. and he already sounds exhausted and desperate.

"Again, Gail, please allow me to apologize, on behalf of the whole club. If there's any— Well, no, I'm afraid not."

Jamie's talking in his calm-cool-concierge voice, but he is

neither calm nor cool. He's hunched over his keyboard, hair askew, clutching the phone receiver with both hands, like someone negotiating a hostage release.

"Do you need anything?" I whisper. "Lemons?"

I give him a hesitant wave. Jamie waves back quickly, then clenches the hand into a fist and quietly thumps it on the desk.

"*No*, Gail, as I said, that is simply not going to work for us."

He squeezes his eyes shut while the other voice squeaks furiously at him through the phone.

"I'll go," I whisper. "You look, um, busy in here."

Jamie nods, eyes still shut.

"Later?" I add, backing out of the room. "The Martha?"

Jamie keeps nodding. I retreat silently into the hall.

"Wait, Alice—" Jamie says. "Gail, sorry, one moment."

He covers the mouthpiece. "You okay?"

I shut my eyes. I hate that tone.

"You don't need another day off?" he adds. "Today, I mean."

"*No*," I declare, perhaps a bit too firmly. "Thank you, really. But I prefer—"

"Yes, Gail, pardon me." Jamie pivots back to the phone, whacking his sticky keyboard. "No, just holiday mayhem around here. *Exactly*."

He waves me off with a big, flapping hand. I head toward the grill, where they're test-driving an online reservation system (approved by the board, "with the understanding members are under no obligation to participate, and may continue to make reservations via telephone and fax"). The first week was a breeze, and today we have the perfect conditions to see how things fare when the clubhouse is full, and the members are tanked. It'll be a headache, but I'm up for a headache today.

Tasks! I think, bucking myself up.

I zoom past the lounge at the end of the gallery, stepping sideways as a couple strolls out, arm in arm. One of them gasps, stopping me cold.

It's them. Patrick and Susannah. They're not alone either. Patrick's parents are with them—the whole group in linens and pastels, the women holding sun hats. Susannah blanches, and Whit and Patrick both look resolutely blank. Liv is the only one still smiling—that sparkling, wicked-queen smile.

They really don't care, I think. *Even today they're here, bright and early.*

Patrick clears his throat and turns left, guiding the rest of them away.

"Happy Fourth!" Liv trills as she passes.

I watch them process down the gallery. All around me, the clubhouse is steadily filling up, the members arriving in festive clusters, everyone chatty. None of them care, I realize. It's just Fourth of July, nothing more. It shouldn't surprise me. It shouldn't make me want to scream and smash the windows. What the hell did I expect?

I change my mind about bothering the grill team. I'll bother Mr. Brody instead. Today's a good day to stay in the basement.

"Time for your break, I think," says Mr. Brody.

I shake my head, not looking up. After scanning all morning, I've slipped into a state of pleasant numbness, no thoughts in my head but *Scan. Save. Repeat.* Even the cacophony of the jam-packed clubhouse is little more than white noise now.

Mr. Brody, on the other hand, is starting to fray at the edges. He was visibly pissed to see me this morning, and we both know he can't stay here watching me all day. The members are already buzzed, and there are kids running down the gallery—and he hasn't made *one* of them cry yet.

"Now, now," Mr. Brody continues, turning strident. "Best not to skip it. Big day."

Big anniversary too, I think, still silently scanning. *If I didn't know any better, I'd say it was getting to you.*

"I think you'll find, Ms. Wiley," Mr. Brody huffs, "that you are obligated to take a break every—"

The phone on his desk rings with a shattering *brrrrill*, and he snatches the receiver.

"Yes," he barks. Another huffing sigh. "Fine, I'm en route. No, you'll have to discard them. Because it's lime *rounds*, not wedges."

He drops the phone into the cradle with a clang and stands up, tugging at his vest.

"They screwed up the punch, huh?"

"Indeed, they did," Mr. Brody snips, blowing past me like a storm cloud and through the doorway.

"Whoa," Jamie says, appearing in it, seconds later. "Hey, did he—"

"Limes. He's on it," I answer, robotic, feeding another page into the scanner.

"Thank God." Jamie rests a hand on his chest. "You doing okay?"

I nod, ignoring the lilt of concern in his tone. I'm in the zone and I want to stay here.

"Alice?" he presses. "Alice, stop."

"Jamie, I'm fine." I turn from the screen, annoyed. "I'm—"

"No, stop. *Look.*" He points to my laptop screen, an open-mouthed smile on his face. "Told you."

I look back at the computer, skimming the page on the screen. It's another page from the members rolls—I've scanned hundreds by now, and the info never changes. You get one or two new members a year, but even then, it's all the same names.

"*What?*" I whisper, searching the screen. "What is it, I don't—"

But then I do. I lift the laptop, squinting at the entry scrawled in Mr. Brody's tight cursive:

Gordon Fairchild (Vivian Fairchild)—R
10 Little Farm Lane
Ashborough, New York

I stare gaping, first at the address and then the *R*. That's a first—but the meaning is obvious. Members almost never resign, as doing so signals one of two things: dire financial circumstances, or a major social gaffe.

"What year is that?" Jamie asks. "Early 2000s?"

I check the ledger's spine. It's 2002—the year *A Death on the Hudson* came out. I turn to show Jamie.

"Bingo." He nods. "Where is Little Farm Lane though? It rings a bell, but—"

Jamie's cell phone buzzes in his jacket.

"Shit," he says, fumbling for it. "Sorry, wedding emergency"

It must be if he's got his phone out on the floor.

"I'll catch you up later," he continues, typing as he talks. "You won't fucking believe it."

"Oh. The date?" Jamie looks up, and I nod. "She told me."

His eyebrows shoot up and he starts to ask the question, interrupted by another buzz from the phone.

"We'll talk at the Martha," I remind him. "You're still leaving at six, right? Jamie?"

He mumbles a vague affirmative, eyes still on the phone. Jamie is technically off once cocktail hour starts—but no one is really off on July Fourth. Someone shouts for him from down the hall—something about straws—and Jamie looks up, jamming the phone back into his pocket.

"Go," I say, but he's already going.

I watch him jog down the hall toward the straw emergency, then I turn back to the address on the computer screen. I know why the street name rings a bell. Because it's two streets down from mine—the one where Theo and I grew up. Jamie would've passed it hundreds of times on his way to our place. Our woodsy nook of Ashborough was small—only a few dozen homes. And one of them was Gordon Fairchild's. It's a rattling discovery, though I'm not sure why.

There's a brief lull in the clubhouse around 4:00 p.m. as the members dash home to change into their black-and-white formal wear. They start streaming back in an hour later, the footsteps above both lighter and sharper now that everyone's in dress shoes.

I take the staff steps to the main floor and carry on down the dim staff hall. I'll leave for the Martha soon, but not just yet. I need to see something first.

I push open the heavy staff door to the library—a swing door built into the back of a bookshelf. The room is reliably vacant at this time of day, and if you can stand the combined heat of the fireplace and late-afternoon sun, then it makes an ideal spot to spy on the lobby. Already I feel perspiration beading above my lip and beneath my eyes. I keep my back against the book-lined wall and look out into the lobby, my gaze fixed on the front entrance.

It's still early, I think. *They're probably not here yet.*

But then, as soon as I have the thought, they are.

Liv and Whit Yates lead the way—he, tall and dapper in a tuxedo, she in a skimming satin gown with a subtle train at the back. The crowd shifts, making way for them as they stride across the room and greet another couple, receiving cheek kisses and two glasses of champagne. I can hear my own breath sharpening as I spot Susannah in a white dress, blank-faced and holding her clutch with both hands.

I knew she'd come. And still, I can't believe it. The Susannah I knew wouldn't have come to this party if you dragged her by her hair.

I've got to get to the Martha. I wait until Susannah is standing with the Yateses, then, keeping my eyes on her back, I pivot and step out of the library. Just as Patrick Yates steps into it.

"Fuck!"

We stumble clumsily against each other in the doorway, and the smell of lime and woodsy cologne waves over me. He's holding his phone against his ear.

"You f—"

He stops, realizing. We stand in a frozen stare-down, close enough that I can hear the tinny voice on the other end of his phone. He holds a fizzing glass of something in his other hand—gin and soda by the look of it—though half of it's splashed on his lapel now. Up close, he looks older than he does in photos, but still younger than he is.

"Excuse me," I say.

Patrick lowers the phone to his chest, turning sideways to let me pass. And as I do, he answers.

"Nope," he says. "No fuckin' chance."

The air goes out of my lungs, and I stop with a slight wobble a few feet past the doorway. With all my might, I will myself to look back.

Patrick has the phone against his ear again, but his eyes are still on me. He waits for me to turn, then he raises his glass.

"Cheers," he says, perhaps to me or to the person on the phone. Then he grins that boyish grin and brings the glass toward his mouth.

"Happy Fourth."

Chapter Thirty-Four

Jamie hurls himself into our booth at the Martha, his elbows and knees audibly whacking against the wood.

"Hey." I look up from my phone, surprised. "You made it. How—"

"Here's my theory," he begins, incensed. "They moved up the wedding so Susannah can't testify."

"Wait, Jamie, just—" I hold up my hands.

"No, listen." He grabs my beer, chugs half, then continues. "You know that thing about how spouses can't incriminate each other, legally? I think Patrick knows you're getting close. I think *Alex* probably convinced him. See, first Patrick tries to scare you with the notes and shit, but Alex must have—"

"Jamie, stop. Just listen." I push my beer back to him. "And quiet down."

Bit by bit, I walk him through my very eventful Tuesday: meeting Alex at the airport, locating Barbara across the river and, finally, hearing Susannah's big news at the fundraiser.

"It's nothing to do with me—well, not directly. They moved it up because of the magazine story."

I watch the wheels turn in Jamie's head as he absorbs the great heap I've dumped on him.

"'Kay," he says, his words slow and stretchy. "But she didn't tell me that."

"Sounds like the story only just got booked."

"Three weeks out? I don't think it works that fast."

"It doesn't," I reply sharply. "Jamie, I've worked for high-profile people; it takes months for something like that to come together, even when it's one photo and a five-minute interview."

I've already thought it all through. It won't be a five-minute interview, and I bet it has been in the works for months—possibly even before the engagement. In terms of publicity, it's been a rough year for Patrick and the Yateses, and I'm sure their team's had all hands on deck, searching for good-press opportunities. And this one's as good as it gets.

A lush, high-summer wedding at the club. The club where Caitlin died—that's how they'll put it. No mention of "killing," alleged or otherwise. It'll be "the tragic death of his high-school sweetheart," or maybe they'll water her down to "classmate" or "friend." Patrick will make his long-awaited comment, answering with some brief but poignant statement, crafted and calibrated by a league of publicists and lawyers, ensuring he conveys adequate grief but *not* responsibility. And that's how it'll happen. Caitlin's death becomes his tribulation. The murder becomes a mere paragraph in a bigger, brighter story, starring a sober and reformed Patrick, and his radiant, hometown bride. A blue-blooded redemption.

Jamie considers this for a long moment.

"Unless you blow it up first," he says carefully. "You were planning to go to the press anyway. Right?"

"Yeah," I scoff. "But I'm not going to *Vanity Fair*. At least not now."

"Why not? Same magazine that ran that 'Blue-Blooded Killer' article back in the day."

"Yes, and now they're basically running a public apology. Jamie, no matter what quote Patrick gives them, it's a *wedding* piece."

"So they're flip-floppers," Jamie counters. "Give them a call. Flop them back."

"With *what?*" I demand. "My creepy note? My useless police records—sorry, *stolen* useless police records? The only new info I have so far is the fact that Alex lied. And I didn't even record him saying so."

"So call him and get him to say it again!" Jamie says. "Bring him in on it. You and Alex contact the magazine together. Maybe you even go in person. I could—"

I shake my head.

"I tried, his phone's already off. He's in-patient for a month—a month at least, he said. Besides, you didn't see him." I picture Alex: his bloodshot pallor, his slippery, ever-shifting mood. "*I* believe him, but he's— I don't know, he's not okay. He's disturbed."

"Right." Jamie shifts in his seat. "Gordon Fairchild then. You've got his address now. I know you're not a fan, and I get it—he cashed in on Caitlin, and it's gross."

"Gross?"

"Really gross—sleazy, tacky as fuck—and everyone around here knows it. But everyone *else* read that book. The guy's got clout. People know him, and they believe what he has to say."

"You're right," I agree. "He's the 'authority' on the topic."

Jamie shakes his head.

"You're the authority. He's just the name they know."

Jamie's right. The fact that I'm the child witness is an open secret in the village, but outside of it, I'm an unknown. If I go to the press I'd run the risk of being dismissed as an attention seeker. At the very least, there'd be a lengthy vetting process before anyone trusted me or my evidence enough to publicize it. *Why now? Why didn't she say something sooner?* As if that question weren't the answer itself.

"Fine. I'll give it a shot, Gordon. Might as well knock on his door," I say. "I'm still betting he's moved though. Little Farm

Lane is barely outside the village—practically shouting distance from the club."

Jamie grabs our empty beer glasses. "I'm gonna get you a refill," he says. "And some fries. You want fries?"

He gets up without waiting for my answer.

I check my phone—8:42 p.m. Not long until fireworks. Not long until this day is finally done. I scroll through my texts. Theo messaged me hours ago, and I still haven't replied.

> Ordered the moo shoo in your honor. Jules and the boys say hi. It's the first year Simon's watching the T-Zone marathon with us. Too soon? Anyway, we miss you. Happy Wednesday.

His sign-off makes me smile. "Happy Wednesday" is another family tradition. It was little things that caught me off guard after the murder—like the way people say, "Happy Fourth!" by way of greeting on that day. The first anniversary, it upset me terribly. I burst into tears at the grocery store checkout. The second year, I woke up, shuffled out of my bedroom, bracing for another hideous, panicky day, and saw Theo waiting in the living room. He held a makeshift sign above his head, with "Happy Monday" printed on it, in a big, goofy font.

"Hooray! Happy Monday!" Theo shouted, waving the sign.

I didn't get it for a second, and then I did. And then, I laughed. And he did. And then Mom came out of her room, saw the sign, and she laughed too.

He never made another sign, but we've maintained the tradition of wishing each other a happy Monday or Wednesday, or whatever day of the week it is. It helps to remember that although today is many other things, it's also just a day in the week. It will end, and tomorrow there will be another.

Still smiling, I text Theo back:

> Happy Wednesday, one and all.

Jamie returns from the bar, stopping beside our booth, a distant look on his face.

"Are you going to sit?"

Jamie nods, but stays put. He frowns and tilts his head, as though puzzling through a math problem.

"Or maybe speak?" I continue.

"Yeah." A slow smile spreads across his face. "I have a really bad idea."

Chapter Thirty-Five

I'm only half-convinced by the time we leave the bar.
"Sleep on it," Jamie says in the parking lot. "We've got a couple weeks to find the holes."

One comes to mind right now.

"What if they change their minds and move it indoors?"

"Doubtful." He points his key fob at his car, unlocking it.

"Really? They changed the *wedding* date."

"Fair point." He taps the hood of his car and shrugs. "Yeah, like I said, it might not work. But let's figure it out tomorrow. I have to check in at the club before heading home—make sure they're pushing water. No one ever remembers."

Who cares! I think. But then I see how beat he is.

"Go." I wave him off. "Tomorrow."

Jamie's idea is way beyond bad. It's high-risk and comically improbable—chock-full of potential holes. But I'm pretty sure we're doing it.

"The rehearsal dinner," Jamie explained in the booth. "That's how we'll get in the archive. Well, you will. I'll have to be—"

"Wait, wait," I said, coughing on beer. "Back up. A lot."

"Okay. You would work the rehearsal dinner."

"What?"

"Quit interrupting. Yes, it only works if you're on staff that night. I could put you in the break room—for shirt changes and touch-ups." He grew more animated. "I'll need someone for that anyway. The guys are gonna melt out there"

He sat back, thinking it through.

"We'll need hairspray, maybe an iron." He pointed at me. "Do you know how to tie a tie?"

"Slow down."

"It's fine, I can teach you."

"Stop!" I peeked out of the booth. "For starters, why would I try to sneak into the archive during the rehearsal dinner? When all the Yateses are in the clubhouse—literally, everyone and their relatives?"

"Because," Jamie answered, grinning, "they're not having it *in* the clubhouse. They're having it outside. Sunset dinner, on top of the hill."

I turned my head, dubious.

"Outdoor dinner, at sunset? Who thought that was a good idea?"

"I know, mosquitos and glare, super romantic—but c'mon, think. No members in the clubhouse, *and* we'll know exactly where they are. Everyone will be right outside where we can see them."

"And if someone comes in to use the bathroom? Or get away from the bugs?"

"Then you'll have a minute or two while they walk from the hill to the clubhouse. That's why it's perfect—they're close, but not too close." Jamie pointed across the table at me. "Shouting distance—that's what made me think of it. You'll be able to see them coming."

"Great, but Jamie, even if all this works, we still don't have a key."

Jamie heaved a breath, nodding.

"That part—yeah. That part's harder. I'm going to have to get Mr. Brody to give me his keys."

"*Give* them to you? Voluntarily?"

Jamie nodded.

"It's the only way. We'll never be able to steal them. He wears them on this key-clip thing like a fuckin' latchkey kid. He'd never give them to you, obviously, but he might give them to me in an emergency."

"What kind of emergency?" I asked, doubtful.

"I don't know—something with the freight elevator? I'll just have to fake some random crisis and tell him I lost my elevator key."

I shook my head.

"Not random. It has to be something specific and urgent, so he won't have time to fiddle around and get that one key off the ring."

We both sat, silently staring at each other. Then, the answers hit us simultaneously:

"Gin," said Jamie.

"Lemons," I said.

I call Jamie from the car, five minutes after leaving the Martha. He answers on the first ring.

"What if it rains?" I ask without preamble. "Then they'll *have* to move the dinner inside."

"It won't," Jamie answers, not missing a beat. "Where are you anyway?"

I roll down my window, letting in the fragrant, grassy breeze.

"Still on Revolution," I answer. "I'm not even at the lake yet. Where are *you*?"

Most nights we both take Revolution Road to the intersection by Rippowat Lake, one of us following the other in a kind of unofficial escort on the rambling, unlit backroad. We usually wave good-night at the turn-off, Jamie heads toward his place in Ashborough's town center and I turn back into Briar's Green.

"Heading for the highway," says Jamie. "Aren't you? I'm not messing with Route 9 tonight."

Down the road ahead of me, a cop car shoots across the intersection, siren whooping—on its way to confiscate some sparklers.

"Shit. I wasn't thinking."

"Good luck, soldier. Have fun driving on the shoulder. Anyway, it won't rain at the rehearsal."

"Right, but what if it does?"

"It won't," he repeats simply. "We don't get rained out. Not since Roosevelt left office."

"Oh—wow, you're not serious." I hear him chuckle on the other end. "Don't tell me they're still saying that."

"Of course they are!" Jamie cackles. "Club tradition!"

Club *myth* is more like it—one of the silliest. It starts with some ancient beef involving FDR and an ill-fated club luncheon he attended, the summer before his fourth term. I don't know what faux pas he committed (perhaps a comment about socialized healthcare or women's rights) but it was bad enough that he was allegedly never invited back. That, or he was too tied up with WWII to attend every country club lunch. Either way, the story goes, the club was rained out for the rest of the season—every terrace dance and golf tournament ruined. The bad streak continued the following spring, when the Easter Hunt was canceled by an off-season hurricane, and everyone feared another spoiled summer. But when FDR died three days later—"Left office" as the members like to say—the clouds instantly parted.

"And hasn't rained on a club party since," I finish.

"It hasn't!" Jamie comes back, indignant. "Look it up!"

My laughter trails off into a sigh. The more doable this plan becomes the more anxious I get.

"You there?" Jamie asks.

"Yeah, but— Hey, listen. I don't want you to do this. It's too—"

"Alice—"

"*No,*" I say sharply. "It's my call, and I'm saying it's not worth it. I know you want to help, but you live here. You work here. You've made a whole life, and I don't want you jeopardizing it for me."

He waits a moment, letting me finish.

"Hey, egomaniac?" Jamie says lightly. "What if I want to help *because* I live and work here?"

I blink, my cheeks warming. I can hear him smiling.

"Just—you sleep on it too. Deal? If I get caught, you're my accomplice."

"Ooh, say that again?"

The heat spreads from my cheeks to my neck. I reach the intersection and hang my arm out the window into the velvety cool air.

"You know, there's one thing I never really understood," says Jamie. "About the murder."

I idle at the stop sign, listening.

"Why do you think he did it?" Jamie continues. "They hadn't even been dating that long, right? I don't get the motive."

A memory rises unbidden—one of those split-second dioramas: Caitlin stumbles slightly leftward, briefly unbalanced by Patrick's grip around her wrist. He lifts his free hand, pausing—not even for a second, but long enough to notice—then he knifes it down across her head.

"Do you know the term *malice aforethought*?" I ask, my foot still on the brake.

"What?" Jamie answers. "Is that like *premeditation*?"

"Not quite. It's broader than that—it's from the Middle Ages. It's the term they used to distinguish murder from other kinds of killing."

"Like manslaughter."

"Will you just listen?"

"Sorry."

"Anyway, no one could really define it, but everyone agreed that malice aforethought was what made a homicide a murder."

I pause, waiting for Jamie to interject again. He keeps quiet. I hear the distant rush of a car passing him on the highway.

"The strange part is that it stuck. Malice aforethought is still in the criminal code, and people are still arguing over what it means."

"Are you going to tell me?" Jamie asks carefully.

"*No*, that's the thing. The current legal definition is basically intent to kill or seriously hurt someone, or to act with reckless disregard for human life—something like that."

"Sounds about right."

"But it's not. Malice is a feeling—a desire. It's like love, right? This massive, powerful thing that can swallow up your whole life. You can't boil it down to a simple definition. But you know it when you see it."

I bite down on the inside of my lip, cringing at myself in Jamie's silence.

"Okay," he answers evenly—eventually. "I get that, I guess. I'm still lost on Patrick's motivation."

"Yeah," I say, shrugging. "Me too. But I don't think it's worth trying to make sense of it. Malice isn't logical."

Don't make me ramble on about love again. Please just get it.

"But you know it when you see it," Jamie repeats. "And you saw it."

"Yes," I say, relieved. "Unmistakable."

He pauses again, longer this time.

"Jamie?"

"I'm here," he says. "Alice, I n—"

"What?" I wait. "Jamie? You cut out for a second."

I glance at my phone screen. Full service.

"You're in a dead zone," I say louder.

Jamie's voice cuts in again, garbled and choppy.

"—if he did. Okay? Are you—"

"I can't *hear* you." I'm nearly shouting now. "Jamie, hey. *Jamie.*"

A string of high-pitched beeps comes screeching through the phone so loudly that I flinch, my foot briefly lifting off the brake pedal. I slam down on it again, holding the phone an inch from my ear. The beeping stops and there's a strange *whoosh*, followed by a second of dead silence. I hear a muffled thud, a distant, arcing howl and then two soft clicks. The call cuts out.

Chapter Thirty-Six

Jamie's phone goes straight to voicemail, and I hang up, dial again, and it doesn't even ring. I give it one more try, and then I put the phone down and slowly ease into the intersection. A police car comes screaming down the road, heading in the direction of the highway—but that doesn't mean anything. Jamie's phone cut out barely three minutes ago; even if he was in an accident, they wouldn't be on their way yet (right?). Besides, the cops are all over the place tonight, handing out firework fines. Like the saying goes, you can't even get a speeding ticket on Fourth of July. On this particular night, you can get away with just about anything.

I check the road in both directions, then hit the gas and turn left, speeding toward the club. Those sounds I heard—that piercing squeal, that sickening whoosh—that could've just been traffic. Or perhaps Jamie *did* have a near-miss while we were talking and decided to just put the phone down and drive. Better safe than sorry.

I make it to the club in decent time, despite the handful of cops that shoot past, nudging me toward the shoulder. I take the service driveway up the back way, craning my neck as I reach the top of the hill and the staff parking area comes into view. I circle it, searching the crowd of cars for Jamie's.

"Hey," someone calls as I crawl along the front of the lot. "Alice?"

I screech to a stop and turn to see Cory leaning out from the staff entrance. He waves urgently.

"Alice, hold up, there's a situation."

"Oh my God, what happened?" I roll down the passenger window.

"Do you know where Jamie is?" Cory asks. His voice is as dull and unbothered as ever, but his face is alert—almost stressed.

"No, that's— So he's *not* here?"

He said he was coming back first, right? To make sure the servers were pushing water? I run through the timing again. He should be here by now.

My stomach twists as Cory shakes his head.

"Damn, thought he was with you."

"Cory, what's going on then? What situation?"

"One of the wives is throwing a shit fit in the gallery." Cory glances behind him. "She's drunk and pissed at her husband. It's getting kind of loud."

I sit back, gathering myself. This guy.

"So? Go deal with it. Talk to them." I shake my head. "Did Jamie call?"

"I tried dealing with it," Cory snaps, ignoring my question. "She told *me* to fuck off, swear to God."

I put the car in gear. This is a waste of time.

"I don't know, Cory, try harder. Bring them some cake and coffee—that's what Brody does."

"Uh, that's a little below my pay grade," Cory calls as I reverse into a turn.

"That's not the expression!" I shout, heading back toward the service drive. "And no, it isn't!"

I pull back onto Route 9 and call Jamie again—voicemail. It's been over forty minutes now. Something is officially wrong. I aim for Ashborough, thinking I'll go by his apartment. I don't know the address, but I know it's the same complex he grew up in—somewhere off the shopping center, near the Carvel. I have a vague memory of it, having been in the back of the car when

Mom picked Theo up there, probably hundreds of times. I'm trying to picture the number on the door when I pass a familiar sign on my left: Riverside Hospital.

"Shit," I whisper, stopping in the middle of the road.

I look back at the sign, gnawing the edge of my lip. Then I signal left and pull into the ER lot.

"Say again?" the woman at the front desk asks. "You were in a car accident?"

She scans me, uncertain.

"No, not me. There's *been* an accident," I repeat. "On the highway—the Taconic."

She turns to a nurse seated at a computer a few feet behind her, typing. The nurse shakes his head without looking away from the screen.

"I don't know what to tell you," the woman says. "I couldn't give you any information unless you were a relative anyway, but—it's been a quiet night."

I nod, thanking her absently as I turn for the door.

"You could try Valley Medical," the nurse calls. "They're the closest emergency surgical unit."

I pause, confused. Valley Medical is something like twenty miles north. *Why would they bring him all the way there, and not a local hospital?* But then the word *surgical* sinks in.

I drive to Jamie's apartment first. I still don't remember which unit is his, but I don't have to. There's only one without a car in the driveway.

I smell charcoal, I think, my pulse pounding. *I hear fireworks on the river. I see a darkened window.*

I drive north toward the highway, my phone on speaker. I punch buttons with my thumb, navigating Valley Medical's phone menu, trying not to look at the time. I imagine Jamie laughing at me. *You went to the hospital? Seriously?* He'd say something about how the amateur sleuthing had gotten to me. Then he'd give me the perfectly reasonable, obvious explanation for what had happened.

Except I can't think of one that doesn't end with something terrible happening to him. And the idea of something terrible happening to him—on this night, in this year—while I listened on the other end of the phone, seems too surreal a coincidence.

There's a click on the line as someone answers my call.

"Emergency," the voice says. "Nurses station."

"Hi, I'm trying to find a friend of mine who may have been brought in."

"Are you a relative or emergency contact?"

"No, I—"

"I won't be able to help then."

"No, I know. But is there any information you *can* give me?"

"Not regarding patients. Is that all?"

"No, wait."

I strain for a reason.

"I was at a bar with my friend," I spit out suddenly. "We left at the same time, around ten."

The voice waits. I wince into the silence.

"He wasn't drunk. I just— He split off and took the highway. He was somewhere near Ashborough—"

The nurse cuts in.

"And he was in an accident?"

"I think so. I think I heard it." I cringe again, preemptively. "We were talking on the phone."

Another long pause. I can hear the hospital in the background: overlapping voices, distant beeps, the click-clack chatter of keyboards.

"I'm looking," the nurse says finally.

"Thank you, thank you so much," I say, though my shoulders tense up.

"We did have a car accident around eleven. Came in via ambulance."

"Oh my God, really? You did? Are they—" I clear my creaking throat. "Were they discharged already? Does it say that?"

"You're not an immediate relative, correct?"

"No." My voice wobbles. "A friend."

The nurse sighs hard into the receiver.

"Then I can't disclose details. But nobody from that accident was admitted," she says. "Or discharged."

"Oh."

"Do you understand?"

"You mean he's still there? In the ER?"

"No, ma'am."

Now I hear it—it's there in the "ma'am." Solemnity. A little sympathy. The nurse waits another moment, then speaks again.

"I'll have to hang up now. I'm sorry."

My lungs pull in a sharp breath. I drive in a daze, muscle memory guiding me back south on the highway, toward Briar's Green.

Inch by inch, reality descends. Jamie is dead. A few hours ago, he was sitting in a pub with his feet propped up, his face flushed and animated, making him look even younger than his thirty-two years. He'd had iced tea and some soggy fries—the last meal he'd ever eat. I was the last person he'd ever talk to. And it's all my fault. I involved him. I'm the reason he was out tonight. I'm the one who called.

I come to a red light at a four-way intersection. It takes several seconds before I register the orange flare on the road, just past the traffic light. I hadn't been thinking when I turned back south on the same highway Jamie was on. I've driven directly into the scene of the accident. It's real. Even from here, I can see how bad it was.

The light changes, and I roll slowly through the intersection, nauseated as I navigate around lingering shards of plastic— bumper parts, maybe. The car is gone, and most of the mess has been cleaned up, but it's clear there was a mess. The road glimmers with smashed glass, and there's an acrid stench in the air—that ominous mix of oil and burnt mechanics.

A lone police vehicle remains, its red light twirling silently. The driver's side door is open, and the officer stands beside it with a small, chunky laptop perched on the roof. Her hair is tied back in a braid, and at first, I think of Jessie. Then I see the uniform: a State Trooper, not a village cop. (*But oh my God, Jessie. Who will tell her?*) The officer glances back, waving me onward.

I roll down my window.

"Everyone all right?"

"Just go around please, ma'am," the officer says, not looking back. "Thank you."

I don't want to though. I don't want to see the rest of it.

My knuckles go white on the wheel as I gently press the gas, rumbling forward, my eyes straight ahead. Passing the police car, I glimpse something shiny on my right. I hold my gaze forward, trying to stop thinking of what it might be: twisted metal. Mirror shards. The glasses he kept above the visor.

"Alice?"

My foot jerks to the brake and the car stops with an *eek*, my head thwacking against the headrest as I look out the open window.

It's an emergency blanket—the same crinkly, shiny kind they gave me.

And it's him. It's Jamie.

Chapter Thirty-Seven

I fumble for the car door and get out, stumbling toward the shoulder.

"Are you—"

"Totally fine," says Jamie.

I list forward, slamming into him with a hard, clumsy hug.

"Ah, shit." Jamie pats my shoulder. "Alice, my ribs."

I jump back. Jamie waves to the officer.

"It's okay. This is the friend I was with before."

The officer nods, turning back to her laptop.

"Jamie, I thought—" I'm still half-numb with shock. "What the hell happened?"

"A hit-and-run is what happened. Someone T-boned me with a massive SUV."

"Why aren't you at the hospital!"

"I'm really okay—nothing's broken," he assures me. "Just really fucking bruised."

I see it now. He's not fine. His bottom lip is swollen and bleeding. The top of his shirt is unbuttoned, revealing a gash across his throat and collarbone.

"The seat belt," he says, gesturing to it. "Trust me, it could've been worse. I pulled forward a little, just before he hit me."

"What, you *saw* the car coming?"

"No, no," Jamie says. "I barely saw it after—fucker had his

headlights off. No, I just saw the light was about to change and took my foot off the brake. Jumped the gun a little, but it probably saved my life. He didn't hit dead center, just the back of the car."

My eyes clamp shut as the scene runs through my mind: Jamie's head whips sideways, the seat belt taut against his throat. A shattering boom as the car makes impact, a sudden hail of glass.

"I must have thrown his aim off," Jamie continues. "He must not have realized I'd moved. Jerk was going so fast he probably couldn't tell."

"What are you saying exactly?"

"He just kept going, Alice," Jamie answers, the swollen lip blurring his consonants. "He didn't stop—he floored it. I didn't see the front of the car, but it must've been wrecked. And he just kept going."

"You're saying it wasn't an accident?"

"Not a chance."

I call over to the officer, now sitting in her open car, talking on a cell phone.

"Have they found the driver yet?"

"We're working on it," she says. "Among other things—it's a holiday, you know."

"Let's get you home," I tell Jamie. "How much longer do they need you?"

"Huh? Oh no, I'm good to go," he says. "I was just waiting."

My throat tightens.

"For me?"

A great burst over laughter overtakes him, and Jamie cups his neck and bends, laughing and grimacing at the same time.

"For *Uber*," he says. "God, you really are an egomaniac."

I spend the night—what's left of it—in Jamie's living room. While he dozes on the couch, I open my laptop and click blearily between my open tabs—Twitter, Facebook, the *Hudson Valley*

Journal site—refreshing and scanning for updates. So far, I've seen no mention of a hit-and-run or a black SUV, not even on the local crime blotters. Shouldn't there be a public notice? Some sort of appeal for sightings? Regardless, someone *would* have spotted it, unless it really did just vanish into the woods.

My phone buzzes, jolting me alert.

Did you see my email?

I blink at the message with scratchy eyes. I don't recognize the number—it's a number though, not asterisks. Another message pops up beneath.

Check your email. The other one.

It clicks: Jeremy. He'd told me he used scrambling services like this—the kind that doesn't "star out" numbers. Then I remember another thing Jeremy told me: email only. No phones. He'd only contact me that way in "life-or-death situations."

I open a new window on my laptop, logging into my Jeremy-only email account with shaky fingers. The message is there, time stamped just before midnight last night. The subject line is ominous, even for Jeremy:

Did you see?

The email itself is even more chilling. It's just a link, and beneath it, three words:

This is bad.

I click the link, and then I'm looking at another local news site—not the *HV Journal*, but one from upstate: the *North Country Register*. I scan the page for something familiar, and find it in a brief paragraph, halfway down the homepage:

Patient Reported Missing from Black River Facility

Jefferson County police are seeking information on the whereabouts of a man reported missing yesterday, having failed to arrive for a scheduled intake at Fairview Treatment Center, in Black River, NY. Alexander Chapman, of Briar's Green, NY, arrived at Watertown International Airport at 10:40 a.m. on July 3, where a Fairview staff member was waiting to escort him to the facility. Chapman, thirty-four, was seen collecting baggage shortly after deboarding, but his escort was unable to locate him in the arrival area. Fairview administrators reported Chapman missing twenty-four hours later, having failed to locate or contact him. When reached for comment, staff did not specify Chapman's medical or physical condition, but noted that, "As with anyone in need of in-patient care, we are deeply concerned for his safety. We ask that anyone who comes into contact with him to please contact us or county authorities, for the sake of Mr. Chapman's own well-being."

My phone vibrates again, and Jamie stirs. He sits up carefully, a hand against his bruised ribs, blinking around the dim room.

"What's up?" he says. "Is it morning?"

"Not quite."

Jamie scrubs at his eyes, registering my expression.

"What, did they find him? Did they find the car?"

I tell him no, then hand him my laptop. I watch his face go still, eyes darting, as he reads the paragraph.

"Coffee?" He stands up slowly and shuffles to the back of the apartment.

I look down at my phone and see Jeremy's final text—another three-word message:

Be careful. Please.

Chapter Thirty-Eight

Jamie's giant bachelor TV is tuned to a local news affiliate, the volume low. It's nearly 8:00 a.m., and the news about Alex is spreading, albeit slowly. The *HV Journal* picked up the report, and there was a brief mention on the regional NPR station, among a list of other area-news items: coyote captured on college campus, historic lighthouse reopened after flood repairs, local man reported missing upstate.

Both of us are under-slept and jumpy. Jamie plugged Jessie's thumb drive into his laptop to review Alex's interview and search the other files for any mention of him.

"It's weird, right?" I ask again. "You'd think there'd be more coverage on such a slow news day."

"They only reported him missing yesterday." Jamie shrugged. "Not much else to cover—as far as *they* know."

My head throbs at the thought of it. I haven't called the Fairview Center, or the Jefferson County police, to tell them about my meeting with Alex—not yet, anyway. Part of me wants to, immediately. Alex is vulnerable, and on the outs with some very powerful people. But those are the people who sent him to Fairview—who made the arrangements and paid the fees. For all I know, they're up there now, making further arrangements with the county police. I do know they've done it before.

"No mention of the car either," I say, looking back at the television.

Jamie snorts.

"No shit." He rubs the side of his neck. "No one's 'seeking information' on that car, 'cause no one's looking for it."

I shut my laptop, reaching for my bag. "I'm going to run back to the Alcott. I'll change and come back to take you to the rental-car place. Okay? Jamie?"

Jamie pauses, leaning closer to the laptop, his eyes fixed on something.

"Huh?" he answers in a distant voice. "Oh, the, uh, yeah."

"Half an hour, okay?" I hitch my bag up on my shoulder, waving at him. *"Okay?"*

He shakes his head. "Alice," he says, a smile spreading on his slightly swollen lips. "I found something."

"On the drive? There's nothing about Alex in the—"

"Not Alex." Jamie shakes his head. "Brody. It's Brody's interview."

Jamie turns the laptop toward me. I skim the page—as bland as I remember it.

"Yeah? There's no intel here. He didn't tell them anything."

Jamie shakes his head.

"He answered the questions as they were asked."

"Yes, Jamie. That's generally how interviews work."

He points to a paragraph toward the bottom of the screen.

"Read it, smart-ass. The second-to-last question."

I exhale loudly, leaning closer, a tiny swirl of anxious excitement spinning in my stomach.

Offc. McElroy: And from your vantage point, standing in the ballroom, did you observe Caitlin Dale leaving the party?

J. Brody: I did not.

Offc. McElroy: But you did see Patrick Yates leave at some point thereafter?

J. Brody: I did.

"See?" says Jamie quietly.
I shake my head. But then . . .
"Wait."
I see it. I think I see it. It's like an optical illusion that won't stay in focus.
"The officer thought he was *in* the ballroom," Jamie says, standing, unable to hold back any longer. "See? Look at how he phrased it."
He points to the line.
"'From your vantage point, standing in the ballroom.'"
Jamie grins, continuing.
"But that's not where Brody watches during parties, right? He stands just *outside* the room."
Always. Mr. Brody might dip into the ballroom to attend to a member or correct a server's misstep. But otherwise, he holds his post just outside the doorway, in the gallery, shifting down the hall in tandem with the party as it progresses from the yellow ballroom, to the green and blue rooms and, finally, to the pink.
"The officer knew Brody supervised," I say, thinking aloud. "So, he just assumed—"
"And Brody didn't correct him," Jamie interjects. "But that's not the point."
I picture the scene from above as though looking down into a dollhouse.
"He would've been outside the pink room," I say, my heart speeding up. "He'd have been—"
"At the end of the gallery, right by the basement stairs," Jamie finishes. "Right fucking there."
That's exactly why he stands in the gallery, not the ballroom

itself. From there, he can better track the comings and goings. He can spot trouble brewing at the party—or just outside of it.

I turn to Jamie.

"Do you think he could've seen all the way to—"

"Yes."

"Are you sure?"

"No question." Jamie nods. "Standing there, you barely have to turn your head. Just look down and it's a clear view. You can see the door to the men's locker room, the supply closet—that whole end of the basement hall. Including . . . ?"

Jamie grins again, waiting for me to finish the thought.

"Including the north exit," I say.

The one that leads to the pool.

Chapter Thirty-Nine

July 5 is always quiet. Kids come to the club with au pairs and nannies to play in the pool while their parents sleep it off at home. The clubhouse is vacant, save for the regulars: the library men, napping under their newspapers, and the clutch of widows who camp out at the grill all afternoon, shooing flies away from their fruit salad. Jamie gives most service staff the day off and the club operates on a skeleton crew. But Mr. Brody doesn't take days off.

"Look, five o'clock and the lounge is empty," Jamie adds, peering down the hall. "Perfect conditions, I told you."

But he sounds less certain now.

We went back and forth all afternoon, debating when and how to approach Mr. Brody. In the end we settled on immediately, and guns blazing. No point trying to subtly outwit him—the man who'd so gracefully sidestepped direct police questioning, obstructing justice so politely that no one felt a thing.

Jamie follows as I cross the gallery, pausing at the top of the basement stairs.

"Wait." I hold a hand in front of him. "I just have to state the obvious. If you come with me, Brody will know you're involved. He's probably guessed what I'm doing already, but now he'll know for sure, and—"

"And he'll know I'm part of it," Jamie continues. "And he'll tell the board, and they'll want me out."

"And you're okay with that?"

"I'm here, aren't I?"

My eyes drop to the thin red ridge peeking out beneath his shirt collar—the only visible evidence of last night's incident. That, and the slightly pouted mouth.

"This is a big call," I add. "Jamie, you just climbed out of a car wreck."

"Yeah," he answers quickly. "So quit bugging me."

He puts a hand on the brass banister, and heads down the basement steps.

"Ms. Wiley, I wasn't expecting you," says Mr. Brody as I open the door. "Bit late in the day to darken my doorway."

He sits behind his desk, half-hidden by a newspaper, his chair turned toward the wall. This is as close as Mr. Brody gets to leisurely.

I step inside and sit in his guest chair, uninvited. No way to do this politely anyway.

"We need a minute of your time."

Mr. Brody looks up. *We?*

Jamie shuts the door behind us.

"I have to ask you some questions about the July Fourth party in 1999," I continue, spilling it all out in one breath. "The night my cousin Caitlin died."

I let it hang in the air, taking in Mr. Brody's placid gaze. He doesn't move. He just looks back.

"Ms. Wiley," he begins, inserting one of his performative *ahems*. "You are neither a member of this club, nor a full-time employee. As such—"

"Sorry, no," I cut him off. "I know you withheld information from the police. I'd like you to give it to me."

Mr. Brody's face doesn't change. But his head does. He tilts it forward slightly, his eyes fixed on mine. It's so quiet that I can hear the faint wheeze in Jamie's nose with every rapid breath. I didn't think I had more adrenaline in me, but every inch of my body is wide-awake and rattling.

"Pardon?" Mr. Brody says.

"You were standing in the gallery, outside the pink room," I say flatly. "Not in it."

Mr. Brody remains still, head bent. Silence swells in the room.

"Come on," I press, slipping for a moment, getting loud instead of firm. "I'm not saying you lied outright."

"I should hope not," Mr. Brody interjects, quiet and clipped.

"You just didn't correct the assumption," I continue. "You were by the back stairs when he left the party. You would've seen him leave, *and* which way he went."

Mr. Brody holds steady, taking his time to reply. First, he just lifts a finger.

"*Could* have," he corrects. "You've made an assumption too."

I seize up again. He's right. I'm assuming Mr. Brody looked to see which way Patrick went. But I think it's an accurate assumption.

"You're telling me that Patrick Yates walks out of the party, and you don't even turn your head?"

Mr. Brody breaks into a polite smile. "My dear, whatever you've gone a-hunting for, it's not hidden in my cupboard."

I ignore his fairy-tale riddle-speak and hold my face neutral and unreactive. I can do that trick too.

"That was indeed a terrible night in our history."

Brody puts a hand to his chest. *Our history*, it seems to say. *Not yours.*

"But it was many years ago. I mean no disrespect to that unfortunate young woman." He nods soberly. "Or to you. But again, you assume too much of me."

I run his answer through my head again. Is it me or did he have it just a bit too handy? The little nod, that pat on the chest—and how smoothly it slid right out. This from the man who snapped over a screw-up with the punch yesterday.

"What's that then?" I ask. "My assumption."

I'm stalling—playing for time while I suss out the bullshit.

"Well," Mr. Brody begins, all too happy to expound. "Firstly, that I can recall the details of a party hosted twenty years ago, the very moment you barge into my office. Secondly, that I can track the whereabouts of each member in attendance on a given night. Sadly, my dear, I am not omnipotent. More's the pity."

It's coming to me in glimpses, the way it did when I read the text of Brody's interview—the truth glinting between the lines. I just can't quite make out its shape.

"Fine. You didn't see where Patrick went," I say, still stalling. Another minute and it'll click. "He passed you on the way out and you—you were just looking in the wrong direction."

Mr. Brody's smug smile curls into a sneer.

"Are you under the impression that is what a butler does? Simply stands beside the party like a house cat?" he snarls. "That is indeed what the officers thought—why they asked such inane questions. I imagined you knew better, but perhaps I overestimate you. Are you so ignorant, Ms. Wiley, that you assume my work extends only to the parts you see with your own two eyes?"

Mr. Brody waits, daring me to answer. I couldn't if I wanted to. Jamie remains dead silent.

"I wasn't in the gallery at that very moment, Alice," Mr. Brody continues, his voice raised and rapid. "I've no idea where I was, in fact, because there are countless tasks with which I am charged during a party. Perhaps I was orchestrating dessert service in the kitchen, or reassuring the bandleader that there'd be no further disruptions by silly girls with silly song requests—quite a few that night, I recall. I do remember making a trip to the subbasement for an extra case of gin. True, that sort of errand usually falls to the barmen, but I'm certainly not above helping when staff is overburdened. Regardless, I assure you, I spent very little time in the corridor, 'just looking' at the guests."

The air goes rigid in the silence that follows. The tiny muscles around my mouth begin to quiver, and I can't stop them. I would rather set my hair on fire than cry in front of Mr. Brody—this vile, poisoned, pathetic man—but already, the tears are trembling in my vision, one blink away from spilling. And Mr. Brody sits there waiting like a proud conjurer.

"But—" Jamie says beside me, cracking the quiet. "But then you did lie."

"I beg your pardon?"

"Or else you're lying now," Jamie says. "You're saying you were somewhere else—in the subbasement, the kitchen, far away from the party. But when the police asked—"

"No." I grasp Jamie's forearm, my head whipping back to Brody. "Not lying. You're just not telling the truth again."

It really is an elegant trick: scolding us for making assumptions he wants us to make. Answering the questions exactly as asked. I easily could have missed it. But I've seen this trick before.

Mr. Brody shuts his eyes heavily, in a great show of exhaustion, before launching into a half-hearted rebuttal that I don't even hear.

"They asked if you saw Patrick leave," I interject—softly, patiently, knowing he knows what's coming. "You said yes."

Chapter Forty

Mr. Brody stops talking, but he doesn't look up. His eyes stay downcast as he gives a stagy laugh, feigning incredulity.

"You said yes," I repeat, waiting.

"Ms. Wiley," Brody begins. But then—nothing. His sentence stalls out.

"'I may have been in the kitchen,'" I say, repeating his line back to him. "But you weren't, were you? You were somewhere else."

He doesn't answer. He just keeps his eyes down—as though I can't tell from the rest of his body. He's caught and cornered, no choices left but one: Will he surrender, or go down fighting?

"You did see Patrick," I say, prompting him. "Just not in the gallery. You saw him somewhere else."

Mr. Brody doesn't speak. Instead, his chin drops to his chest.

"Brody," Jamie murmurs softly, as stunned as I am.

I walked in half-expecting to be outmatched by Mr. Brody. Even as an adult, I couldn't quite shake the childish belief in his all-seeing, all-knowing power. But now I get it. He's just a petty fake, clinging to his sense of superiority. He withholds answers because you don't deserve them—you didn't ask the questions right. He's no mighty ruler; he's the man behind the curtain. It's about time someone rips it clean off.

"Were you in the locker room?" Jamie asks, taking a step forward. "Or on the grounds somewhere? It was eight thirty, right?"

I nod silently. Patrick left the ballroom around 8:30 p.m. That timing is certain, based on what I saw, what Theo saw and even the statements taken on the scene, from the otherwise tight-lipped members. I read through the notes on Jessie's drive, appalled by how similar their vague "recollections" were phrased: *He was there when the band began playing, but all the young folks had vanished by the time they took their break. Teenagers. Never a dull moment.*

"You were on the terrace," I say, my gaze refocusing. "It's got to be that."

"The terrace," Jamie murmurs to himself. "I didn't even think."

I never would've put it together either, were it not for those bland, scattered statements on Jessie's drive. It was one of those invisible, unacknowledged tasks that brought Brody out onto terrace—the kind of thing no one thinks of when they picture an aging butler.

While Mr. Brody shifts alongside the party as it progresses, the waitstaff follows behind it. With the first three ballrooms emptied out, they shut the interior doors for cleanup. Since the ballrooms are visible from the terrace, they need to be tidy before the party moves out there for fireworks. It's always struck me as such a silly, draconian rule that I know it must be Mr. Brody's.

"You stepped out to check their progress, right?" I demand. "To watch the cleanup from the terrace?"

"That is my role, Ms. Wiley," Brody says, his jaw so tight it sounds like he's speaking through a mask. "Supervision."

"Right." I think of Aunt Barbara's words. "You keep everyone on their p's and q's."

I see the club in my mind's eye again, lighting up like a dollhouse: Mr. Brody stands watching at the terrace railing. The staff hurries to tidy the ballrooms. The sky darkens from dusk to full dark, and down in the basement, Patrick leaves the club-house through the north exit.

And then what? I think. *Which way did he go?*

I move the figure of Patrick around, trying to place him within Brody's sight line. He couldn't have taken the slate steps down the hill—he'd have been virtually invisible, especially in a black suit.

"The floodlight," Jamie answers. "The one by the basement door, above the golf carts."

"Floodlight?" I say, confused. "But I didn't see—"

"No, you wouldn't have. It's automatic. Turns on at six and off at nine." Jamie's head bends toward me, but his eyes don't move. "It's for the golfers—games run late, maybe they've had a few."

The tableau before me: Mr. Brody's spots a suited figure in the floodlight, leaving the basement.

"How far did you see him go?"

Mr. Brody flinches, but says nothing.

"Did you see which way he turned? Did he seem—I don't know, anything. Anything you remember." With effort, I soften my voice to a plaintive pitch. *"Please."*

Mr. Brody goes pale and hollow eyed.

"The pool."

"You mean, the pool gate?" says Jamie. "Or—"

"Shh," I hiss.

Mr. Brody shakes his head—a tiny, shivery no.

"Not the front. The side. Into the trees."

I see the scene progress as Brody narrates: Patrick walks across the damp grass, aiming for the narrow thicket of evergreens just to the left of the pool—a practical feature, providing shade and buffering the sound of shrieking children.

"They go through there sometimes," Brody continues. "To drink and all that teenage rot. But he was alone. That awful boy. He never should've been there."

"And then?" I coax. "He cut through the trees and then what? Did he hop the fence? How did—"

"*Into* the trees, Ms. Wiley," he answers, turning his empty eyes on mine. "Not through."

Another assumption, I scold myself. But Mr. Brody doesn't. He carries on, his gaze still aimed in my direction, but not at me.

"I saw him step into the trees, and then, one of the waiters—a new boy, too young for high season. He came running for me, panting about some emergency. *Running*, in clear view of the party, and so I had no choice, you see. I had to step in that very moment."

I don't see—not entirely. There's some part he's skipping over, some detail he's left out.

"And then?" I prompt. "You—went to handle the emergency."

"Hardly," Mr. Brody mutters. "Party nonsense—such fuss over nothing."

I wait, unsure which part to press him on.

"When did you next see Patrick?" Jamie asks, each word landing firm and measured.

And exactly right. I know it the second I hear it. *This* is the right question.

Mr. Brody knows it too. Whatever umbrage left in him evaporates, and he answers Jamie without resistance.

"After. During the fireworks. When he came back up the basement stairs, sweating in that wrecked suit. That's when I was in the gallery. After it happened."

I sit forward again.

"After what happened, Mr. Brody?" I speak up, reaching for him through the fog.

He pauses—not hesitant, but perplexed.

"After he killed her, Ms. Wiley," he answers, a mild lilt in his voice. "Only just, I imagine. I'd barely laid eyes on him when that awful screaming started from outside—you, screaming like nothing I'd ever heard. Yes, I assume just minutes after he killed her."

Jamie and I look at each other, both of us caught on the same word. And even in his absent state, Mr. Brody seems to hear it too.

"I assume," he says wearily, "because I did not see the killing with my own eyes. I saw enough to be certain. And to remain certain, despite what the authorities and family believed. But only you and he, Ms. Wiley, can claim to know."

Minutes pass in ringing silence. Mr. Brody's words still fill the air like woodsmoke, settling into our clothes and hair and lungs. Eventually, I feel the ground beneath my feet again, and realize we can leave—we're done. We did it. I turn to Jamie, nodding toward the door—then pause, my chin aloft, as something catches my eye: that strip of red on Jamie's neck, thin but vivid, his pulse beating behind it. Something knots up in my chest, hard and knuckly, like a fist.

I turn back to Mr. Brody.

"I'm going to the authorities tomorrow, to begin the process of having my cousin's death reinvestigated."

He looks at me bewildered. I've never seen him look so human.

"I'd like you to come with me," I continue. "And tell them what you just told us."

He draws a long, audible breath. "Ms. Wiley, I've entertained these accusations only because of your intimate involvement in the matter. I suppose I should forgive your behavior, given your troubled history. But I believe you've been forgiven far too much."

"Understood." I turn back to Jamie, signaling toward the door. "Ready?"

"Yep." His voice matches my casual tone, but his eyes dart back and forth, alarmed.

I open the door, looking back to Mr. Brody over my shoulder.

"If you change your mind, call me before tomorrow morning."

He rears back, flummoxed by my informality.

"You have a legal right to amend your statement," I add. "Possibly an obligation, but I'm not sure."

He stands, imperious again, but still speechless.

"See you tomorrow afternoon then."

I let the door slam behind us and head for the stairs, nudging Jamie to pick up the pace.

"What just happened?" Jamie asks.

"I gave him a chance."

"Alice." Jamie stops at the bottom of the stairs, turning me by the shoulders. "Explain."

I put my finger to my lips, and glance down the hall. Still empty. No sound of nearby footsteps or showers running in the locker rooms. I turn my back on Jamie, unbuttoning my blouse.

"Uh," he says.

"Shh."

I unbutton all the way down to my sternum, smirking to myself as I recall that batshit staff dress code Jamie sent me on my first day—the rules for female staffers twice as batshit, naturally: no dyed hair, no visible kneecaps and absolutely no pockets.

No problem, I think. *We've got a solve for that.*

A phone's not as easy as stashing a thumb drive, but in a pinch it's doable.

"No fucking way." Jamie stares awestruck as I turn around, holding it up to show him.

I check the screen, smiling again.

"Looks like it's all there."

I hit the red button and stop the recording.

"Shall we?"

Chapter Forty-One

"Now I feel like a criminal." I crane my neck, checking the driveway again.

"What? You *are* a criminal." Jamie takes a bite of pizza. "You've been one for, like, a month. Stolen police files? Who the hell knows what else."

We're sitting on the terrace steps—one rule I never dreamed of breaking. We waited until the few lingering members had gone home. Jamie called it at seven thirty, releasing the dozy kitchen staff and sending the doormen home to sleep off the rest of their hangovers. Then we ordered a pizza, got a pitcher of iced tea from the bar and carried it all outside for an illicit sunset picnic.

"Did you mean it about going to the cops tomorrow?" Jamie leans back, propping his elbows on the step behind him. "Or was that just to see if he'd refuse?"

"To see if he'd double down, yeah," I answer. "And no, I'm not going to them. Not tomorrow anyway."

"Seriously?" He nods toward my bag and the phone tucked inside it. "Because I'd say that evidence counts as novel *and* compelling."

I nod, smiling.

"That's why it's going to the press first."

"Explain again, Scarface? I haven't slept in two days."

"Well, the recording is good. It proves Brody's original interview was bullshit, and it makes him another witness. His story lines right up with mine—"

"Lines up with Alex Chapman's too," Jamie adds, and both of us fall silent.

"Right," I continue. I don't want to think about Alex right now. "And Theo's! Brody's story also has Patrick walking toward the pool. *And* it's got him returning to the clubhouse after."

"And the floodlight."

"Oh my God, the floodlight! So good."

"You're welcome." He nods soberly. "So what's the issue?"

"It's just not enough."

Jamie turns his palms up, his mouth a questioning circle.

"It *might* be enough to initiate a new investigation," I explain. "Maybe. But it's not a guarantee. And that's not the goal here anyway."

Jamie cocks an eyebrow.

"The end goal is Patrick." I look at him head-on. "And this isn't enough to keep him from slipping through the cracks again. I need more witnesses—more of those blanks filled in."

"I'm gettin' too old for this shit."

I reach over the pizza between us, nudging his shoulder.

"Sorry, had to."

"This is the first domino!" I continue, gesturing with my slice. "Brody's story goes public, and that convinces other witnesses to speak up. 'Compels' them, rather."

That's the idea, anyway.

"You know that thing you said about Gordon Fairchild and clout?" I add, recalling our conversation at the Martha.

"Alice, I—"

"No, Jamie, you weren't wrong." I wave his apologetic face off. "A good story isn't enough. You need a reason to make people believe it."

Jamie turns forward and squints at the vivid sun, melting into a Popsicle-pink puddle on the horizon.

"Your call, Scarface. I'd say you're solid though."

He looks over with a half smile, and a jittery delight bounces in my stomach.

"And if you get the incident report?" Jamie looks forward again, but his smile holds. "You're golden."

"I think we've pretty much killed that plan," I say, reaching for my iced tea. "That plan requires both of us still having jobs here in two weeks. How long until Brody gets us booted?"

"Brody's a dead man walking," says Jamie. "He's not going to have much pull with the board once his big speech runs in the *Post* or wherever. We might be out too, but he'll be out first."

I sit back, taking in the deepening sunset, thinking all this through.

"It really hasn't hit you yet?" asks Jamie. "Alice, you did it. It's check, and they have no moves."

I blink at him.

"Sorry, I switched from dominoes to chess."

"I thought it was checkmate in chess?"

"Yeah, no, but first it's check. Checkmate's when they realize, or— Hey, can you just let me have this one?"

"No, Jamie. *Please* explain chess to me."

He looks back with a friendly glare.

"My point is it's inevitable now. You'll win."

"The *Post* though? You really think I should go to them with this?"

"I think," Jamie says slowly, "you should give it to *The Club Kid*. Let them play it on the podcast, start to finish. No edits. That's what I'd do, anyway. But go anywhere you want with it. Like I said, you already won."

The sunset shifts into its final act, shooting blinding golden rays across the valley.

"Another ridiculous idea," I reply, smiling.

"My specialty."

"I'll sleep on it," I say. "I don't think I'm in a fit state to make decisions like that now. And you—"

Jamie leans over, his face a shadow in the melting daylight—but I can see his smile when I lift my head and close the gap between us. I feel it linger for a second when our lips meet. I worry for a moment that I'll giggle. (*Am I kissing Jamie Burger on the hill?*) But then the thought evaporates, and I'm not worried about anything.

The light's turned dusky when I open my eyes. Jamie pulls back a few inches, picking up the conversation where we left off.

"Yeah, I'm beat too," he says, low and serious. "I've really got to head home."

"Oh." I sit upright, disoriented. "Okay. Yeah, let's—"

"Alice," he says in that same serious tone.

I wrench my eyes back up to his face. He kisses me again, and then looks at me with a lopsided grin.

"You drove us here."

Chapter Forty-Two

I wake up early on Friday morning, my eyes snapping open at the unfamiliar sound of Jamie's quiet, humming snore. I look over my shoulder at him, sound asleep with an arm slung over his eyes. I hold still and watch him for a long moment, part of me still astonished by the sight of Jamie Burger's bare arm and bedsheets, let alone the fact that I am waking up in them. Surprised in a good way—a giggly way. I smirk at the ceiling, imagining the look Susannah would give me. *You what?!*

That brings me back to earth. I blink away the image, angry at my own careless subconscious. I sit up and ease out of the bed, properly awake now. I gather my things from the floor and dresser as I make my way out of the bedroom. I back out slowly, one hand on the doorknob, watching Jamie's still, sleeping form. *Later*, I think. *He'll understand.* My gaze drops to the mottled cast of bruising on his ribs, visible even in the dim room. I pull the door shut silently. He knows I have things to do.

I take a hasty shower in Jamie's cramped bathroom, put on yesterday's outfit and twist my hair into a wet bun. The apartment is still quiet when I step out and sit at the little round dining table to put on my shoes. There's a small pile of mail on the glass tabletop, and I grab one of the envelopes and scribble out a quick note:

Went to knock on G.F.'s door. Text me when you're up, and I'll come back to help with rental car, etc. —A

I hover over the page, wondering if it reads too businesslike. Maybe I should scratch out the "etc." and throw in an exclamation mark? Then I drop the pen on the table and force myself to leave it. Things to do, bigger fish to fry, etc.

Gordon Fairchild is indeed a big fish, this summer at least. He was big in the summer of 2002 too, when *A Death on the Hudson* first came out, but his star never rose further in the intervening years. He'd succeeded in profiting on Caitlin's death, but evidently bungled the chance to capitalize on his own successful book—the first and last he ever published.

Caitlin's death was always going to be a story, and after *Vanity Fair*'s "Blue-Blooded Killing" piece and the initial blast of news coverage, it became a big story. But it was Gordon's book that ensured it *stayed* a story—the kind that ebbs and flows in the zeitgeist, fading into the background for years then having a comeback, but never actually ending. It was always right there in the bookstore—rarely on display, but always available somewhere between *Helter Skelter* and *In Cold Blood*. I've only skimmed two chapters, but I'm confident in saying it has no business hanging out with either of those books.

I picked it up in River Road Books last week, and hid out in YA, thumbing through it for an hour. They'd placed the new edition proudly in the front window, with other "Summer Crime Classics."

"Classic" is debatable, but there's no denying it was a hit—in part simply due to good timing. Murder scandals were knocked out of the news in September 2001, but by the time *A Death on the Hudson* debuted in July 2002, they were having a comeback. Americans were evidently eager to escape the horrors of terrorism and invasions, and kick back with a good old-fashioned, homegrown tragedy—something simple, with blonde girls and bad boys. And that's just what they got:

> To the outside world, Patrick was a handsome young man with a bright future. But in his own family, Patrick was always a bad seed. In elementary school, he was suspended for a playground attack on a fellow classmate (unprovoked, I'm told), during which he elbowed the little boy so hard in the face that he broke the poor child's nose. He discovered girls at an early age, but his father—always consumed with his own political career—never bothered to teach him how to treat them right. Before setting his sights on Caitlin, Patrick had blown through half of his high school's female students, and he was not opposed to flirting with their little sisters or even their mothers. But after the ugly business of his highly publicized DUI on Martha's Vineyard in 1998, Patrick was under strict orders from the patriarch to straighten up and quit messing around. And Caitlin Dale, with her straight-A grades and pristine reputation, was not the kind of girl you messed around with. She was, as everyone said, "the kind of girl you married."

I'd braced myself for outrage when I opened the book, but I'd closed it more confused than angry. It was almost too ridiculous to anger me. It read like a lengthier version of the supermarket tabloid pieces they'd run on Patrick years ago—the kind no one took seriously (right?). Aside from the basic facts of the murder, everything in the book seemed trope-ified and formulated to titillate the masses. Gordon's descriptions of the villainous Yateses seemed both over-the-top and lacking in the subtle details of their true villainy. He'd expounded on Whit Yates's political ambition in almost sociopathic terms, and likened Liv Yates to Lady Macbeth no less than four times.

Patrick came off like some wicked child king, who killed for the sake of killing, simply because he could. Even I thought it was a bit much.

I've made a conscious effort to ignore Gordon Fairchild for the last twenty years, so I made sure to do a cursory Google catch-up on him before leaving this morning. But all I discovered was that I needn't have bothered avoiding his press appearances and interviews, because he hasn't done any since 2002—not even when the book's new edition came out. A certain faction of his readers seems to take this as a sign of the great danger he lives in, having betrayed the hallowed Yates family and broken ranks with "the Briar." (An alarming number of Amazon reviews mention how "brave" he is for this "takedown" of the elite.) But others suggest that Gordon's silence is an ill-advised attempt at cultivating mystique. "Salinger Syndrome" as one particularly snarky critic put it. "And Salinger, he is not."

Turning my car onto Little Farm Lane—a verdant, sloping street just over the village border—it occurs to me that no one's considered the third, most obvious option: Gordon Fairchild was already a rich guy when he wrote that book, and then he got richer. He didn't do press or write anything else because he didn't have to.

If I had a house on this street, I'd retire early too, I think, winding slowly down the hill.

Despite its proximity to my own childhood street, this one is significantly nicer. High Top Road looked like an unfortunate mistake you'd shake your head at while driving by. (*Who put all those ugly duplexes there? No fences or anything—what a shame.*) Little Farm Lane still has the whiff of elegant seclusion carried over from Briar's Green. It's a notch more rambling and woodsy, which gives it even more charm.

I park a few yards back from Gordon's property and step out into the stifling humidity. That part's the same at least. It always feels hotter over here, thanks to the brackish breeze that creeps up through the woods from the river, trapped and earthy beneath the dense canopy of leaves.

I walk along the stone wall that rises out of the road—probably a remnant of the original "Little Farm"—until I reach the driveway I recognize as Gordon's. At least, I sort of recognize it. I checked the address on Google Street View but Gordon's made some drastic updates since that image was taken. The latched wooden gate is long gone, as is the weathered iron mailbox embossed with the number 12. There's no mailbox at all anymore, nor any visible number. And the old gate's been replaced with a massive slab of steel—clearly new, and so shiny it makes me squint. There's even a sticker slapped across the front: Hudson Home Security Solutions, with an 800 number below. For all my eye-rolling at the village's aesthetic laws, I have to admit this looks criminally hideous.

"And *why*?" I say aloud. Then I think of the girl from my train ride last month, shouting across the aisle about how *obsessed* she was. I suppose that could make a shut-in out of anyone.

I approach the small speaker box just left of the gate and press the metal button, already hot to the touch. A minute passes before a crunchy squeak comes through the speaker, followed by a distant voice.

"Yes."

There's an audible period at the end—a distinct *lack* of a question mark.

"Hello," I say. "I'm looking for—"

"Is that you?"

I step back, startled, looking around. My eye lands on a metal cube on the top left corner of the gate—a small, but not at all hidden camera. The moment I turn toward it, the voice comes back. It sighs.

"Fine then. Come in, Alice."

I step back as the metal gate swings slowly open. Gordon stands waiting in his front doorway, a shaggy sheepdog at his side. Neither of them seems happy to see me. Gordon looks like an off-duty professor, in belted khaki shorts and leather flip-flops that make a loud shushing sound on the stone floor as he steps aside and lets me into the entryway.

"I don't have much in the way of refreshments," he says, turning left and walking down a short hall, leaving me to follow. "But then, you didn't come for tea."

I hesitate briefly, then shut the door behind me and head down the hall and into Gordon's large, cool kitchen. The house is airy and serene and I'm annoyed at myself for noticing its loveliness. The dog settles in the wide opening between the kitchen and the living room, and behind him I catch a glimpse of a glass-paned wall that looks out over the treetops all the way to the river.

"It's fine," I say as Gordon fills a glass with water from the tap. "We can just talk. I don't need anything."

He slides the glass at me like a crotchety bartender.

"It's a hundred and ten in the shade out there. And I don't have air-conditioning."

I give in and take the glass, drinking it down in two gulps.

"Thank you," I offer. "May we begin now?"

He nods, his face unchanging. "You're working at the club this summer, yes?"

I look back, mirroring his own flat expression.

"Am I supposed to ask how you know that?"

"I only ask because it surprised me. I can't imagine why you'd go back there, this year especially."

I lift my eyebrows, waiting for him to say more—to say it explicitly.

"And with your brother being who he is now," Gordon continues, "I'm sure he's not thrilled either."

"That's right," I say, ignoring his little indirect jab. "You must remember us from when we lived over on High Top. I'm sure it's strange to see us all grown-up."

"Him, I see all over town—or his name anyhow, on all those yard signs. But you don't live here anymore. So yes, it is a bit strange seeing you in my kitchen. Why are you here, Alice?"

For your clout, I think, though at the moment, I'd rather die than say so.

I'd expected him to be—at the very least—mortified in my presence. I'd expected some sort of stilted, shame-faced apology when faced with an actual relative of the person whose death he'd so brazenly exploited. But Gordon just seems annoyed at me for taking up his morning.

"Patrick's getting married at the club this summer."

"That much everyone knows."

"*Vanity Fair* will be there. They're doing a story on the wedding."

Gordon nods, waiting for more.

"What?" I stumble, irked and confused. "You knew that too?"

"No, but it doesn't surprise me. Whit Yates—he's a doer. And he knows good press is worth more than a legal win. All that new media coverage about the murder," he continues. "The new book edition, that—that internet radio show, you know, *The Club*."

"*The Club Kid*," I correct him.

"Asinine," Gordon mutters. "Yes, all that. Like I said, the Yateses don't run around suing, even when they have a case. They're savvier than that. And surely, you see that something like—"

"Like having his wedding covered by the same magazine that blew up the murder story," I finish dryly. "Yes, I get it. That's why I'm here. I want to get it killed."

Gordon lifts one eyebrow.

"And?"

"And—" I shake my head. *Is he serious?* "And I have information that's compelling enough to do so. I'd like you to deliver it with me."

I'll let him think this is just about the wedding story. I'm not sure he needs to know everything I plan to do.

Gordon looks back with a softly knitted brow, lips parted. Finally, slowly, he shakes his head.

"No, dear."

"Excuse me?" I lunge toward the counter. "Jesus, all that money you made with that bullshit book about her, and now you won't lift a finger?"

Gordon's dog startles awake. He lifts his head and gives an anxious little whine.

"Duncan." Gordon signals him to lie back down, but the dog ignores the gesture, rising up and trotting to Gordon's side.

"Let's sit."

Gordon nods toward the living room. I wait—I don't need to do what he says. *But I do need his clout.* Silently, I follow.

He gestures to a set of lounge chairs beside the glass wall, settling into his with a heavy sigh.

"I'm guessing you haven't read my bullshit book?" he begins, eyes slightly downcast. "Of course not, apologies. Well, as you know, I was a member back then. So I knew the Yateses. Only slightly—just enough to say, 'I knew them.' We knew the Dales a bit better. My wife, Vivian—my late wife—she played doubles with your aunt for a time. Vivian was the aristocrat. *She* was the reason we were invited to join the club, but truth is, she wasn't much interested. I was the one who insisted. I was ambitious."

Gordon rubs absently at a cramp in his left thigh.

"Ambitious, and half in the bag most of the time," he adds. "I wanted to be a writer. Then your cousin died, and the stories were coming out. I saw a chance and grabbed it."

"And?" I prompt, and his eyes flash hard at me.

"I understand your anger, Alice, but just give me a goddamn minute, all right?"

His voice is calm but brittle, and I rock back slightly in my chair.

"*And*," Gordon continues, "I got it. I got the book deal. Then Whit Yates found out about it—I don't know how, but I'd only just signed the contract when he showed up and gave me what for."

"You mean—here? He came here himself?"

Gordon takes a deep breath, his eyes wide with memory.

"Hard to imagine it, I know." He nods. "He was a sitting senator back then, recall. The idea of him making open threats—unheard of. He never *had* to. Everyone deferred to him regardless."

Gordon looks up with a bitter half smile, touching his chest.

"Understand, it wasn't valor on my part, crossing him. It was plain ego. That, and—well, I didn't grow up here. You hear about men like that ruining lives, crushing people like flies, but you see, I didn't realize the mighty myth was *real*. Not until it came banging on my door."

Just the thought of it makes my mouth go dry.

"What did he say to you?" I ask quietly.

"He said enough—enough to make a believer out of me. I was scared shitless, but angry too. This was my big shot, but Yates had me by the throat. I was hellbent on writing the book, but I just couldn't put pen to paper."

He turns up his palms, and I wait for him to fill in the rest. He doesn't.

"But you did," I add. "Eventually."

Gordon shakes his head.

"I didn't. Each time I tried, I choked. I did that for a whole damn year before I went crawling to the publisher. They put me in a room with a ghost—a real writer. And I sat there and ran my mouth while *he* wrote the book." He sits back and points at me. "And you're right. It is bullshit."

I search his inert face.

"I don't understand."

Gordon holds my gaze and shakes his head.

"There's nothing new in that book—not about the murder. Those details I got from the news, same as everyone. I didn't add any revelations because I didn't have any. I didn't talk to anyone—not that anyone would've talk to *me* by then, but I didn't even try. And I didn't see what happened, Alice."

He leans forward, a hand on his chest again.

"I promise you that. Others did, I'm sure, but Viv and I left the party early that year. I'd started too early and by the end of dinner— Well, she wanted to get me home before I could embarrass her."

"Wait, wasn't that the whole point? That you were there?"

He sighs.

"It's like me saying, 'I knew the Yateses.' Only technically true. But yes, that's what got me the job. I was a member, and I was there. And I had plenty of that insider shit—club gossip and color. That's what they really wanted from me." He pauses for a short grunt of a chuckle. "I didn't get it until later, when I saw that line they stuck on the cover: 'The real story from the man who was there.'"

I look at him, my lips parted and dry. I understand what he's told me, but not why.

Gordon stands, agitated again.

"There you have it," he says. "I'll show you out."

He heads back into the kitchen, Duncan trotting behind. I stand, slowly, still confused. Now he's throwing me out?

Gordon stands waiting at the sink, his hands splayed on either side.

"Okay, but—it worked. You're the authority on the murder. I mean, as far as the public's concerned."

Gordon nods, not looking at me.

"So why won't you help me? You don't even have to do anything. You just have to show up."

I'm giving you another shot. Why don't you get off your ass and take it?

"I'm sorry, Alice."

"This time you *will* have evidence. *I* have evidence, and I can share it with—"

"I said *no*, goddamn it."

"Why?" I demand, my voice jittery.

Gordon's face hardens.

"For one thing, my authority, as you call it, is one fact-check away from falling apart. I didn't actually write a book; I just aired some dirty laundry. I sat on a couch and called Whit Yates a pig, and said I was there when I wasn't."

This time, it sinks in: he really is all bullshit, and the Yateses—the whole village, probably—know it.

"They didn't sue over my book because it wasn't worth it. It didn't include anything about Patrick that hadn't already been said."

Nothing novel or compelling, I think. *Nothing credible.*

"But if I go out there and start making new accusations? Reveal this new information you claim to have. What happens if your evidence comes out of my mouth?"

"Then Whit Yates shuts it down. I know, but—"

"Shuts it down by lunchtime. Legally. Easily. He'd call me a fraud, and he'd be right. I'm not going out there and giving them more ammo."

Duncan whines at his side again—the sound of a strained violin.

"You're scared," I say simply.

"All the time. Every day of my life."

I think of those conspiracy-minded Fairchild fans, imagining him living in hiding. Turns out they're right, just for the wrong reasons. I think of the shiny new gate out front—the one with no number or mailbox. I wonder if he used to have one. I wonder if he ever found a note in it.

"Gordon," I begin, stepping toward him. "It's not just the magazine piece. I'm here—"

"Enough!" He raps his knuckles on the counter.

Duncan yelps, and I jump back.

"I'm sorry, Alice, but I'd like you to leave now. And don't come here again."

I take another step back and bump into the kitchen island.

"Fine," I mumble, alarmed and frustrated and out of other

options. Duncan watches as I head haltingly back into the hall.

At the front door, I glance back one last time, still half-expecting to Gordon to stop me. *On second thought, to hell with it.* But all is still and silent enough that I can hear the morning birdsong outside. I reach for the doorknob and twist.

"You do have things to lose, Alice," Gordon calls, spinning me around. He stands at the end of the hall, his face no longer angry—merely cold. "Consider it, before you do anything you can't take back. You have a life. You have family—not much, I know."

He cups a hand on Duncan's head.

"Take it from someone who doesn't have any. Not much family is better than none."

Chapter Forty-Three

"So do it yourself," says Jamie again. "Forget Gordon, you don't need backup."

He keeps typing as he speaks, this refrain so familiar he doesn't have to think about it.

"Says the guy who suggested I needed backup," I reply. "Going to Gordon was *your* idea."

Jamie looks up from the monitor.

"Two weeks ago. A lot can change in two weeks. Anyway, it was a bad idea. My specialty, right?"

A lot can change in two weeks, but the trouble is, it hasn't—not since those frenzied first days of July. Alex Chapman is still missing somewhere near the Adirondacks. The car that smashed Jamie's into oblivion has yet to turn up. Mr. Brody is still downstairs in his lair, and we are still sequestered in our closet—the three of us in a silent standoff and all of us still employed. Then again, there's nobody here to fire us.

"It's just the lull," Jamie says, eyes fixed on his screen. "Happens every year."

He keeps saying this too. When the clubhouse suddenly emptied out, he shrugged it off cheerfully. ("It's because of the wedding. Everyone took their August trips early.") But it wasn't just here—the whole village had gone still, and half the stores were shuttered. Today it's so quiet you can hear the horses, restless and whinnying down at the stables. The sky is low and rumbling, always just about to rain.

It's been like this for weeks. I felt the shift that morning, leaving Gordon's house—that sudden drop in air pressure. There's no name for this strange phenomenon that rolls through every Hudson Valley summer like a mild plague. The atmosphere turns dense and tactile, gathering itself into a storm that never breaks—just looms and roils above. Breathing is effortful, and sleep impossible, and you start to get the awful feeling—you'd never say it, but you *feel* it—that it's always going to be like this. The world has stopped spinning, and you'll be stuck forever, choking in this purgatory

And that's exactly what I'm doing. I'm choking—just like Gordon did. The recording of Mr. Brody's confession is still sitting in my phone, unknown to anyone but me and Jamie. I haven't sent it anywhere. I can't even make myself listen to it again. That's how hard I choked.

I drove away from Little Farm Lane with every intention of tracking down *The Club Kid*'s producers—maybe contacting the magazine too. I'd started playing it out in my mind, picturing the conversation in some anonymous café. But—no, that's not how it would go. There'd have to be a phone call first, where I convinced (or compelled) them to meet me at the anonymous café. How would I do that? How would I even get someone on the phone? Would I leave some creepy voicemail? *I have information. I think you'll be interested.* No, of course not—in order to even get a phone number, I'd have to write a creepy email first. The more I thought about it, the more implausible it sounded.

"Who in their right mind would reply to that email?" I say aloud, restarting the conversation we've had a dozen times.

"Any journalist," Jamie says with a thin wire of frustration. "We've been over this. You know this."

"Think it through. Wouldn't you assume I was a crackpot?"

"But you're not."

"And those *Club Kid* people probably receive four hundred crackpot emails an hour."

"But you're *not*."

Jamie hooks a finger into the collar of his shirt. He yanks it sideways, displaying the spray of broken blood vessels still lingering on his neck.

"Want me to talk to them?" He lifts an eyebrow at me. "I'll write the email, no problem."

In the distance, one of the horses lets loose a ribboning cry. I jerk upward at the sound.

Jamie sighs.

"They're fine. They act funny when the weather turns—" He gestures upward at the discomfiting gloom. "When it gets like this—something about barometric pressure. They run around in circles."

Aren't we all.

"It's just not enough—one recording," I say in a guilty whisper. "It's too big a gamble. You read Jeremy's report."

This was the second blow. Jeremy sent his background file on Patrick last week. Up until then, I might've chalked my doubts up to anxiety. But there was no chance of that after reading Jeremy's email—a spooky one, even for him.

Alice,

As promised, here's the background on Yates. Sorry it took so long—I really scraped the barrel on this one. I was hoping I'd surprise us both and turn up something useful. No dice. It's the old-money problem, like I said. They're too damn discreet. You smell smoke, but you'll die trying to find that fire—even with a guy like this, who reeks of it.

Hope you don't mind me saying again, but I'd proceed with caution. Chapman vanishing is bad enough, but the fact that they haven't found so much as a security-cam shot of him—that's the real alarm bell. People go missing all the time, but it takes real means to disappear someone. I can't tell you what to do, but I'm going to bow out now. If you intend to pursue this further, I'll ask you not to contact me again.

Anyhow, PDF and invoice attached. Per your contract, please delete each email individually before deactivating this account within thirty days.

Take care,
Jeremy

The report was five pages long, and as underwhelming as Jeremy said. His email itself was far more incriminating than the "dirt" he'd managed to dig up on Patrick's last two decades. Most of the records were traffic violations—all paid. To my dismay, Jeremy had also included discharge papers from the two treatment programs Patrick had completed. Rehab hardly qualified as dirt, and just looking at the documents made me feel filthy. What made it worse was the little note Jeremy had added: *It's your call, but I wouldn't go public with stuff like this. Makes you look like the bad guy.*

"But you're not," Jamie says for the umpteenth time. "And Jeremy said he wouldn't find anything. He told you that up front, right?"

"He did, but—"

But he also told me to back off for my own safety. He said he wouldn't do "boots on the ground" work because it wasn't worth the risk.

"Hello?" Jamie prods. "Alice?"

"That's it. I need to get more intel myself. More substantive evidence, or at least more witnesses."

"Okay," Jamie says slowly. "And when were you planning to do all that? Because the wedding's next week."

"I am well aware."

"And you literally aren't working," he says, adding in a rush, "which is fine. Not much you can do this week anyway."

"Okay, boss. What are you trying to say then? What would you like me to do?"

He gives me a warning look.

"That's your call. All I'm saying is now's the time to make it."

We stare at each other for a long, crackling moment of silence, neither of us certain which way the conversation will tip. This too has complicated matters—this thing between the two of us that we've yet to name in daylight. I knew it would that first evening—flirting over pizza like a couple of middle-schoolers. But it seemed like such a harmless complication that I'd followed the impulse all the way back to Jamie's apartment. We were adults; we'd figure it out. Why not have one sweet, messy bit of fun in this grim summer?

This is why. Because we haven't figured anything out. We're stuck in a holding pattern, like the rest of the village: each day, we muddle through work hours, having strange, stilted conversations like this one. Then we clock out, and without saying anything, we leave the club together, sometimes for the Martha, and sometimes for his place. From sundown on, everything's easier—it *is* sweet and messy and fun. Then I wake up at dawn, drive back to the Alcott, and a few hours later we both walk into work and *wave* at each other.

Jamie gives the desk blotter a final, firm tap.

"Okay, I don't know how to say this, so I'm just going to say it." He swallows. "You don't have to do this."

I look at him sideways. His shoulders shrug up even higher.

"I'm just saying, you *can* bail. On Patrick—on all this."

"Seriously?" I say, incredulous.

"*Absolutely.* No judgment."

"No, I mean is this seriously your move? You think if you call me chicken, I'll—"

"What? No. *No*, that's not what I—"

"I'll just snap out of it?"

"Wow." He turns back to his computer. "You know what? Never mind."

"No, go on." I lean back in my chair, crossing my arms, my heart thumping. "Go ahead."

"Forget it."

"Come on, Jamie. I'm listening."

"Yeah. Got that."

"What does *that* mean?"

I watch him click absently around his computer, eyes fixed forward.

"*Jamie.*"

"Shit, Alice!" he bursts out. "You're not doing anything. You're talking about evidence and witnesses, but you're not out there knocking on doors. And that's *fine*! That's probably—"

"Whose door, Jamie?" I ask, my voice clear and unchecked.

"But this lull, right here?" Jamie jams a finger on the desk, blowing past my question. "*This* is your window. It's not going to be easier in a couple days when everyone's back in town, plus a few hundred wedding guests. It's going to be chaos, you know that, right?"

"Whose door should I be knocking on?"

He tosses his hands up.

"Your aunt's? Your brother's? I don't know, *anyone's*? Isn't that literally what Alex said?"

"Right, and now he's *literally* a missing person."

"Yeah! And I got run off the fuckin' road! You're scared because this is scary shit. So how about you get over yourself and call it off already?"

"You know what? I'll take it from here." I gesture at the air between us. "This part I'm calling off."

"Okay. What?"

"You've got doubts—totally fair. You're out. I've got it."

I get up, gathering my things.

"Where are you going?" Jamie says wearily. "Alice, don't be a child."

I pause to look at him, watching regret bloom on his face.

"It's after five," I answer calmly. "And you're right, I've got doors to knock on."

Chapter Forty-Four

Theo's office doesn't look like a lawyer's. It looks like the home of a nineteenth-century ship captain, which is what it used to be. The building was rezoned more than sixty years ago, but none of the occupying businesses have had the funds to remodel. Thus, the old canning pantry serves as a copy room, and the communal fridge stands inside a six-foot-tall fireplace in the parlor. Theo works on the second floor, in a dressing room once belonging to the lady of the house. He stores his files in her old armoire.

"Who goes there?" Theo calls as I approach, my footsteps creaking loudly in the empty upstairs hall.

He's hunched at his computer, and his desk is a swamp of paperwork: thick bound documents, legal pads and sticky notes everywhere, their corners fluttering lightly in the breeze from the window fan. The lights are off, the room lit only by the glow coming off Theo's monitor. He leans in close, eyes flicking back and forth as he scrolls through lines of text.

"What's with the darkness?"

Theo startles back in his seat.

"Alice?" He squints. "What is it? Did something happen?"

"Nice to see you too. Can I come in?"

Theo shakes his head, apologetic. He waves me in, gesturing to the visitor's chair.

"Sorry," he says, reaching to switch on the desk lamp. "They issued a brownout warning."

"Ah." I nod, understanding. "'Tis the season."

Growing up, rolling brownouts were a frequent occurrence, especially during this stagnant stage of summer. If the forecast looked particularly hot, the power company would issue a warning, telling residents to be prepared for reduced power throughout the day. Mom always said it was better than having a blackout, but I disagreed. A blackout meant candles and board games, but brownouts were eerie—the lights suddenly going dim and buzzy, the blades of the ceiling fan circling slowly. Everything worked, but not quite.

Theo peers at his watch, frowning.

"Man, I didn't realize it got so late. I'm just trying to catch up on my day job."

"Jules told me." I lift the paper bag in my hand. "She made tomato sandwiches."

Theo takes the bag, waiting for me to explain.

"I need your help, Theo."

He nods, his face calm and serious. "I'm listening."

"It's about Patrick. I— Okay, you know that podcast?" I press on, too nervous to pause for his answer. "I emailed them this afternoon and told them, you know, who I am."

It was only two hours ago, actually. They haven't even replied yet. The fight with Jamie had shaken me out of my funk, and I'd rushed back to the Alcott on a surge of adrenaline. I found a general contact form on *The Club Kid*'s website, then dug around for direct addresses for two of the show's producers. I sent a simple message saying I was a relative of Caitlin's and I had new evidence I'd like to discuss with them. It was so easy—how had it ever seemed complicated?

"So, I'm going to be speaking with them—soon. Probably Monday?" I continue haltingly. This part isn't so easy. "And then I'm going to village PD. To request a formal inquiry."

Theo's face registers nothing.

"You mean, you're requesting a case review," he replies in a level tone.

"Yes, but—" I clear my throat. "Yes, but ultimately, I'm seeking a formal reinvestigation. Specifically, into Patrick's involvement."

Theo sits forward, shaking his head, patience dwindling.

"Alice, they don't just do that because someone asks. They can't. They need new witness statements, DNA, some form of—"

"Compelling evidence," I finish. "I know. I have that."

Theo turns his ear toward me, as though he truly can't believe what he's hearing.

"I really do. Mr. Brody saw Patrick too. He saw a lot actually, and I have it on tape—"

I hold up my hands, bracing for Theo's backlash, but he doesn't even raise an eyebrow.

"But Theo, here's the big thing: *he* saw Patrick walking to the pool too."

Theo's rakes his fingers back along his scalp, tugging his hair in a fist. His gaze shifts into a distant stare, and I wait. I know this part still eats at him. When he stepped forward to speak up, he expected—as any fifteen-year-old should—that the adults would listen. Hell, he probably expected praise (that's what adults usually gave him). Instead, they'd all gone silent. He'd never say so, but I think, for him, that was the biggest shock.

"Mr. Brody saw Patrick from the terrace," I add quietly. "He saw him go into the trees—those evergreens by the pool fence? That's how Patrick snuck in."

I wait for a shift in Theo's expression—some sign that it's sunk in.

There's a third witness. It's not just us anymore.

"No shit," Theo whispers. "Of all people."

I nod.

"It lines up perfectly with what *you* saw. Except you had an even better vantage point. You said you were out behind the clubhouse somewhere?"

"I think I said top of the path, yeah."

"Right!" I scoot forward in my chair. "Brody could only see Patrick from behind, but *you'd* have seen him in profile."

Theo just keeps nodding, wide-eyed.

"So," I pause. Here goes. "I need you to tell them that—again, I mean. So it goes on the record."

Theo's eyes refocus. He looks at me, exhausted.

"Alice, I have to tell you something."

My back goes straight and goose bumped.

Theo rests his elbows on the desk, scrubbing his palms against his face.

"I didn't see him," he says. "I didn't see him walking to the pool."

He pauses, searching my face for understanding. But I don't understand.

"I saw him leave the party," he continues. "When he left the ballroom—that was hard to miss. He had that look on his face. But—yeah. That's it."

For a minute, I just sit. I hear the whir of the fan. I smell the ancient wood varnish. I feel the hard edge of my chair digging into the back of my thighs.

"You mean—you saw someone else then?" I ask, my voice loud and hollow. "Like you thought it was him and didn't realize until after?"

Theo shakes his head.

"It wasn't a mistake. I lied to them." He swallows. "To you too. I'm sorry."

My brain is still trying to fix it—to reorder the facts in a way that will disprove Theo's admission, simple as it is.

"Why would you do that?"

"Why?" He almost laughs. "Because I could see what they were doing. It was obvious, the second the cops came. Everyone was already saying she drowned! Meanwhile, you're sitting there with bloodstains all over you."

A whiff of that earthy, iron stench wafts up from my memory.

"You were this little kid, and they were treating you like—" Theo shakes his head, disgusted, lost in his own memory. "I still think about it—those assholes trying to railroad you. 'Oh, she probably passed out, doesn't know what she saw.' And everyone just let it happen! Nobody even stops to say, 'Hey, she's shivering. Can we get her some dry clothes?' 'Hey, maybe have this conversation elsewhere, you fuckin' amateurs?'"

Nausea churns my stomach. Theo continues.

"I kept thinking, 'They must have him already. That's why they're taking their time. They already have the guy.'" Theo does an exaggerated shrug. "Nope!"

My thoughts move in slow motion, jammed in the tangle of old memories and new information.

"I'm trying to remember," I say. "I must have been so out of it."

"*No,*" Theo says sharply. "You were not out of it. I wasn't, and neither were you. Got it?"

He reaches over the desk, waiting for me to look up.

"You were so brave, Alice, I couldn't believe it. You'd been through this nightmare ordeal, and you managed to report it immediately. You sat there and talked it through. Do you know how rare that is?"

I hate this. I hate the way he's soothing me with praise—shifting the focus from his lie to my bravery. And I hate how good it feels to hear it.

"So, the cops were taking statements," I say slowly. "And you approached them, and—just came up with that? On the spot?"

Theo sits up, his hand dragging back across the desk.

"Basically." He shrugs. "I wish I *had* thought it through more. It came out so fast that afterward, I couldn't remember exactly what I said. I remember sitting in the car, trying to replay it in my head. I was so damn scared. And then for months, every time the phone rang . . ."

He sucks air in between his teeth, rubbing his forehead with the heel of his palm.

"Jesus, I was terrified."

A dense breeze murmurs through the window, filling the quiet room with the smell of hot pavement and fertilizer.

"I can't believe you never told me."

Theo looks up, his face apologetic, bordering on anguished.

"I always thought I would." His voice crackles. "I just—didn't. I'm sorry, Alice. It's inexcusable."

I stand, my skin unsticking from the seat with a sting I notice but don't quite feel.

"Well, I've got Mr. Brody's thing. So that's, um. That's good."

"You're still going to do this, Alice? You're sure?"

I shrug.

"Wouldn't you?"

Theo drops his head, smiling sadly into his lap.

I turn for the door with conscious effort, keeping a hand on my chair. My reflexes feel dull and glitchy—my whole body in a brownout.

"Let's talk when you're ready, okay?" Theo calls after me. "Maybe family dinner?"

I think of Gordon Fairchild—his ominous reminder: *You do have things to lose, Alice. Not much family is better than none.* As if I didn't know already. I knew just how many ways there were to suddenly, brutally lose someone. But now I see how it can happen slowly—how ties aren't always cut, but sometimes simply start to fray.

"Yeah," I answer Theo without turning around. "Sounds good."

I'm not sure yet which is worse: losing someone, or knowing you're about to.

Chapter Forty-Five

I wake up at sunrise. The sun gleams off the river, my stuffy hotel room already so warm it feels like midafternoon. If this is what 6:30 a.m. feels like, today is going to be a record-breaker—a brownout day for sure.

Brownout, I think. *Theo. Theo lied.*

I still can't make sense of it—any of it: Theo lying, and to me, and about *this*. Thinking about it feels like trying to walk on my hands.

I check my phone, quickly skimming my inbox for any response from the *Club Kid* producers. Nothing yet—thank God. I'm still determined to move forward with the plan, but I need to get my head on straight first. How does Theo's revelation fit in here? Do I tell them? Do I tell the cops? Does it matter to anyone but me?

I switch on the TV, eager for the idle chatter of morning news. In the bathroom, I peel off my T-shirt and start the shower, letting it warm up (a little, at least), while I brush my teeth. The TV voices drift in, the words unintelligible over the roaring shower. All I can catch are snippets of sentences and the vague tonal variations of different segments: bubbly host patter, the coo and giggle of a viral-video story involving an animal, and then the sudden drop in volume as they pivot to thirty seconds of actual news.

That's when I hear it.

Hovering above the sink, I shut off the faucet and hold still. I hear it again, clearer this time.

I shut my eyes and breathe for a moment. I smell the flowery bar soap. I see the reddish-black insides of my eyelids. What do I hear? A name, coming from the television. Again.

". . . found early this morning on the edge of Lyme Island Preserve, a forested island at the head of the St. Lawrence River, just east of Ontario Bay. The clothes were damp but neatly folded, suggesting they'd been there no more than a few days. The note was sealed in a plastic bag, inside one of the hiking boots, along with a driver's license—which, authorities have now confirmed, belonged to Alexander Chapman."

I stand in front of the television still holding my toothbrush, a scratchy towel tucked around me. On the screen, a handful of cops mill about in a small, unpaved clearing on the edge of a dense forest. They're wearing jackets, which strikes me as odd, standing in my sunbaked room, my thighs already sticking together. Then I remember how far north they are. And that they're on the water.

My phone vibrates on the bedside table, and I shuffle over to it, keeping my eyes on the TV.

"Hello?"

"Are you seeing this?" says Jamie.

"I'm watching now."

A map appears on the television, showing an island the shape of a lopsided diamond. There's a red circle on the eastern edge, highlighting the spot where Alex's belongings were found. The anchor continues, speaking in a sober, wrapping-up voice:

"A maritime unit recovered Chapman's kayak, partially submerged in a nearby cove, before suspending the search due to high waters. They hope to resume within the week."

The screen cuts back to the newsroom.

"And now an update on this *heat*! Pete, what do you say? Are we gonna break a record or what?"

I grab the remote and mute the television, dropping into the floral-print armchair beside me.

"Shit," I say, mostly to myself. "When did they—"

"A few hours ago," Jamie answers. "They got a tip."

"What?"

"No." Jamie sighs. "Not like that. It sounds like Alex called them himself. Before he did it."

My phone buzzes against my ear—Jamie's sent me a link.

"Just read it," he says softly. "I'll wait."

I open my texts and see the small preview of the article, its grim headline cut off halfway through:

Briar's Green Man Feared . . .

My stomach sinks. I think of Alex at the airport—his strange, swinging temper. The way he just unspooled his story for me.

"He said something, before he left." I put the phone back to my ear. "He said he wanted to make a different choice this time."

"Huh," says Jamie. "Alice, that could've meant anything. You couldn't have known he was planning this."

"No. But I knew something was wrong."

I lean back into the overstuffed chair, shutting my eyes against the bright sunlight.

"You know what's awful?" I say, eyes closed. "What else is awful, I mean."

"What's that?"

"I feel *relieved*."

Jamie chuckles quietly on the other end.

"I'm serious. It's a tragedy, and I'm fucking furious. This family, the way they used him up? God, you should have seen him at the airport. He was this shredded wreck—he could barely function. It scared me, the thought of him out there on his own."

"Yeah," Jamie interjects calmly. "And now he's not. That's the relief. I get that."

I drop my head back, staring up at the ceiling, dappled with bursts of light bouncing off the river.

"Seriously?"

"Sure. I wouldn't walk around *telling* everyone. Okay, egomaniac?" He pauses—not for a laugh, because it's not a joke this time. It's just a gesture. "But yeah, I get it. When you know someone like that, you worry all the time."

I hear the gentle questioning in his tone. *Are we okay? Whatever we are?* I don't answer, because I don't know.

"How'd it go yesterday?" Jamie asks, carefully breaking the silence. "Did you talk to anyone?"

Another covert question. I told Jamie I was leaving him out of it, and here he is asking: *Can I come back in?*

"I did," I answer, cracking the door. "I emailed the podcast people too."

The sun starts prickling on my bare shoulder, and I stand, shuffling over to the tiny dresser. I tuck the phone against my shoulder and yank the top drawer open, the wood tacky and swollen in the heat.

"Whoa," he says, either stunned or impressed. "And?"

"Nothing yet, but it's early. And then—"

I turn to glance at the muted TV, a truly hideous thought arising: How might this news complicate my own plans with the press? And if I tell them that I'm the child witness, will I also have to disclose my meeting with the alibi? Just before he got on a plane and vanished?

"And then?" Jamie prompts, snapping me out of it.

"Yeah," I sigh, fishing socks and underwear out of the drawer. "And then I talked to Theo."

"What?"

"Yeah. That's a whole other story."

"Alice, what happened?"

I shove the drawer shut and it jams with a squeak, the left side sticking out at an angle.

"Alice?" Jamie says sharply.

"God, I don't—" I mumble, banging the drawer with the side of my fist. "I don't even—"

My phone buzzes against my shoulder and slips to the floor, thudding on the thick rug. When I pick it up, I see a text bubble from a number I don't recognize. But this time, I know exactly who it is.

Jamie's tiny voice calls my name again.

"Hey," I say in a rush. "Jamie, I have to go. I'll tell you later, okay? Tonight—the Martha."

I hang up on the sound of his exasperated exhale, and quickly read the text again.

Check your email.

It's Jeremy. Jeremy who doesn't text—who "bowed out" and asked me, politely, never to contact him again. And he's using my regular old non-secret email address.

Alice,

I'm not billing for this so don't worry. I guess you've seen the news about Chapman. Awful business. I still say it looks more like a disappearance than a suicide. You wanna disappear someone, you do it in the woods. And this guy disappeared in the woods on an island, in the middle of an international water border. It's a little too perfect, y'know? Kinda like Yates's record.

It's been eating at me ever since I sent you that light background file. I don't like a light file, especially when I know there's more out there. Yates is rotten—you can smell it on him. So I gave it one last shot, and this time I went old-school. I pulled his recent phone records to do a manual search for red flags. I thought I might catch him calling old dealers. I didn't—no suspicious numbers. But I did spot a very surprising one. Do you recognize it too?

I peer at the image he's pasted beneath: a scanned list of outgoing phone calls from last week, with one number circled, halfway down the page. I do recognize it. I asked Jeremy to get it for me earlier this month. It's the landline registered to Barbara D. Dale. She didn't answer when I called. But she picked up the phone for Patrick. What's more, she stayed on the phone with him for twenty-two minutes.

Jeremy's clocked this too. I glance at the little note he's scribbled beside the phone number:

22 mins? Barely takes one to say "sorry." What do you think he used the rest for?

Chapter Forty-Six

Google Maps still claims it's twenty minutes to Aunt Barbara's house. I get there in seventeen. Seventeen! A lot shorter than your leisurely phone call with the guy who killed your daughter!

I turn the cranky old car in between the hedges at the top of the long driveway, and leave it parked there, deciding to walk the rest of the way. This is an ambush, after all.

My shoes crunch loudly on Barbara's gravel driveway, and I slow myself down. I cannot be livid when I knock on the door. But I am livid. Twenty years and she hasn't spoken a word to us. But she gave him the time.

The house is large for one person—a white, Mediterranean-style rectangle, built on the far end of a cliff-side street, overlooking the Hudson. This side of the river has a different feel to it—the streets are wider, and the driveways are all hedge lined and ungated. The trees aren't so tall and overgrown, allowing for more breeze and sky and a hell of a lot less humidity. But I don't know what possessed her to stay here all these years. She may be across the river, but her view is Briar's Green.

I'm about ten feet away from the front door, when suddenly, it opens.

"Alice?"

Aunt Barbara stands in the half-open door, her eyes narrowed.

"I—" I begin, the sight of her startling me out of my angry fugue. "Hi."

She stares at me, unblinking, her lips parted.

"What is it, Alice? Are you all right? Is Theo all right?"

She asks in a quick, mechanical tone, as though getting it out of the way.

"Everyone's fine," I say, firming up my own voice—remembering why I'm here.

Aunt Barbara holds still, looking at me. She closes her mouth.

"May I?" I gesture to the door. "I won't stay long."

She takes a step back into the dark entry, her mouth a pinched line. Finally, she opens the door.

"I was having tea," she says as I step into the cool front hall.

I wait for her to ask if I'd like some, but she just extends an arm out and turns crisply on her heel, leading me down the hall. She looks—well, she looks so much like *her*. Aunt Barbara always reminded me of the Roman statues I'd seen on school museum trips: tall and broad shouldered, her hair piled atop her head in thick auburn swoops. It's paler now, and glinting with silver strands, but overall, she's shockingly familiar.

"The house is nice," I say—some childhood reflex kicking in at the sight of the aunt I once adored.

It is a nice house, though very different from the one she shared with Uncle Greg and Caitlin. Their home had knotty hardwood floors, almost soft to the touch from a century of polishing. There were photos on the walls and a broken grandfather clock in the foyer, which chimed at odd hours, and the whole place smelled a bit like fireplace. This place smells like nothing at all. The floors are dark and make no sound beneath our footsteps, and there's nothing on the walls but sandy-cream paint.

"That's right," Aunt Barbara says in front of me as we enter the open living room. "You've never been here before. I've never invited you."

I stop in my tracks. Barbara stops too, turning halfway back to me.

"Man," I say. "I don't know why I expected you to be nice to me."

There's a caustic satisfaction in her plain, unguarded rudeness. The child in me could sob; the rest of me—the angry, aggrieved adult—is utterly relieved. I don't have to be nice to her either. At least we don't have to fake it.

Behind her, I see glimpses of the river through the wide windows of the living room. A glass door opens onto a veranda, accented with shrubs and small potted trees. There's a table too, but something tells me she won't invite me out there either.

"What did you expect, Alice?" she asks. "Sincerely?"

"Good question. I guess this seems about right." I give a shrug. "This is how I'd act if you showed up on my door—not that you know where it is. Or anything about me."

She lifts her chin, taking me in.

"The city, I heard. You do some sort of admin work."

I feel myself blanch.

Holding her hard gaze, she gestures toward a glass coffee table and a pair of white sofas on the left side of the room.

"Shall we?"

I take the sofa facing the windows, and Barbara settles in the opposite one, her frame sharply backlit by the sun. She perches at a slight angle, one elbow on the back of the sofa and one ankle resting on her knee. I remember this—the funny way she sat on a sofa. On someone with less confidence, it would be an awkward pose, but it just made Barbara look cool. It made her look even more like Katherine Hepburn—a resemblance everyone noticed, and she always laughed off.

She waits, her jaw set and readied.

"Right then. You're fine. Theo's fine." She lifts a hand. "Let's have it."

I open my mouth to give it to her, but instead, an apology comes out.

"I should've called first," I say, my eyes drifting. "I'm sorry."

Barbara drops her chin and looks at me from under heavy lids.

"Oh dear, we're not going to do that, are we? Sit here saying 'sorries' to each other?"

It makes me chuckle, I can't help it. All these details I'd forgotten: her scolding glare, her sharp propriety. The interior steeliness I'd admired, even as a child.

"No, no," I say, composing myself. "'Sorry' is dull conversation. I remember."

She gives me an approving nod, and it feels so surprisingly good that for a second, I want to drop this whole thing. For a second, I think I *would*, if it meant I could be her niece again. But it doesn't look like that's on offer. She didn't even offer tea.

So, I suck in a breath and do what I came to do:

"I'm here to ask about the phone call," I say, my face up but my eyes on the coffee table.

"When your mother was ill? Alice, I don't know what Theo told—"

"What? *No*," I retort, my back rigid. "Not the phone call Theo made to tell you your sister was dying. I actually do *not* want to talk about that."

"All right," she says calmly. "Good then. Neither do I."

I pause, gathering myself.

I hear seagulls. I smell my sweat. I see a glass coffee table, and a puckered face reflected in it.

"Your phone call with Patrick Yates. That's why I'm here."

I watch Barbara's shadowy figure in the glass tabletop—still and silent, but something in it shifting. When I look up, her taut face has gone bloodless. She turns toward the wall, looking at the empty space where no pictures hang. The hollow room is so quiet that I hear the faint pop as she parts her lips. But no other sound comes out.

"Patrick Yates called you on—"

Barbara raises a hand, stopping me.

"You know what? I'm not going to ask," she says. "I'd rather not hear your explanation."

"I found out—incidentally. I didn't mean to invade your privacy."

"Well, as long as you didn't *mean* it." She recenters herself on the sofa, anger burning bright in every gesture. "Go on then, Alice, out with it. Fire away."

I knit my hands together in my lap, and give them a tight squeeze.

"First, I'd like to know why he called you."

"I didn't ask."

"What do you mean? What did he say?"

"He said a number of things, none of which is your business."

She turns toward the wall again and exhales a fiery breath through her nose.

"I'm not asking for every detail," I say. "But I do need to know."

"You don't, actually. You'll survive."

I can feel myself shrinking and squeeze my hands tight again.

"If you tell me, I'll go. I won't bother you again."

I wait for her to cross her arms and tell me not to be maudlin. But she doesn't even look at me.

"I think he—" Barbara sighs at herself, annoyed. "Alice, I really do not appreciate this."

I hold my ground and fight the instinct to apologize. Again.

"I'll tell you what I recall, but only because I'd like this conversation finished sooner rather than later. Are we clear?"

I nod.

"Honestly, I think he called so he could say he called. So he could tell himself he'd made the effort. He's getting married and racked with guilt, naturally. So he called to 'acknowledge' how hard it must be for me."

Barbara looks up, rolling her eyes.

"God," I say, repulsed as well. "That is—*gross*."

"Agreed."

"What did you say?"

"I said, 'That's very big of you, Patrick. Kindly fuck off, and congratulations.'"

A bubble of pride swells in my chest. I hope she did actually say some of that.

"Oh, you know, I told him it was fine," Barbara says, waving a hand. "It makes no difference if he's married or not. It won't change anything that matters."

I see the tears now, slipping down her cheeks and under her chin. She clutches a hand to her throat.

"It's not right though," I say, sadness clouding my own anger. "You being so fair to him. He doesn't deserve it."

"Oh, good Lord, Alice, no one gets what they deserve. None of us did."

She gestures at the air between us.

"Your generation *astonishes* me," she blusters, her eyes still tearing. "This righteous obsession with justice—as if you invented the concept! As if you were the first people on earth to look around and realize things aren't as they should be."

"Okay?" I say, my shoulders slowly rising. "I don't know. Kids these days."

She shoots me a look like a poison arrow.

"You aren't though, are you? You're not children anymore. But it's taking you so goddamn long to grow up."

I straighten up. I'm not here for a scolding.

"What else did he say?"

"What else? Nothing. He just wanted to atone."

"And that took twenty minutes?"

Aunt Barbara freezes. Then her eyes start darting left and right in cartoonish confusion.

"Did it, Alice?" She scoffs. "It sounds like you might know better. I wasn't watching the clock."

"I do know better. I think he confessed to you."

It's the only thing that makes sense. I knew it, Jeremy knew it, and looking at Barbara, I can see she knows it, too. What else would keep her on the phone that long?

"I think he did feel guilty," I continue, my voice steadying. "Like you said. I think it got overwhelming. With the wedding, yes—but also the anniversary, and all the press this year."

And me, of course. Nosing around. Getting close to something.

"I think he wanted to unburden himself, and he used you to do it," I finish.

Aunt Barbara sits in bewildered stillness.

"I would tell you how ridiculous that sounds, but I don't think there's much point."

She shakes her head, both weary and disturbed.

"'Confession'—my God," she mutters, looking past me. "If he'd confessed to *anything*, he'd be in handcuffs by now, or dead. Dead if I had my way."

Her eyes drift back to me, that leery look on her face again—like she's wavering on something.

"Well." Her expression snaps shut again. "Time to go, I think."

She unfolds from the couch in one swift motion. She's done with this, and with me.

"No, I—"

But she's halfway down the hall already. I rise, obedient, and follow.

At the front door, Barbara folds her arms.

"No need for niceties." She steps back to let me pass. "Off you go."

I wish it didn't sting so much—this frigid goodbye. I wish a lot of things.

"Bye." I step out onto the stone landing, letting the door swing shut behind me.

She catches it.

"Alice."

I stop short and look back.

"It really doesn't matter," she says in a husky, tremulous voice. "All right? Do you understand?"

Her face is full of something. Anguish? Fear? It twitches at her eyelids and the corners of her mouth.

"What doesn't?"

"Never mind, just—" She turns away sharply, eyes shut tight. "Just try to remember that. Yes?"

I search her face another moment, then nod.

"Good," she says. "And watch where you step."

Aunt Barbara lets the door close with a thud. Before I turn back to the driveway, I heard her lock the dead bolt.

Chapter Forty-Seven

"Just checking in," says Jamie. "Home yet?"

I'm sitting in standstill traffic on the bridge—the same place I've been for an hour.

"No." I prop my elbow onto my open window, faintly woozy from gasoline fumes. "There's an accident or something. I'm stuck."

Half the cars have cut their engines. Arms swing idly out of windows, snippets of chat and podcasts drifting through the heat. The sun hangs low in the sky behind me, rose-gold rays bouncing off the rearview mirror, filling my vision with sunspots.

"Sounds about right," says Jamie. "You should see the scene here. It's like the whole village came home from vacation at once—and brought half the eastern seaboard with them."

Behind him I hear the familiar clutter of voices, and the kitchen door swooshing open and shut as servers bustle past.

"It's barely cocktail hour, and we're overrun," he continues. "Brody kicked all the kids out to eat on the lawn—which was genius, actually. We've got so many out-of-town guests, we had to bust out the reception chairs early."

I turn, gawking at the cars around me. Oh God, is that what I'm stuck in? Their wedding traffic?

"Guess that's it for the lull," I grumble, dropping back against the sticky seat. "And they're all just hanging out, drinking martinis? Is anyone even talking about Alex?"

Jamie makes a nervous, chuckling sound.

"Not now!" he says—an answer, and an order.

"Of course not," I mutter.

"So, the way it's looking, I'll be here all night," he says. "I'll have to skip the Martha."

"Oh. Yeah, that's— Don't worry about it."

Guilty relief settles over me. The last twenty-four hours have been exhausting enough. The last thing I want to do is talk through it all, even with Jamie.

"I know we really need to talk. It's just—"

"Jamie, it's fine. It's work."

There's a clang and a holler in the kitchen behind him, underscoring my point.

"Shit, that's the dishwasher again." Jamie sighs. "I gotta go, but—how did it go?"

I open my mouth to answer, and my breath catches. My eyes spill over with sudden, stinging tears.

"Not great," I warble. "She gave me a bunch of bullshit and threw me out."

"Whoa. You think she lied? About the call or—"

"Yes." I nod, swiping my red, running nose. "She lied, I'm almost sure of it. And I don't know why."

This too is a relief: saying it aloud. I don't know why Barbara is lying. I don't understand any of this. Theo's confession, after all these years. Gordon's hostile warnings. Brody standing his spiteful ground. And Alex, doing what he did. I can't blame myself for that, but I can't say I played no role. Alex spent his whole life holding in secrets, then broke like a dam in front of me.

"God, I really am an egomaniac," I say through a choking laugh. "Talking about evidence and witnesses—like I know what I'm doing."

"You know what you're doing," Jamie says. But this sounds like bullshit too. Kind-hearted bullshit.

"I've just been *bothering* people, Jamie. I'm not 'investigating.'"

"That's not—"

"Sure it is," I cut him off. "You know why? Because I already know what happened."

Jamie goes quiet. The kitchen chatters and bangs in the background.

"I just don't know why everyone's still doing this—protecting him. Letting it go."

Why am I the only one who can't? That's the only answer I need.

"Look, Alice, I— Two seconds, I'm coming!" Jamie returns, his voice short and practical. "I've really got to go. But listen, the rehearsal dinner? I still think you should work it."

"Jamie, even if we get into the archive, *and* the incident report is actually there? I don't know if it'll make a—"

"It will."

"I haven't even heard back from the podcast people."

"You will. It's still the weekend."

"What happened to 'Alice, you don't have to do this'?"

"You don't," he answers firmly. "But do you still want to?"

I look around at the traffic jam—this clamor of people so eager to dance, in black tie, on her grave.

"I need to try. That's what I came to do."

"Okay then," Jamie instantly answers. "Let's."

Chapter Forty-Eight

It's still early morning when I get to the café, but Susannah has once again beaten me. She waves from a table in the back, where she sits with a scone and a coffee—the only customer at this hour.

I suggested the Bluebell Café because it was new and unfamiliar, and just south of the village in Berrytown. It was also the only spot open at 8:00 a.m. on a Thursday, which was the only time Susannah could do. She'd seemed pleasantly surprised to get my text. Of course she'd still like to have coffee. But could it be an early one? She was pretty booked up, *haha*. I'd looked at her message, imagining the reply I might send in another life: "Two days before your wedding?! I thought you'd be wide-open!" Instead, I'd written back saying simply: "That's fine, I have work at nine. Will find a spot." In that other life, I'd be running around between hair appointments and final fittings with her. And I wouldn't need to have this conversation at all.

Tomorrow night is the rehearsal dinner—and very likely, my last at the club. Jamie and I will attempt to break into the archive and get the incident report. I'll be doing the actual break-in part (alone, I've insisted), and I'd estimate there's a 70- to 80-percent chance I'll get caught. I've decided it's worth the risk if there's a chance I'll find a piece of physical evidence. Either way, my summer job ends this week. Next week I'll be meeting with two reporters—one from a national newspaper and the other from a New York–based news blog—as well as the producers of *The Club Kid*.

They replied to my email first thing on Monday, and we were on the phone within the hour. The reporters were even faster, and once they'd verified that I was who I claimed to be, it was only a question of when I could meet. I wanted to say immediately. *Give me an hour—forty minutes if traffic's good.* I wanted to be in a cold conference room, handing over my documents, playing my recording and dictating my own story into their microphones—every detail, once and for all. I wanted to get it done.

But then I thought of Susannah. I thought of what she said the night of Theo's fundraiser, when she'd asked me out for one last uncomfortable coffee: *I'm just trying, Alice. I don't think I could live with myself if I didn't.*

I'm not sure I could say the same. The more I see of the new Susannah, the more I'm convinced the old one is gone—dissolved into this straight-haired stranger in cotton-candy pink. But I owe her every chance to prove me wrong. And this is my last one.

I wave back to her from the counter at the front of the café.

"Double espresso, please?"

The kid behind the counter yawns, dragging himself off his stool with obvious annoyance—a young Cory in training. He fiddles with the espresso machine, and I keep one eye on Susannah. She looks every bit the bride, right down to the blush. Her hair is gilded with cinnamon highlights. Her face looks fresh from a serious facial—not just blushing but shiny and still a bit swollen. She checks her manicure over and over, handling the scone like a landmine. In another life, I'd laugh at the way she's gingerly pulling off chunks.

The kid slings my espresso at me, forgetting to put it on a saucer. I leave him to his phone, carrying the scalding cup to Susannah's table.

"Nice place," I say, sitting down.

"I know," she coos. "Isn't it just darling?"

She beams at the wall, admiring the decor—a cluster of bird paintings and a plastic clock.

"Is it?"

Susannah's smile turns sour.

"Sorry," I say, shaking off the acerbic tone. "I didn't mean to be—whatever."

She cocks an eyebrow at me, the old her peeking through for a moment.

"Do-over?"

"Do-over," I agree. "But come on, those paintings are weird. And the guy is—"

"Oh, the coffee guy sucks." She nods. "The coffee's good though."

We've done it again—fallen into the familiar grooves of friendship, forgetting ourselves for a moment. I consider letting it go on a bit longer. But it'll only make this harder.

"Susannah," I begin. "I'm going to leave you alone after this. I promise. If that's what you want."

Her face tenses. I continue:

"But I need to tell you something."

She sits back, folding her arms.

"A few weeks ago," I say, as evenly as possible, "Patrick called my aunt Barbara."

Susannah holds completely still.

"Caitlin's mom."

A blink. Then she shuts her eyes and rolls her head as if working out a kink in her neck.

"Uh-huh, okay." She knits her eyebrows, looking at me. "Sorry, what?"

"He called Caitlin's mother," I repeat.

"That's—" Susannah shakes her head. "Alice, what is it you're trying to tell me?"

"Apparently, he felt he owed her some sort of penance, or atonement."

Susannah looks toward the bird paintings, her mouth making soundless shapes. For just a second, I feel real hope. This was my last shot, and it landed. Susannah's woken up. If I accomplish nothing else, at least I'll have done this. *What the hell was I thinking?* she'll say. *I've got to get out of this.* And I won't ask any questions—not now, or ever. I'll just help pack up her things and haul them to her parents' house. I'll just help.

"Okay," Susannah declares. "Got it."

She whips back, her hair flying over her shoulder, freshly trimmed and bladelike, slicing through the vision.

"Well," I say, straining to read her taut face. "What do you think about that?"

"Um. None of your business?" she says with a crisp little titter. "The phone call *and* my thoughts on it."

She picks off a hunk of scone and pops it into her mouth.

Why is everyone still doing this? Why are we pretending he is a normal person, and this is a normal situation and I'm *the one ruining everything?*

"Okay," I reply. "But I think we're past that, right? Propriety and stuff."

Her eyes flash at me. I glare back, stung and emboldened. Hopelessness will do that.

"Is that it, Alice?" she asks. "Is there more?"

"Sure. Plenty."

I shrug.

"Alex Chapman?" I toss out. "Any thoughts on him, or no comment?"

Her face drops slowly, eyes widening.

"Why in God's name would you—"

"What? He was Patrick's best friend; you must have known him."

"I did," she answers, swift and firm. "Not well, but certainly better than you."

"But it's full steam ahead with the wedding plans? What's Patrick going to say about the best man's mysterious, tragic suicide?" A macabre thought hits me. "What's he going to tell the *magazine*?"

"We're not doing the magazine," she spits. "We pulled out, *because* of Alex. Out of respect."

She lifts her eyebrows at me: *Ever heard of it?*

"And yes, we're still getting married. We considered changing dates again but—"

Susannah straightens up again, glancing past my shoulder at the door.

"Actually, no. I'm not doing this with you." She gives one downcast, decisive nod. "I tried, but I guess that's that."

She stands, tucking her hair behind her ears with a tidy flick and reaches for her purse. I watch in silence, both furious and enthralled. Something's cracked the seal on Susannah's prim new facade, letting out the real her.

"I'm sorry this has been so hard for you—I really am," she says, fussing with her bag. "But it's not actually my problem, and I can't take it on. I'm going to have my own family. I'm getting married."

There's a split-second stumble before her last sentence. Not even a pause—just a slight hitch in her rhythm. You'd have to know her well to even catch it. And you'd have to know her very well to see the subtle change in her face: the slow-motion blink as she briefly shuts her eyes.

To know what it means, you'd have to know her like I do.

"Oh God," I say. "Susannah, no."

She freezes, her anger faltering.

I press my face into my hands.

"You said you moved the date up for the magazine, and I just—" I scoff into my palms. "I just believed you." I thought she'd had a facial.

"It *was* because of that," Susannah insists, an edgy urgency in her voice. "Alice, I'd only just found out about the baby when I saw you at that fundraiser."

The baby.

I drop my hands, defeated. I thought I'd hit the bottom, but here I am in free fall. *This* is hopelessness.

"Alice?"

I stand, picking up my own bag, my chair squealing against the floor. I'm about to sob or vomit—not sure which, but I have to get out of here.

"You're right," I tell her. "That's that."

Or maybe I'll scream.

"If you'd let me, I'd like to—"

I cut her off with a brisk shake of the head, repulsed by the thought of it—letting her *explain*.

"I don't know what is wrong with you," I say, barely above a whisper. "But something is very, very wrong."

I charge out of the café. Outside, the world has woken up. Commuters stride past, heading for the train. Parents steer their children down the sidewalk, the kids all dressed in camp shirts or swim gear, buzzing with summer energy. I skirt around them, storming into the tiny parking lot tucked between the café and the pharmacy next door. I'm head down, aiming for my car, when Susannah's voice hits me in the back.

"Hey!" she shouts. "Alice!"

I wheel around, ready for a fight—and a fight is what I find.

"Susannah," I warn as she steps into the parking lot. "I—"

"No, shut up, I'm done listening to you."

She's on full-blast now—her most outraged and unguarded self.

"You know why I suggested getting together again? So I could tell you in person."

She gestures sharply to her midsection.

"So you wouldn't find out from someone else. I'd *barely* found out myself and I was already worried about how you'd take it. Meanwhile, you're all over town, talking to everyone, getting stuff from the cops. You make this big display, dragging the whole thing up again. I'm thinking, *Okay, she's upset. But we're adults. We've all got baggage."*

"Baggage?!"

My voice breaks on the word, cracking into a shriek. A handful of startled faces turn from the sidewalk, then quickly look away.

"Susannah, listen to yourself," I implore. *"Baggage."*

She holds her hands out, her eyes wide and reeling, searching for my point.

"He killed her!" I bark. "Patrick, your fiancé, killed a girl. A girl you knew, Susannah! A sixteen-year-old! He killed her. You *know* that, and—"

"I don't!" she screams—really screams. "I don't, and I—"

"What? You what?"

"I know what happened to Caitlin." She forces the words out through gray, trembling lips. "And it was unspeakable. But I—I don't think Patrick did it."

Her eyes crack open, and she looks at me through dark, gleaming slits.

"I never did," she says.

Chapter Forty-Nine

For about ten years after the murder, I didn't know how to tell the truth. What I mean is that I just told it plainly—no softening the edges or politely hedging. If I thought a dress was ugly, I said, "I think it's ugly. The ruffle especially." I knew there were kinder words, but I couldn't make myself use them. Either I said nothing, or I said the whole unvarnished truth. Of all the oddities and compulsions I developed, that one probably wrecked my social life the most. Try going through adolescence fainting on people and saying you hate their haircuts.

One night, when we were twenty-two, Susannah called me out on it. She'd come home for a visit after graduation, and we were out in the city, buying drinks we couldn't afford. We were two cocktails in and chatting with the bartender while he mixed our third—a special, off-the-menu concoction he'd invented himself. He handed them over, waiting with a smile as we each took a sip. I nearly gagged.

"This tastes like raw egg," I said, setting the glass down. "And pennies."

I'd had to speak over the noise of the bar, so really, it was more like shouting in his face. The bartender's smile fell like a popped balloon, and he quickly disappeared to the other end of the bar. Susannah burst into peals of laughter.

"Okay, this was the most revolting thing I have ever consumed."

She stuck out her tongue. "But your honesty made me feel bad for the bartender. Can't we just pretend we're allergic?'"

It wasn't an overnight fix, but that was the moment I started learning to catch myself.

"Believe me," she said. "I wish we could all do it your way. But bullshit's just one of the rules. You can't trust liars, but—you also can't trust people who don't know how."

Chapter Fifty

I toss an empty can of hair spray into the bin, wincing as it clangs against the others.

"Come on," I say and wave over the next waiter—a new one I don't recognize. "Shut your eyes."

The server dutifully covers his face with his hands. I crack open a fresh can of Aqua Net and spray down his wavy blond hair, pressing it back into place. I've converted the library's oak bar into a grooming station, stocked with combs and safety pins, and enough aerosol product to fuel a chemical-weapons program.

"You're good," I cough, turning away from the acrid mist. "Don't forget to blot."

He gives a stiff thumbs-up and wheels around, speeding toward the lobby.

"Do *not* run," I bark. "Next!"

Jamie wasn't kidding. He really did need me for the rehearsal dinner. In fact, I've been on touch-up duty all week. Thanks to the swelling heat wave and the hordes of early-bird wedding guests, club attendance has effectively tripled, and the staff have been sweat-stained and overwhelmed all day, every day. I've been posted up in the boot room with blotting papers and stacks of fresh undershirts, shoving Gatorade at teenagers like a JV soccer coach. Jamie's hired virtually every kid in town with a valid license, along with a dozen temp servers, scavenged from local catering companies. Jamie himself has been a passing blur, zooming around the clubhouse to put out fires and fill in gaps: uncorking at dinner, fetching cars from the lot and plunging the powder-room toilet every ninety minutes or so. I've barely seen him all week, but when I have, he's been holding a plunger.

"Okay, gang." He strides in from the lobby, hands pressed together. "Halfway through salads, and we're all still standing."

Tonight, it's a whole other level of chaos—the edgy, silent kind, where everyone's sweating before they step foot out into the buggy heat. The rehearsal guests are outside under the tent, and the clubhouse is echoing with hurried footsteps and ominous, distant bangs from the kitchen. It sounds a bit like a haunted house, complete with the occasional sob as another server comes back from an encounter with Liv Yates. The wedding coordinator declared all staff be "camera ready": no wrinkles, no frizz and, please, no blemishes. But it's clearly Liv Yates who's enforcing the order.

"She's already made two of them cry over hair issues," I tell Jamie once the servers leave—quickly touching a hand to my own head, ensuring my French twist is still tidy. "And this thing about the handkerchiefs being floppy?"

"I know," he says. "And the tie knots—I know."

On top of the grooming rules, everyone's decked out in wedding-weekend attire. I'm only here for hair spray duty, and even I had to borrow a blazer to throw over my regular work top and skirt. The floor staff are dressed in freshly tailored suits, accented with lavender-gray handkerchiefs, and silk ties, dyed in the club's signature green and tied in Patrick's signature knot—that fussy four-in-hand.

"I spent the first hour redoing everyone's," I say. "God, even *yours* is lopsided."

Jamie tugs it absently, then checks the lobby exit. I glance at the staff door—both clear.

"I think we have a window," he says. "They're starting speeches."

My heart jumps to a staccato beat. It's not panic or trepidation this time. This time, I'm champing at the bit.

"You put your bag in the office?" Jamie murmurs.

"Bottom-left drawer of your desk." I nod. "You stashed the rest of the booze downstairs?"

"This morning," he replies with a nervous smile. "The perks of sleeping at work."

Jamie decamped to one of the upstairs guest rooms earlier this week, citing the mayhem at the clubhouse (not to mention all the wedding deliveries). When the liquor arrived yesterday—including a whopping fifty cases of gin—Jamie took receipt himself. As usual, he set aside a quarter of them in the subbasement, where the backup booze was kept. Then, in the wee hours of this morning, he sequestered another two quarters. It was a party crisis waiting to happen.

"For real, we're going to need that gin soon," he adds. "We did something like three hundred martinis at cocktails—the parents are tanked."

I pause, catching his eye.

"Which parents? His?"

"Hers, mostly. Her dad is—" He glances toward the window, shaking his head. "I think they're nervous."

A blistering sadness comes over me, imagining the sweet, bewildered Joyces out there in the WASP nest. But thinking of them makes me think of Susannah. And I can't think about her right now.

"Brody's out there?"

"Oh yeah. Hasn't left his post since appetizers. The way Liv Yates is on everyone—"

"Right, sure, he needs to show her he's on them too."

"I'll let them finish topping glasses. Five minutes—then I'll rush him and ask for the keys."

The last time the club ran out of gin was The Descent of 2016—a disaster Mr. Brody will recall well. It's the reason they keep so much in reserve. So when Jamie comes running (another red flag), we're banking on him to panic just enough to hand over his keys without asking questions.

Jamie's already backing toward the lobby, glancing toward a distant shout from the kitchen—something about the sorbet.

"I'll text when I've got them," Jamie says. "Stay close."

He turns and jogs out into the lobby, heading for the gallery. I rush after him.

"You're positive this is the window? No one's making moves for the bathroom?"

Jamie pauses on the other side of the grass-green carpet.

"Nah, not during speeches. Susannah's mom is up next, and she's already weepy. No one's walking out during Mother of the Bride."

I flinch again, thinking of her. The upside to all this chaos is it's allowed me, occasionally, to stop thinking about Susannah, and her admission in the parking lot. Susannah did not believe—had *never* believed—that Patrick killed Caitlin. It was such an implausible statement that I just stood there in a wordless daze. She too seemed stunned by her own words, and we'd both just wobbled there for a moment, eventually drifting apart toward our cars.

It took hours for the shock to wear off. How had she kept her doubts hidden for so long? Why tell me now? Above all, how could she, of all people, possibly believe Patrick was innocent? I couldn't find a single logical answer, until finally, the obvious one hit.

She didn't. She doesn't. She's full of shit.

There's no complicated explanation. Susannah just changed sides. She's just going along with the official story, like rest of the village—like Caitlin's own parents—because it's easier, and because she's with Patrick. And *why* is she with him? Perhaps I've overlooked the obvious there too. He's a powerful, handsome and profoundly wealthy man. She wouldn't be the first to look the other way in exchange for all that. And haven't I been self-deluding too? All this time, looking for a deeper, darker story, instead of facing the sad truth. We were friends; now we're not. People change. People lie to each other and themselves. It's that simple. I'm the one complicating things.

"Hey."

I whip around, startled, and see Cory, holding his green tie.

"I heard you know how to do this?"

I can hear the frantic bustle echoing from down the hall. But Cory, as ever, seems immune to the stress around him.

"You don't know how to knot a tie?"

"I can *do* a regular one." He rolls his eyes. "Just not this stupid, old-school one—four-hander, or whatever. I guess the mom complained about it."

"Four-in-hand," I correct. "Did you try YouTube?"

I know he hasn't. Everyone else at least tried to do it themselves, but Cory's not a real staffer. In four weeks he'll be done with doorman duty and go back to being a member kid, as bratty and entitled as ever. The least I can do is give him a hard time.

"Can you do it or not?" he huffs. "I gotta get back on the door."

I sigh and wave him over, quickly looking at my phone, face up on the bar—nothing from Jamie yet.

"Look up," I order Cory, taking his tie.

He'd never get it from YouTube anyway. The whole point of this knot is it's a pain in the ass. It took me a few tries to get it just right, my muscle memory rusty after twenty years.

"How is it out there? Still on speeches?"

"Huh? I guess. Can't see much from the front door."

I glance discreetly toward my phone. No vibrations. Nothing on the screen.

"How do you even know how to do this?" Cory asks, sighing at the ceiling, impatient and bored.

"It was a thing at school," I reply absently. "Patrick's thing."

Cory's chin drops.

"No shit, you were at Wheaton with Yates?"

The look on his face—like he's only just realized I too am a person, just like him.

"Different year." I nudge his chin. "Head up."

"Did you know that girl he killed?"

It's the casual certainty in his voice. The nonchalance. *That girl he killed.* It's just a fact. He doesn't even say it quietly.

"Yes," I answer. "I knew her a little."

"So fucked up," Cory says to the ceiling.

Again, that mumbled, offhand certitude, like it goes without saying—this thing I've waited decades to hear someone else say.

I give the tie a final pinch, then step back to check it, though my eyes are filmed with tears.

"Good enough."

"Cool," Cory says, already turning toward the staff door—oblivious as usual.

I put a hand to my abdomen and tell myself to breathe.

I smell the fireplace. I hear the crowd laughing outside. I see—

My eyes come to rest on a bookshelf by the door—on one shelf in particular. *I see*—I see a row of books that don't quite fit in. They stick out, just slightly, over the edge of the shelf. And though the spines are leather bound and dusty like the others, they aren't actually books. They're binders.

Chapter Fifty-One

I shove the first one back onto the shelf and grab for the next binder with fast, shaky hands. I tear through the pages, looking for dates before anything else. No, this one is too recent—the first entries are from 2010.

But this is it. This is what we've been looking for. I don't know what's in the archive, but it's not the incident reports. They've been here for the taking, the whole time.

I open another and flip through. Judging by the brittle pages, no one's taken them off the shelf for years—maybe even decades.

Each sheet is topped with the date, time and incident type, followed by a brief summary—most of them one or two paragraphs in Mr. Brody's familiar script. The majority are common infractions: someone wearing shorts inside at the grill, kids joyriding in golf carts, the occasional fender-bender in the driveway after a party. I'd estimate half the entries are regarding late dues or unpaid bar tabs, but I know I'm in the right place. Flipping through pages, I catch flashes of words like "injury" and "intoxicated" and more than one mention of shouting.

I crack open a fourth binder, brush past the first few pages and then suddenly, it's there.

Date: *July 4, 1999*
Time/Time of Day: *Evening*
Location: *Pool*

Incident Type: Death
Summary: The body of Caitlin Dale (daughter of member Gregory Dale) was recovered from the pool shortly after the fireworks display, during the annual Independence Day party. Ms. Dale had been excused from the party by her mother (Barbara Dale) earlier in the evening, following complaints of disruptive behavior and presumed inebriation. Upon excusal, she exited the clubhouse and absconded to the pool area, along with her cousin (non-member guest/child). Shortly thereafter, a young man was observed departing the north exit in evident pursuit. Per further accounts, he then attacked Ms. Dale, who was killed during the encounter. Local authorities were alerted and arrived shortly thereafter.

I read it again, confused. I turn the page, looking for more, but there is none—that's it.

"Alice!" Jamie calls in a hissing whisper. "Alice, *fuck!*"

I turn and see him bounding across the lobby at a sprint.

"I've been texting you!" he barks, frantic. "Come on! I've got the—"

I shake my head rapidly.

"What?" he says, stopping in the door. "What is it? Alice, I *have*—"

"I have the report, Jamie." I hold up the binder. "They're in here."

His eyes widen and he grasps the door frame.

"It's not—" I look back at the report once more. "I can't believe it."

"What?" says Jamie softly. "What does it say?"

I walk to the doorway and thrust the binder at him, my hands still shaking. When he takes it, his start trembling too.

I watch him read it. And read it again. His brow furrows, he peers closer and then he looks up at me.

"It doesn't say his name."

I shake my head, affirming. The incident report—the only key evidence left, as far as we know—does not say Patrick Yates's name anywhere. It's damning in every way except the one that matters most. It says she was attacked and killed—it even says the killer pursued her. But it doesn't say his name.

"Also, see there's a parenthetical beside everyone else?" I murmur, pointing. "'Daughter of member,' 'non-member guest'? There isn't one for him."

"Yeah. It just calls him a young—"

"*Ahem.*"

We both freeze at the sound. I look up at Jamie's pale, frightened face. Then we both turn toward the lobby, where Mr. Brody stands, hands folded in front of him, taut as a plucked piano string.

"What?" I call, my voice high and warbling. "What does it matter?"

Brody inhales, fury humming off him. I hold my ground.

"Alice," Jamie breathes. He bends his head and turns his face away from Mr. Brody's glare.

"No!" I snap, still facing Brody. "It makes no difference. All it proves is he's a coward."

Mr. Brody slowly crosses the carpet.

"My keys," he says to Jamie, his eyes still on mine, motionless and wide.

Without a word, Jamie fumbles in his pocket, fishes out the keys and drops them into Mr. Brody's hand.

"I'll leave you to finish this up then." Mr. Brody nods. "Looks like you're just about done here."

He turns his back on us and crosses the lobby, resuming his swift, silent pace.

"Jesus," Jamie exhales. "You really said that."

"Yeah. It felt *great*."

I take the binder out of Jamie's arms.

"So much for the big break-in. Sorry you dragged all that booze downstairs."

Jamie nods absently. He looks out into the lobby.

"Hey." I wave for his attention. "You have to get back out there."

"Huh?" He turns back, still shaken. "Right."

"Jamie, don't worry about the report. It was a long shot."

But even as I say it, I remember: Jamie's got other things to worry about. Like finding a new job after spending his entire career in this one. I rest the binder on an end table and reach for Jamie's hand.

"We'll figure it out. Let's just get through tonight." I squeeze his clammy hand, nodding toward his neck. "Let me fix your tie."

Jamie blinks, coming out of the daze. He touches a hand to his collar, where his crooked tie has come undone.

"Ah, shit."

"It's fine." I pull him toward me. "It needed a re-do anyway. Chin."

I slip the loosened tie off, lifting Jamie's collar, glad to be helpful for a change.

"See, it was worth hiring me after all. No way you'd find another admin who can do a four-in-hand knot."

I steal a glance at Jamie, his face upturned toward the ceiling and still visibly tense. But he manages a half laugh.

"I should put it on my résumé," I continue, my voice overly chipper. "I could list it as a special . . ."

That's when the first thought hits me. Not even a thought—just an image. It flashes in my mind for less than a second: a younger Jamie, gangly and big-eyed in the cloakroom, standing like a scarecrow in a suit that doesn't quite fit, his tie askew. He has that same expression: mouth flat, nostrils flared—not frustrated, but upset. Upset and on the verge of tears.

"All good?" Jamie asks—the adult one—pulling me back into the here and now.

"Yeah," I answer slowly. "Almost done."

I watch my fingers work the tie, circling the wide end around again—the trickiest turn in the knot. Once again the scene appears: young Jamie's cheeks flush as Caitlin pokes at him. Is he really here all alone? Won't he need a grown-up to drive him home for bedtime? And then she'd turned to me:

Is this your little boyfriend?

Her voice sounds different in this memory—sharper, more giggly. But then, I haven't dwelled much on this part of the night. (Why would I? It's not the part that mattered.) So maybe my recollection is off. Was she really that mean?

"No," I say, speaking the thought aloud—startling myself and Jamie.

He glances down.

"What?"

"Nothing." The word stumbles from my mouth. "Done."

What had Mr. Brody just said? *I'll leave you to finish this up.* Had he been talking to me?

I let go of Jamie's tie and quickly turn back to the bar, surveying my array of combs and cans of hair spray. I need to put some distance between us.

"When did your dad pick you up that night?" I ask. "The night of—"

"A little after nine," he says before I finish. "Just before the fireworks."

A tiny gasp comes out of me. Jamie doesn't say anything, but I know he's heard it. When I turn around, his face is soft and almost drowsy—as though we've had this conversation countless times.

"I thought so," I say, a soft quiver rising my voice. "I just wondered—why didn't you wait?"

Jamie doesn't answer yet. He waits for me to ask the rest.

"Because you told us—" I'm shaking all over now—jerky adrenaline tremors "—when we came to the cloakroom. You said you were going to watch the fireworks too."

He'd been babbling, painfully nervous in front of Caitlin.

They're not paying me. But I get to stay for the fireworks.

That was the whole point. That's why he'd spent July Fourth in the cloakroom and not at some kid's party, or at home with his dad.

Jamie watches silently as I eye him up and down, appraising him against his younger self: tall for his age, all knuckles and long strides. From behind, his baggy suit might have looked like a deliberate choice—like the oversize shirts and jackets Patrick favored. His messy hair might've looked intentionally grown out. And the face, when I saw it, mottled red and twisted in rage. I'd never seen such an expression before, and yet I knew that face instantly—not because it was famous but because it was familiar.

"Oh, Alice. Please."

My feet start moving before I realize it. Three quick steps and I'm at the door. Jamie lurches back, allowing me to pass, but then he grasps my forearm and we both freeze.

I look down at his hand around my wrist. I remember how we all froze back then too, when it was Caitlin's arm in his grip. Then I see Jamie's other hand clench into a fist, and something in me starts to shriek.

"Alice," he says again, but I'm already running.

And then I'm past him, in the lobby. And then I'm at the front door. And then I'm through it, brushing past Cory, and then I'm outside in the hot, windy twilight, and the tent is a raucous blur, and the imprint of Jamie's fingers throbs around my wrist. I stop short at the top of the driveway, looking down at the open gate. And then I run again.

Chapter Fifty-Two

It was Jamie. The thought beats louder in my head with each slap of my shoes against the asphalt. I run down Route 9, past the edge of club property and through the village center, aimless but unable to stop. I pass the bookshop and the ice cream stand and the Wishing Well, its candy-colored stained-glass windows darkened. I run past the last streetlamp and keep going, running into darkness, the memory of Caitlin's death breaking into pieces and scattering into the night.

It was Jamie. It was a hurt, angry kid, in a body much older than he was. Caitlin had been mean to him. She'd mocked him in the cruel, specific way that only an older teenage girl can do to a younger teenage boy. And then he'd seen her scolded too—drunk and chided by her mother for playing silly, childish games. Had it made him feel powerful and bold to see her punished? Or had he always had violence within him, waiting like an unstruck match?

I run down the dark street until I reach the turnoff at Station Hill Road. I veer right, skittering down the slope, across the street, into the parking lot and up the staircase to the old wooden overpass above the tracks. I thunder across the splintered floorboards, down the steps to the platform and run until I reach the solitary bench in the middle. I put out my arms and crash to a stop, bent over and heaving for breath.

Not Patrick. Jamie.

Of course, Jamie. My God, how had I never seen it? How had I never even wondered? Why else would he have helped me—gone to such lengths, taken such risks? Who would do that but the terrified man who'd once been the angry boy who'd done an unspeakable thing? I'd been hell-bent on proving Patrick's guilt, once and for all. Of course Jamie would do anything to help me.

The pieces come back together easily. I sit on the bench, struck by the awful, obvious truth. I'm the one who got everything wrong about Caitlin's death, and Caitlin's killer. I stare out over the water, the village looming behind me, forever changed by what I've done.

Not until the first hints of daylight seep into the dark sky do I know what I have to do next.

I wait for sunrise, shivering in the brackish river breeze. Even now, the thought keeps coming back:

He didn't mean it. He couldn't. I know him.

But what the hell do I know? Who am I to judge what he, or anyone else, is capable of? Jamie's just another person I thought I knew. He's just another person I got very, very wrong.

Chapter Fifty-Three

The taxi lets me out behind the village library—tiny and closed, as usual in the summer—and I walk the rest of the way to the club. I reach the bottom of the service driveway just as a large green truck turns onto it. I step off the road, watching from behind a tangle of honeysuckle, as the truck rumbles up the hill.

That'll be the floral team. The wedding vendors are all scheduled to arrive before eleven, and finish setup in time for a final cleaning before the reception starts. The club staff gets a late start today—a mandatory morning off to keep out of the way (and mitigate the fug of body heat in the clubhouse). I'm not supposed to be here at all.

I made it back to the Alcott before 6:00 a.m.—a short, throbbing walk from the station, my feet swollen from last night's sprint across the village. I sat in a cool shower until the water ran icy, then swallowed three aspirin and two cups of hotel-room coffee. I dragged my suitcase out from under the bed, and packed—everything but my last clean work skirt and one of the bland white blouses I bought during my first week. ("Is it *true* white though?" I'd teased Jamie. "I demanded the whitest they had!") My insides twisted at the memory, the acrid threat of coffee burning back up through my sternum, and I had to brace my hands against the bed and breathe it back down. Then I stood up, got dressed and forced my throbbing feet into my linen oxfords, one last time.

Now the stiff backs dig into my heels as I near the top of the service driveway, approaching the clubhouse from behind. When the southeast corner appears in my view, I step off the path and wade into the trees, walking the rest of the way through the woods. The morning is loud with late-summer sounds: gossiping birds, chipmunks and squirrels rustling through bushes, and cicada song pulsing behind it—a manic rhythm that thrums around the clock this time of year. You just have to get used to it.

But only for one more day, I tell myself, picking my way across the mossy ground. This time tomorrow, I'll be back in the city, safe and where I belong. I considered just staying right there at the station until the first southbound train arrived. I'd leave my stuff at the Alcott and deal with it later, or never—who needed *stuff*?

I did, of course. My stuff wasn't just stuff—it was notes and recordings and stolen police records. And it wasn't just at the Alcott. I had a few transcript copies there, and some others at Jamie's apartment (what was I thinking *printing* things?). But everything important is still inside the clubhouse, including the phone I left behind when I fled the library. And the most important things—my laptop, my files, Jessie's original thumb drive—are sitting in my bag, in the bottom left drawer of Jamie Burger's desk.

The trees thin out as I reach the edge of the thicket, giving me a clear view of the staff parking lot and the rear of the clubhouse. I wait in a crouch a few feet back, listening for voices and scanning the scene for movement. The florist's truck is parked at the loading dock, but the back is closed and the engine's cut. They'll be inside, rushing to set up before the next team arrives. The only other car in the lot is mine—my borrowed old

Volkswagen, sitting smack in the middle, red and conspicuous as a nosebleed. What if I don't get in and out before the club staffers start trickling in? How long before Jamie knows I'm here, and how long until he finds me, and what happens then? For the second time since sunrise, I think about just getting in the car and going. Forget my evidence; I'll just bail. I'll leave an anonymous tip on some anonymous tip line, then go buy a new laptop and find a new job and let the cops handle Jamie however they want.

I allow myself the fantasy for ten whole seconds, then I leap out of the woods and bolt across the parking lot. I race into the boot room and head down the staff hall. I don't slow down until I reach the staff entrance to the library.

I peer in, relieved to see the fire isn't lit yet—a sure sign that the coast is clear. I pause at the sound of distant voices echoing from one of the ballrooms, and the brief buzz of a hand drill. Whatever they're doing, they sound busy. Still, I have to be quick.

I scan the library, seeing it's already been cleaned and freshened, the wood surfaces gleaming and pleasantly reeking of polish. Someone's tidied up the bar and cleared away the tissue boxes and hair spray I laid out last night.

As expected, my phone is gone too. I didn't have high hopes, but I still feel a sinking ball of fear at its absence. I check behind the bar, along each wall of bookshelves, and under the sofa and reading chairs, and then check them all again, just in case—nothing. The only question now is what Jamie will do with it—the recordings, the texts, the numbers in my call log. Would he risk using it to implicate Patrick? Maybe. But it might be easier to point the finger elsewhere. No matter how you frame it, my phone is pretty damning evidence of what *I've* been doing.

One of the voices shouts to another, sounding a bit closer now—in the gallery, I think. I quietly back out of the library and into the dark staff hall. I turn and take off at a jog, heading toward the west side of the clubhouse and Jamie's office.

I pause in the doorway. Jamie's desk chair sits swiveled to the side, and I picture him leaning back in it, drumming his fingers on the blotter. How many hours did I sit in here with him? Laughing at his jokes, telling him the truth about so many things. And then, oh God, the little crush I'd given in to—the sweet, harmless diversion I'd allowed myself. I'd thought it was fun, the way we never talked about it head-on. I'd liked the way we weren't dating, and never even used words like that—almost pretending it was forbidden (My boss! My brother's friend—oh no!). It felt sexy and complicated in a high-school way, and how I'd relished that escape from the hideous, mundane mess I was mired in. Didn't I deserve a stab at youthful sex and romance when my *actual* youth was so devoid of anything so carefree?

The fact that I thought it was simple, and something that I chose—that's the worst part. That's the part that makes me bend over the desk and heave. I stand there retching, bringing up nothing, and then finally, one ragged sob. And then I get it together.

I scoot around to the back of the desk and open the bottom drawer. Cool relief runs down my back—it's there. My bag is there, thank God. I slide the laptop out, just to ensure it's in one piece and still locked. I unzip the bag's small inner pocket and find the thumb drive right there where I left it, nestled among tubes of lip balm and keys. The files are there too—it's all there. I slide the laptop back inside, moving quickly again, and hoist the bag onto my shoulder. I nudge the drawer with my knee, and as it slides shut, I notice something else inside: my phone.

It's sitting there, right where my bag was. As though someone tucked it underneath for safekeeping. It still unlocks when I thumb in my passcode, and nothing's been deleted or changed as far as I can tell—the battery's nearly full. I look down into the drawer again. He just *left* it there for me? The back of my neck goes prickly at the thought, and I hold still over the drawer for a moment, wondering if I'm going to heave again.

"Ms. Wiley."

I yelp at sound of his voice. Mr. Brody doesn't even twitch.

"I could have you arrested," he says, glaring from just outside the doorway.

"I—I don't think you could, actually," I answer. "But don't worry, I'm leaving today."

The tremble in my voice fades as I reply, the realization dawning on me: I'm no longer the slightest bit scared of him.

Mr. Brody doesn't move as I pass him, close enough to smell the powdery scent of his aftershave. I stop and turn to face him, emboldened by the knowledge that I'll never have to again.

"It wasn't Patrick."

"I *never* said that it was, Ms. Wiley—not to you or to anyone else."

Registering my surprise, he continues. "I told you I saw Patrick Yates before and after the presumed killing, and indeed I did, among others."

That awful boy. That's what he said. *He never should've been there.*

"I told you I believed he'd killed the girl, and so I did, for many years. I believed *you.*"

Only you can claim to know.

"That was *my* grave mistake, Ms. Wiley. What of yours, eh?"

Mr. Brody takes a lunging step toward me, so sudden that I stumble back against the paneled wall.

"But then—you knew," I mutter, stunned. "When? Why didn't—"

"Why didn't *you,* Ms. Wiley?" he demands in a quaking whisper. "My God, all these interrogations—why did you never question *him*? Hmm? All this time, all this spectacle and fuss you've made, and he was there at your side. Perhaps you might consider that before demanding answers of me."

He pulls away, shrugging back into composure before nodding a curt farewell. He hesitates then, tilting his head. His eyes narrow, but when he speaks again, there's no menace in his voice. Only idle curiosity.

"And now you have the truth—awful though it is. I wonder, what will you do with it?"

Chapter Fifty-Four

I sit on the floor of the airing cupboard, my back sticky against the door. Early-afternoon sun creeps across the floor, streaming in through the window, amplifying the smell of mouse droppings and mothballs. But I don't dare open it, and risk someone noticing. I've made it this far. A couple more hours and I'll be out of here, one way or another.

Mr. Brody left me backed against the wall of the staff hall, his ominous question lingering as he walked away with visible satisfaction. I waited until he rounded the corner, then slowly inched forward. I took two silent, toe-heel steps down the staff hall, heading in the opposite direction.

Front door, I thought—more an instinct than a fully formed idea. *Closest exit.*

I made it to the lobby entrance before I heard the first familiar voices bouncing down the staff hall. One of them was Cory's—I recognized his snorting laugh. I froze in the doorway for a prickling, terrified second, my mind blanking out. Then I bolted across the lobby and up the staircase to the second floor. I turned left and darted to the end of the hall, heading for the airing cupboard. I pulled the door open and threw myself inside. At first I could only hear the gasping of my own breath and a tinny ring in my ears. When it subsided, I heard more familiar noises from below—doormen chatting in the lobby, and the distant wheeze of vacuums rumbling down the gallery.

Now the whole clubhouse is rumbling beneath me as the staff dash about, tending to final touches before the wedding guests arrive. The airing cupboard was a good instinct, but not the best idea. I can hide in here indefinitely, but sneaking out is another thing. I'll have to wait until cocktail hour, when it's good and crowded. The staff will be busy getting drinks in hands, and the guests will be busy drinking them. I'll wait until it sounds loud and chaotic, then slip out and head for the boot room, and I'll be out of here, finally and for good.

And then?

What I have to do then is tell. I'll start with village PD, because I want my new, amended statement on the record right away. I want it saved and stored forever in the system: *I was wrong.* That's the part that feels like swallowed glass—like an emergency. The urge to say it out loud, to someone's face, is overwhelming. And once I tell the authorities, I'll tell the media. I'll keep my meetings with the podcast producers and the reporters. I still have a story for them. *I was wrong,* I'll begin. *We all were. That's the story.*

That's how it starts, at least. I don't know what happens next—when or how they'll come for Jamie. I don't think it's a question of "if" though. Jamie isn't a Yates. He's a normie—a janitor's son. The village will be all too glad to point the finger at someone else—and such an ideal target. *There was always something funny about him,* they'll say to each other. *They always had a feeling.*

In reality, it's that same snobbery that let Jamie go unnoticed in the first place. No one questions the fidgety kid in the cloakroom, so worthless to them—so accustomed to his worthlessness that he's working unpaid, drinking free soda in lieu of dinner. Yes, Theo and I were outsiders, and yes, the club members looked down on us, but Jamie they didn't even see. And neither did I. And probably for the same reason.

The truth is awful, as Brody said. But at least I know what to do with it. First the police. Then the press. Then I don't know. Then I'll have to go figure out the rest of my life.

A clanging bell rings in the distance, startling me awake. I jolt upright against the door, blinking in the blinding late-afternoon light. The cacophonous bells tumble over each other, and suddenly I recall what they're for.

I pull myself up by the doorknob and walk on pins and needles to the window. Outside, a line of SUVs and town cars snakes up the drive. The first wave of guests has already arrived—I see a handful strolling the lawn, and others on the terrace. The sounds of bubbly chatter float up as the church bells finally fade. I step quietly back to the door and press my ear against it—no need though. The clubhouse is audibly bustling with footsteps and whispered instructions and the tinkle of champagne flutes. I listen, wondering if this is the moment, and then I hear a cheer go up outside. I feel a dreadful sinking as I peer out the window again—but I have to look.

There they are: Patrick driving his dad's baby blue Jaguar up the hill, and Susannah leaning out the window, waving with both hands. Her smile is huge and victorious. Even from here, she is as happy as I've ever seen her. I still recoil at this strange sight—I can't help it—but there is a tiny flicker of warmth too. I don't know that I'll ever be happy for her, but I do know that she deserves happiness. And maybe (*maybe*) I can accept that she's found it. Maybe I don't have to be the shadow over it.

I can't think of Patrick in such generous terms. I can't pretend I want him to be happy. But I do owe him a debt. *I was wrong.* I owe him that.

I watch the Jaguar crest the drive and pull up to the front entrance, disappearing from my view. More cheers rise up from downstairs, and I realize it's time. The guests are flooding toward the lobby, and for the next few minutes, all eyes will be on the couple. This is my best shot at slipping out.

I lift my heavy bag, ensuring the zipper's tight. Then I open the door, glancing left as I step right. It happens in a flash: a shadow appears on the edge of my vision, and before I can take another step, I slam hard and directly into Jamie Burger.

Chapter Fifty-Five

My vision blurs bright white and I cup my left eye, the pain so huge that I can't even move.

"Alice, shit—are you okay? Alice?"

I stare at the floor as the world reemerges. Then the panic strikes. My breath turns shallow, and I'm suddenly, acutely conscious of the fact that I'm standing at the dead end of the hallway with my back to the wall. I know I have to run.

"Jesus, Alice, I need to talk to you."

Jamie's face is gray, his eyes rimmed red and underscored by deep, bruise-purple rings.

"I . . ." he begins, then—nothing.

I run. For the second time, I run from him in wholehearted fear for my life. *No*, I think. *The third time.* I picture my little-girl hands grasping at the damp ground as I scrambled up the hill and away from the pool.

I reach the other end of the upstairs hallway, careening onto the staff steps, still gripped by the feeling that I am both here now, and out on that hill in 1999. I've slipped through a hole in the timeline of my own life, living and reliving—only now I know who I'm really running from. Now everything makes sense: they didn't believe me, because I was wrong. It wasn't a cover-up; it was a massive, ridiculous oversight—the kind that can happen in insular, affluent corners of the world.

I reach the main-floor landing, pausing for an instant, peering through the nearest staff door just in front of me. Someone's left it open and from here, I can see all the way down the gallery—now filled with wedding guests. A dark-haired man stands with his back to me, chatting in a circle near the open staff door. He seems to feel my eyes on him and turns to glance over his shoulder.

"*Alice,*" comes a voice from above—Jamie's angry, urgent whisper.

My body jerks into motion again, hurtling down the next flight of stairs, and out onto the subterranean level. I stand frozen at the head of the basement hall, my eyes darting between the north and south exits. If I take the south, I'll be plainly visible to any guests coming up the drive, as well as the doormen at the front. But if I go the other way, I'll—

Footsteps thunder down the stairs behind me, coming fast.

Panicked, I dash across the hall, shoving through the nearest door—forget the exits, I just need to hide. I shut the door and hurl myself against it, my ear pressed to the green-painted wood. I listen for Jamie's footsteps, breathing as quietly as I can.

Behind me, someone scoffs.

My eyes refocus, and I realize where I am: the men's locker room. I can tell from the clear, crisp sound of the scoff that the room is almost empty—*almost* the perfect hiding spot.

"Jesus," he says. "I should've guessed."

I push myself off the door, my sweaty cheek unpeeling with a soft thwack. Then I turn around.

He stands at the sinks, facing me through the mirror with a paper napkin in his hands. He balls up the napkin, tosses it in the trash and turns to face me.

"What now, Alice?" Patrick asks.

Chapter Fifty-Six

"Y'know, I knew this was coming," Patrick continues. "But I never thought you'd actually crash the wedding."

My gut churns with a queasy swirl of fear and anger and physical repulsion. I can't bring myself to speak, or even open my mouth. I have no idea what might come out.

"If we're going to do this, let's get on with it," he says. "I'd rather not spend my entire wedding day with you."

I stay silent. Patrick sighs, then looks down, cracking an aggravated smile—that same one-sided smirk. As a teenager, it made him look mature and debonair. Now it makes him look younger, even with the weathered skin and faint dullness in his eyes. It shakes something loose in me, this glimpse of the boy he was.

"It wasn't you," I say, my voice barely above a whisper.

But he hears me. The smirk vanishes, and Patrick's face melts back into a somber stare. He takes a breath and lets it out slowly.

"No," he answers heavily. "Of course it wasn't."

I shudder.

"Did you know it was him?"

Patrick hesitates. "I was pretty sure, yeah."

"Why didn't you say something?"

Patrick holds still, regarding me with caution. It hits me that I'm making him nervous.

"Because I was pretty sure," he answers, watching me. "But I wasn't positive."

I could scream—I want to, desperately. *Say more! Make me understand!* Instead, I force my head into a nod.

"It didn't click right away," Patrick says. "I knew they'd talked. I knew how she could be—all the senior girls, I mean. I was a freshman once; it's like torture."

I file this away, afraid to interrupt.

"I never found out what she said to him," Patrick adds. "But I saw him at the cloakroom after, all fucked up about it."

"What do you mean?" I interject, unable to stop myself. "What did he say?"

Patrick turns his palms out, shrugging.

"Nothing, really. He just had that look, like he was going to set the place on fire. Definitely wanted to set *me* on fire. I was like, 'Oh hey, what're you doing here anyway?' And he lost his shit. Called me an asshole or something." Patrick's eyes go distant. "I didn't even remember at first. Not for weeks. They'd already closed the case."

"That doesn't matter. You still could have reported him."

Patrick nods, solemn and deliberate. He looks like his father now—like a politician who's been through this issue a hundred times, repeating his official stance.

"I wasn't positive—not a hundred percent. And you don't go calling someone a killer unless you're sure." Patrick glances at me again. "At least I don't."

"But you must have known she didn't drown," I press. "She wasn't that drunk—you knew that. You were with her practically the whole night."

Patrick's gaze shifts downward, considering.

"Not the whole night," he says at last. "I was also—"

He leans back against the sink.

"I was with someone else too," he says. "In here. That's where I was when it happened."

I wait, confused. The sauna alibi? The one I know is bullshit?

"No, you weren't," I retort—then catch myself and try again, more carefully. "I know you weren't with Alex, okay? I know what Alex said was—"

Patrick holds up a hand.

"I'm not talking about what Alex said, and—yeah, I think you'd better just leave him out of this." He shoots me a look of simmering rage. "I'm not discussing Alex. Not with you. Not today."

Patrick holds me in a hard look. I nod.

"So you were in here with another girl," I state evenly.

"I was with Barbara."

Barbara who? I think, blinking at him. *There weren't any Barbaras at school.*

Patrick looks back, silent and neutral, waiting for me to puzzle it out. For me to realize he's talking about my own aunt. Caitlin's mother. My mother's sister—*my* Barbara.

"You—" I stumble.

I see the clubhouse from above again, looking down at it like a dollhouse as another room lights up—the locker room this time. I see the figures in there—Barbara's auburn hair and Patrick's, dark and shaggy—but I can't conjure the rest.

"You had an affair?" I hear myself say.

Patrick makes another noncommittal gesture with his head.

"It wasn't an affair," he counters quietly—that unmistakable mix of self-righteousness and shame. "We had sex a few times. It was stupid—nothing. It *would've* been nothing if things hadn't happened the way they did."

A vague, protesting syllable bursts out of me, and hangs there—the rest of the words, whatever they were, forgotten. My train of thought is getting away from me, derailed by this new, unthinkable fact.

"I was a little shit back then, okay?" Patrick spits back, bridling. "Not a killer."

I look at him, pulling my focus back into the room. At least now the phone call makes more sense—the mysterious twenty-two minutes. Whatever he said to her, it wasn't a confession.

"Why did you lie to the cops then? If you had a real alibi?"

He leans back, smirking.

"Why didn't I tell them I was fucking my girlfriend's mom? You mean *after* you told them I killed her?"

He chuckles to himself. I wait it out.

"Yes," I reply. "They'd have confirmed your story with Barbara. It would have been uncomfortable, but it would've made your life easier in the long run. God—it might've changed everything."

They might have investigated properly. They might've found Jamie sooner. This might have been a private tragedy with an ending.

"Twenty years," I murmur, my mind still reeling with what-ifs. "If you'd just—"

Patrick lunges forward.

"Do you hear yourself?" he barks, a drop of spittle arcing through the air. "I'd just watched them pull my dead girlfriend out of the pool. I was in shock—and there's this kid screaming that I killed her."

He jabs a hand at me, the other one gripping the edge of the sink.

"I was fucking delirious! I kept thinking it was a mistake and it wasn't her, or that she wasn't completely dead, and they just had to, you know, get her heart going again. I mean, for like a week, I'd be like, 'Did they check? Are they sure?'" He shakes his head and exhales a shaky sigh. "So no, no, I wasn't thinking about alibis. I wasn't worried about convincing people that I wasn't a murderer—because, again, I *wasn't*."

He leans back and clamps his head by the temples with his thumb and middle finger.

"So yeah, when they questioned me—I mean, it hadn't even

been twenty-four hours. I was still totally out of it," he mutters. "Totally useless, couldn't even talk really. Not that it mattered."

"What does that mean?" I ask carefully.

"What it sounds like," he snaps, still holding his head by the temples. "What you fucking know already. My dad had the whole thing worked out before they even talked to me."

He trails off into a mumble, the venom drained from his tone.

"He thought I'd done it too. My dad. Didn't even ask before he went and made the deal."

Patrick looks wilted inside his wedding suit. His gaze drifts past me, hazy and soft.

"I walked in there, and—God, all their faces. They thought they were letting me get away with something."

His phone buzzes, startling us both. He turns away and answers in a lowered voice. I can't hear what he's saying, but it's obvious who he's talking to. I see his smile in the mirror—a real one.

No, I plead in silence. *No, we're not done.* I need this strange détente to hold, just one more minute. My mind is still tangled with questions. *What kind of deal exactly? Did you tell them the truth—the cops, your dad? Did anyone believe it?*

But Patrick's standing straight now, slipping the phone back into his pocket. He checks his reflection in the mirror, touching a hand to the buttons on his jacket. Then he clears his throat and turns back to me.

"I'm going back to my wedding now."

He strides forward, heading for the door behind me. I don't move.

"Why did you have it here?" I ask. "The wedding. Of all places."

Patrick answers without hesitation.

"Because it meant something to Susannah. Or to her parents. And—sorry, what the fuck is it to you?"

"Don't *you* think it's a little strange? A little—" I gesture around the room, feeling my shoulders rise "—complicated?"

"Nope. I love her. It's not complicated." He leans in close. "And I didn't kill anyone. So why shouldn't I come back here?"

The corner of his mouth lifts into a small, mean hint of a smile.

"You though?" he murmurs. "I honest-to-God don't know how you could."

He makes for the door, but I hold my ground. *This can't be it. I need more answers.*

"Wait. Patrick."

He stops with his hand on the door and sighs, his annoyance plain.

"How did you know it was Jamie?" I ask, stepping closer. "You said you were pretty sure, but how? Did you see him walking to—"

"Who's Jamie?" Patrick frowns.

I stand there, frozen, looking through him. Everything in me goes still.

He waits another moment, then shakes his head and walks out.

Upstairs, the guests cheer, welcoming Patrick back. The roar of their united voices rumbles the ceiling above me.

Not Patrick. Not Jamie either.

I was a freshman once, Patrick said.

I thought he'd just mistaken Jamie for a freshman. He was so tall.

I knew they'd talked. He had that look—like he was going to set the place on fire.

Again, I assumed it was Jamie he'd seen by the cloakroom. Jamie was the one working there.

I stand still and force myself to think in slow, deliberate thoughts: it could've been anyone. There were tons of other Wheaton kids there—freshman, seniors, lower-school students. Just because it wasn't Jamie does not mean it was *him*. I can't jump to conclusions like this anymore. I don't know anything.

My relief is shallow and short-lived. It lasts only until I open the door and see him sitting there, on the bench in the hallway, by himself.

My brother smiles at me, tears standing in his eyes. He raises a hand.

"Hey, Alice," he says, his voice high and watery. "I need to tell you something."

Chapter Fifty-Seven

He followed us. He saw us leave the party—Caitlin with her chin held high, pissed at her mother for scolding her in front of everyone, and me, trotting along beside her. He'd been keeping tabs on me since dinner, watching us at our separate table, on the other side of the room. He'd been curious at first, then concerned by the way Caitlin kept whispering to me—suddenly treating me more like a friend than a little cousin. It bothered him.

"She had this hold on you," says Theo. "You were obsessed with her."

As if it had been Caitlin's fault for being an older, beautiful, confident girl.

He hadn't realized I'd been drinking until the dancing started. He watched Caitlin and I spinning each other around, doing goofy dance moves and laughing loudly. He'd never seen me behave like that—certainly not at the club—and as more party-goers took notice, he started to get nervous.

"I was pissed off too. It was embarrassing, you know? We were guests and you—because of *her*, you were making an ass of yourself, in front of all those people. And Uncle Greg too—you know how I was back then. He was the closest thing I had to a dad, and I thought, *Shit, they'll never invite us again.* I just imagined losing all that because you'd made this big, stupid scene, and I knew it wasn't your fault. She was playing with you like a toy—dressing you up like that, making you perform for her, getting you drunk for the fun of it."

Then Barbara intervened, and Theo watched the tense exchange. He been relieved when Caitlin stormed off, but then he saw she'd taken me with her. He kept his distance, following just close enough to see us, but not close enough to hear or to be heard. He watched us leave the clubhouse, alarmed to see us heading for the rear path. It was dark. I'd been drinking and so had she. What if we went to the pool? He'd slipped out the north exit and waited in the shadowed doorway, craning to see the bottom of the path. He just wanted to make sure we stayed on the grass—that we didn't wander too far. Then he saw Caitlin jogging toward the pool gate, laughing and waving for me to follow.

"I got really scared then. The way you were walking . . ."

He took off after us, barely registering the floodlight clicking on behind him. He hurried down the side of the hill, nearly running as he reached the bottom, and quickly ducked into the evergreens beside the pool. From there, he watched with mounting panic as Caitlin hitched up the hem of her dress and stepped into the water. She stood on the top step, up to her ankles, and she was saying something to me. He couldn't make out all the words, but her voice was loud and insistent. She was telling me to come in too.

"And then she fuckin' did it. I couldn't believe it," Theo recalls, staring into his open palms. "I was waiting there in case you slipped or something. But she actually *pushed* you in."

"What? No." I shake my head. "No, Theo, that's not what happened."

He looks at me, his forehead knotted, his eyes wide and desperate.

"I fell in," I continue. "She was getting out of the water, and she slipped on the step. I reached out to grab her and just lost my balance."

Theo turns his head sideways, his eyes still on me. He shakes his head.

"Alice," he scoffs. "Look, I know you think she was this goddess who could do no wrong, but—that's just not what happened. Maybe she pretended to slip, I don't know. But she *grabbed* you. She pulled you forward, and then—" He leans back and mimes a hard shove. "She pushed. In fact, I think she pushed hard, to make sure you hit the water and not the banister or the edge of the pool. I thought about that a lot after."

"You did?"

"Oh God, constantly. For years. I kept trying to convince myself that maybe she *had* wanted to hurt you. And then it wouldn't be as bad, what I—"

Theo cuts himself off, squeezing his eyes shut and shaking off the image.

"But I knew it was a prank—just the kind of mean prank she'd do." He sighs a ragged sigh. "But you *could* have been really hurt, you know? And in that moment, I thought you were."

Theo had waited only a second as I thrashed under the water. Then he fumbled out of the thicket, clumsy with fear and rage. He tried to run, but the grass was slick beneath his dress shoes, forcing him to walk, which only made him angrier. He was going to ream her out. He'd make sure I was okay first, but then he was going to let her fucking have it. She thought she could do whatever she wanted, didn't she? She was like every other spoiled, snotty, upper-school bitch, acting like she was better than everyone just because she had big tits and blond hair and old money. And the sick part was that no one ever stopped her. Everyone fucking worshipped her, just like they worshipped Patrick—only she didn't even have the excuse of a famous family. She was just a high and mighty cunt who had it coming to her, and *he* was gonna be the one who gave it to her.

I was gone by the time he got to the pool—already walking

up the rear path back to the clubhouse. It didn't matter. He took one glance in my direction, and then I was all but forgotten. He exploded at Caitlin: Who the fuck did she think she was? What sick game was she playing? How about she pick on someone her own size?

Caitlin had looked at him, confused but not frightened. Theo lunged at her, and only then did she rear back with a surprised shriek. He grabbed her wrists, not knowing why, and held on as she tried to pull away. They lurched and shuffled in the awkward pose, Theo's panic rising now, in tandem with his rage. He shouted in Caitlin's face—called her a nasty bitch, in a growling voice he didn't know he had in him. She yelped again, then twisted away and broke free.

She'd stood there, bewildered, catching her breath, and Theo thought it was over—this fight, whatever it was. Caitlin's mouth began to tremble, and Theo waited for the tears. But then, she laughed. It was breathy and nervous at first, then she was properly giggling. And then, seeing the wide-eyed shock on Theo's face, she laughed and pointed. She laughed so hard her eyes shut and she bent forward. And in that moment, Theo, for the first time in his life, had balled his fist and stepped forward and slammed it into the side of Caitlin's face.

She'd stumbled back, stunned silent. It was a hard punch, but a clumsy one. She was hurt, but not terribly—just a red mark on her temple and the top of her cheekbone. But she was incensed. She stood up straight and marched toward him, shouting at him, hurling expletives. Theo felt himself react, surprised by his own swinging limbs. He had the strangely lucid thought that they were two angry animals—all reflex and survival instinct—and then he wasn't thinking at all. He wasn't even angry anymore; he was just shoving and snarling and hitting as hard as he could. He didn't even hear the sound of her skull on the cement. He didn't realize what he'd done—what he was still doing—until he saw the blood.

It pooled swiftly from the side of her face, a lopsided halo.

He reached out, but stopped short of touching her. His hand throbbed, the pain slowly bringing him back to consciousness. He nudged Caitlin with his toe (had he been *kicking* her?) and said her name. He nudged again, harder. She wobbled, but wouldn't wake. Her mouth parted and he caught sight of blood-stained teeth. Panicked now, he nudged again, only this time it was more like a kick. Her body rocked back slightly, then rolled forward, the momentum tipping her over the edge and into the pool. Theo stood, frozen in terror. Then he heard the sound of running footsteps from somewhere on the hill. He turned from Caitlin's lifeless corpse and fled into the dark.

"I didn't want to, Alice," I hear Theo say. "I swear to you. It just spiraled."

He puts a hand on my wrist, and I jerk. He quickly pulls his arm back, then lifts both his hands up and looks at me, despairing. He covers his face with his palms.

"I didn't plan to hurt her like that," he says, weeping and muffled. "I never even knew I could."

Theo drops his hands into his lap and sits back against the wall.

"It's unforgivable," he says, looking straight ahead. "But if you'd been there—I don't know. I wish I could make you understand how it just—"

His hands go out in front of him again, like he's reaching for something he can't quite see.

"It happened. It just happened."

I make myself look at him, sealing this moment in my mind.

"Why are you here, Theo?"

"Jamie called me. He told me about last night."

"Jamie *knew*?"

"No, not technically. I never told him everything. But he—at some point, he had suspicions."

When? In high school? Did something click years later? Did someone tell him something?

Theo shakes his head, reading the thoughts on my face.

"I don't know." He shrugs. "I never asked. We just stopped talking."

"Who else?" I ask, wishing I didn't have to.

"A lot of people, I think," Theo says, eyes downturned. "No one says so—you know how it is here. But I'll get a look. Or one of those comments, you know? 'Staying out of trouble?'"

He cringes.

"You tell yourself you're paranoid," he adds.

"Jules?" I ask in a tiny voice.

Theo's face pinches.

"I tried. I came close to telling her a few times. But no, never managed it." He swallows. "Fucking coward, I know."

I think of Jules telling me about how stressed-out Theo was this summer—because of the campaign, the work piling up. I wonder if he told himself that too.

Still leaning back against the wall, he lolls his head toward me.

"Hey," he says wearily. "Let's do the rest at the station, okay? They'll need this on tape anyway."

I hold still until he looks at me, his face all trepidation. I give him a reassuring smile—I can't help it. He's my brother, and this is it. Everything changes on the other side of this moment. So I smile. I tell him I love him. Then I reach into my pocket and take out my phone.

Theo looks down at it, the recorder still running.

"Atta girl." He sniffs and nods, and then he smiles too. "You win."

Chapter Fifty-Eight

I sit in the back booth of the Martha Washington, keeping one eye on the door. It's strange to be here in the middle of the afternoon, with the bright August sunshine pouring in the foggy windows, highlighting the splintered floorboards and the faint haze of smoke from the sputtering fireplace. I check my phone for messages—nothing new—then put it back on the table, face down. I'm still breaking the habit of idle scrolling. I check the news each day, and my phone is always on in case of updates or calls from the lawyers, but other than that, I tend to stay offline. It helps to stay in the moment and remember to mind my own business. I've got plenty.

It's been a week since I drove Theo to the station and watched as he turned himself in. The surrender itself was an awkward scene. The young officer behind the desk hadn't quite understood at first, and Theo had to clarify that he was not the victim of a crime, but that he'd committed one—a felony—and he'd like to report it. There was some commotion as calls were made, and a handful of cars came zooming into the lot, sirens wailing. Finally, the chief arrived, appraising Theo with a look of muted disappointment. Then he'd silently waved him to the back. I haven't seen or spoken with him since.

I sat on the bench in the station for half an hour, lulled by the chaotic bustling around me and the pleasant feeling of being invisible. Then, someone said my name.

"Alice?"

It was Officer Jessie. She shook her head, wide-eyed.

"I heard about Theo, but I didn't know you were here."

I just nodded. I was suddenly so tired.

Jessie sat down next to me, her face thoughtful. It occurred to me that this was the first time I'd seen her go more than a minute without grinning.

"Do you need a ride home?" she asked.

"No," I said. "My car's out front."

"I'll walk you to it then." Before I could protest, she stood and nodded sternly toward the lot.

This was how I learned that it was Jessie who'd slipped a note in the mailbox that morning: "Take care, Alice."

"I'm sorry," she said, a hand to her chest. "I felt awful scaring you, but I had to do something. You weren't safe in that house."

She paused to let me catch up. I'd run through the morning in my mind. Had she waited until I was alone in the house? Had she been keeping tabs on me that closely?

"Wait, why?" I asked. "What do you mean *you* had to do something?"

"I knew what you were doing. I knew the specifics—I'd processed your request for the records." She'd sighed, her face pained. "And I gave them to you."

"You stole them for me," I said. "That was—"

"Oh Alice, I know. It was reckless, giving you that drive."

"Brave, I was going to say, but—yeah, that too."

"*Completely* reckless. If he'd found it while you were staying in his house?" She shut her eyes and shook her head rapidly. "I should have been straight with you, or just told you to get out of there."

She put a hand on my arm and squeezed.

"But I knew what you were doing," she repeated, with a small, tearful smile. "And I wanted you to do it."

"I don't understand," I said eventually. "Anything."

And Jessie—whom I'd underestimated from the moment I saw her sunny, bright-eyed face—explained.

She'd always known about the rumors, but only in the non-specific, unsaid way that most people in the village seemed to know. She'd never consciously considered whether or not they were true (if so, surely someone would've done something about it back then). But she didn't really think about the murder at all. It was a club thing, and club things were not the business of outsiders, especially those with names like Jessie Applebaum. It was just lore to her, until five years ago, when she'd the joined village PD. There were still plenty of cops on the force from "back then," and now they were all her superiors. It was a slow, uncomfortable realization, but she couldn't shake it. She certainly couldn't *ask* about it. But she kept an ear out, always listening.

"The way they talked about Theo—or no, not 'talking.'" Jessie paused, squinting into the dusk. "It was just the way they *were* about him. Like, he got written up in the newspaper once, for some big case. And a few of the older guys were passing the paper around, but in this very deliberate way. Not casually—not like 'Here, I'm done with it'—and it was that one specific item they were reading. Something like that happens once and maybe you don't even clock it. But then Theo was blowing up and getting all this press, and those weird moments were happening a *lot*. Little comments too."

Jessie was clocking *everything*. But what could she do? The more she noticed, the harder it was to ignore. The rumor was slowly gelling into something like fact.

"Then, one day, someone made a crack about Theo getting canceled," Jessie told me. "It was nothing. 'Oh, he better quit getting famous or they'll cancel him.' This was when 'canceled' was the big new buzzword—they were always making shitty jokes about it, like it was the most hilarious thing. But when someone made the joke about Theo, nobody laughed. Total silence."

Jessie shook her head, staring past my shoulder.

"I felt like such a dope," she added. "How did I not get it until then?"

"God. If you're a dope, what does that make me?"

"No, Alice, that's different. I didn't—"

I waved off her hurried apologies. My brain was already soupy with information, unable to absorb any more.

"Doesn't matter. You got it. And then . . . ?"

"Then—well, then I met Jamie," Jessie sighed. "And you know that part, I'm sure."

"That part?"

She looked at me, surprised.

"He didn't tell you?"

I shrugged. I could feel myself growing foggy. Another five minutes and I would need someone to drive me.

"Huh," said Jessie, then paused, considering. "Well, that's his story. I'll let him tell it."

I hear the door swing open and look toward the front of the bar. Jamie turns to the bartender and lifts a hand in greeting, then drops it as he sees me. He makes his way to the booth and folds his hands on the table.

"Hey."

He's dressed in khakis and a button-down, rolled up to the elbows.

"Day off?" I ask.

He shakes his head.

"Had my interview at the station."

This time around, everyone's getting questioned, and not just by village police—who'll soon be under investigation themselves. Every law enforcement body in the state seems to have a stake in the shocking confession of Theo Wiley, congressional hopeful and civil rights champion, who allegedly—and horrifically—killed his teenage cousin. Each day more cars and cameras appear in the station parking lot—I make a point of driving by, even if I don't have to be there. Theo himself is keeping quiet and, by all accounts, completely cooperative. The media seems to expect a drawn-out legal fight, but Theo won't mount one—that much I know. I think of the look on his face when he surrendered and said goodbye. I won't say it was gratitude, but it wasn't merely resignation either. He was resolved.

I'm all sorts of things. Relieved, of course, and gratified to see so many people not only taking interest but action. And I'm devastated too. And angry, and guilty, and hopeful, and worried. There's a strange, gloomy calm above it all, knowing the storm has passed. I can take my time picking through the wreckage.

"I'm sorry," I say.

Jamie sits back against the booth, his shoulders softening. "Thanks," he answers flatly, his eyes on the table between us. "You okay?"

"Sure." I shrug. "Not really, but—"

"Yeah. Me too. Not really, but . . ." He glances up briefly. "Guess I'm sorry too. I should've told you months ago."

Or years ago, I think. *Or decades.*

Jamie shakes his head, reading my silence.

"I didn't know, back then. I knew there was a rumor," he begins. "But I never believed it. There were a lot of rumors about that night, especially that first year. God, one week, everyone at school was saying it was a mob hit."

He exhales sharply—part laugh, part exasperation.

"The one about Theo—yeah, that one stuck around. But it's not like everyone was talking about it all the time."

Not in front of you. His best friend.

"I thought it was just local talk or whatever," Jamie continues. "Theo was this hometown hero, and I thought it was just the village trying to take him down a peg."

Jamie looks at the table.

"But I guess—no, I did. I did sometimes wonder, just for a second. I'd see how he'd get laser-focused sometimes—like when something didn't go his way with a case. Or, one time, Isaac had a teacher who put him in a time-out—I don't remember why, but this was like a kindergarten thing. And Theo was fucking *livid*. It was all he could talk about for a week—this shitty teacher who had no business being anywhere near children. The school should fire him. The school should be shut down. Eventually, I was like, 'Yeah, but Isaac seems okay, right?' And I was at the house that night—Isaac was *fine*. He was goofing off, singing some song from school. But then I said that thing to Theo, and Theo bangs his hand on the table and goes, 'That's not the point!'"

Jamie's face tenses at the memory.

"And I kind of—" Jamie sits back with a jolt. "Isaac too. He looked all scared, then he just started wailing."

Jamie opens his hands and sighs.

"But I don't have kids, right? So, what do I know? And it wasn't like he did that every day."

I have the thought again, but this time Jamie says it:

"Or maybe he did." Jamie blinks slowly, shaking his head. "I wasn't there a lot."

"Me neither," I add quietly.

We look at each other for a long moment, the awful, unknown possibilities hanging in the air. Then he continues:

"So yeah, I'd seen him snap a few times, but I never connected it to Caitlin. I never even thought about it—not until Jessie."

"Did she know who you were when you started dating?" I murmur. "Theo's friend, I mean."

"*No*," Jamie says. "Not until a couple months in. Meeting friends and all that."

He hedges for a moment, glancing up at me.

"It's a little weird, talking about my ex-girlfriend," he says with sudden sharpness. "After the thing with us—whatever. I don't even know—the thing where we were having sex for, like, three weeks and you'd sneak out every morning? And refused to talk about it?"

His sideways glance becomes a glare—the wary, scornful look you'd give a nosy stranger or an uninvited guest. Someone you don't need to be nice to.

"Just saying, next time, maybe have the awkward conversation. Maybe get on the same page with the guy you're sleeping with before you suspect him of murder."

I bend my head, acknowledging the hit.

"Okay. Maybe tell the girl what *you* know about the murder," I say in an even tone. "Yeah?"

Jamie launches into a response, but I shake my head. We'll get to that part, but we need to finish this part first.

"Go on." I nod. "You were dating Jessie."

"Anyway," Jamie says in a calmer voice, his fingers drumming the table. "Jessie knew I had some old Wheaton friends, but I guess I'd never mentioned Theo by name. Then I did, and—boom."

"What?" I prod him—no need to be gentle now. "You had a fight?"

"At first, yeah," Jamie answers. "She accused me of keeping it secret from her—the fact that I knew Theo. I was like, 'Why the hell would I do that?' And she just said it: 'Because he killed a girl.'"

I knew it was coming, but I still flinch.

"Sorry," Jamie mumbles, rubbing at his hairline.

"It's fine, he did," I answer sharply, waving him on.

"That was the first time I'd ever heard someone just lay it out like that—plain and simple, no hesitation. She kind of yelled it, actually. And I did the whole knee-jerk 'What are you talking about?' thing. But it wasn't even a fight, really. As soon as she said it—" He shakes his head. "It was like she hit the light switch. And now . . ."

He rears back with a look of dawning, dreadful recognition.

"Is that when you looked into getting the case reopened?" I ask. "Was that Jessie's idea?"

"No. No, she had other ideas—wearing wires, getting the higher-ups involved. I thought that was batshit ridiculous. One thing at a time, y'know? Let me do some research *before* calling the district attorney." He exhales a light tsk. "*That* was the fight. Jessie was dead set on this stealth plan. She said *my* way was too risky—that Theo would catch wind of it somehow."

Jamie looks away, and I wait for him to say it: *And she was right*.

"So I told him myself," he says, gazing impassively into the hazy air.

I hold still, replaying the sentence in my head.

"Yeah." Jamie gives a jerky, defensive shrug. "I was pissed. I'd known this guy my whole life, and she—"

He cuts himself off, looking back at me—suddenly remembering that I'm the one he's pissed at now.

"Whatever. I told him," Jamie says. "But only the part about getting the case reinvestigated—nothing about investigating *him*. We were getting beers after work one night, and I just mentioned I'd been looking into it, casually. Just to see what he'd say."

"Jamie," I whisper.

"And he freaked out," Jamie continues. "In a big way—a *weird* way. 'You think you're some hero? You think anyone cares?' He wasn't even making sense, but it was like he couldn't stop. It was that tunnel-vision thing, but aimed at me this time. I got up to leave and he was still going—ranting. So I just left."

Jamie shrugs again, slowly this time.

"Like I said, I already thought it was him. But after that, it was real. All those years—it had been him the whole time."

I still can't find the words to name it—the seismic shift that happens when you understand that someone you have loved unconditionally has also been a stranger to you. The way it fractures the very lens with which you look back on your own life. The desperate urge to mend it, knowing all the while that glass cannot be uncracked.

"What did you do?" I ask, though part of me already knows.

"Nothing. I dropped it—panicked, I guess," Jamie answers in a hollow drone. "I figured it would come out anyway, with Theo becoming this big shot. It wasn't on me to blow the whistle. I could just move on with my own life. Why nuke it all over what *he'd* done, right?"

Jamie sits back as far as the shallow booth will allow.

"Right," I say quietly. "Then I came home."

Jamie doesn't reply. He just exhales, long and hard.

"Yeah," he says finally, looking past me. "Yeah, you did. And I should've told you—I'm sorry. I shouldn't have gone along with your whole Patrick vendetta. I know I owe you an explanation, but I don't have one right now—not a good one. I'm gonna need a minute."

"Give me the bad version then," I say, cutting through his bluster. "Try."

Jamie puffs and leans over the table, his elbows landing with a hard thunk.

"It's like—it's the what-if. You can be ninety-eight percent sure, but as long as that two percent is there—I don't know." He looks away, still scowling. "I told you, it sounds like bullshit."

I watch him, angry and shifting in his seat. Then I shake my head.

"No," I say. "I get it."

I would've done the same, I think. *I would do the same right now.* If someone walked into this bar—some random girl from high school, anyone—and told me Theo hadn't killed Caitlin, I would shut my mouth and listen. Even with his confession still ringing in my ears, I would want to believe. I would leap at the thinnest shred of hope that it was somehow someone else. I might just settle for the fantasy of it—just play along for a month or two, and relish the relief.

Maybe Jamie's reasons are entirely different. I don't know—I don't need them. I'm not much interested in reasons anymore.

Epilogue

On the Sunday of Labor Day weekend, I drive to the club for the last time. My bags jostle in the back seat of my rental car as I wind up the sloping front drive. I'm heading home today. I've already checked out of my little economy-express room at the Berrytown Motorway Inn, where I've been since early August. I had to stay local those first few weeks ("No sudden moves," the lawyer said), but the Alcott was officially out of my budget now that my budget included a lawyer. Berrytown was barely six miles away, but I slept better on the plastic mattress of that roadside motel than I had all summer in the village. Partly, because it had air-conditioning.

I pause at the edge of the club's staff lot (technically off-limits to me now), then pull in and park in my usual spot. There are only a handful of cars here anyway. Even for a holiday, things are sleepy in Briar's Green. The press is gone, and there's only a smattering of tourists this year—the village's historic lore dampened by the smack of current events. And after the full-tilt chaos of August, the villagers themselves have picked up and left in a huff for a nice long weekend of peace and quiet.

"A lot of them were specifically asked *not* to," Jessie told me on the phone last night. "I know for a fact there were three no-shows at the station today."

Jessie and I have kept in semiregular touch this past month, forming a cautious friendship. With Caitlin's case now officially reopened, we both find ourselves in awkward, uncertain positions. Jessie's technically on desk duty, though the only thing on her desk is a phone. I'm technically free to leave, though I've been asked (not ordered) to stay within the state. We've both been questioned by a cadre of investigators, and we'll both likely face some sort of charge regarding the files she stole and I knowingly accepted. Depending on how things shake out, that could be the least of our worries, but for now, we're just names on a long list of people who may or may not be important.

"*Three* no-shows," Jessie repeated. "Can you imagine?"

"If they were members? Sure."

"Seriously? You can be jailed for failing to turn up for a scheduled interview."

But they won't be, I thought. It didn't need to be said.

It doesn't really bother me—a few entitled members flaking on their interviews. They'll all go in eventually. They're doing it right this time, bringing in every potential witness and anyone who can speak to Theo's affect and behavior as a teenager: teachers, classmates—even our old neighbors.

Gordon Fairchild called me himself, two days after Theo surrendered. The cops hadn't yet contacted him, but he was planning to go the station and volunteer his information.

"What little I have," he'd added in a stilted voice. "But I felt I should tell you first."

Gordon hadn't known the truth in 1999. He'd been certain that Patrick was the killer and his father had covered for him. *That* was the open secret, he thought, and he had every reason to. Patrick was a reckless little shit who crashed boats and drove around unlicensed and drunk—and at seventeen, he already had an unsavory reputation when it came to women (not just girls, but *women*). Gordon had no trouble believing, and he got all the proof he needed when Whit Yates himself turned up to threaten him over his tell-all book deal. The Yateses were the ones to fear, as far as Gordon knew, and he'd been consumed by it.

"I was looking over my shoulder, always," he told me. "Looking for *them*, you understand? Never at anyone else."

By the time *A Death on the Hudson* came out in the summer of 2002, Gordon was, in his words, "a full-time paranoid drunk." He'd stopped going to the club long ago, though his wife, Vivian, continued to play doubles every week with her longtime tennis friends—until the day his book came out, and they'd simply not shown up. Both Fairchilds were outcasts in the village now, and estranged from each other at home. Thus, despite his book's success, Gordon was living in isolated panic, holed up in his office with his liquor most of the day.

"I only left the house because the damn dog made me," he said. "This was two dogs ago—our first sheepdog, Hal. He was a nuisance about his morning walk. So, that much I'd do."

Gordon stuck to the neighborhood, never going farther than a few streets past his own. He went out in the early hours, when no one else was out, save for the occasional jogger or bleary-eyed teenager heading to swim practice. At that time of day, there was no risk of conversation or even a wave. If you saw someone more than once, you might exchange a nod. It was safe.

High Top Road was part of his regular route that summer, and Theo—home from college and working at the local garden center—was one of the kids he'd nod at. Gordon barely knew his name, and had no idea of his connection to Caitlin. He only recognized him because of the green T-shirt and khaki shorts Theo wore to work every day.

One day though, Gordon went out even earlier. He'd been up all night, unable to knock himself out, and the dog had started pestering him before the sun was even up. It was just past daybreak when he turned the corner and trudged onto High Top

Road. Gordon had paused at the sight of Theo—the green-shirt kid—standing in his driveway. Except he wasn't wearing his green shirt. He was still in his boxers. Even stranger, he was holding something in his hands—a suit jacket, all crumpled up.

"It was the strangest thing. He was trying to tear it apart. He had one of the arms out in his fist, trying to pull it off. It was such an odd sight, it stopped me in my tracks. He was out by the trash bins—that's why, it must've been trash day. I couldn't see his face at first—he was turned sideways—but I suppose he must've heard me. He turned all of a sudden and gasped. And his face—I can hardly describe it. I thought he might scream, honest to God."

Gordon tugged the dog's leash and walked back home. Vivian was in the kitchen making coffee.

"I said, 'I saw the strangest thing just now.' And I told her about it—the suit, his face. Things were cool between us then. We weren't talking much—just day-to-day business. But she stopped what she was doing and looked right at me and said, 'The boy on High Top? Wiley?' I told her yeah. She didn't say anything—just stood there, holding the box of filters. Then she came over and put her arms around me—she called me 'honey.' That stopped me in my tracks too."

Then Vivian sat Gordon down at the breakfast table, and told him about the rumors she'd heard around the club—back when she was still going to the club.

"It hadn't come out right away. You know how those people are—all that riddle-speak and *'pas d'avant.'* But it did emerge, in bits and pieces. So-and-so saw him leave the clubhouse, others saw him coming back from the pool. Vivian told me someone—I don't know who, but someone had seen him in the powder room, holding his jacket over the sink. Scrubbing at it—a spot of something, I suppose."

I asked Gordon to stop there. He'd started to apologize, and I said no, it wasn't that. I wanted every detail, but I had to absorb these details first. Sometimes you need the truth in bits and pieces.

That's what I'm doing now—gathering the bits and pieces. I have no deadline or agenda anymore, and I admit, it's a strange feeling to walk around without an axe to grind. It still dawns on me at least once a day—while sitting at a red light or rinsing my hair in the shower—that I'm not the child witness anymore. I'm the adult sister. I'm the one who got it wrong. I suppose I'm the one who finally got it right too. Which of those things matters most? I don't know yet. I'm between identities.

The whole story is being rewritten now, quite literally. "A Blue-Blooded Killing in Briar's Green" now has an italicized clause beneath the headline:

This story does not reflect recent developments regarding the death of Caitlin Dale. Certain statements may be factually inaccurate or lacking in relevant detail. Please refer to current coverage on our homepage.

There's a similar caveat edited into each episode of *The Club Kid*, and the hosts have announced a new season starting next month, featuring new guest interviews and ongoing updates on "this story's shocking new chapter." As of now, I will not be one of those interviewed guests. Again, nobody's told me I *can't* speak to the press (yet), but I don't need to be told. The story may be ongoing, and it could be for years—Theo could spend the rest of his life in and out of court—but in terms of the public narrative, it's pretty clear how things are shaping up. Right now, the general consensus is that it was obvious: Patrick was an easy target—a victim of his family's name and notoriety—while Theo was the stealthy villain in disguise, who played the underdog for political gain. *He* was the favored son of Briar's Green all along. He was the one they were protecting.

"Hogwash," Barbara said when I told her. "They were protecting themselves."

She'd called me out of the blue, ten days after Theo's surrender.

"One point I'd like to clarify," she'd begun, rushed and chilly at first. "I did not know about Theo. Understood?"

"Yes," I'd answered without thinking. "I mean—no?"

Barbara had sighed and gone quiet. I thought she might've hung up, but then:

"All I knew was that Patrick wasn't involved," she said. "Not that Theo had been. It never even crossed my mind until Patrick himself suggested it."

I sat there with my mouth open, still catching up. I'd never expected to hear from Barbara again, let alone hear *this*.

"You mean—"

"He came to me, weeks later," she continued. "Quite hysterical. He demanded that Theo be questioned—that Greg and I go to the police and insist."

She scoffed on the other end. A dark, throaty chuckle.

"Did you believe him?" I asked carefully.

She paused again—not a calculating silence, but a thoughtful one I somehow recognized. I pictured her, perched on the couch, one ankle resting on her knee—her Katherine Hepburn pose.

"I could hardly believe my own thoughts back then, Alice. Nothing makes sense when you've lost a child. It's anarchic." She cut herself off and took a steadying breath. "No, I don't think I believed him. Even if I had, I'd never have trusted it—not enough to speak aloud, let alone to some police officer. To do that to my sister? To all of you? No. I'd have needed more than Patrick's word."

At this part I went silent.

"It was selfish," she added firmly. "Fine. But I'd lost enough."

I couldn't understand. But I couldn't argue either.

"And when I came to you this summer?"

Barbara replied without missing a beat:

"You'd grown up. *You* had made the decision to do this—come back and get to the bottom of things. Whatever you found there, you'd decide what to do with it."

I wanted to ask her if she thought I'd made the right decision. But I held my tongue, conscious of the tenuous new link between us—distinct from the one we once had as a child and her aunt. I'm not sure what we are to each other now. But I hope we figure it out.

As for my own status as an aunt, the future is less certain—hopeful would be a stretch. So far, Jules has not returned my two brief voicemails or the email I sent, nor do I expect her to. I probably wouldn't, if it were me. I told her I would continue to reach out every few months, unless she asked me not to. I have no expectations. I just want her, and the boys, to know I'm here. I'm still family, if they want me to be.

I know Theo would want that. It's the one thing he's asked of me. A week after his surrender, I got a call from the front-desk clerk at the Alcott, alerting me to an envelope that had arrived for me in their mail. It looked "official," he said—clearly, a Briar's Green euphemism, though I couldn't translate it until I picked it up and saw the bright-red stamp on the front: "Inspected and mailed from the Lower Hudson Detention Center." I'd quietly thanked the stone-faced clerk, and waited until I was back in the car to open it. Inside was a single sheet of paper, with a short, tidy note typed at the top:

> Don't worry about me. You did everything right. You're going to be fine. This is a chapter. It's not your whole book. Would you remember that? And, if I may, would you please remind my children every now and then? It's not their book either.

The response came to me instantly—a snippy, adolescent voice in my head: *God, Theo, obviously. Like you even have to ask.* The little reflex of annoyance passed through me like a chill. I cried in the parking lot for a while, then put the letter back in the envelope and left. I doubt I'll hear from him again, unless I write back myself. I don't think I will. Still, it's good to know I've got the address.

I didn't expect to hear from Susannah either—and was astonished to wake up to a lengthy text from her, three days ago. She and Patrick had reportedly canceled their honeymoon when the news broke, and have been tucked away on his family's Long Island property. They'll be returning next week, according to her message. She wanted to write before things got too "complicated."

> The lawyers say no contact, so I'm trusting you'll keep this private. So is P.
>
> All I really want to say is that I didn't know. I thought it was gossip. I overheard a lot of club gossip when I was growing up. My parents heard things. Sometimes they saw things. One night I heard them talking about something my dad had seen in the men's locker room. I was terrified that dad might lose his job, so I never repeated it, even to you. But I had reason to believe that Patrick was with someone else when Caitlin died.
>
> Patrick confirmed my suspicions himself, shortly after we started dating. I asked him directly, and he told me everything. I knew about the affair. So yes, I was taken aback when you told me he'd called her. But not for the reasons you thought.
>
> I confronted him about that phone call too, by the way, and he was completely honest. That's the kind of man he is, whatever you believe. He owns his mistakes and atones for the harm he's done—and yes, he's done his share. My husband is not perfect, and neither am I. But we don't keep secrets from each other. He knows I'm writing you this message, and he's pissed about it. I can live with that. I cannot live with secrets anymore.

I've read the text a dozen times, but haven't yet replied. The more I think about it, the less I have to say. There's nothing left to argue over, and all the questions I could ask seem unimportant now. Why muddy the waters further, when I could just walk away? If those are the final words of our friendship, they're pretty good. And it feels right to let her have the last ones.

With her and Patrick and the rest of the village returning after Labor Day, it also feels right to be leaving now. Once the holiday is past, it's back to reality—and after my summer hiatus, I have a lot of reality to catch up on. I have to find a job. I have to plan for the very real likelihood that no one will want to hire me, what with my name attached to a still-unfolding scandal. I have to crunch the numbers and see how long I can stretch what's left of my savings before I put my apartment on the market. And for some reason, I'm oddly excited. It turns out uncertainty isn't all bad. It's scary, not knowing what the future holds. But at least it's the future I'm thinking about.

With that in mind, I turn off the car and get out. Just one last pit stop, here in the past.

Mr. Brody sits bent over his desk, writing in one of his ledger books. He looks up, squinting at me.

"Ms. Wiley?" he says. "You surprised me."

For once, I realize, it's actually true.

"I'm on my way home. Back to the city, I mean." I inch forward, resting my fingertips on the back of the visitor's chair. "But I was hoping—"

"Sit," he says, gesturing to the chair. "Please."

He closes the binder and slides it to the side of the desk, watching with a thin smile as I step around a stack of papers and settle into the chair. Then he nods for me to begin.

If only I knew how.

"The last time I was in here," I heard myself say, "when you told us what you saw that night on the terrace. Seeing him sneak out and hide in the trees."

I look up, watching his face as I say the next part.

"When you said that, did you know I was recording you?"

"My dear," he chuckles. "As I said, I am not omniscient. Merely old."

He searches my face, his smile dwindling, but still wide enough to show his teeth. I think it's the first time I've seen them.

"I ask," I say, my own voice turning stern, "because I'm still trying to understand what you knew. And when."

Mr. Brody nods and clears his throat—not the phony little *ahem*, but an actual, human cough.

"Ms. Wiley, I may not have told you the whole truth, but I have never told you a deliberate lie," he says, his voice light and clear. "A small distinction, granted, but as you and I both know, it's the little things that make the difference."

I look at him. I should've just left.

"What I mean, Alice, is that I made my own mistakes that night," he says more quietly. "And I had my own uncertainties about who I saw and when."

I think of the incident report—its glaring lack of specificity. No names, no physical descriptions.

I told you I saw Patrick Yates, he'd said. *And I did, among others.* Others. More than one.

"They were thick as thieves, those two—always together, always up to something," Brody says. "I was none too pleased about Jamie working in the cloakroom that night, knowing your brother would be at the party. On top of everything else, I'd have to keep track of them too."

I can see it in my memory: Brody, always looming in the near distance, his glare always pointed in our direction. But we were used to those disdainful looks at the club. We stuck out like sore thumbs in our borrowed shoes and clothes that never fit right.

I look up, something clicking.

"The suits?" I ask, thinking aloud.

I see Jamie in his father's jacket—he'd stuck out too that night.

"Well, no," Brody says, nodding his head sideways. "Not that alone. All the young men wore those baggy suits back then—dreadful fad. But yes, I take your point. One can always tell."

He averts his gaze, and I feel my cheeks heat up. Of course it wasn't just our clothes. It was our haircuts and our names and the stench of our self-consciousness. One could tell just from the way we carried ourselves. One could spot an outsider from a mile away. And standing on the terrace that night, Brody was much closer than a mile.

I look at Brody. He looks back, his face heavy with despair.

"I didn't know which one of them it was."

I picture him, glowering at the shadowed figure striding toward the pool. He might have missed those crucial little details, like hair color or exact height. But then, why bother to look that closely? As far as he knew, it was just one of those nonmember boys making trouble.

"'That boy, who never should have been there,'" I murmur, recalling his own words.

"He shouldn't have been," Mr. Brody adds in soft agreement. "Neither of them."

I straighten up, my cheeks still burning, and wait for him to meet my eye again.

"So you knew it was Jamie or Theo, but you didn't know which. Is that right?"

He nods.

"No inklings whatsoever? Over the years?"

"Certainly, I had them," he says evenly. "There were rumblings about your brother, as I'm sure you know by now. And Jamie's behavior this summer—forgive me, but all this snooping and scheming with you. Barging in here with you to interrogate me."

He gives a bewildered shake of the head.

"I tell you, I did not know what to make of it. But the

kettle was boiling." He lifts his hands from the arms of his chair. "Nothing to do but wait for the whistle."

"Nothing to do," I repeat. "Really, *nothing*? For twenty years?"

Mr. Brody considers for a long moment, his expression calm. He knits his hands together and rests them on the desk.

"Had I an explanation, I would give it to you gladly. All I have is the fact of those twenty years—all the life that's happened. Days go by, each one full of other business, other tragedies, and that is how the past becomes the past."

His eyes shift downward, and he draws a tired breath.

"Which is another way of saying that I have no excuse," he adds. "You did the right thing. I did not. Mea culpa, Ms. Wiley. And well done."

Outside, the sun has turned from stinging bright to warm, rich rays of orange, glimmering through the trees. The crickets are already chirping, getting a jump on sunset. The days are steadily getting shorter, and I can smell the first notes of fall, even through the heat. I pause beside my car, and take a deep breath of it. Then I open the driver's side door.

"Hey!" a voice calls from somewhere behind the clubhouse. "Alice, wait up!"

I stop with the door still open and shield my eyes against the sun. Jamie calls my name again, and then he appears on the edge of the parking lot, jogging toward me. He's dressed in a blue T-shirt, sweating around the collar—not even close to dress code.

"Where were you?" I ask, eyeing him.

"Birthday party at the stables," he says, pausing to catch his breath. "They needed hands—everyone's out of town."

He frowns, noticing my bags in the back seat.

"Wait, are you leaving right now? Seriously?"

I look at my luggage with a pang of uncertain guilt.

"No text, nothing?" he asks, squinting. "A little dramatic, even for you."

"No, I—" I was trying to do the opposite, for once. Trying to make a quiet exit. "I was going to call you."

It sounds wimpy. We both hear it.

"Uh-uh, in the car," he says, and opens the passenger door. "We're doing this in air-conditioning."

I stand still as he gets in the passenger seat and shuts the door. "This?" I ask.

"*Air*-conditioning," Jamie repeats.

So I get in and start the engine, cranking the air on full blast. We sit in sweaty silence until the vents blow cool, and then Jamie leans forward, adjusting the knobs. I flip my visor down against the sunset, now blazing over the river.

"What's the game plan?" he asks.

"Uh, drive back," I answer, looking forward. "Shower. Sushi, maybe."

"Cool, any plans after that?" He gestures at the horizon. "In terms of the rest of your life?"

"Not really. I'm open to suggestions."

I glance sideways at him. His expression turns sincere. I don't know how much more sincerity I'm up for today.

"Can I just say I'm sorry?" My eyes drop to his shoulder. "Can that be it for now?"

A heavy silence hangs in the car, until finally, Jamie breaks it.

"Hmm," he says in a musing voice. "What happens if I say no?"

"God," I say. "Jamie Hotdog."

Jamie's head goes back, eyebrows raised. "*Whoa*, I forgot about that nickname. That was good."

"I think it was supposed to be mean."

He shrugs.

"Yeah, but it was cool. It was funny. I remember I was mad that I hadn't thought of it myself."

The corners of his mouth go up as he nods, thinking back—like it's that simple. I sit and watch him smiling at the memory, his face so wide-open and content that I stop breathing for a second. I reach out, squeezing his shoulder, hard and quick.

"Okay," I say in a farewell tone. "I really do have to go. I have to unpack and get groceries and everything."

I put my hand on the gearshift, but he doesn't take the cue.

"Do you need a hand with groceries?"

"No," I say.

He widens his eyes, exasperated or pretending to be, or a little of both.

"Well, can I give you one anyway?"

I feel my smile bending into a grin.

Why not? I think. *Whatever this is—why not?*

I can't think of a reason. I might be giving up on reasons for a while. If I've learned anything these past three months (and the twenty-ish years prior) it's that there's rarely a good reason for the things that happen to us, or the things we do. I haven't earned the great fortune I've been given or the brutality I've witnessed—or even this moment right here: sitting in the sunset, in an air-conditioned car, with gas in the tank and someone beside me.

I don't deserve any of it—this minute, this life. But I'm the one who got it, and I can't give it back.

I put the car in gear and go.

★ ★ ★ ★ ★

Author's Note

The first inklings of this story came to me about eleven hours into a fourteen-hour plane trip, in July 2019. It was hardly an idea—just a few names and settings, and a vague idea about nostalgia and a twist. I was seven months pregnant and flying home from a semi-spontaneous trip to Saint Petersburg, Russia, where I'd spent the week touring Romanov palaces and indulging my lifelong fascination with imperial history. It was a trip I'd always dreamed of taking, knowing it would likely remain a daydream. History geek or not, it's a little bit weird for an American woman to fly off to Russia by herself, let alone a super-pregnant American woman who makes her living as a writer and journalist. I felt a surge of excitement when booking the trip, along with a sharp zap of anxiety. Was this a ridiculous idea?

A few days before leaving, I'd gone to my doctor to get a formal letter clearing me to fly. I didn't actually need one. Most airlines only require a note during the final month of pregnancy. But I wanted one anyway. "Is this a ridiculous idea?" I'd asked, anxiety zapping me left and right, half hoping she'd tell me to bail. "Is it *really* okay for me to go?" She'd taken a long pause, then shrugged. "I can't see why not," she said, and gave me my permission slip. I left the office still racked with uncertainty, keenly aware that she'd only answered my second question.

I felt the same way the following spring, when I decided to take that little inkling of a story and turn it into a book. In truth, I was even more nervous. That sounds *profoundly* silly, I know, but writing a book, just like having a child, is an all-consuming, life-changing gamble. So many things can go wrong, even if you do everything right, and although you're responsible for making and growing and delivering it, you don't really know how it'll turn out. There's only so much you have control over, so y'know, maybe play it safe and don't jet off to Russia in your third trimester? Maybe *don't* commit years of your life to some vague wisps of a story idea you had on an airplane. On the other hand, why not?

I thought having an actual child—who, I might add, turned out to be spectacular—would resolve these conflicting ideas about the stories we choose to tell. I thought I would lean hard to the safe side, not *just* because parenthood would surely make me more neurotic (it did!), but because parenthood would make my time exponentially more precious, and I wouldn't want to waste a minute of it noodling with a story that might go nowhere. I was right about that too. The very thought of wasted time is chilling to me now.

On the other hand? I now know just how spectacularly well a gamble can go. My daughter was a wispy little inkling once, and I cannot even fathom my life had I not followed it. Not all inklings lead you somewhere so magnificent and joyful; sometimes the ridiculous idea is also bad. But the same is true for the so-called safe bets. There's no avoiding humiliation or failure or (I know we're not supposed to say this but oh well) regret. So, when faced with a flat-out ridiculous idea, you may as well consider it. I hope you will—in fact, I'm asking you to. Please, *please* do.

I know this isn't how the author's note usually goes. It's usually more about the book itself, not the circumstances of its creation—and I don't think it's supposed to make demands of

AUTHOR'S NOTE

the reader. But it's not every day you get the chance to publish a novel, so before I send it out into the world, I'm going to go ahead and slip this little note in the back for anyone who cares to read it. If you're reading it after finishing the book, this note is for you, with my great thanks. If you've found it while killing time in a bookstore because it's raining and you forgot your umbrella, this note is for you too. And as with everything else I do, it's for my daughter too.

Please give the ridiculous idea a chance. You don't actually need a permission slip, but if it makes you feel better, then here you go—printed out and everything. Even if it doesn't work out, I bet it'll make for a good story.

Kelsey Miller
January 23, 2025
Brooklyn, New York

Acknowledgments

This book owes many thanks to many people, and I must start with John Glynn, my editor, and Allison Hunter, my agent. I started this book in mid-2020, thinking it might take me seven or eight months to finish. Both John and Allison were excited and wholeheartedly supportive from the jump, and they remained stalwart as my seven-month project stretched into four and half years. Allison, thank you for reading my massive, messy early drafts, for pointing me in the right direction and out of the wrong one, and for pushing me when I'd run out of steam. John, thank you for taking this manuscript and turning it into a book. I relied on your wisdom and belief in this story so many times over the last four years. Without your guidance and care, this would still be a clunky, unfinished idea knocking around my desktop. Thank you, so much.

My enormous thanks to Hanover Square Press, Peter Joseph, and the incredible team of people who've supported both me and this book. Further thanks to Trellis Literary Management—I am so proud and lucky to call myself your client.

I am forever grateful to the teachers who taught me to write—by which I mean they taught me how, and taught me to just do it. My particular thanks to Julie Faulstich, who made me realize I loved writing, and to Jack Murnighan, who told me I should do it for a living. My great thanks to the editors with whom I've been lucky to work over the years, including Neha Gandhi, Joanna Goddard, Anna Maltby, Christene Barberich, Molly Stout, Kelly Bourdet, Leila Brillson and Lindsey Stanberry.

Thank you to my family, who were *always* in favor of creative work—even when my field of choice was musical theater (the really loud kind). Thank you for instilling in me the foundational belief that life as an artist was doable, and worth the effort. What a tremendous gift.

To the friends who held me up throughout this journey—I will never be able to express my gratitude: Mary Childs, Laura Stampler, Caitlin Abber, Elizabeth Kiefer, Jonathan Parks-Ramage, Chrissy Angliker, and Deborah Siegel. You showed up for me over and over and over again. I can only hope to do the same for you.

To my husband, Harry Tanielyan, who rode the ups and downs and long stretches of this road beside me. For your steadfast love, for cheering me onward again and again, for giving me a good shake of the shoulders when I needed it, and for so much more: thank you.

Finally, to my sweet, dazzling Margot: thank you for being exactly who you are. I am so lucky to be your mom. *Lucky* doesn't cover it—not even close.